Dedalus Europe 1995
General Editor: Mike Mitchell

Night of Amber

Pour Aurore,
bien cordialement,
[illegible]

Translated from the French
by Christine Donougher

Night of Amber

Sylvie Germain

Dedalus

Dedalus would like to thank the French Ministry of Culture in Paris and The Arts Council of England in London for their assistance in producing this translation.

Published in the UK by Dedalus Ltd, Langford Lodge, St Judith's Lane, Sawtry, Cambs, PE17 5XE

ISBN 1873982 95 X

Distributed in Australia & New Zealand by Peribo Pty Ltd, 58 Beaumont Road, Mount Kuring-gai N.S.W. 2080

First published in France in 1987
First published by Dedalus in 1995

Printed in Finland by Wsoy
Typeset by Datix International Limited, Bungay, Suffolk

A C.I.P. listing for this book is available on request.

THE AUTHOR

Sylvie Germain was born in Châteauroux in Central France, in 1954. She read philosophy at the Sorbonnne, being awarded a doctorate. From 1987 until the summer of 1993 she taught philosophy at the French School in Prague. She now lives in Paris. Sylvie Germain is the author of six novels, a short narrative and a study of the painter Van Meer. Her work has so far been translated into sixteen languages.

Sylvie Germain's first novel *Le Livre de nuits* (*The Book of Nights*) was published in France to great acclaim in 1985. It has won five French literary prizes as well as the TLS Scott Moncrieff Translation Prize in England. The novel ends with the birth of Night of Amber and his story is continued in *Nuit d'ambre* (Night of Amber) in 1987. Her third novel *Jours de colère* (*Days of Anger*) won the Prix Femina in 1989. It was followed by *L'Enfant Méduse* (*The Medusa Child*) in 1991 and *La pleurante des rues de Prague* (1992), published by Dedalus under the title of *The Weeping Woman on the Streets of Prague*.

Her latest novel *L'Immensités* was published in 1994 (Dedalus edition in preparation for 1997).

THE TRANSLATOR

Christine Donougher was born in England in 1954. She read English and French at Cambridge and after a career in publishing is now a freelance translator and editor.

Her many translation from French and Italian include Jan Potocki's *Tales from the Saragossa Manuscript*, Octave Mirbeau's *Le Calvaire*, Sylvie Germain's *Days of Anger* and Giovanni Verga's *Sparrow*.

Her translation of Sylvie Germain's *The Book of Nights* won the TLS Scott Moncrieff Prize for the best translation of a Twentieth Century French Novel during 1992.

Her current projects include translating Marcel Bealu's novel *The Experience of the Night* and editing *The Dedalus Book of French Fantasy*.

To Gregoire

What is going on behind that door?
A book is being leafed through.
What is the story of this book?
The realization of a cry.

Edmond Jabes

And Jacob was left alone; and there wrestled a
man with him until the breaking of the day . . .
And Joseph asked him, and said, Tell me, I pray
thee, thy name.
And he said, Wherefore is it that thou dost ask after
my name? And he blessed him there.
And Jacob called the name of the place Peniel: for,
said he, I have seen God face to face, and my life
is preserved.

Genesis, 32, xxiv–xxx

CONTENTS

Night of Trees 3

Night of Wind 63

Night of Stones 131

Night of Mouths 215

Night of the Angel 283

The Other Night 337

No, the book did not close. It could not end, could not fall silent. Yet the war, the war that kept endlessly recurring, had left men bereft of words, utterly bereft. The war that had now reduced to ashes the names, bodies and voices of millions upon millions. The war that had reduced to nothing the souls of so many of the men ruling in these murderous times.

The book tossed in the ashes and blood, like a sleeper tossing in a nightmare sweat. The book raised itself in a desert world crushed by so low, so heavy a sky, like a wounded man raising himself from the ground he no longer recognizes, after being thrown upon it with extreme violence.

The book of names that had fallen into oblivion, into silence – the book of names that had turned to cries. Breathless cries.

The book of names now saving themselves from oblivion, from silence. The book of shattered nights that page by page, step by step, word by word, once more resumes its odyssey. Braving land and sky.

The book did not close. It set off again, one page at a time, at the pace of a man girded with the tatters of his memory, whose shoulders were built to carry other men. It set off again, once more, as ever, at the pace of a man with a stubborn heart. It went on its way, braving the night.

'With his mother's cry, Night took possession of his childhood, one September evening, never again to leave him, running through his life from age to age – and proclaiming its name to forthcoming history.'

For the night that seized him, and the cry that entered his flesh, there to sink its roots and there to do battle, came from infinitely further back.

Oceanic night of his ancestors from which all his people had risen, generation upon generation, had taken on names, lovers and battles. Had cried out. And fallen silent. And renamed themselves.

Had only fallen silent and renamed themselves the better to establish the strange resonance of their cries, of their names.

Oceanic cry of his ancestors that went back to the beginning of time in a volley of countless echoes.

Cry and night had wrested him from childhood, alienated him from his own, stricken him with loneliness. But thereby made him irremissibly at one with all his people.

Mouths of night and cry confounded, mouths wounded by memory and forgetfulness.

An out-of-time wound that presided over the emergence of the world and opened its history like a giant book of flesh leafed through by wind and fire.

A wound that was even out of this world, rending the stellar night like a great book of stars penned by violence and light.

A great book constantly being written without ever reaching the final word, the final name, the final cry.

A great book constantly being deleted, then written again in reverse, without ever reaching the first word, the first name, the first cry.

And the book continues for ever, making its pages flap and its words run on. And the night continues for ever, letting its nebulae appear and its shooting stars fall.

Charles-Victor Peniel, whom everyone would call Night-of-amber-Wind-of-fire, in his turn entered into writing – a passion of writing. One page among other pages, destined, like all pages, to be read by the Angel, until obliterated. Until torn and turned back again.

NIGHT OF TREES

1

For it was terrible, that mother's cry, when they brought back her son's body. Her first-born son. The child of her youth, conceived on a day of rain and marvellous nakedness. The child that beat the drum of expectation in the days when the enemy occupied their land and kept his father so far away. The child she had suckled, and who for so long had slept, played, and grown at her side when there were just the two of them. The little companion who brought hope and joy right into the heart of the war zone. Her first-born son, flesh of her flesh, love created by her love. Little-drum.

It was truly a terrible cry, uttered with all the strength in her body, that seemed to rise from deep underground and reach the outer limits of the sky. A cry from the far side of time. The cry of a madwoman, a woman turned animal, who had become some elemental thing.

The father came. He saw the stiff wet body of his son, lying in the arms of three hunters who stood in the doorway with their heads bowed. Three men in hunting gear, with muddy boots and their arms covered in blood. Their game pouches were empty, and their dogs lay whining outside by their shotguns that had been thrown into the grass in the rain. They were holding the child's body so awkwardly and clumsily, they looked as if they were about to drop it.

At that very moment he saw his wife's body writhe and stagger as the cry rose within her. And he sprang towards her and caught her in his arms. He hugged her fiercely against his body, a living man's body, as though to keep her from the death of their son. But she broke free of his embrace and ran to the child. She grabbed the little body with such sudden aggressiveness that none of the hunters had time to react. And she ran off into the rain, carrying her son in her arms.

Before they reached the doorstep, she had disappeared. They, too, rushed out into the rain, and searched for her in the yard, on the road, in the fields, but could not find her. She had completely vanished. As though dissolved in the grey downpour from the September sky. Then Baptiste, known as Crazy-for-her, fell to his knees in the middle of the path, and wept.

And Charles-Victor, the second son, was left standing all alone at the front door, his five years suddenly weighing on him more heavily than a century. All alone. Abandoned. Betrayed.

For he had in an instant been betrayed by everyone: his dead brother, his demented mother, his weeping father. Did no one, then, care about him? He drew himself up and in the innermost depths of his heart, the heart of an excluded child, he shouted at them all, 'I hate you!'

For three days groups of men with dogs searched for Pauline and her child. Night-of-gold-Wolf-face, the man death had disdained, led the search. He seemed bigger and stronger, and more wolf-faced than ever with his gleaming eyes, his sharp teeth always bared as in love-making, and his tousled hair.

They found them on the evening of the third day, in the heart of Love-in-the-open Wood. There she was, more she-wolf or vixen than woman, crouched against the trunk of a huge pine-tree with low branches that steeped her in their blue-green shadow. She held clasped to her womb the now slimy, purplish-blue cadaver of her son. The smell of the child's decomposing body, with its enormous belly all swollen with dark gases, mingled strangely with the smell of ferns, mushrooms, sour strawberries in the moss, and mouldering chestnut-burrs. In the green shadow of the boughs Pauline's eyes had the very steady gleam of broken flints.

She was filthy and ragged, with her hair stuck to her face like yellow lichen; her skin was bark-coloured, her lips cracked. She seemed to be a part of the pine, to merge into its trunk, to cling to its roots. She had to be dragged from the tree's embrace. She was now silent, but the whole forest around her observed the same silence. It was the time of day when the stags began their raucous belling and prepared to butt each other. Their cries of rutting and of rivalry seemed to issue from the trees. You expected to see them all wrest themselves from the ground and start marching like an army of tutelary warriors ready to battle it out with each other in order to win the child and offer him their immortality. Soon the noise of their bellows filled the air for miles and miles around with fantastic loudness. Never before had such raucous, sonorous belling been heard in all the land. Never before had the trees so amazed people and terrified them.

And all the while he cried at home. It was not for his son that Crazy-for-her wept, it was not for Jean-Baptiste that he called, but for her, only for her. And little Charles-Victor in his bedroom heard his father weeping. That weeping on the other side of the wall sounded like the endless booming of the sea. And he felt a hatred welling up inside him, for his demented mother, for his father who was so weak, and for his dead brother.

Pauline was carried back to the farm like a bundle of dirty rags. During the night they nailed down Jean-Baptiste's coffin – the smell of his corpse was upsetting even the animals in the stables – but the child's smell permeated through the sealed planks; he imposed it on the whole house. The walls, objects, curtains, clothes, all committed this stench to memory. The smell of him filled the night, like the fabulous roar of the trees uttering their war cries.

When Crazy-for-her saw his wife looking like an old, hunted and wounded animal, he did not recoil, or say anything. He went up to her, and smiled. He approached her with a smile whose sweetness was mingled with pain. He took in his arms his filthy wife's wretched, disgusting body and hugged it to his own body, a living man's body. And cradled her like a child.

Charles-Victor clenched his fists so tightly that he bruised his fingers and scratched his palms. The smell of his brother on his mother's dress, skin, hair – even on her lips and eyes – made him feel so sick that he spewed. And it felt as though he were spewing up his heart. And his childhood.

While Mathilde took care of laying out the corpse, Crazy-for-her took care of his wife. He gently removed her torn clothes, stripping her completely naked – this, a new, tearfully upsetting nakedness. He slowly washed her passive body, tended the wounds that stones and brambles had made on her knees and arms, then washed her hair. When he had finished cleansing her body of mud and blood and the smell of death, he put her to bed and lay down beside her. He began weeping again in the night.

And Charles-Victor again heard through the wall the endless booming of the sea. And he heard from beyond the walls, travelling all through the night, the clamour of the trees locked in combat. He remained with his fists clenched, so as not to cry, too, so as not to scream. Did nobody care about him, then? He hated them all, insanely. Eventually he got up, went over to his brother's empty bed, climbed on to it, tore back the blankets and pissed on the sheets. No other tears for his brother!

Crazy-for-her did not go down into the room below, where Jean-Baptiste's coffin lay. He did not go and keep vigil over his son. And neither did anyone else. The smell kept everyone away. Only the trees kept vigil with their continuous song.

Crazy-for-her stayed with his wife, watching over her tormented sleep. He held her hands and stroked her brow. He stifled her moans with his mouth, the mouth of a living man. And he wept into her hair, as though to wash it clean of more filth and grief and blood, with his tears, the tears of a living man.

When they removed the coffin the next morning and took it to the cemetery, Crazy-for-her had to make a huge effort to leave the bedroom where his wife lay, and follow the procession. Charles-Victor dressed himself. Before, until these last few days, it was his mother who washed and dressed him, and everything. Those days were gone for ever now. He waited for his father by the door, standing very erect, with clenched fists and a hardened mouth. Crazy-for-her looked at him as if he did not recognize him. For a long time he stared sorrowfully at this very small boy standing there, so stiff and silent, with all his clothes awry. He wanted to speak to him, to say something, to take him in his arms, but he had no words or gestures left. Since the hunters had appeared in the doorway, he existed only for his wife. He had actually forgotten about Charles-Victor. He did not even think about the dead child. All the horror and grief for that death had descended on the boy's mother, leaving her shattered and drained. And he was only pained by her suffering; he grieved only because of her. It was only because of her, for her, that he wept. From the moment he saw her writhe and stagger, and turn into a cry, the world had receded into misty haze and he could no longer find a way to approach other people. And anyway, he had no desire to. All his desire was now invested in her alone. He had forgotten the others; there was no other closeness but closeness to her.

Yet he did sense that the little boy was suffering, that it was all too much for a child. But he sensed this almost outside of himself. He had to make an enormous effort to feel this.

No, really, he had no words or gestures left for anyone else, not even his own son. He had no more tears, even for his dead child. For he had given everything to his wife, and to her alone would he give, ever more. He was no longer his own master; from now on, his entire body – the body of a living man – was totally dedicated to the woman who lay upstairs in the bedroom.

She was now his child, his little girl, his only love. And he felt a sudden desire to scream. To scream at Charles-Victor to disappear. To scream that he wanted to be left alone with his wife. His only child.

Then, seeing his father's grief-stricken face, Charles-

Victor said simply, 'We must go now. The others are waiting. It's raining.' And he thought, actually with gleeful anger, 'I'll say it's raining! Even the sky's pissing on big brother! That's good!'

The others were indeed waiting, stamping their feet as they stood round the funeral hearse beneath big black umbrellas, which they held tilted. There was Night-of-gold-Wolf-face, Thadée and young Tsipele, Nicaise the farm hand, Mathilde and a few more besides.

The hearse advanced slowly through the pouring rain. They did not take the children's bypath, which was all muddy and of no use now anyway: since the destruction of the old Montleroy cemetery during the last war, a new cemetery had been opened, not in the churchyard but on the outskirts of the village, on the main road. The dead were constantly being denied any fellowship with the living: they were banished now to this patch of land enclosed by a high concrete wall, as if to some pariahs' camp, at a distance, far away from the houses, from the living, and the church. But this completely new cemetery was still empty; the last war had caused so many deaths – with the bodies, at that time, having to be heaped hastily into an emergency common grave dug at the bottom of the old cemetery – that not a single candidate for burial had since been found in the whole region. Those who had survived the calamity of war had kept going, as if they had to double their own lifespan to avenge all those lives taken before their time, by gunshots, bomb-blasts and artillery-fire.

So where the funeral procession ended up was in a big empty field. When the coffin was taken out of the hearse, the grave diggers had just finished digging the hole in the corner by the north and east walls. Jean-Baptiste was the first; he came as a pioneer, a founder. It fell to a little eight-year-old boy to assume the peculiar responsibility of inaugurating the big, new, rectangular cemetery marked out with concrete blocks. He was the first to die after the war, just as his little brother, Charles-Victor, was the first to be born. He brought his childhood as an offering to all the dead to come. Little-drum was doing his work as a forerunner for the last time.

They all stood there, stiff and awkward, around the dank grave.

It was then that she appeared.

As if her son were calling her again. Deep in her sleep, she had heard they were digging a grave. A grave in which they were going to bury her son. In her sleep she had sensed they were digging. They were digging a hole in the earth, in her womb. They were digging in her entrails, in her heart. Then she woke with a start, covered in sweat, her splayed hands flailing the emptiness and silence. She got up, dressed hurriedly, and ran all the way over to the new cemetery.

And now here she came, cutting across the field, out of breath. Shining in her aged, drawn face was the broken-flint gleam of her eyes.

They saw her running towards them, bare-headed, through the rain. She was not even wearing any shoes. She went straight up to the edge of the grave. Crazy-for-her tried to hold her arm but she pushed him away. With the look of a mad dog in her eyes, she stared at the four men lowering the coffin with ropes.

She watched, as the black oblong box, swaying slightly, slowly disappeared into the hole. It was such a small, narrow box. Was it possible that such a tiny box could contain her child's body? She did not understand.

No one spoke. All that was to be heard was the monotonous sound of the rain drumming on the wooden lid at the bottom of the grave, and Pauline's heavy breathing. Someone threw the first spadeful of earth. It was as if someone had just thrown earth in her mouth, in her womb, as if she – his mother – were being buried alive. And the rain, the rain kept beating on the wood, like a final drum-roll.

Crazy-for-her once again saw his wife's body writhe and stagger. He did not have time to restrain her. She threw herself into the grave. It was not earth that should cover his flesh; it was for her, his mother, to cover her son's flesh with her own. And the thud of earth on wood was echoed by the duller, heavier thud of flesh on wood.

There was a clamour and a scuffle. Thadée dragged Charles-Victor away from the grave. Crazy-for-her climbed down the ropes into the grave and brought Pauline up on his shoulders. She was unconscious. He felt the rain entering his body, streaming inside him. Weeping into his heart. To what depths would he have to descend to fetch his wife and bring her back, to a living man's love? He remembered that day, that wonderful day, when Pauline had pulled him down into a ditch and had surrendered herself to him in the rain-soaked grass. He even remembered the giddiness of that day of extreme nakedness, that beautiful day of insane love. What had happened all of a sudden? Why had sorrow replaced that former joy? How had it come about that a love so crazed with desire now quivered only with fear? Yet the rain was the same – a gigantic drum rolling with deep hollow resonances.

There was yet another sound, deeper than the grave-side mourners' clamour. It came from beyond the concrete walls of the cemetery, originating from a long way off, rising from Love-in-the-open Wood. It was a single cry, more raucous than any other heard during the night – the bellow of victory. The long battle between the trees was over.

And as the mourners were leaving the cemetery they beheld a squat tree with sturdy branches and dark foliage and a grey-barked triple trunk, coming down the hillside. And this tree moved in the manner of a giant. It crossed the fields and meadows, and came straight along the highway to the cemetery. It entered the big empty enclosure and went up to the grave that had just been filled in. Then it came to a halt, and there, in the very loose earth of that hastily dug mound, it plunged its roots to re-establish itself. It was an age-old yew tree, its branches studded with luminous, bright-red berries.

'Your child is saved,' Thadée told Baptiste, pointing to the tree over the grave.

'Your child is fortunate,' said Night-of-gold-Wolf-face, 'for that tree is female. She will cast a gentle shade over him and give him peace. I've lost many a child who has no tree to watch over them. Nor does anything remain of my wives. No tree came to bring them this: the earth's love.'

But Crazy-for-her Baptiste thought only of Pauline. As for Charles-Victor, he immediately declared, 'I hate trees!'

Charles-Victor stayed for a while with Thadée, joining Tsipele and Chlomo in the part of the farm where Two-brothers used to live. Thadée had expanded and refurbished this section of the outbuildings that he now occupied with the two children of his former comrade in the camp where he had been held. And these children had become his own. He had taught them to raise their heads, to look other people in the face again, to meet their gaze, and to restore some zest to their youth, to their lives. Yet, even though they had finally stopped holding hands all day long, they remained taciturn and a bit distant, and very closed in on each other. From having stayed too long in the depths of that cellar, they seemed to have retained a tendency towards gloom and silence.

This gloom they still carried within them deeply troubled Thadée. The density of darkness he sensed in them intrigued him as much as the mysteries of the night sky, which he continued to investigate in books and through telescopes. But it was with Tsipele especially that he felt a great unease, a feeling that sometimes even extended to suppressed panic. For, in her, as she grew up, this mysterious gloom had turned to beauty. The young girl had cast off her childhood, her body maturing into a womanly shapeliness of delicious curves. As it progressed, this metamorphosis of Tsipele's body caught up in its vortex Thadée's gaze and his mind, slowly overwhelming them with amazement, admiration and finally desire.

He often caught himself thinking that Tsipele was not

his daughter, although he treated her as such, and that in any case he was far too young to be her father. There was in fact only some ten years' difference between them. But he also had a strong sense that what made the young girl untouchable for him had nothing to do with age; it was because of something else – an immense discretion, as indefinable as it was fierce. And he battled constantly against the onslaught of his amorous feelings, refusing even to name his desire. He battled all the more with himself, knowing he was already defeated: his heart was basically of the same stamp as that of his brother Crazy-for-her Baptiste. A heart too undivided, made for a sole, absolute love. A stubborn heart, as tenacious as couch-grass, prepared to undergo a thousand endurances, a thousand tortures and pains, to keep the woman who had brought his desire into being, once and for all.

Charles-Victor refused to share a room with Chlomo; he wanted to be alone, completely alone. He had to plumb the utmost depths of the solitude in which he had been cast by his family, and forgotten. The utmost depths and beyond if possible.

He was still baffled. A few days before, his mother was still his mother; a kind and gentle mother whose love was equally divided between him and his brother. Such a kind and gentle mother, who took care of everything: who washed and dressed and fed him, and lingered a while at his bedside every evening. A few days before, he was a real little boy, considered as such and loved as such. But then all of a sudden his mother had broken down, collapsed, and now it was she who was considered a child, and made a fuss of. And his father had fallen apart, too; he was no longer a father to his son, only to his wife.

His mother was no longer his mother, but a child to his father. And yet she did still remain a mother . . . but not to him, the youngest; she was a crazed mother to her dead son. Exclusively. His mother's love had shifted. It was no longer equal. His mother's love had all gone down into the grave where his brother had been thrown. That maternal love was rotting in a grave.

Her dead son. His brother. His big brother. The big brother who had never forgiven him, Charles-Victor, for not having been born a girl. That little girl with blonde braids, and almond-shaped eyes the colour of dead leaves, he had so longed for – was it she that he had gone in search of underground?

'Well, let him go, then, let him go,' Charles-Victor said to himself over and over again, with his clenched fists buried in his pockets. 'Let him go to the devil, and his mother, too!'

Jean-Baptiste, the older brother. The first-born. The one whose mother had so fondly called him Little-drum.

'Yes, little drum of shit!' Charles-Victor said to himself. 'Go and roll your drum among the dead and give us a bit of peace!'

Some old women at the cemetery said to him, ' Ah, poor little fellow! You must pray for your unfortunate big brother.' He detested them as well, those women with their nasty smell of grey flesh and dusty woollens, with their rheumy eyes and whining voices whistling through their black tooth-stumps. No, he wouldn't pray for his big brother.

'Pray? Like hell, I will! I'll piss on him, on his dirty little dead face. Nah!' he kept thinking with rage. So, let the old women go rambling on with their yucky prayers, if that's what they wanted, he had better things to do! Piss on all traitors. His brother, mother, father – they were all in it together, all in the same grave. A rubbish tip. He could not tell them apart any more. He could not distinguish between death and madness, between tears, screaming and silence. And there was his father, huh, the big crybaby, who did not even see him – and he was the little boy! His father, on the other side of the wall, making that noise, like the endless booming of the sea. The booming of the winter wind.

A broken-flint gleam in his mother's eyes; blinding tears

in his father's eyes. Earth and darkness in his brother's vacant eyes. Gazes averted from him. The gazes of traitors. Well, never mind, Charles-Victor decided, he would invent his own gaze, a gaze much stronger than any that these three had, with their pathetic moping expressions.

'I,' he said to himself, 'will look through my bum-hole!' And so it was that he invented a magic, triumphant third eye for himself, in his underpants.

His father, too, was baffled. He, too, came up against the void, the unthinkable. He could not even think of his dead son. He perceived his two children as from afar, so very far away, without even knowing which of the two was dead or alive. He had scarcely seen the rain- and blood-soaked body of his son who had been shot by hunters. What he had seen, and kept seeing, was her: Pauline. Her body, twisting and reeling, with that piercing cry.

He stayed with her, all the weight and warmth of a living man lain beside her.

For a long time the mother stayed in her room and remained silent. She did not move, or speak, and kept her eyes closed. She lay resting like stagnant water. Not moving. Not speaking. Not feeling the life inside her. The life that pulsed with nothing but suffering now. Not thinking. Pretending to be dead, so as not to be susceptible to death.

And his only care was for her. He washed her and fed her.

Yet at night she would sometimes wake up, her face chilled with sweat, and scream, 'Jean-Baptiste! My little boy!' She would thrash about in the sheets, trying to get away, to run over to the cemetery, to lie on the ground and cover her child. She cried, 'He's cold, I can feel it. He's calling me. He needs me. He's so cold, all alone under the earth, I must go and warm him. I most go and comfort him . . .'

Then he, her big watch-dog of a husband, who always kept guard against these attacks of sorrow, had forcibly to restrain her in his arms, and fight against his invisible son. He smothered Pauline's cries under his mouth, a living man's mouth, and made love to her the better to regain possession of her body by chasing away the dead son, banishing him far away. But against his wife's new nakedness, his own orgasm was no less different; it was a sorry orgasm, consisting of tears. He inseminated her with his tears.

All the time that his mother's illness lasted, the mysterious death-illness that just as much consumed his father, Charles-Victor stayed in Thadée's house. But he spurned his uncle's affection just as he had rejected Tsipele and Chlomo's friendship. He lived there like a feral child, with his peculiar ways and fierce looks. He hated any kind of sympathy, mistrusting everybody and everything. Demonstrations of affection sickened him.

'I know their sympathy,' he said to himself, 'it means less than nothing, it's all rubbish and lies. A nasty grown-ups' game. Idiots and rotters, every one of them. They only pretend to love you to let you down all the more afterwards. I'm not going to be had again.'

And then his uncle was the spitting image of his father. The boy resented him for looking so much like the traitor. As for what he thought of Chlomo, seeing all the attention he got from the lovely Tsipele made the boy unspeakably jealous of him. What was the matter with her, that she sang songs to her brother and told him stories in a language that he, Charles-Victor, did not know? He was jealous of that language, of the beautiful sad lyrics he could not understand.

'That witch Tsipele,' he said to himself, 'now where did she get such words and tunes? Surely down in that cellar where she and her brother lived for years like rats! Underground for all that length of time! Just like corpses. So it's another dead person's trick! That means they're on Jean-Baptiste's side. Against me. I hate them.'

And so he contrived to surround himself with imaginary

enemies, to convince himself he was unloved, detested by everybody, more alone in the world than a lizard in the snowy wastes trapped alive in the ice. All this because he could not get over his mother's demented cry and his father's sobs, and their turning their backs on him. Anyone would have thought that the hunters, when they shot his brother in the forest, had let their bullets continue to ricochet against all the rest of the family.

'I do wonder,' he would sometimes think, 'what those three fools could have mistaken my brother for, to make them shoot at him like that? A badger, a fox, a crow, or a duck? A baby wild boar, perhaps, or a bear cub? But he was just a son of a bitch! That's all. And anyway they turned him into a skunk. A horrible skunk that went all blue.'

He relentlessly immured himself in rage and hatred, defining the territory of his solitude and defending its approaches. The better to establish such a territory, he went off in search of the most deserted spots, the wildest retreats. He found some terrific ones.

He chose three places as sanctums of his utterly barbarous solitude, and he made these places his kingdom. He declared himself a prince. Prince-very-dirty-and-very-naughty. This was the title he gave himself to institute his domain and begin his reign as the betrayed child saved from abandonment by rebellion and anger.

His first and largest possession was an old factory built on the far side of Love-in-the-open Wood, at the bottom of the hill by the river. The factory and its huge warehouses were nothing but ruins now, left to rust, surrendered to the silence and to the water since being bombed in the last war. There was a prevailing tang of damp-corroded iron, of cold, and rancid grease. He liked these smells, especially that of the iron, because of the suggestion of blood in them. Among the metal girders of the semi-collapsed framework heaps of bats nested in clusters. He was not at all afraid of these scowling creatures with their disgustingly smooth wings and piercing cries. He called them 'my lovely little beastie queens', and he yelled out crazy orders to them beneath the collapsed roof.

'Hello, there, my darling beasties!' he was in the habit of calling to them when he arrived at these vast premises so resonant with emptiness. 'Did you sleep well? Got to wake up now, my lovelies, it's time to go and suck the blood of all the cretins in the neighbourhood. Come on, now, wake up, you dreadful lazybones, you hairless rats, you ugly graces of the night, or I'll pull off your claws and wings!' He would address them at length in this way, with a mixture of insults, threats and endearments, straining his neck to look up at the ceiling. The only effect of his yelling was to scare the wild cats lurking in the corners and the other little creatures crawling around everywhere.

Then he inspected his 'metal nation' – huge obsolete machines, rusted tools and objects mouldering in the brackish water left by the rain or the flooding of the river.

'Hey, you things!' he shouted, hitting them with iron bars. 'You wake up, as well! Do your stuff, make a bit of a racket for me! Come on, you things, arm yourselves, get moving, go and strip the bark off all the trees. Let's have some excitement, some loud noise, some action! To arms, you things!'

And he took pleasure in wading in that dark greasy water dyed orange with rust, in extracting from it the pitted objects decaying there, in breaking the last pieces of glass by throwing bolts or stones at them. And he shouted himself hoarse in that silence-seeping emptiness devoid of any murmur of sound but for the viscous lapping of the water and the rustling of the bats when they awakened. He shouted out words whose meaning he did not always understand, and even words that did not exist. He blasted them out, like showers of stones, for hours on end. He hollered them until he lost all sense of language, until his voice cracked and he was overcome with dizziness.

It was during that time that words became like objects to him – rough, massive, metal objects that did not mean anything but struck home. In complete silence. Striking against fear and death. Striking against his mother's cry, his father's sobs, his brother's stink.

'Yah! Listen to that, mother! I can yell, too! My yells are louder than yours, and travel further than yours. Yah! And you, father, snivelling like a sissy in a funk, listen to this: yaaah! And you, too, darling little dead brother with a stomach swollen with blue gases, listen to this: yaaah! Listen all three of you to the great thundering of my orphan voice that will smash your bones and knock your teeth out!'

And the emptiness shattered his cries into even greater volleys. He listened to the repercussions of his voice echoing back and responded to them even more loudly: 'Who's talking? Who dares to reply? Is that you, angels? What do you want?' He could spend hours conducting these absurd dialogues with the echo angels.

But he soon set out to conquer new territories. He was constantly discovering fantastic vestiges of the last war, including a huge blockhouse in the depths of the forest, perched above the factory. This blockhouse was now no more than a vast refuse dump overgrown with nettles, brambles and ferns. Here, it was not rust that ruled supreme, but decay. So he forged for himself a language appropriate to this atmosphere of decomposition, consisting of shapeless words of glaucous sounds and glutinous accents. He slavered these words and spat them on to the walls – in his brother's face. For his brother never ceased to haunt him, from one place to another, and he had constantly to do battle with him all over again. But here, there was no echo; all sounds were deadened the moment they issued into that close air saturated with moisture. So in this place he did not so much shout as growl or gurgle with hollow rumblings in his bowels. And through all these noises he kept inventing, wresting from his throat and belly, he experienced in his flesh and in his heart strange sensations born of closeness, sweat and mud. While his cries in the big factory warehouses, reverberating in the emptiness and cold, had taught him to feel the networks of his muscles, nerves and tendons tensed to the utmost, here in the bunker, filled with fetid warmth, he tried out the texture of his flesh in its sliminess and extreme sponginess. And his stomach rose to heave in his mouth, melting on his tongue and bursting against his teeth like an overripe fruit.

In the course of ferreting around in these concrete lairs now spurned by history and by men and abandoned to vegetal oblivion, he discovered a tunnel with narrow-gauge rails running into it, on which stood an old disused rail-inspection car. From then on, he devoted himself constantly to getting this car in working order and clearing the tracks of obstructing detritus and stones. This tunnel went deep into the earth, then after a long stretch underground it emerged right in the middle of the forest. The rails continued on a winding course through the trees but suddenly disappeared into the undergrowth. A mud-filled crater marked the abrupt terminus of this railway. The jagged ends of the rails lying twisted at the edge of this little bog bore witness to an explosion that must have occurred towards the end of the war.

Charles-Victor made this rail car his chariot of glory, his battle-tank. 'I can also go right down into the earth, like my brother! But that purple skunk can't move. He's rotting and letting his bones crack like dry branches. But I can walk about, I can run underground, I can trundle along like an iron sun into the bowels of the earth!' And he gave out wild piercing cries of glee at the helm of his chariot, to frighten his brother, that decaying blue carcass nailed into his coffin under the roots of the yew-tree. He called the old rail car with its screeching wheels 'my ballerina with a fiendish bum and golden tootsies' and equipped it with a storm lantern.

He rode his fantastic mount through the underground labyrinth, exploring these dark passageways by the sole light of his storm lantern. He liked these solitary rides into the earth's cold darkness, yelling into its entrails, fraught with silence and damp shadows, torrents of abuse and threats in defiance of the dead. He even berated the roots of the trees – the big traitors who had taken his brother's side. He would have hacked them all off had he been capable of it.

If only he could hack off all the roots of the trees, with an axe or a knife, and make all the roots bleed like chopped-up muscles. And make all the trees fall down with a great shattering of branches as he went by. So that not one was left standing, and the forest was turned into a great battlefield. A field of disaster, a field of vengeance.

His lamp, swinging and jangling at the front of the line car, splattered the darkness with intermittent pools of bright yellow light. He liked to see these orbs of light dancing on the walls, momentarily snatching from the darkness glints of things – bits of broken weaponry, rusted helmets, fragments of human bones.

'Hey, there, dead people!' he shouted, swinging his lamp. 'Wake up, I'm coming by! Just look how clever I am with the light, lovely circles of yellow piss, real shooting stars! Hey, there, dead people! I command you to look! His Majesty – that's me! A little order in the ranks there, stand to attention, if you please! His Majesty is passing in glory through your cesspit. And watch out, you band of old carcasses, I've got my eye on you all! And you, too, trees! It's terrible, my eye, it sees everything. It spies on you mercilessly through my bum-hole.'

He saw everything with this third eye. This fierce, magic, anal eye. Most of all he saw what did not exist. And he exhausted himself fighting against hordes of imaginary enemies visible only to this ruthless, rectal eye.

And he discovered yet another place, perfectly suited to his third eye's lunatic gaze. This place was the most squalid and most cramped of his domains, and for that very reason the most splendid: an old hut made of rickety planks, with its door now held in place only by a broken latch; a truly royal, secret chamber that housed his throne. It was an old privy, stuck on the edge of a piece of waste ground on the outskirts of Montleroy – before the war, this is where the village inn had stood. It had long been a large inn, a cross between a bar and a dance hall, where the men of the village gathered in the evening to smoke, drink, and play cards or billiards, and where dancing took place on holidays and special occasions. It was called Eugene and Marcelle's, after its owners. Although the Marcelle in question died before her time, leaving her husband Eugene all on his own, the cafe retained its dual name. Eugene the widower was a very decent fellow who took everything literally, and solemnly stuck to it. So he never called into question the little phrase he had uttered as a young man on his wedding day, which so many others, however, pronounce unthinkingly; he had agreed to marry Marcelle 'for better or worse'. He remained true to this promise, as to all the others he had made. Moreover, it had not been at all difficult for him to do so, for his experience with his wife had been only for the better. The worse had not come until she died; though so loyal and faithful a companion, she had deserted him. She had suddenly left him all on his own, alone to the point of tears.

'Dead or not,' he obstinately repeated to the foolish drinkers who made the mistake of talking to him of remarrying after he was widowed, 'Marcelle was my wife and always will be. With these things, there's no going back on your word. It's for ever. Anyway, who's to say Marcelle isn't still there, behind the counter, and if she can hear you, it must be giving her a turn, poor thing! So enough of your idle chatter. No one's going to take the place of my Marcelle, and that's all there is to be said.'

And Eugene the Widower never did take any other woman into his bed.

On the other hand, he did not hesitate during the war, in the middle of the occupation, to take into his cellar or attic anyone seeking refuge or somewhere to hide. Nor was he surprised to see the Germans turn up at his place one evening without warning and smash down the doors he had just closed. They came armed, with dogs, and immediately overran his house from top to bottom. All the time they were carrying out their search, Eugene the Widower did not let go of the broom he was holding when they came bursting in. He stood rooted to the spot, among his tables that bristled with upturned chair-legs, staring dolefully at the little pile of dust and cigarette-butts that he had just begun to sweep up. He knew what lay in store for him, and he meekly awaited it. He suddenly saw three young men wearing nothing but their shirts file past in front of him with their arms raised. One of the men was trembling, even his lips trembled. The soldiers shot them on the doorstep, right under the sign 'Eugene and Marcelle's'. Then he smelt petrol, and amid the soldiers' shouts he heard a peculiar sound, quite out of the ordinary. The sound of a huge fire flaring up, just like that, all around. It was suddenly very hot, incredibly hot. The windows, the big mirror, and the bottles and glasses standing on the counter and shelves all shattered. A tremendous ruddy laugh encircled him. The table caught fire, along with the upturned chairs, and the billiard balls cracked on the green baize full of holes. And he was still holding his broom.

The moment when his broom also caught fire, he felt, as it were, a very gentle, loving hand laid on his shoulder. He looked round and asked under his breath, 'Marcelle? Is it you, my love?' The sole response was a great onslaught of flames that leapt at his face.

But little Charles-Victor as yet knew nothing of this past, albeit so recent. For him, the entire world was a vast wasteland with no other history but the one that he invented. He was the postwar child, born after all the wars. He was also the child of the post-brother era, the era that came after his mother's cry and his father's sobs. And that was enough for him. That in itself meant another war, a child-scale war, with cries and words for weapons.

The cries, he had honed amid the silence and rust of the old warehouses, bellowing them, until he was hoarse, from the depths of his blockhouse, chanting them at the top of his voice to the juddering rhythm of his rail car on the underground track. But here, in this privy that had escaped the enemy's blaze, it was words that he was to discover – the power and mystery of words. He was to discover how to play with them, savour them, and knead them like clay.

Weeds had overgrown the little wooden shack once painted blue, a blue now so washed-out by the rain, so eroded by the wind, so dirtied by the droppings of birds – whose nests made of twigs wobbled under the edge of the corrugated-iron roof – that a spectrum of other colours had come to the surface. Depending on the light in the sky, sections emerged of faded purples, shades of lavender or pale ink-blue, almond or absinthe green. Sometimes it was even possible to detect indeterminately pinkish patches or tracts of yellow. This fading blue in its slow demise had developed an infinitely subtle play of subdued tones that delighted Charles-Victor.

'My lovely dainty shit house!' he exclaimed with admiration, as he inspected the rickety walls of his shack.

He would shut himself away for hours on end in this godforsaken house of his at the back of beyond; in the dregs of his heart. The smell that pervaded this place was as marvellous to him as the multi-shaded blue on the weather-worn doors. It was a curious mixture of noxious odours – worm-eaten wood, damp earth, sheets of old newspaper putrefying in the urine and excrement at the bottom of the latrine. Spiders had woven huge webs in the corners of the ceiling; he wondered at the delicate intricacy of these finely worked veils of death that flies and mosquitoes came and spangled with their quivering wings.

A wooden box with a large round hole in the middle of it served as a seat. This latrine pit was for him a fabulous chasm – an empire of dark emptiness and the most thrilling vertigo. 'The eye of God,' he had dubbed it. The eye of God, that great Artful Dodger who was always ogling at men from underneath them in order to rob them in passing of their own creation – their shit. And counterbalancing this horizontal hole gaping hugely over the darkness of the earth was another, much smaller, vertical hole right above the door. This little window, the sole aperture for light – narrow rays of which nonetheless filtered in through the countless cracks between the wooden planks – was heart-shaped. Depending on the time of day, the sky was stencilled in heart shapes of every colour. 'The sky is very fickle-hearted,' he concluded, 'a weather cock philanderer.'

There were plenty more in the way of hearts: crude drawings on the walls of completely crooked hearts, pierced with arrows and garnished with initials – veritable little heraldic devices celebrating nothing but old passions, past desires, long-lost kisses. There were also other drawings and graffiti covering the walls with obscenity. It was at this academy, with no other instructor but the wind blowing all around and whistling over the tin roof, and on wooden slates such as these, with the scribblings of ribald drunkards, that Charles-Victor was schooled in words. He did not understand all of them and diligently read and reread these enigmatic phrases, tracing each letter with his fingertips, and spelling them out aloud. But though he did not understand everything entirely, he had an adequate sense of the power engraved in these words: a power connected with their very outrageousness and crudeness, and glorified by an aura of taboo. For of this he was certain – he felt it fiercely, deliciously – all these drawings and graffiti spoke only of things that were taboo: men's penises and women's breasts, smutty declarations, insults and obscenities of every kind. All these words – words naming the body and desire, the body and its pleasures, its parts of darkness, its magic hardening, its hidden juices – he made his own. They were word-matter, raw, fecal, seminal matter, living matter.

He tore pages from his school exercise-books, to use for a secret diary that he wrote on his lap, sitting on his privy, in full view of the glowering eye of God. He called it 'Diary of a Pooh', and entered in it all the salient facts of his constant battle against his blue skunk of a brother, against his mother's cry and his father's sobs. An imaginary battle, unchecked and endless, aggravated by its very isolation; a battle fought with rude words and obscenities, against phantom enemies. A battle pitting word against word, body against word, a knife battle.

But he became involved in another battle, a real rough-and-tumble battle. For he found an adversary who was quite his equal, in the person of a little girl hardly any older than himself. She was a young gypsy who happened to be passing through the area. Her family had set up camp on the banks of the Meuse, not far from the village. Just like him, she, too, ran wild in the fields and forests, and kept away from school. But she ran barefoot, and was also completely naked under her coloured petticoats that were all stained and torn. Charles-Victor came across her in the old factory warehouses; she was playing hop-scotch amid the ruins and the old machines.

'Hey! What are you doing here?' he shouted the first time he saw her. 'This is my territory. Go away!'

But the little girl stuck out her tongue and replied, 'See if I care! Everywhere's my territory.' And she continued leaping about, tossing her head, with its black tousled mop, making her grubby-flowered petticoats flare out like petals.

'Hey!' he exclaimed. 'You're not wearing any knickers!'

She laughed, not in the least embarrassed, and retorted, 'So what? My bum's just fine the way it is!'

Charles-Victor was actually of the same opinion, and without more ado went rushing towards the girl, with great yells.

Her name was Lulla. Her slanted eyes were a very soft and luminous green, and she was always bare-bottomed. He called her Lulla-my-brawl and fought with her like a crazed pup. He liked the green, green sparkle of her eyes, the already bitter taste of her skin, and the smell of fire and wind in her never-washed hair. He liked her wild ways and her pretty, impudent laughter, and above all the blithe shamelessness of her buttocks that remained the prize of all their tussles.

★

Lulla-my-brawl. She was his first pal, his first playmate, sharing his games, dreams and adventures. And his first love. He did her the honours of his three domains. But he never spoke to her of his brother, Jean-Baptiste, the great blue Skunk that nonetheless continued to haunt him. Nor did he ever take her on his rail car, his chariot for waging battle against the trees underground. Lulla-my-brawl was allied with life, desire, joy; he sensed this too powerfully to want to drag her along on his rovings in the land of the dead. And besides, he so hated his blue skunk of a brother that he was jealous of his hatred, as a lover is jealous of his love. He could not share it, even with his only friend. He, Prince-very-dirty-and-very-naughty, ruled over a dual kingdom: one of play and desire, of the body and pleasure, together with tough and alluring Lulla-my-brawl with her she-devil's bum; and one of anger and hatred directed against the blue Skunk, whose pestilence still blighted the air, and perpetually blighted this forsaken child's heart. And his dual kingdom remained strictly segregated, for he was just as jealous of his hatred of his brother as he was of his passion for Lulla – for Lulla's buttocks which he liked to bite, scratch and fondle. For each brother, a sister: for the dead brother buried in the earth, the sister that did not exist, the invisible fair-haired little girl; and for him, the living brother, an unruly gleeful sister with a pretty pert bottom. So he ruled over this dual kingdom by the power of words apprehended and explored in their dual nature: death-words snatched out of the earth and mud, out of the blue belly of his dead brother, and life-words stolen from the flesh and that which was taboo, from the walls of the privy, and above all from Lulla's lips and bum. In fact he regarded the little girl's pudenda as a second mouth containing deep inside it fabulous words as yet unknown to him.

He, the hurt, betrayed child, survived, thanks to this magic power of words – the only power he had, which he kept wanting to double, to multiply, to intensify.

2

On the far side of words, beyond all cries, was Night-of-gold-Wolf-face. He, too, had been a postwar child, but he was not so much born of a woman's womb, but rather a war wound. A wound that had never closed again, never healed. He owed his entry into the world to a sabre cut. And he had come into this world in the middle of the night, stealing a star on the way. A star that broke up into a strange constellation, whose dispersed points of lights in the course of time occasionally died out. Seventeen points of light, ten of which had already died out, fading into darkness. And these ten extinguished lights were as many sons and daughters laid to rest, surrendered to absence.

Children, and wives, that had passed away. With the death of each one, he became ever deeper immersed in silence, in the loss of words.

Night-of-gold-Wolf-face, for whom death had no use, whom death had rejected. And old age seemed to have no greater use for him. At over seventy-five, he remained as he had always been, his body firm with strength and vigour, his shaggy hair an unchanging red-brown. He may have looked even taller and sturdier than before, and his face, with its weathered, wrinkled skin, remoulded by age, was yet more striking. Only his voice, his voice more than anything else, had changed. As if the loss of speech that had afflicted him for a long time after the death of Ruth and their four children had left its mark on him. A mark of coldness, of dull greyness. A certain mattness of silence. Unless it was the taste of death, with which he had filled his mouth one night in the clearing in Dead-echoes Wood, still making his voice sound so curiously husky. That terribly bitter and persistent taste that made him always keep his lips drawn back somewhat tightly over his bared teeth, as in love-making.

He no longer lived at Upper Farm. Since his failed

suicide attempt in Dead-echoes Wood, he had never again set foot in his house. The house where he had lived for more than half a century, where he had known love four times – one of these a very great and wonderful love – was no longer his. All of a sudden it had become a forbidden place to him, a blasted spot. The stones of his house enclosed nothing but darkness now; a terrible acid darkness in which the women he loved had dissolved, one after the other, struck down by death, madness or war. Dissolved in black, acrid excretions of blood. He had bequeathed his farm to his children – his few surviving children – Mathilde, Baptiste and Thadée.

Mathilde had claimed her father's room, and her father's big bed. The very bed in which she and all her brothers and sisters were conceived and born, and where her mother had given up the ghost one spring morning. The bed thrice sullied by her faithless father's new, successive loves. Two of these usurping wives had died in it, like her mother. The third had gone to perish far away. She was said to have disappeared in smoke and ashes, like a common-or-garden bundle of firewood. Yet it was she, more than any other, who had left the deepest impression in the bed. It was she, the foreigner, who had eventually driven her father out of his room, away from the house. For it was the memory of her body, her arms, mouth, breasts and belly, that her mad father had fled like some wounded animal, crazed with grief. Mathilde was aware of this, angrily so. But she, with her rebel virgin's body, her female body excised by rage and defiance, would manage to drive out any ghosts and restore this room to the dimensions of none but her mother.

Baptiste and Pauline were in the room that had once been the girls' room, and their two children had the one that had always been the boys'. Thadée moved into what had formerly been the refuge of Two-brothers and Nicaise, in old Jean-François-Iron-rod's shack.

They had all done up their own rooms, repainted the walls, tried to give a new atmosphere to the big farm that had survived the war, to wrest it from the past. But the patriarch's shadow nevertheless persisted; a great shadow cast like a veneer of golden night upon the walls, shutters, doors and furniture. Despite being wrested from the past, Upper Farm retained its memories.

And besides, had not the cry, Pauline's crazed cry on that late-afternoon under the teeming autumn rain, re-established a link with this suppressed past? Had it not restored eloquence to memory? A deeply buried eloquence, consisting of echoes and responses.

The ever broken cry, perpetually renewed, reverberating through one life after another.

Night-of-gold-Wolf-face had done battle with this cry; he had strangled it. He had left his home. He continued to work his land all around the farm, sometimes even venturing into the middle of the yard, but he never entered the house. There was no indoors for him any more, no within. The whole world had turned itself inside out like a glove. A glove of human skin, with the flesh rawly exposed. He was for ever more turned out of doors.

The house where he lived stood beyond the fields, on the hillside facing Upper Farm. This house was not even part of the village of Blackland, but of a mere location on the map that went by the name of The Three Spellbound Dogs. No one from thereabouts could have explained precisely the origin of this name; it dated back to some obscure legend from the time when men, through carelessness or curiosity, began to meddle with the occult powers of Evil and suddenly found themselves transformed into beasts. These spellbound dogs were none other than the werewolf manifestations of three reckless monks who had supposedly taken the risk one day of reading a dread and mysterious tome forbidden to novices – or so the story went, without being given any real credence, but without being taken too lightly either. No one could have put a date on that day that went back to the darkness of time, nor could anyone have given details of what book of magic was involved. Some old women claimed it was the Bible that these three over-inquisitive young monks had tried to read backwards, as if this reversed reading of the Holy Book were to reveal to them the secret of Creation. But they had been struck down half-way through by God's anger. The fact remains that the name stuck, as firmly attached to those few acres of land as the old beech trees growing on it.

Here, there stood a huge residence of lightly ochred stone; it was called Beauteous-shade, because of the immense shade in which the surrounding beeches and oak-trees enveloped it. It was true the house had once been beautiful, in the days when the Roumiers lived in it. The Roumiers were horse-breeders, for generation upon generation. Breeding horses so strong and plucky that they had, in the previous century, to the greater glory of the Roumier family, accompanied the Emperor's Old Guard to Russia. But it was not only the sturdy little horses with coats the colour of wolf-pelts that had developed a liking for adventure and faraway places: the Roumier sons, too, had then started to emigrate. One had gone to Canada, another to Africa, and a third to Asia. But just like the little war-horses that had gone off to serve the Emperor, the Roumier sons never came back. The little horses died in the cold; the Roumier sons put down roots in their various distant lands. Then when the father died, the house was left with no heir to claim it, and slowly it withdrew under its great vault of shadow and silence. Beauteous-shade has thus fallen into a vacant and very damp slumber for close on a century, in the course of which its walls and beams and floorboards had gradually surrendered to decay and ruin. And of its original name the house retained only the shadowy part.

Then one fine day, after the last war, the decrepit doors and windows opened again. The person who opened them was the last surviving heir of this family now scattered to the four corners of the globe; she was the daughter of old Roumier's youngest son, the one who had settled in Asia, in the Gulf of Siam. To have come back and taken up residence in the shade of the beeches, over the Meuse, she must surely have been as ruined as the abandoned house. It was in this dilapidated dwelling, with the inheritor of this shady pile, that Night-of-gold-Wolf-face found refuge. He did not even remember how this had come about. It did not matter. Nothing mattered any more. He let the days pass, events occur, people and things come and go, without paying them any attention, without giving any thought now to their meaning.

She called herself Mahaut de Foulques, claiming to be of an age and with a past as fanciful as her name. But even more freakish was the character of this woman who had turned up one fine day, from heaven knows where, in the middle of The Three Spellbound Dogs. She would immure herself in her house for weeks at a time, with all the shutters closed, then suddenly fling open all the doors and windows again, and go wandering off through the fields and forests. Whenever she set off like this on her rambles, walking briskly with little hurried steps, with her nose turned skywards as though to sniff the wind and the bellying clouds, her eyes sparkling at so much rediscovered space and brightness, she would chirrup away continuously, quaintly nodding her head. Anyone that saw her would not have been able to say whether this chirruping was some confused monologue, quiet singing or laughter. All they could say about it was that she sounded like a reed warbler. And did she not, like a reed warbler, always head for watery places? Ponds, pools, and above all riverbanks. Her wanderings always led here: she would crouch in the damp thickets, with her arms clasped around her knees, and for a long time remain motionless in the waterside shadows, quietly modulating her strange monotonous song.

Modulating the painfully haunting song of her memory. Tec tec tiritiriti . . . zec zec zec oowoyid oowoyid oowoyid oyid oyid . . . Her memory; her love, her sorrow. Her memory congested with dark rustling forests, saturated with dampness and sickeningly, deliciously, heavy smells, battered by warm rains. Her memory steeped in green shadows of near-blackness and watery light ruffled by birds. Tec tec tec tiri tiri ti . . . Her memory splashed with stains of scarlet – coral-tree and tamarind blossoms, conflagrations of trees and creepers set alight in the jungle, pools of blood, and red-tiled roofs, buffaloes with clay-covered flanks – and the great river with its sluggishly flowing, brick-coloured waters. Her memory reddened like the mouth of a beggar constantly chewing his betel leaf. Oowoyid oowoyid oowoyid . . . Memory swollen with mud and unrestrained desire.

She remained there for hours on end, gazing at the river, towing her memory against the stream, against the tide of time and history, just as the river Tonlé Sap, when in spate, suddenly reverses its flow, directing its waters, swollen by the monsoon, into great lakes to the north, inundating fields and forests. She went back over her life, returned to days gone by, to her lost happiness. She returned to her youth, steeping herself in her past. She would remain there until nightfall, crouched in the undergrowth, on the very edge of the river, with her head resting on her knees, staring with a fixed gaze. Zec zec zec . . . An extremely fixed gaze, until there arose all around her the great lake-forests and songs of out there.

She was said to be a liar and a fantasist. People did not like her bogus airs and graces, her foreign ways, her exile's gaze, her peculiar reed-warbler's chirping. They were sceptical of her name; they speculated about her past; they made fun of the way she dressed and joked about her skin that was too white, like breadcrumb soaked in milk. Sometimes she was stricken with violent fevers – sudations of memory. It was then that she would lock herself up in her house, with all the shutters closed. She said she was sick. She was mainly thought to be a bit daft, and it was not long before she was given a nickname that dismissed the arrogant pretentiousness of her own name: Milady Crackpot, she was known as locally.

But she was not at all bothered by the rumours and sarcastic comments made about her. To her, all these people from the surrounding villages of Montleroy and elsewhere were just like those troops of monkeys uttering their piercing cries in the depths of the dark forests: a noisy rabble.

Dark, airless forests with no paths. The forests of her memory. Impenetrable, suffocating. Yet she had lost some part of herself out there. Some part of herself had remained there, tangled in the creepers and giant ferns, in the stridulation of insects, the susurrations of humidity, the harsh cries of wild peacocks. Some part of herself kept returning out there, relighting fires at the foot of those giant trees shrouded in moss and vegetation. Oowoyid oowoyid oowoyid . . . Her memory quietly intoned its chant, giving chase in the gloom of the past to the fug of forgetfulness, to the furtive emergence of some lost image, some past sensation that would sometimes flash by, very quickly, just like slender lizards with translucid skin scuttling across the walls. Zec zec zerrr . . . Her watchful memory would pounce on the image, catch the lizard – and be left with nothing but the tiny, immediately shrivelled-up tail, and the images would be gone again. Oowoyid oowoyid oowoyid . . . Her frantic, stubborn memory would start singing again.

As for Night-of-gold-Wolf-face, it mattered little to him to know exactly who this woman was that he had fetched up with. She could call herself whatever she liked, or what anyone else wanted – Mahaut de Foulques, Roumier, or Milady Crackpot, he did not give a damn. Let her wander the tortuous paths of her sick memory until she dropped, let her invent all the names she pleased and imaginary glories without number, let her fabricate her past – it was none of his concern. He himself had no memory any more. He had spewed it up in the depths of Dead-echoes Wood at the end of the war. A gruel of red grain, sweat and tears mingled together. A gruel of rat poison. He had poisoned his memory. He was dead to his memory, dead of too much memory. A memory distorted by grief, for ever laid to waste by the fury of a name: Sachsenhausen. He had to destroy his memory that had been turned into a monstrous beast by the black alchemy of history. A memory made to resemble those giant rats that towns visited by plague for a long time once used to breed: it had eaten away his heart.

Now every day rang hollow for him, every night resounded with emptiness. And along with his memory, he had also spewed up time. For him, time did not exist any more. He had dropped out of time. The years could continue to pass, accumulating on his shoulders, nothing in him bowed or weakened. Every morning he rose exactly the same as the day before, unbroken in his age, unbroken in his strength. 'That Wolf-face,' people would go round grumbling, 'will live to be more than a hundred. He's a werewolf. He's made a pact with the devil!' And old women crossed themselves in terror at the mere mention of old Peniel's name.

Quite to the contrary, Night-of-gold-Wolf-face had made no pact with anybody – neither God nor the Devil! Not even death had any use for him. All that he had done was to team up with Mahaut. But who else could he have encountered, other than this woman who had suddenly pitched up out of nowhere, coming to roost in a derelict house in the shade of the huge beeches at The Three Spellbound Dogs. This woman with her white skin and warbler's voice, whose memory went rambling through fabular forests.

It was not love that united them, nor even desire, but a shared sense of being away from the world, of being banished from everything, and everybody, and from themselves. It was a shared violence, of forgetfulness for one, of memory for the other. It came to the same thing. Perhaps they had never actually seen each other? They collided with each other. They were just two bodies adrift with forlorn hearts. They collided with each other like wild animals, always fleeing, and only ever possessed each other in haste, with distraught gestures. They only came together the better to tear themselves apart, yielding their bodies then to total separation. Their lovemaking was unconnected with desire, had nothing to do with tenderness, but now and again threw them, blindly, into physical contact with each other, as though in a ritual fight, then just as abruptly cast them far apart again. They only made love together the more thoroughly to lose themselves, from all and sundry, to make their banishment from themselves even greater. And they never kissed when making love, as if fearing that from the mere contact of their mouths deeply buried, blocked-off words and names might suddenly break out again and rise to burn their lips. They made love hastily, with a kind of callousness, as though in a low-class brothel.

And when Mahaut gave birth to two sons, that, too, was something that happened at a distance, a very great distance, from themselves. Right up to the last, she had no regard whatsoever for her pregnancy – had she not left her real body behind, on the banks of the great river with its turbid waters the colour of dried blood?

Two new sons marked with the Peniel sign. The last-born sons of Night-of-gold-Wolf-face. They were not given any first names.

'The names of saints and archangels are unlucky,' said Night-of-gold-Wolf-face.

And Mahaut said, 'They don't count, children don't. They don't exist, they don't need names. Names are something that come to you with age, something that grows with your body. They can call themselves what they like, later on, when life has given them something of a history.'

Yet since the two latest offspring of the Peniel tribe had to be referred to somehow verbally, in the expectation of better names they were known as September and October, the twins having been born astride of these two months. They had their whole lives ahead of them to identify themselves in terms other than the time of year. And once again it would actually be life that determined what they were called. One was to become September-the-long-suffering, and the other October-the-most-bitter.

Charles-Victor was three years their elder. But not until many years later was he able to make their acquaintance and strike up a friendship with them. Although they spent their entire childhood just a few kilometres apart, they never met and never played together. Like a strategist selecting his combat zones, so Charles-Victor had opted where to play his rebellious games, in solitude and secrecy. And anyway, he had enough to do, with the constant battle to be fought against his blue Skunk of a brother, his big namby-pamby father, and his mother's cry, to have either the time or the desire to fraternize with his younger uncles. Besides he had a horror of twinship, and took pains to hunt down any resemblance in himself to the gamy corpse that was his brother, in order to extirpate it on the spot. He wanted to be a real live person, wholly alive, and not one of those survivors stricken with melancholy and stinking of dead bodies like all the other relicts of the living in his family. A real live person, free and unique, without any obligation to share with a double. So, let his uncles play together, in the absurd mirror they held up to each other.

And then, even if he had wanted to spend time with his young uncles, he would not have been able to. Mahaut did not like children, and her two surprise arrivals were enough of a nuisance and a disturbance in themselves. She certainly did not want to have any more around her, running about shrieking.

'They're like monkeys, children are,' she said, 'leaping and climbing everywhere and squalling the whole time and, what's more, stealing anything left lying around.'

She was particularly frightened they would steal her memory – and what else could they have stolen from that dilapidated house furnished with junk? She had brought back from her faraway lost paradise nothing more than a few fabrics, some pieces of silk, a few pots of make-up and bits of jewellery. Just enough to brighten her hours of nostalgia and dress up her memories, like cadavers groomed and pomaded for burial.

But what if her sons were in any case to deprive her of the very thing that was already slipping away from her all the time: her past, her youth, her life out there. Out There. Out There. Her Far Eastern yesteryear, her glory as a White Woman in the colonies.

For they had nothing in common with her past. They had been sprung upon her, without warning, at the age of over forty – and two of them, what's more; yelling and wriggling about like little macaque monkeys, and always hungry. Why were they not born Out There, in the big white city, with blinds the colour of mango leaves, steeped in ruddy shadows and the smell of fruits with succulent flesh, of brightly coloured flowers, of spices and brine. If they had been born Out There, in the days of her wealth, happiness and youth, she would have loved them . . . perhaps. She would have dressed them in white, taken them for walks along avenues so broad and quiet, and in the big public gardens of the smart European quarter. And later on, they would have become traders, like her father and her grandfather, or planters, or bankers, or even civil servants, with their entree to balls and parties at the governor's palace. Ah, if only they had been born Out There . . .

But she might also have gambled them on some game of chance, just as she had gambled all her other possessions, and might have lost them. And ultimately that was precisely what it was that she had so loved Out There: that perpetual invitation to gamble and lose. That invitation to lose everything, to lose yourself. That delicious languor it gave to feel you were in a legendary elsewhere. But why had they turned up here, in this dark house in this godforsaken place, so impregnated with cold? They were not even any use for playing roulette with. On what number, what colour could she have placed them? What good would it have been here to present them tied together with a purple silk ribbon round their necks, crying out gaily, 'I lay my golden-eyed pair of twins on the 3!' No, they had definitely arrived too late, choosing the wrong place and the wrong mother. They were going to grow up and force her to look where she certainly did not want to look. They were going to wrest her from her dream, distract her from her past and misdirect her towards a future she wanted nothing to do with. Her past was enough for her, her memory served as present and future. Her memory – her legend, her eternity. So where did these two little monkeys fit in? Where was the justification for their existence? Nowhere. In any event, not in her life, not even in her heart.

Her heart had remained Out There, back East, and did not want to look westwards. Her heart belonged entirely to her memory, and her memory, already, to oblivion, like those guardian spirits seated in their ruined temples in the depths of primeval forests made muggy by warm rains and choked with gigantic creepers and tree ferns. And this oblivion, too, was part of the legend, like the most vacant, sacred thoughts of the stone gods whose eyes buzzed with insects – clusters of green tears.

But this memory that constantly mingled memory and forgetfulness, reality and dream, and above all falsehood, was even more vigilant than the stone dragons, the fantastic serpents with fan-shaped heads, the tigers, the fabulous sculpted birds at the gates of neglected gods: it only allowed the servants of her madness access to her heart. So she would have to disguise her sons as servants. Then maybe the two little monkeys would find a place in her heart – or at least in the service quarters of her heart.

As for Night-of-gold-Wolf-face, he had not much more of a welcome to offer them. His heart was devoted entirely to absence. He who had so dearly loved his wives did not even look at this one, his fifth and last wife. Nor did he listen to her. His warbling wife, dressed up in baggy black silk trousers and bedecked with precious stones, could chatter away till she was blue in the face, he did not hear her. He who had so dearly loved his children and grandchildren hardly paid any attention at all to these, his last-born sons. He let them grow up all on their own, in the shade of the big oaks and beeches. As it was, he felt he himself had grown closer to trees than men. He loved the strength and calmness of the trees; he loved their silence, the density of their shade. He loved knowing them to be bound to the earth and spread against the sky, sending their roots ever deeper into the ground as they grew towards the clouds. Yes, he often thought, Little-drum was fortunate, having a female yew-tree come to grow over him. He was going to pass into the roots, the sap and the leaves, to regain colour as myriads of yellow flowers in the spring, and even more so as red berries in the autumn. He was going to experience the taste of the earth in all seasons, the taste of the rain, snow and wind. Night-of-gold-Wolf-face had no other desire but to become a tree, to surrender himself to the earth. To have done with the fuss and folly of mankind, with the unbearable suffering of this world, the wrath of history. To have done with God's anger. God's cruelty. And anyway, had not his shadow the quivering golden hue of the great maples when they were in flower? The shadow that had protected him for so many, many years. What would happen to this light shadow after his death? Would it break away from him to go and attach itself to someone else's footsteps, or would it follow him into the earth, enveloping him like a shroud? But the shadow was already a shroud, bearing the imprint of his grandmother Vitalie's smile, the imprint of her love.

In fact throughout their childhood his last-born sons had no other companionship but that of trees and bushes, and knew no other love but that of plants. And it was in their company that September was taught the very mild patience that was to make him always so open-hearted, and October the great bitterness that was to afflict him, even to a state of gloom.

*

October. The sullen child overwhelmed once a year by a surge of violence. Was it because his mother had deposited in him her surfeit of memory, the sickness of her desire? Or was it because he was born at dawn on the first day of October, the month that, Out There, in his mother's lost paradise, opens with the launch of an offensive, carried out by its fantastic army of winds, rains and storms, against the plain of the Mekong Delta. Or was it that he was the last-born, last-begotten son of Night-of-gold-Wolf-face, already in his sixties at the time? That he had come into the world so late, at the very last of his father's spent desire, at the very tail-end of this already widely scattered line of descendants?

The fact remains that every year, at the time when he should have been celebrating his birthday, he was violently overcome by an extraordinary frenzy, depriving him of all reason, all moderation. He even lost the power of speech, or rather language began to return to its source within him, like the waters of the river Tonlé Sap reversing their flow. He regressed all the way back to the prattlings of an infant full of anger and terror, until eventually he re-released his birth-cry. But then it was not silence that finally established itself; all at once the cry would return, and another alien language emerged that only Mahaut could understand. This would last for about two weeks, during which time Mahaut would shut herself away with her son – her supernatural son, the holder of her memory and even more than just her memory. Her son, made fertile and delivered anew, like a gift of the Mekong. She jealously closeted herself with him in some isolated room in the house, keeping both Night-of-gold-Wolf-face and September at a distance. For then, the child thus invested with this other language, thus fabulously visited, became exclusively hers. He became even more than a son to her; he became a people, a geography, a climate. He became a god. A marvellous gift of the Mekong. He became a shadow theatre in which her memory at last found expression. She veiled him in the smoke of joss-sticks, set out all around him as though around an image of the Buddha. Like a forest of grey, impalpable trees.

Then the reflux would begin. The alien language within him would subside, withdrawing word by word and returning to oblivion. At the end of this reflux the child would then give way to a state of exhaustion fraught with fevers, fears and nightmares. And Mahaut would gradually turn away from him. She would stop the incense burning and eventually chase him out of the sacred room. She would cast him aside. He was just a little macaque monkey again. He was no more than a child fallen out of favour, for the gift of the Mekong had deserted him. He could no longer speak anything but an ordinary, profane language, a language she detested.

Only his brother September, who had been awaiting his return, would seek him out again, to offer his affection, and bathe his face with cool water to wash away his extraordinarily sour sweat. Only September knew how to say to him, 'There's nothing to be afraid of, I'm here. As soon as you're well again, we'll go back and play in the shade of the big trees. We'll both speak the same language. I'll tell you stories that will make you forget the cries of our mother's gods.'

But though October managed to forget the language of these foreign gods, he could not forget the violence of their passing, and he spent all the rest of the year in secret dread of their return.

3

Pauline's illness lasted for months, and she spent the whole time confined to her room with the shutters closed. Then one morning she got up, wrapped herself in the big cashmere shawl in shades of orange-red that Baptiste had given her when Charles-Victor was born, and she opened the shutters a fraction. The light blinded her and made her reel. But she remained at the window with her eyes half-shut and her hands clasped on her chest. Her body slowly recovered its stature and balance, and regained its senses. She glimpsed in the distance the dark blue, almost purplish forests shaking off the last shadows of night and sending a flurry of screeching crows soaring into the sky. The earth looked pink to her. She noticed the figure of a man on the road, and recognized Night-of-gold-Wolf-face. She suddenly recalled their first encounter, and the very simple way in which he had taken her in when she came during the war to seek refuge on his farm. He was on his way to the fields. The flock of crows flew over him, veered towards the marshes, then disappeared. Night-of-gold-Wolf-face, her father-in-law. All at once a great pity overwhelmed her, for that old man stricken with forgetfulness and anger, who had so often come to grief on the very brink of death without ever completely foundering. What could he be thinking? But perhaps he did not even have any thoughts now. He went on, come what might, never deviating from his path and always working hard. He kept going, in the margins of time. But by what necessity, she wondered, does he keep going like that? Was fate the power that kept him stubbornly alive, full of endurance and bitterness? Or was it some mystery of that perverse and terrible grace with which God oppresses men? But the moment that Night-of-gold-Wolf-face left the road and struck out across his fields, Pauline's thoughts, too, left her. She trembled at the glimpse of all this daylight, this end-of-winter brightness that she could feel, so fresh and keen, in her fingertips, and so light on her face. She could not yet focus her attention on anything, or follow a train of thought, or keep an idea in her head. With her whole body and mind, she groped towards this new lease of life and air and light, gently reaching her through the barely opened shutters. She had just recovered from her extremely long death-illness, and she still felt very weak, like a woman after childbirth. She moved a chair to the window and sat there, with her hands lying in her lap, her palms turned upwards.

'And now,' she thought without even seeking an answer to her question, 'what is to become of me? So life continues, and I must follow suit? So I haven't died from the death of my son? I'm here, I survive, as old Night-of-gold-Wolf-face has survived all his bereavements. What I am going to do with this reprieve? What can I do with my life? Will God eventually have pity on us? God? How strange everything seems suddenly, even the thought of God . . . Strange and agreeable . . . Unimportant . . . ' She closed her eyes and dozed off.

Down in the courtyard, outside, someone was watching her. It was young Chlomo. He had climbed an elm in search of a nest that he had noticed a magpie building in the topmost branches. He liked hunting out the nests of these birds, as shy as they were thieving, for there were always curious treasure-troves of glass and bits of metal to be found in them, with which he would then amuse himself, creating mobiles or making jewellery to give to his sister.

There he was, clinging to the trunk, half-way up the tree, among branches covered with delicate clusters of pink stamens. He had seen the shutters of Pauline's window open, and this had surprised him, for since the death of Jean-Baptiste, this room had always remained closed. He kept looking, suddenly more curious about this window than the magpie's nest. Then in the dimness of the room, by the fractionally open window, he caught sight of Pauline's bewildered face. He did not immediately recognize it. Pauline's face seemed to have no more substance than a ray of moonlight. All her features had, as it were, faded, leaving the strange golden shadow of her eyes, an undulation of subdued light. He recognized this glimmer, impinged upon by obscurity and silence, that slowly comes into eyes for too long hunted down in darkness and fear, for he had it in his own eyes in the days when he lived in hiding with his sister down in a cellar. And slowly, inexorably, the echo of a song began to rise within him, a distant song and yet so near. One of those songs Tsipele used to murmur to him quietly, very quietly, to suppress the madness of fear and the desire to cry, when they were both cowering behind crates and barrels. One of those songs that do not even dwell in the memory, but like tears repeatedly swallowed gradually dissolve into the blood and penetrate to the heart's core. One of those songs that maybe are not even songs any more, but sobs whispered on the very brink of silence, a secret and translucid trickle within . . . '*Aiee lu luli Nacht un Regen . . . lu luli Nacht and Vint . . .*'

He remained there, perched in the elm tree in the cool pink shade of its flowering boughs, and his body grew more crackly than the bark. '*Aiee lu luli ai li luli Nacht . . .*' He, too, was a lost child, far from his mother, a little boy for a long time marked out for death. How well he knew that bewildered look Pauline had! He knew it to the point of tears and trembling. He did not even know any more who was looking at whom. '*Aiee lu luli Nacht and Regen . . .*' Nor could he tell who was the child and who the mother or sister, who was dead and who the survivor. Everything became confused, slowly spinning round, receding into darkness. '*Geien sei in shvarze Raien . . . geien, geien . . .*' They had all gone, grandparents and parents, black figures packed into rows, crowded on to trucks, then separated from each other, and burned in ovens . . . So whose face was that, scarcely visible at the window? His mother's perhaps? He clung even more tightly to the tree. He became a branch of the tree; his heart beat inside the trunk. The clusters of stamens turned into so many eyelids with tears contained behind them. '*Aiee li lulilu . . .*'

But what he saw suddenly released the tears, like budding flowers. Did he in fact see it with his own eyes, or through those many closed eyes in the rustling pink around him? For what he saw did not exist – did not yet exist.

He saw it in Pauline's vacant gaze: he saw that she was carrying a child, a new child, a little girl. But a child so recently conceived, not even the mother had any inkling of it. He forgot about his song, and the elm-tree, and the magpie's nest. He slid down the trunk and as soon as he reached the ground he raced off, and just kept running, in a state of keen excitement. All at once he felt happy, tremendously happy. Inexplicably happy. When he was completely out of breath, he dropped to the ground on the edge of a field and lay stretched out in the bed of a furrow in the damp rich earth, and the smell of the earth made him even more elated. He began to laugh, with a new kind of laughter. A real child's laughter, at last. The morning brightness bathed his face and blinded his eyes. He laughed. His breathless heart palpitated in his chest. The world opened up around him – earth and sky. It grew increasingly light. He was done with fear, with the terrible mustiness of the cellar that for years had cast a pall over his childhood. He laughed. He felt free and light. He had seen the child so recently conceived that no one yet knew about.

But what had he actually seen? In truth, nothing. He had caught sight of Pauline's white face, steeped in absence, in the shadow of the shutters. And that face momentarily illuminated by the countless pink flames of the clusters of stamens trembling on the branches of the elm had opened up to him, the hunter of magpie treasures. He had been dazzled by the fragility and mystery of that face; he had stolen its secret. For that face had unknowingly confessed to being the bearer of a promise: a child was to be born. And it was to be a little girl even more beautiful than that

April morning. And then and there, he made that little girl, only just present on the verge of existence, his joy, his hope, his love.

This was what he had seen, without understanding any more than that. And he laughed, rolling his head in the earth, in the bed of the fresh furrow. Maybe he himself was born just at that moment.

Pauline emerged from her room and her silence. So, there she was, one morning, walking through the house again, and talking. Indeed, she talked about everything – everything, except him: Little-drum. Day or night, his name was never mentioned. She did not wake up during the night any more. She did not dream or cry out. Something inside her had broken the terrifying power of the dream, had silenced the cry.

Then she wanted to see Charles-Victor again, to have him back with her. But it was too late. The child had grown so wild his heart was now a wasteland bristling with nettles, brambles and broken glass. When she tried to approach him, to give him a kiss, he broke away with anger and revulsion. For to every part of his mother's body – her hands, her face, her hair – clung a nauseating smell of blood and putrefied flesh. The smell of his brother, the smell of betrayal. And he wrote in his Dairy of a Pooh: 'Mother's back. Her skin's all white and soft like curdled milk, it's revolting. She gives me smiles that turn my stomach and hugs me like a snake. I don't want her smiles and hugs, and I don't want her. I'm an orphan and I want to stay that way. In any case I've found my own house. It's a wooden shed with a little window, a lovely shit house that would make any king green with envy. It smells of piss and pooh in my house, and it smells good, much better than mother, who stinks of curdled milk and skunk's blood. I want to stay in my house full of bluebottles, big blue cockroaches and nice soft white maggots. And if mother comes and sticks her old weasel-face in my little window, I'll rub dirt in her eyes and mouth. Hurray! I'm

Prince-very-dirty-and-very-naughty, and I'm an orphan and I'm very happy. Mother can go to hell, I don't want her any more.'

Pauline eventually grew to fear this wild child with spiteful, almost cruel eyes. She saw that his heart was closed, and try as she might she could not find a way into that heart. Yet she said nothing. She decided to show patience. She felt guilty; guilty of all the ills that had befallen them: Jean-Baptiste's death, the distress for too long suffered by Baptiste, Charles-Victor's infuriated loneliness. During the war when she was separated from Baptiste, she was able to be strong, to wait and hope. And Baptiste had returned to her. But the strength she had then was lost to her, for it did not reside within her. That strength resided in her first-born son, the child she had watched growing up at her side: Little-drum, who was so good at beating up expectation and hope. Little-drum had fallen in peacetime. Silent now and for ever, he lay buried in the earth. And yet she had to be strong again, to face up to time, to the amazing whirl of time that seemed constantly to be ebbing and flowing all at once. Then she remembered the God of flesh and mercy she used to pray to, kneeling at Jean-Baptiste's bedside. That bed was now and for ever empty. But had not that God of flesh and mercy emptied Himself of Himself? Well, she would return to Him, she would kneel beside all that emptiness – the emptiness of God, of her son's bed – and she would pray. But she had no words left, no words equal to all that emptiness, and she did not know how to pray any more. All she could do was get down on her knees and bury her face in her cupped hands. Then a terrible silence reigned inside her. Even worse than silence, it was a coldness of her entire being, a very great coldness that rose in her heart and travelled through her whole body like a fantastic wind whistling across a plain, blowing everything away. Then she forced herself to go to church again. But the mass also remained an empty ritual to her.

The church at Montleroy still bore traces of the devastation suffered during the war. Now without its belfry, it stood very silent in the midst of an expanse of pitted ground left untended. Along one of its half-collapsed perimeter walls was the communal grave where all the dead in those days had been thrown in a heap.

Pauline went to Montleroy every morning, making her way straight to church. The church of St Peter, who three times denied his master. But now who was denying whom? During those yet so recent days when the blood of the village menfolk had dyed the water in the wash-house red, those days without number when the flesh of men, women and children had darkened the sky, covering it with ashes, and on the day that became everlasting when the body of her first-born child was brought to her like the carcass of some poor hunted animal – during those days, who had denied whom? Was it not God who had denied mankind? Was it not God who had consigned hordes of people to death in total abandonment?

Pauline went every day to church, endlessly turning this question over and over in her heart, without ever being able to put it to anybody, without ever getting even remotely close to an answer. Who is denying whom? Who is betraying whom? Who is abandoning whom? The question floundered in the void, turning back on itself, against itself.

Yet in its hollow and haunting resonance the question became a dialogue. But was Pauline's silent appeal to the person facing her every day in church really a dialogue? And did they even face each other, these two equally distressed people, positioned at opposite extremities of the question? Pauline Peniel. Joseph Delombre. And the question between them: who is denying whom?

Father Delombre had arrived only a short while ago in Montleroy, his first parish. He was still young and had only recently been ordained. But that he should have been received into holy orders at all amazed the few parishioners who still went to church, and who soon numbered even fewer. Father Delombre stammered appallingly. He could not deliver the least sentence without halting words and syncopated silences, to such a degree that what he said became completely meaningless, even more so than the spluttered sermons in days gone by of old Father Devranches, who was always being seized with coughing fits. Whatever subject he broached in the pulpit, from Christ's Passion to the Last Judgement, a restlessness would immediately begin among the congregation, a murmur of irritated groans and semi-stifled laughter. His flock soon lost patience, and not being able to obtain from the bishop the removal of this disastrous preacher, they ended up by quite simply deserting the church. Apart from a few somewhat deaf old women who, out of zealous habit, continued to make their dozy appearance in the pews on Sunday, Pauline was the only regular church-goer. But even if Father Delombre's speech impediment had been any more extreme, she would no more have been put off. The haunting question that pulsed inside her like the pendulum-swing of a timeless clock claimed all her attention. And perhaps it was even the case that in her state of total desperation the priest's stuttering words were closer, as though familiar, to her.

But how much closer still was Pauline to Father Delombre's heart? For in this woman who walked down the hill from her distant farm every day to come to church, always to kneel there in the shadow of the pillars, he sensed the very presence of his own destiny – of all destiny. And he sensed the meaning of his vocation open up to face a challenge. She was the other, the infinitely close and distant, the woman in whom all at once and with the utmost intensity the enormity of his responsibility was made evident. And he heard the question that endlessly tormented Pauline. But he heard it pre-empted, turned against itself – and against him. Against everybody. The question he heard through her was the question that Christ had three times put to Peter: 'Do you love me?'

'Do you love me?' God asked him through Pauline's

distress. And to him that meant: 'If you love me, rescue this woman from her distress, untie the knots of her question, save her and her family, save them from suffering and anger.'

Such was the secret dialogue that passed every day in silence between Pauline and Father Delombre.

'Who is denying whom?' she would ask.

'Do you love me?' was what he heard.

A dialogue conducted in profile – a dialogue involving three voices, three silences: Pauline, Delombre and God.

Yes, they spoke in profile, unable to look at each other, not daring to confront each other, for each feared the other's face, each sensed that in the other's face would appear The Face, impossible to look upon, the same Face that had sweated onto the shroud, branded the shroud, then disappeared.

Yet there came a day when Pauline dared to look up at Father Delombre and speak to him, but it was in the dimness of the confessional-box through the small wooden grille. Even though they were so close, all they could see of each other were sections of their faces. Delombre tried to look at the face of the woman who had come to kneel close beside him, but he could only make out isolated fragments, chequered with shadow. A face devastated by doubt, shattered by fear and grief. A face cast before him like pieces of jigsaw. But what could he say with his equally fragmented speech? What response could he give to the muffled cry that she kept repeating over and over again, as though to convince herself of her refusal.

'I don't want this child. I don't want it, I don't want it!'

For what Chlomo had seen was true: Pauline was expecting another child. As soon as she became aware of her condition she was overcome with fear, and refusal. She did not want another child. There was too much grief inside her to be able to give birth again. Her entrails remained scarred by the death of her son. And anyway, what kind of a child would be born of silent weeping? Her first son had been conceived on a day of rain, bare skin and desire. He had been killed on another day of rain. But this new child had been conceived in nothing but its father's tears, in a bed of sadness, without desire. Utterly without desire, for she lay lost to herself, in a state of indifference, when this new child was conceived. She did not want such a child. She did not want any more children, ever. It was against this fear, this refusal that Father Delombre had to fight. He had to save the child, to find for it in the mother acceptance and welcome, and to rescue it from death's darkness and its father's tears.

'I don't want it! I don't want it!' Pauline persisted in repeating, with her hands clutching at the wooden grille.

And every time she said it, that other cry, full of entreaty, echoed in Delombre: 'Do you love me?'

'Do you love me?' Joseph Delombre kept hearing, and that voice without a voice that pleaded for itself through Pauline's very recalcitrance was so urgent, so sweet, that he had to respond to it each time with equal urgency and sweetness.

Perhaps in the end it was that very voice that began to speak through him, covering up his own poor halting, jarring voice. The words he uttered through the wooden screen did not even come from him any more – the voice spoke within him, tenderly, hurriedly. A murmured cry combating Pauline's rebellious cry word for word.

'It's not yours to say any more what you want or don't want,' he told her, 'for the child does not belong to you. Do we even belong to ourselves? No, we belong to each other, we are one another's. But this bond of belonging is terrible, you see, because it's not reciprocal. We belong to others, but no one can belong to us. That's the way it is: we live in a state of total disequilibrium, and if we don't fall, despite such disequilibrium, it's only because God is sustaining us. And the more we dispossess ourselves, the more we cease to rely on our own strength, our own will, then the more God gives us His support.'

'But I'm scared,' Pauline repeated, 'scared, so scared! It's not even my will that's in mutiny, it not my strength asserting itself, on the contrary it's something very weak and cowardly in me . . . it's my fear . . . a huge, sick, blind fear . . . I just can't . . .'

'Then give this fear to God,' replied Delombre, 'only in Him can such a fear be cast away, relinquished, redeemed . . .'

'It's impossible. My fear and God are one and the same. He has become my fear. Life has become my fear. How could I possibly give my fear to the very one who is my fear?'

'By renouncing the fear, by abandoning yourself to it totally. You're fighting against your fear too much, you're protecting yourself from it too much – and badly. This terror and sorrow inside you are beyond your strength. It's no use resisting; you're defeated in advance. You're already defeated. The moment you finally admit this, that you're defeated, when you give up your pointless struggle, then, only then, will you be free of this fear. Let the child develop inside you, let it have its chance . . .'

'Chance? What chance?' Pauline immediately cried. 'What about my chance? And my son Jean-Baptiste, killed as a child: what chance did he have? And my second son who's become more vicious than a wild dog: what's happened to his chance? Eh? And my father-in-law, old Peniel, and his wives and all his children: what chance did they have? Life has continually robbed that man, completely despoiled him to the point of utter ruin! Where was his chance? What about that of my parents, who died in the bombing during the war? What chance have we Borromées and Peniels ever had? What chance do men have? And yours, where is it, tell me, where's your chance? Answer me!'

'Adversity, however great, can never destroy the chance we're given . . . Because . . . because . . . the chance we're given has nothing to do with happiness, it's not a victory, it's not related to being strong . . . the chance we're given, do you see, lies in the opposite of all that, in the deepest . . .'

'I don't understand you!' Pauline broke in.

But he persisted, with desperate earnestness. 'I don't think I really understand either . . . but it's something I sense inside me: we are given a chance, it exists. However much we're deprived of that chance by the misfortunes that befall us, it can never be completely lost. Never! For it's associated with sacrifice. It's not a matter of victory, or gain. Especially not gain, in fact. On the contrary, it's the ultimate loss. The chance we're given is . . . is . . .'

'It's a chance to be defeated, then? Is that it?' Pauline cut in harshly. 'If it's not a chance for happiness, or victory, or a chance to be strong, then it's a chance to be defeated. That's absurd.'

'It's neither one nor the other,' he continued breathlessly. 'It's associated with peace. An inner peace, a rediscovered, intimated peace . . . allied to . . . to grace . . .'

'When everything has been crushed, killed, massacred, destroyed, the word peace has no meaning any more! Where grief, sorrow and suffering reign, peace cannot enter, for it's too late by then. Irreparably too late. Chance! Peace! These are words devoid of meaning in a place like ours, regularly laid to waste by war, and especially in my family that's been relentlessly persecuted by fate. Go and ask old Peniel what he thinks of peace and being given a chance! Ask everybody around you! They'll all tell you with anger and disgust that these words are worse than meaningless – they're obscene and offensive. Yes, offensive!'

'We're not talking about the same thing,' Delombre then admitted, slowly raising his head. Sometimes he even placed his hands on the grille, as if he wanted to touch the face screened by it. 'The chance we're given,' he said, 'is simply, when the world disintegrates, when everything collapses around us, and we plummet into the void and into darkness . . . the chance given to us then is to realize that God lies in the depths of that void . . . that He is that very darkness . . .'

'But Christ himself rebelled, and cried out against the God who had abandoned him!' protested Pauline, at the limits of her resistance. 'He, too, succumbed to fear.'

'Yes, he did. But in the moment of his death he added: "Father, into thy hands I commend my spirit" . . . He died in the hands of God, in the empty, flayed hands of God. Even his suffering and fear he commended to God . . . otherwise he could not have died . . .'

'But he himself was God,' Pauline retorted, as a challenge and reproach.

'He was God, and he is God. But in the moment of his death he was also a man. Just a man. As weak and vulnerable in his flesh and in his heart as you and I . . .'

Pauline always left the confessional abruptly. She would get up all of a sudden, sometimes even in the middle of a sentence, and rush off without a backward glance, hurrying through the church. And he would remain where he was for a while, all alone, not moving, his knees aching on the little wooden bench. He listened to the sound of her hurried footsteps, the creaking of the door, and the return of heavy silence.

'I failed to find the right words,' he would say to himself then. 'I was unable to talk to her. Her doubts are stronger than my faith, her rebellion greater than my hope, her suffering more intense than my love.'

And he emerged from these arguments each time more upset and overwhelmed with sadness than the previous occasion. And fear overcame him, too, as if Pauline, in rushing off so suddenly, had left it with him, had pitched it into his heart. But he did not fight against this fear, he let it flood over him, crush him, finally casting him face down on the ground with his arms outstretched, in the silence of his room. He then felt so destitute, at such a loss for words, that he could not even pray. He remained there, lying on the floor, with his eyes and mouth closed, enduring the fear until it spent itself inside him. Until he found the strength again to answer 'yes' to that unrelenting question awaiting him at the confines of fear as soon as day broke: 'Do you love me?'

His reply was a murmur.

★

Pauline kept the child. She stopped fighting. She gave in. But the day she decided to allow her pregnancy to come to term she also stopped going to see Father Delombre. She sent him a letter, a very brief note that said only this: 'You win. I'm carrying the child to term. But this child is alien to me. Nothing matters to me any more. For it's not a chance that I've been given, but something cold, dry and bitter. Indifference. Now let each of us follow our own path. Mine doesn't lead anywhere at present. And I fear this is true of all paths. Including yours. Especially yours, perhaps. I don't want to see you again. I don't know whether or not I should thank you for such stubborn patience as you have shown towards me. Pauline Peniel.'

Delombre knew he had not won. He had not won anything. He felt more affected by Pauline's despair, and more destitute, than ever. But he did not try to see her again, to write to her, for that would only have worsened the young woman's suffering. And the reply to the question that haunted him became ever more sorrowful.

Pauline confined herself to the farm again. She felt her belly swell – it swelled like that of her son in the depths of Love-in-the-open Wood in the blue-green shade of the branches. And her eyes regained their former broken-flint gleam.

'Will I give birth to a child that's blue, purple-blue?' she wondered in terror, remembering Jean-Baptiste's decomposing body. But Crazy-for-her was there, beside her, more concerned about her than ever, trying to chase the image of their first son away from their room, away from his wife's body. He clasped her in his arms, he reassured her of his love, he called her 'my little Princess of Cleves', as he used to, in the days when they met among the books at the back of the Borromean bookshop. But every day she grew a little more distant from herself, from her past and present, and above all, resolutely, from the future. She followed in silence a dead-end path: the path of indifference. Not even

Baptiste's love could open other paths to her. As for Charles-Victor, he watched aggressively out of the corner of his eye. Yet there were nights when he woke all atremble, elated to have regained his mother's love that he had lost. He would suddenly be sitting bolt upright in bed, mumbling, his lips burning with the name that had just torn itself from his heart, ready to call his mother, to throw himself into her arms. But he would immediately control himself. He would sometimes bite his arms and knees, drawing blood, to keep back the name, to suppress his cry to her.

Pauline gave birth to a little girl. It was a premature birth, as if Pauline was in a hurry to have done with it, to get rid of that alien burden. Yet the child did not weigh much at all, and it cries were no louder than a kitten's.

Pauline fought. She did not even know against what. Everything inside her was mixed up, confused – past and present, the living and the dead. But the indifference born of this confusion brought her neither calm nor detachment. Quite the contrary, this indifference manifested itself as a thoroughly violent and feverish illness. And it was against this inward illness that she fought. But the illness was strong; no matter how hard Pauline tried to keep it secret, to keep burying it, it was always breaking out again. And this ailment had a face and a name: Jean-Baptiste.

Little-drum. The child that had turned blue, with the enormous belly. He was back again with all his cohort of images, smells, and sounds. Pauline saw the rain falling and three soaking-wet men suddenly cast their huge shadows over the threshold. Everywhere she detected the smell of humus, of bark softened by autumn rains, of rotting flesh. She saw hands fighting off the creatures attracted by this stink of carrion – her own maddened, proliferating hands. She had a taste of black soil in her mouth, the taste of a grave dug in the rain. She heard incessantly the dull sound of earth and stones falling on a wooden surface. She saw the trees, all the trees in the forest, wrench themselves from the ground and begin to march. A tribe of crazy warriors waving their countless limbs armed with birds with purplish-blue beaks.

She fought against this jumble of reminiscences, but in vain. For her memory was diffused in her flesh, lurking in every nook and cranny of her body. It exuded like sweat from her stifled heart.

However, there were the others. There was Baptiste, and Charles-Victor, and now the new-born child. She tried to reach out towards them. But something held her back, indeed was forever setting her at a distance from them, a distance that became an ever greater terror to cross.

Yet she went through the motions of motherhood: she fed the child, washed and changed it. But she did all this as though performing a ritual drained of meaning and desire. Her actions were stiff and carried out with an air of vacancy.

It was then that Charles-Victor came back with a vengeance – not to his mother, or his father, but to the new-born child. It was as if he had just been born. He wanted the child for himself, and himself alone. It was to him that the little sister his blue Skunk of an older brother had so much dreamed of had been given. And it was he who chose her name: he asked his parent to call the little girl Ballerina, after his rail car 'with the fiendish bum and golden tootsies'. For in his passion for words Charles-Victor believed in the magic power of the act of naming. In this way, by imposing on his sister the name of his choice, he bound her to him with a sacred, secret and all-powerful bond.

'Ballerina! Ballerina! My little sister who's all mine!' he cried in the retreat of his ruined palaces: factory, blockhouse and privy. 'To you, I'll open up my splendid realm of rust and debris, and thanks to you it will all be transformed into beauty and for you I'll be good, yes, I, Prince-very-dirty-and-very-naughty, will be good! Horribly good! So good that God himself will start to worry! But I'll only be good for you. Just for you!'

Charles-Victor became neither better nor worse. He just became infatuated with his little sister. She was everything to him. Suddenly the world had a face, the face of another person who had not betrayed him. The world assumed childishness, and a new inclination for play. Everything became possible.

It was at that period that his eyes took on the wonderful transparency of concretions of fossilized resins the colour of honey and light gold. The glistening fleck in his left eye looked even more luminous, almost blazing. But there was still so much shadow and darkness in his gaze that no one would have thought of giving him the name Day-of-amber. Night-of-amber was what everyone called him.

Ballerina was everything to him and he made sure he became everything to her. Since their mother remained haunted by his frightful blue Skunk of an elder brother, and there was no doubt his big crybaby of a father had eyes only for his robotic wife and no time for anyone else, the place at Ballerina's side fell to him, by right. And he knew how to fill this unoccupied place and build an empire there. And he was bent on keeping everybody away from his empire, for his was a jealous love. Tremendously jealous. He kept his uncle at a distance, as well as Thadée and Tsipele, and especially young Chlomo. He could not stand the boy – always prowling round the little girl, trying to sneak her a smile, like some disgusting sweet. Night-of-amber nicknamed him Nosy-shark, and did him the honour of ranking him fourth in his list of enemies, after his blue Skunk of a brother, his treacherous mother and his hopeless crybaby of father. He ranked him with the rabble of trees. He was especially careful to make sure that Nosy-shark, and even that witch Tsipele, did not come and sing to Ballerina their mysterious songs that made you feel sick just listening to them. No way was he going to let the little girl be lulled by those tearfully gloomy and beautiful songs. Language, words, sounds – he, and he alone, would teach them to her, in his own way. He would make her his own by the power of sounds and words. By the magic of words.

But it did not bother Chlomo to be hated by Charles-Victor alias Night-of-amber who was six years his junior. Already, in the past, the older brother, Jean-Baptiste, had shown veiled hostility towards him.

'You mustn't hold it against them,' Tsipele had often told him. 'Jean-Baptiste and Charles-Victor have a jealous heart, they're made that way. In fact I think all the Peniels are like that. Passion is so strong in them, it makes them ill. Jealousy is an illness.'

'But what kind of illness is it?' Chlomo asked anxiously. 'Is it serious? Can you die of it?'

'Sometimes, yes. I think so . . .'

'But then,' Chlomo went on, 'if everyone in the family has the same illness, do you think Thadée is jealous, too?'

'I don't know!' Tsipele replied abruptly, troubled by this question without knowing why.

Chlomo ploughed on, without noticing his sister's blushes. 'He mustn't be, if you say people can die of it!'

'But then who and what would he be jealous of?' she said shrugging her shoulders. 'All that Thadée loves are his books and the stars. You can't be jealous of stars.'

'And why not?' her brother insisted. 'If he really loves his stars very much, perhaps that could make him jealous, and sick, and then he'd . . .'

'Oh, you do annoy me with your nonsense!' she eventually said to cut him short, and she changed the subject.

And had Chlomo himself contracted the obscure disease of his adoptive family? And what about Tsipele? These questions had long tormented him. But since that bright April morning when, clinging to the elm-tree, he had glimpsed, through the pink mist of clustered stamens, Pauline's face glowing with transparency, yielding to him the secret of the child that was to be born, he had ceased to be tormented. He was seized with joy. And the love he felt for the new-born child was so vast, so light, that he knew nothing of jealousy. What did it even matter that Night-of-amber should keep him away from the little girl, with fierceness and anger, and forbid him to touch her, see her, or speak to her? It was enough to know that she was there. It was enough that she existed. And it was by the grace of this simple joy that he smiled with such gladness all day long.

'Ballerina! Ballerina!' he murmured, endlessly chanting the little girl's name as though the better to enchant himself with it, the better to make it his own.

And did the child hear these calls, fluttering round her sleep like exhilarated birds, famished as they might be at the end of an overlong winter. She was still so young, so fragile, this child engendered by her father's tears whom her mother had not been able to carry to term. She remained quietly curled round her unformedness, keeping her eyelids closed and her fists clenched shut. She continued a dream interrupted in the ebbing of the waters from her mother's belly. Only very slowly did she come into the world and into life. And silence reigned within her. She never screamed or cried. She listened to the dull rhythm of her mother's heart still reverberating in her temples. She slept. And her breathing was so light it was barely perceptible. She slept, just present to the world. It was not yet time for her to be able to hear these shouted or murmured calls.

But time was already on the move. Ever advancing, ever in a hurry. It matured beneath the unwakened child's eyelids, slowly colouring her eyes the purple blue distilled in the depths of forests, in the underwood and thickets.

Ever advancing, moving quickly among things and living creatures, jostling them, carrying them along. Time without end was making history, weaving its tale.

NIGHT OF WIND

1

Time. It would make them all travel the world, it would make them spend their days migrating from night to night in huddled flocks. Time kept uttering its cry in the name of the Peniels – its forward cry, its cry of struggle and silence.

Ballerina, the little unwakened child, the unformed child, eventually opened her eyes. They were purple blue and there was a gold fleck in one of them. She learned to walk, and talk, and to love. Her brother monopolized this new love. Pauline lived through their childhood days like a sleepwalker, and her arms reaching out towards them were stiff, meeting with emptiness. And Crazy-for-her followed her around, always and everywhere, ready to catch her, to save her from falling again.

Night-of-amber took Ballerina with him to his rebel hideouts and made up stories for her wherever they went. He never tired of telling her the story of his blue Skunk of an older brother, suggesting that he had become a giant with ferrous eyes, an ogre with a purple mouth and a horribly famished, gigantic belly.

'You know,' he would say to the little girl, who listened to him open-mouthed with fear, 'the blue Skunk is really a dreadful ogre. He eats everything – leaves, tree-bark and roots, but also stones, clouds and raw animals. He tried to devour me, too, but I didn't let him! I'm stronger than he is. That's why you must always stay with me, nobody but me, otherwise he'll eat you as well. Don't trust anybody, not even the trees. Especially not the trees. The trees are his soldiers, as cruel and greedy as the purple ogre. They all want to catch you and eat you up.'

'Then why do we keep going into the forest?' asked Ballerina, terror-stricken.

'To chase out the blue Skunk, of course! To show them

all that I'm the strongest, and you're their queen. I want the trees to kneel before you.'

'I don't want to be queen,' said Ballerina, on the brink of tears, 'I want to go home. I'm scared . . .'

'No, you must stay with me. I'm strong, I tell you, you've nothing to fear. As long as you're with me, no one will harm you. You're the princess and I'm the dragon. Your friendly dragon. I'll kill them all, even the dead!'

'I don't want to be a princess,' said the little girl, ' I want to stay at home . . .'

'What home?' shouted Night-of-amber. 'You and I don't have a home. Haven't you noticed how it stinks at home? It's the smell of the Skunk, because he lives there, too. He's everywhere. He's terrible, I tell you! We don't have a home. We only have kingdoms, and a fine chariot to travel round in!'

And he dragged her off on his rail car, clutching her very tightly against him, shouting great threats at the trees and the Ogre-Skunk. He said to his sister, 'Listen! Listen to how the wind moans! It's chasing all the spirits of the dead out of their lairs, all those nasty, greedy spirits, carrying away their voices thickened with dirty saliva, wrenching their teeth out of their rotten mouths, twisting their black tongues, and smashing their jaws! You have to blow with the wind, and run with it. Even stronger and even faster than the wind.'

But the little girl tightened her lips; she was cold and felt like crying. In fact, on these rail-car rides that Night-of-amber forced on her she often kept her eyes shut. She shut them very tightly, so as not to see anything around her, to forget the oppressive and menacing presence of the trees. She pressed her hands against her eyelids, dazzling herself with little phosphorescent suns.

She was scared of everything – of the wind, the trees, her big Skunk of a dead brother with ogre's teeth, but even more of her brother Night-of-amber who squeezed her in his arms so tightly against him, and gave her kisses in her hair and on her neck.

Night-of-amber loved the wind. He tore about with his mouth open to let the wind penetrate his whole body and blow into his heart, and bones, and blood. The wind was his nourishment, his strength, his spirit. He constructed a huge kite, half-fish, half-bird, out of bits of blue tarpaulin, decorated with fine sheets of glinting grey metal, built on a reed frame. He called it steel-jackdaw or silver-swallow depending on how high he flew it and the patterns he imposed on its flight.

'You'll see,' he said to Ballerina, 'one day my kite will turn into a real bird and soar right up into the sky, singing for real, letting out a single shrill note. It will go and burst the sky and the eyes and eardrum of God. Then it will reign alone, over angels and men!'

'Will it be good?' asked Ballerina.

'Of course it'll be good, much better in any case than that rotten God!'

'But then what will God do?'

'Well, he'll be blind and deaf. And really no use at all. He'll be thrown into the dustbin. And good riddance!'

One day when the wind was blowing particularly strongly the kite was torn out of Night-of-amber's grasp and carried far away, infinitely far away in the blustery sky. For a long time the two children remained motionless, their noses in the air, staring after the canvas and metal bird as it whirled like a lunatic among the clouds, then disappeared.

'The bird's gone! It's going to burst the sky and kill God!' exclaimed the little girl, gripped with fright.

'Bah!' said Night-of-amber. 'Let it go! Anyway, God's certainly not at all good, so there's nothing to lose.'

'Are we never going to see the bird again?' asked Ballerina sadly.

'No, it'll come back. Don't worry, it'll come back,' Night-of-amber calmly declared, putting his arms round his sister. 'It'll come back when it wants to, and it'll be even more beautiful.'

It did indeed come back. But not until many years later.

★

But the wind not only made kites dance and children dream. It also attacked bodies and caused pangs of desire.

The wind cast Thadée face down on the ground. But this wind was not of the earth.

It happened on an extremely still and bright night. Thadée had pointed his telescope at the sky. Whenever the brightness of the night was favourable to the observation of the stars he would go up into the attic where he had set up his strange astronomical equipment, in the very place where Night-of-gold-Wolf-face used to offer his family magic-lantern shows, lighting up his own memory with luminous painted images and his children's imaginations with fabulous tales. But Night-of-gold-Wolf-face's lantern had gone up in flames, and his memory along with it. The magic theatre Thadée set up did not relate to those fantastic images of his childhood, or his father's memory. Those orange-coloured giraffes grazing on clouds in the sky, and the white bear balanced on a wheel, and the pink and red parrot, and the old trains swathed in black smoke were gone for ever – all gone. A different black smoke had swallowed them up, dissolved all those images and dreams. What appeared in Thadée's new theatre were much more extraordinary images, and the memory it related to was so vast, so distant that countless of millions of years were involved.

His theatre was the starry night, his bestiary was galactic, and his fable cosmic. His memory went speeding dizzyingly along the brink of black abysses. The passions that had seized him and his brother in the Borromean bookshop on their sixteenth birthday had never left them. Baptiste had become Crazy-for-her, and remained as from the very first day enamoured of Pauline, the bookshop owner's daughter. Thadée remained similarly true to his love of the stars.

For this love had always kept his dream alive in him, even in the camp at Dachau, where everything else, both men and their dreams, was disappearing all the time. Even now he remembered the vision he had one night in the camp.

They were all rudely awakened from their sleep and assembled in a crowd of numbered shadows for some freakish roll-call. They stood there, reeling with sleepiness and hunger, trembling with cold. It was a very dark and clear, freezing night. The stars in the sky had a remarkable brilliance. He gazed at the sky. Were the numbers, shouted in a language that remained for ever alien and violent to him, calling the stars, in order to establish how many there were? But the stars exceeded all numbers and were surpassingly alien, and their violence was infinitely greater than that of men. The stars never answered, they merely appeared. And their indifference to men's cries, and to their suffering, was truly marvellous that night. Although exhausted with tiredness and cold, Thadée could not take his eyes from that chill, sovereign beauty. And besides, by what authority were the stars to worry about men, when men themselves had no pity for each other? And then, even more importantly, the stars themselves were busy with their own conflicts – giant armies of molten matter always in combat, on the path of destruction, shining to a pitch of dazzling destruction and burn-out.

That was when he saw it: a comet shooting through the night with bright tresses of nebulous light rippling after it through space, like some crazed Lorelei diving into the dark waters of a river.

Lorelei, Lorelei, siren of fire and tears, plummeting from the celestial heights, drowning in the silent waters of the night. Lorelei, Lorelei, robbed of her beauty, deprived of her magic, as if the people she had for so long enchanted with her songs had now betrayed her, repudiated her. Lorelei, too fair and gentle, thrown naked into the abyss opened by her treacherous people, outcast Lorelei, soul of an entire people poised on the brink of annihilation.

And when the metallic voice conducting the nocturnal muster called out his number, Thadée responded by shouting even louder, his voice in its turn become crazed, and almost playful: 'Present!' For at that moment he scorned death's callous indifference, as cruel as it was derisive; he scorned the infinite vileness of his oppressors, regaining mastery of himself at that point of extremity where annihilation and eternity touched upon each other.

'Present!' he shouted, almost with a burst of laughter. Present to the absurd beauty of the world, to life as well as death – all life and all death. Present because still desirous beyond measure. And desirous because all of a sudden aware of being born, and made, of these sprinklings of stars. These sprinklings of stars, fragments of matter and light. Echoes, too, perhaps, of the Void stricken by the voice of the Word that brought forth light: sprinklings of sound and splendour. This shooting comet with its nebulous bravura might be one of the letters of the alphabet that had filed past God when he wanted to create the world, one of the letters God had not chosen as the initial of his creation.

Was that the letter Thav shooting across the sky, the letter that set its seal on the word Emeth, meaning Truth, and the word Maveth, meaning Death? Was it the letter Kaph, at the beginning not only of the word Cavod, designating God's glory, but also the word Cala, signifying the end of the world? Or was it some other letter speeding away like that, a letter that did not even belong to the alphabet? Not even a letter, perhaps, but a mere comma, full stop, or hyphen? The slender hyphen linking the names of men to God's Word. And that was why the names of men were turning into numbers, and ceasing to exist.

Thadée stared at the dazzling white trail streaking away. 'Will nothing happen now?' he said to himself when it vanished. And he turned to his companion, whose gaze also seemed to have vanished, whose eyes glistened strangely, with feverishness and abstraction.

'And did he see the star?' Thadée wondered. 'What did he see?' He then recalled the words his companion had recited to him a few days before: 'I lifted up mine eyes, and saw a man dressed in linen, whose loins were girded with pure gold of Uphaz. His body was like topaz, and his face was the appearance of lightning, and his eyes as lamps of fire, and his arms and his feet like burnished bronze, and his voice like the roar of a multitude. And I alone, Daniel, saw the vision . . .'*

'Is that what he saw?' Thadée wondered as he looked at his companion. 'Is that what he is contemplating?' He gently laid hold of the other man's shoulder. But he was asleep on his feet, drained of all strength, with his eyes wide open.

It was at roll-call the next morning that his companion died: standing beside him, with his eyes still wide open. A man dressed in cotton stripes. His body had no likeness to anything any more, his face was the appearance of lime, his eyes had the dullness of stones, and his silence was like a silent weeping. Or perhaps like a song chanted in his heart's deepest core, a silent prayer to a totally silent God. And he, Thadée, alone had seen this: the death of a man standing right at his side. A man among thousands, millions of others, had died right here, at his shoulder, just like that, without uttering a word, without even a flicker. A man had just died, a figure had just been deleted from the long list of numbers. A man had just died, who was his friend. Only he, Thadée, had witnessed this demise. Then his capacity for survival was further strengthened by the promise he had made to his friend to go in search of his children, to find them and take them into his care. For his flesh was made as much out of sprinklings of stars as it was out of other people's ashes. He survived, and he kept his promise.

The same promise that was now so curiously turning against him. Tsipele, the grey-eyed little girl who had for so long kept her head bowed, clutching her brother's hand, had now raised her head, along with her whole body, and released her hand. She had turned into a woman, and in so doing become a torment to him. This new body that she

* Daniel 10: 5–7

suddenly revealed, while at the same time guarding it with vigilant modesty, maddened his body with insane desire. And under the constant and unrestrained onslaught of this desire, lashing his flesh all over, in order to hollow out of it the imprint of Tsipele's new contours, eventually his body, too, was transformed.

It was a bright night. From his position at the attic window, Thadée let his gaze wander slowly across the field of stars. He felt the need more than ever before to turn his attention away from himself, to direct it as far as possible from his body that was haunted by Tsipele's image. He felt the need more than ever before to develop the keenness of this second sight he had created for himself through his telescope trained on the sky. There were so many signs still to decipher among those trails of stars, so many questions raised themselves, spoiling the mind's astonishment.

His mind. What could his poor human mind understand of these mysteries? His mind could only wander about at a distance, a very great distance, groping its way and stumbling. His mind not only got lost, but also wasted time – human time. Time fragmented, drifted, dispersed like great swarms of meteors scattering across the sky in every direction. His mind verged on oblivion, almost on idiocy. As a result of being deprived of every landmark and every support, of being robbed of words. Because for him, there were no words equal to these phenomena unfolding in the far outer reaches of space and time, no words equal to this total extravaganza. No words, only sometimes a few archipelagic echoes of the stories his companion in the camp, Tsaddik Ephraim Yitsak, used to tell him. His companion who died one morning on the Feast of Purim, leaning on his shoulder like a sleepwalker.

'In the vision I saw by night, behold, the four winds of heaven strove upon the great sea. And four great beasts came up from the sea, diverse one from another.'*

Behold, the wind of heaven began to strive upon the

* Daniel 7: 2–3

great sea of desire, and to raise fabulous stirrings in Thadée's loins, and a magic beast emerged from his memory and began to dance in his heart. For that night the sky was to amaze Thadée even more overwhelmingly than usual, as it had amazed and terrified the ancient poets, becoming for them a vast stage on which were played out the follies and passions of jealous and bellicose gods.

He trained his telescope on the lunar orb. It was remarkably bright. The moon was in its last quarter, reflecting with intensity the glancing light of the sun. This cold, oblique light lent extraordinary distinctness to its slightest reliefs, sharpening its mountains and peaks and deepening its valleys and cirques, plunging into dark shadow its lakes and gulfs and seas. Its big empty seas, their sea-beds lacquered with grey lava, riven with crevasses, their shores raised with high crenellations. His gaze crossed the Sea of Cold, the Bay of Dew, the Bay of Rainbows and the Sea of Showers, travelled over the Ocean of Storms, then drifted towards the Sea of Clouds. Wherever he looked, all he could see were wonderful desert places rugged with ramparts and shadows. Places where nothing happened, places absolved of time and history. Places visited only by a few dying comets and the breath of solar winds. But suddenly Thadée's gaze was drawn to the crater Tycho. It looked as if some luminous phenomenon was occurring there. He immediately focused his telescope on an area all at once unusual. He thought he could see vague reddish patches emerging and moving on the edge of one side of the crater. He believed he might be witnessing a kind of volcanic seism. But what he was witnessing was not at all the formation of a new lunar crater. The reddish patch grew incandescent and began to spin round on itself very quickly, then rolled into the Sea of Clouds, where it appeared to explode like a giant russet-red rose. Then a tremendous clamour arose. A figure emerged from the exploded and consumed ball of fire.

A woman, holding a flame and a fish, slowly unfolded

her limbs. Her skin was utterly smooth, like a rock polished by ice. She had no hair. She began gently to sway her body, then started to stamp her feet, faster and faster, and every time she struck the ground with her heels a tremendous clash of cymbals resounded. Then she began to whirl round, twisting her very long, blue arms. All her skin became tinged with blue. And this blue kept intensifying, as did the clash of cymbals. This blue soon cast a reflection all around, illuminating the sides and the bottom of the Sea of Clouds. Then there was a tide of blue surging across the entire moon, confounding the zone of shadow with that of light. Other sounds arose and voices began to swell all around, like moans. Every lunar crater, sea and basin became a mouth. The woman writhed her limbs, streaming with blue sweat, and rippled her shoulders. Her neck was fabulously long, and her fingers proliferated. She began to emit a deep, continuous cry. Her cry grew louder and was soon accompanied by horns and tubas. Thadée heard and saw all this. He could no longer tear away his gaze, or regain control of his senses. The woman's cry choked, but immediately resumed, modulating into a syncopated chant that was at once violence and entreaty. The blue drained from her body, and the zones of shadow and light returned to the moon. Her belly turned a dazzling, acid white, a shield reflecting all of the sun's brilliance. Darkness soon fell on all the rest of the lunar surface. The entire moon was plunged into eclipse. There was no other light but on that smooth belly, that dazzling shield, which the woman began to strike with her fists.

Thadée was then seized with terror. Only then. He pressed his palms against his ears and shut his eyes. But it was too late. The noise continued, sending out its infinite resonances, as of a bronze gong, and similarly the image of that acid-white belly persisted. It was his own body being struck.

The woman stamped her feet hard, swaying her hips and shoulders.

★

His mother, great lunar Eel, was dancing herself into a trance for him. And this dance constituted the parturition of his new body: the body of a desirous man. He, too, began to spin round and dance, to sway his shoulders and hips, and twist his arms. His mother's voice syncopating her husky cries on the bottom of the Sea of Clouds was the voice of neither man nor woman.

Voice of Dead-fishwoman rising from the depths of time, voice of an extinct star chanting the rhythm of his rebirth. He felt pain, but his pain was also thrilling, and his fear bordered on joy. He felt carried along by the wind, he began to run counter to the rotation of the earth, faster and ever faster. But he did not even know where he was any more, where he was running. The wind chasing him was not a terrestrial wind. It was the solar wind that blows across the moon. He ran in space; he ran upon the darkness. His mother writhed in the wind, shouting, and her belly glistened.

Her belly opened like the wings of a white owl starting to flail the air. And he just kept running, faster, ever faster, swept along by hundreds of new winds. He was out of breath now, beyond all thought, all understanding. His mother's voice grew strident, discordant, her belly became blinding. Thousands of white owls flew out of the woman's belly. There was a great shower of blood. Something in her body gained strength and violence, tautened and swelled. Something from her body spattered the sky: a cloud of white owls that pecked at the fall of blood as though it were a vine. Earth, sun and moon disappeared. A whiteness eclipsed every planet. He felt shattered in his loins. He reeled. Only the wind prevailed. A multiple wind in which every stellar wind was joined. Only the wind prevailed, that threw him to the ground.

But there was no ground left.

Thadée woke at dawn. He was lying flat on his back on the attic floor. He was completely naked. His limbs were spread out like the spokes of a wheel, his sexual organ was still hard. He was cold, and yet dripping with sweat. His skin, in the folds of his groin and in his armpits, was covered with fine silvery scales. Outside it was raining. It seemed to him it was raining stones, big greyish stones, of porous matter.

As it grew light the wind rose. Thadée descended from the attic. He found none of his clothes from the previous day. He stole into his room and slipped into bed. But he felt no desire to sleep, despite the immense weariness that racked his body. He was still hurting in his loins, his skin was burning, he felt shooting pains in the lower part of his abdomen. The others had already got up to start work. He, too, got up, washed and dressed. But his skin remained peculiarly encrusted with fine star-dust. He went out into the yard. Clouds were scudding over the forests and fields. He perceived in the distance the figure of his father, flanked by Crazy-for-her and Nicaise. All three were cutting across the meadows heading out to the fields. 'I should be with them,' he said to himself, but he made no move to join them. He sniffed the wind like an animal. The wind carried smells of damp earth, of chimneys and forests. But it carried yet another smell: the smell of laundering. Then he discerned among all the sounds created and carried by the wind the sharp smack of flapping cloth. He walked round the barn. Behind it, extended an enclosed area where the women had just been putting the washing out to dry. Linen laundered that morning, and still dripping wet, was hung out on lines strung from the barn wall to a few hazel trees planted at the edge of the vegetable garden. On the far side of this laundry area he saw hands moving above the lines. The hands tossed the washing into the air, stretched it out along the lines, and fixed it with a host of little wooden pegs, like may-bugs' wing-sheaths. Thadée could not make out which of the women of the household was at work in this manner. Mathilde, Pauline or Tsipele? He could have called out to her, but he remained at the entrance to the enclosure without saying anything, listening to all that flapping of wet clothes and sheets, breathing in the smell of laundry. At that moment, he felt the flapping of the linen caught by the wind right inside his body. Or rather he had the impression that all the bits of cloth pinned up there were nothing but sheets of his own skin hung out to dry, or for tanning. His skin, his many skins. The countless skins of all his past days, the cast-off skins of all his nights. His skin, his skins, shreds of time, stellar slag. It was then that he was again beset by the strange music of the previous day. Discordant sounds of horns and cymbals. He walked straight towards the washing lines, tearing down the laundry as he went, and throwing it to the ground. Enough noise from these dripping wet flags smelling of soap, these big cast-off drum skins! What army of mad soldiers did they belong to? He was quite capable of silencing them, of making them stop their idiotic flapping that merely proclaimed absence and dryness. He tore them down and trampled them into the ground. The days of cast-off skins were over. Gone were the days of burnt pelts and gutted hides. He walked straight towards the woman's hands amid the pungent smell of soap. Let the more tender days of the flesh begin.

He tore down the last sheet she was just hanging up. Tsipele gave a cry of surprise and a start, dropping the handful of pegs she had stuffed inside her tucked-up apron.

'What have you done?' she exclaimed, catching sight of the long trail of scattered laundry.

'I'm coming for you,' he replied simply.

'But you're crazy,' said Tsipele, bending down to pick up the last sheet. 'Now everything that you've dropped on the ground will have to be washed again!'

Her voice was not so much angry as saddened. She asked again, 'Why did you do that?'

He gave the same reply. 'To come for you.'

She looked at him in astonishment. 'To come for me?' she said. Already she could only speak in an echo. Thadée's desire had cast her voice to the ground along with the laundry he had torn down. She remained crouched on her heels, her fingers outstretched among the pegs in the cold grass. She felt the wind flicking between her fingers, hardening her palms.

They remained like that for a moment, silent and motionless, he standing over her, she huddled in the grass. They did not look at each other. The wind was their gaze. They were cold but unaware of it. The cold became their skin.

The wind all of a sudden dictated their gestures in the same abrupt manner in which it whipped the washing still hanging on the lines. Tsipele thrust her arms out towards him and her hands grabbed at his hips. She did not even know whether with this gesture she wanted to help herself to her feet or else make Thadée to kneel beside her. He slowly crouched down in front of her. Their knees met. She was still clutching him round the hips. He raised his hands to her face and let them hover round it for a moment, without touching her. He lightly stroked her temples, her cheeks, ran his fingers down to her half-open lips. They did not look at each other. Their eyes were so astonished, so scared, they kept avoiding each other's gaze. He pressed his fingertips against her bared teeth. He could not distinguish any more between her teeth and his fingernails, between his body and hers. She in turn raised her hands to his face, and seemed to explore it tentatively.

They remained very close, face to face, without looking at each other, without kissing each other. They touched each other clumsily, almost abrasively. He suddenly hunched up, burying his head into her lap. She fell on her side. The wind, blowing over the grass, skimmed their bodies, enveloping them. He rested his head on her belly, and she curled round him. But their feelings were too violent to allow them really to take hold of each other.

They began to roll across the enclosure under the flapping sheets, dresses and shirts. They crawled through the grass as if the wind kept them pinned to the ground, as if they wanted to chew the earth. They did not stand up until they reached the barn. Then he grabbed her by the hair and said, 'Come! Bring me! Bring me to you!'

It was up into the attic that she led him; he followed her, his hands still tangled in her hair. In the attic a bird that had come in through the open window was circling frantically, with shrill cries. It was a jay. It could not escape and was wearing itself out flying round and round, banging against the walls, screeching in terror. It was moving round so fast it was impossible to catch it. Thadée and Tsipele's arrival only increased its fear. Every time it passed through the broad ray of light cutting across the attic its pink-brown plumage momentarily turned orange-red, and its cry became more piercing. It was athwart that broad ray of light, in the centre of the circle described by the crazed bird that Thadée reached the end of his journeying towards Tsipele.

'In you, I have found my memory,' Thadée often said to Tsipele. She was his memory for she was his desire, a desire that however often realized in lovemaking was never consumed. She was his memory, his inexhaustible desire. A memory as vast as stellar space. Desire encircled by the crazed flight of a pink and orange-red bird, and for ever traversed by a broad beam of moving light. A memory always beaten by the wind, accompanied by a flapping of cloth.

They had a child. Tsipele gave birth to a little girl. They called her Nęah. It was shortly after the birth of their daughter that they left Upper Farm, together with Chlomo. They moved into a house at the entrance to Montleroy. When Thadée left the family farm, he also gave up working on the land. He became a shopkeeper, but the kind of shop that he opened, or rather improvised, was indefinable. It was a cross between a hardware store, a clockmaker's and a stationer's. His shop soon became an eccentric bazaar where clocks were to be found next to pots of paint and the most diverse tools and implements, and where the smell of notebooks and pencils mingled with that of soap and candles. Indeed, perhaps that was all he sold – smells and colours. Simple desire and inexpensive pleasure. And while the women of the village who went into his shop did not always know exactly what they had come for, they invariably emerged having acquired something. Thadée had the gift of transforming the least object into a little bit of happiness. Anyone that set foot among this miscellanea immediately developed a desire for something, no matter what, whether it was a length of green ribbon or a white enamel skimming ladle that turned out to be utterly useless once out of the shop.

Chlomo soon moved on again. He settled in town, where he became apprenticed to a watchmaker. When he left he also took something with him from Thadée's bric-à-brac store. He chose a pile of notebooks with coloured covers.

'So what is it that you want to write in all those notebooks?' Tsipele asked him.

But he did not even really know himself. He liked the notebooks for their brightly coloured, somewhat crackly covers, for their white blue-squared pages with red margins, for the smell of the paper. Maybe he would write in them, maybe draw, maybe nothing at all. But in turning the blank pages of his notebooks he would always think of young Ballerina from whom he was now completely parted. In looking over the blue lines printed on the white pages, he would dream of Ballerina, the delicate child made shy of anyone else's company by the exclusive love of her brother, Night-of-amber the jealous.

Night-of-amber. It was true that he had made his sister timid. He was her sole playmate, and when she was old enough to go to school it was he who accompanied her. He developed a liking for school again, because his sister was there now. From one day to the next he began to work hard, to study with a zeal that surprised his teacher, the old schoolmaster who for more than thirty years had occupied the post once held by Gallium Delvaux, the fellow they called the Switch, remembered with bitterness by those that knew him. Night-of-amber studied with passion because he wanted also to become Ballerina's tutor; since she was past the age of nothing but play and her schooldays had arrived, he had to adjust his hold over his sister to the demands of this new era. So it was he that taught her to read, write and count. He invented weird dictations for her, presented multiplication, addition and subtraction as characters in a story, and dramatized her history and geography lessons as tragedy.

At that time Night-of-amber particularly liked travel stories. He described to the little girl the long trading ships of Pharaoh Snerferu or Queen Hatshepsus built from the wood of the cedar trees of Byblos, or the high-prowed ships of the Cretan merchants crossing the legendary seas by the sweat of slaves chained to their rowing benches, to bring back from distant lands fabulous materials wrested from the earth and from trees, from the bodies and entrails of beasts: gold, turquoise and silver, myrrh and ebony, ivory, oil and purple dye. He was especially excited by all the great explorers and never tired of reeling off to Ballerina the long list of their eminent names.

'Listen, listen carefully!' he would say to her, 'and remember these names, because these people are certainly more your family and mine than this whole pack of morons around us. For a start, forget your father's name and mother's name, for those two are less than nothing. And just remember these: Alexander the Great, Hanno, Pytheas, Marco Polo, Ibn Battuta, Cheng Ho, Vasco da Gama, Christopher Columbus and Amerigo Vespucci, Hernan Cortes, Pamfilo da Narvaez, Ferdinand Magellan, Francis Drake, Jacques Cartier and Robert Cavelier de la Salle, William Barents, Abel Tasman, James Cook, David Livingstone . . .'

All these names were drummed into Ballerina's head like multiplication tables and lists of great rivers and their tributaries – words, just words that did not make a great deal of sense. In fact she sometimes ended up by mixing everything up. Seven times seven is Cheng Ho, eight times nine is Magellan; tributaries of the Loire: the Vienne, the Indre, Pamfilo da Narvaez . . .'

But above all else it was the Vikings drakars looming out of freezing sea mists that enraptured Night-of-amber. He admired those hordes of wild seamen sailing on their dragon-ships, with the points of their swords and the blades of their axes sowing mortal terror wherever they went. Those sailors, more than any others, appeared to him to be warriors of the wind, filled with the spirit of the open sea, obsessed with a desire for space and blood.

Ballerina took little steps, sometimes skipping, sometimes stumbling, through these different areas of knowledge marked out by her brother like some crazy hopscotch grid of eccentrically epic proportions. But there was one area in which Night-of-amber failed to instruct his sister: that of music. Ballerina had from the outset revealed an amazing talent for music and singing, whereas Night-of-amber had no aptitude at all. And very early on she began to work on this gift she had, for she found in it at last a new untrammelled space inaccessible to her brother's domination. Music was her free zone, a separate area outside the giant hopscotch grid drawn by Night-of-amber, outside his so jealousy woven spider's web.

So Ballerina was already beginning to elude him, discreetly, determinedly. When he became aware of sister's carefully engineered escape, Night-of-amber did not try to deter her. For by her escape Ballerina became even more beautiful in his eyes; the path she was forging for herself seemed so narrow and difficult to him, and therefore the right one. For the first time he accepted rivalry, because his rival had no face or body. His rival did not belong to his world, it had nothing to do with images or words, it was totally alien, and admirable. Now, Night-of-amber liked to be surprised, arrested and alerted by the unexpected, as long as this unexpected had grandeur and beauty. For then his own power thus challenged gained a new and keener edge. So Night-of-amber the jealous liked this rival even though it was alienating his sister from him. He liked it as he liked the wind, a free power that races and skims and uproots you. Music and wind: very denuded impulses that give rise to a wandering urge.

Wandering. The woman who arrived at Upper Farm with no other luggage but one cardboard suitcase was returning from an odyssey that had lasted more than ten years. More than ten years during which she had sent no news. Her last, very short letter dated from the end of the war. From the death of her twin sister, Violette-Honorine, who had become Violette-of-the-Holy-Shroud and died in the silence of a Carmelite convent after five years' agony in which blood had seeped from her temple.

On the death of her sister she had immediately left the convent. She had reneged her vows, rejected the brown robe and the name she had taken in submission. Sister Rose-St-Pierre had given up the frock. She had taken back her own name, and discovered rebelliousness. For her heart remained rebellious.

Rose-Héloise Peniel returned to the farm after fifteen years' monastic life and ten years' wandering, holding her cardboard suitcase in one hand and by the other a youth so sickly and emaciated no one could have told exactly how old he was. He seemed to be around that ambiguous age where childhood gives way to adolescence. In fact he was the same age as Rose-Heloise when she left Blackland so as not to be separated from her sister Violette-Honorine: seventeen. But though he looked so young, almost a boy still, this was not because of any surviving charm, any lingering prettiness or innocence. His disturbingly child-like appearance was due solely to his puniness. His features were unattractive, his cheeks too hollow, his mouth too big. He had the pleading expression in his eyes of a whipped dog. And it was this expression that from the very beginning had earned him the name Heart-breaker.

And it was also because of this expression that Rose-Heloise had taken him under her wing. She had come across him in the last of the various boarding schools where she had worked as a teacher since leaving the convent, in a little town in Lorraine. A neglected dunce, at the back of the class. A child that refused to grow up, to become a man, who remained fearfully withdrawn, cowering in his semblance of childhood, for he was one of those ill-born children that from the moment they come into the world find themselves all alone, discarded and thereby robbed of their childhood.

Rose-Heloise had taken pity on him. Or, to be more exact, it was he who had caught her in the snare of his whipped-dog gaze. He had watched her in silence from the back of the class with the same expression as a lost dog, on its last legs. And together they had fled those sad institutions where discarded children are brought up somehow or other.

They had fled. The sad institutions, the dismal towns, the grim weeks punctuated by chilly Sundays. Which of them had followed the other, they did not know. They had run away holding hands – the defrocked nun and the orphan child. They had fled their own past. And it was then that she remembered Blackland, for Blackland, to her, belonged not so much to the past as to a parallel time.

'There,' she said to herself, 'he'll be able to hide his fear, bury it in the earth, create a childhood for himself, and I shall rest from this pointless running away. Perhaps, too, I shall find there other traces of Violette-Honorine than traces of her blood. Blood shed, drop after drop, day after day, because of the folly of men and of God. Blood that even today pains me so much and makes me rebel, against men and against God. The blood that still flows in my dreams every night. That blood – my sister's blood. Yes, I'll go home to Blackland. I can now. I'm like my father. Is my father even alive still? Who will I find there?'

Her father. He was still alive, but on the outermost fringe of the night, of oblivion, far, far from everybody, very close to the dead. He was not living on the farm any more. But everything on the farm bore a memory of him. A silent memory, sealed into the walls and beams, locked inside every piece of furniture. This was what Rose-Heloise felt on her return.

It was Mathilde who greeted them.

'You did well to come home,' she said to her half-sister. 'For us Peniels the world is both too vast and too small. This here is our land, this house is our history.'

And Mathilde might have added, 'And that room upstairs, with the big dark-wooden bed to which our father brought four women, where our mothers gave birth to us, is our body. It's my body. My body of dark wood and coldness that creaks in the night. My frigid body, divorced of rhythms, desire and pleasure. My amenorrhoeic body flaunts its strength and indifference because it remains unfailingly true to a single, impossible love. Father and mother and daughter united. Because true to my anger. My body, armed with jealousy!'

'Yes,' Mathilde said to Rose-Héloise, 'you did well to come home. The farm's so big, and being deserted. We need extra hands. Father has left and now Thadée is gone. The children, too, will be leaving. Yet the farm has to be kept going. The only man of the family still here, Baptiste, is far too weak, and Pauline has been no better than a sleepwalker since the death of her son. So there's room for you, and work to do. For you and for the boy.'

Rose-Héloise and Heart-breaker moved in to take Thadée's place, and began working on the farm. And slowly the earth redelivered to the world their bodies that had for so long remained discarded, and opened up their hearts to time and to the outside world. Heart-breaker finally put his childhood behind him, and Rose-Héloise her grief.

She rediscovered the land. And the land was space, space and wind. The land bore traces that although scarcely visible were readily perceptible to senses other than mere sight. The land bore traces of her childhood too soon lost, and of her youth too hastily denied. The land retained traces of all her family, and especially of her sister, Violette-Honorine. And they were not only traces of blood and roses. Her sister's brisk walk, the most remarkable brilliance of her smile, the almost painful transparency of her gaze, the thorough sweetness and fairness of her behaviour, and the habit she had of raising her fingers to her temple, all these came back to her, as the days passed, at the mercy of the wind. The land became more than countryside; it had a countenance. A huge countenance traversed by many profiles of faces lost and found. A countenance traversed by the wind.

2

The wind. It sometimes came from afar, from very far off, scarcely blowing at all, and advancing slowly, like an animal that has been lying down for too long and finally awakes and starts walking again, but for a while still retains in its movements something of its slumber. On other occasions it rose without warning, springing up with a sudden gust and beginning to whirl violently, to race and whistle.

The wind that blew on Midsummer's Night, no one saw coming. It had been a still, hot day, just like the preceding days. It was a long day, the longest day of the year, steeped in that bright light in which the birds seemed to swim rather than fly, so warm and soft was the air.

All of sudden the wind rose. Did it come from the embers of the already dying fires on the edges of the fields, which the peasants had lit at sunset, or from the stones, or the rivers and bogs, or from the trees whose flowers had just turned into fruit? The wind gathered. All of a sudden it was up. Boundless and dry, it began to blow through wood and across field. The birds no longer swam in the sky, for the air was no longer still, or warm. The air was in spate, and suddenly you could see in the still faintly pink sky flocks of birds being violently carried by the wind. Those that tried to fly against it had their wings broken and were dashed to the ground like hailstones.

Everything was caught up and carried along by the wind. Clouds of pollen and dust and insects spiralled, and whirled, then scattered. Trees were lain flat, their branches parted. Roofs shed their tiles as easily as dandelions shed their clocks, gates banged open, and signs along the roads spun round like weather vanes before being twisted out of the ground and flattened. Lots of cats, chickens and dogs perished, caught up into the air, then hurled in a spin against walls or tree trunks. Cows, bulls and horses tried to resist by huddling together, but many were knocked about and lamed by stones. Bones, branches, shutters, everything came to grief, getting broken.

Pauline closed Ballerina's bedroom door. The little girl had gone to sleep. Night-of-amber was not asleep. He could not sleep, as though able to sense the wind rising. As she went by his room, Pauline heard him tossing and turning heavily in his bed. But she dared not go in. She stood for a moment outside the door, straining her ears, with an aching heart. She listened to her son thrashing about under the sheets, prey to insomnia, and anger. The stubborn anger that it seemed was never to leave him. For how long would he reject her, and treat her as his enemy? How much greater would his hatred against her, his mother, grow? She waited outside the door, her hand scarcely touching the handle, her heart aching more and more. What would he say if she found the courage to go in? What would he do if she went straight up to his bed and sat beside him, and laid her hand on his brow? But she did not find this courage. She let her hand drop and tiptoed away. Her heart ached so much, she felt close to tears. The floorboards creaked almost imperceptibly under her feet, but Night-of-amber heard that slight creak. He detected the presence of his mother outside the door, and sensed her hesitating to come in and see him. And his heart was pounding fit to burst. He buried his head under arms, under the sheets and pillow, and chewed his lips so as not to cry out. But which of the two cries wringing his heart at that moment might he have uttered, for there were two cries within him.

'Come in! Come and kiss me, take me in your arms, come and free me of my anger. Come, I'm your son and I love you madly!'

And the other cry: 'Go away! Keep away from me! If you dare come in, if you dare come near me, I'll hit you. If you dare kiss me, I'll tear your lips! I'm your orphan son who's bursting with hatred of you!'

He could not choose between these two gut-wrenching cries. Ah! She was going away! He heard her stealthy footsteps, the cowardly footsteps of his mother! Then anger erupted inside him, like a deliverance. And hatred, hatred alone, held sway over him once more.

'That's right! Go away! Make yourself scarce! Cowardly mother, shitty mother, mother of a skunk! Disappear from my sight, my life, my body! Scuttle away you little yellow rat, and disappear for ever!'

She tiptoed away. The floorboards creaked like the little bench in the confessional box where she had so often gone to kneel before Father Delombre.

Delombre had won. She had given in, and kept the child. But where was the victory, she kept wondering. The child had not consoled her for the death of her eldest son, nor reconciled her with the other. In fact she was very well aware that the child was a total stranger to her. The child had been a stranger to her from the start, turned against her by Charles-Victor. And perhaps, too, in a more obscure, more terrible way, by Jean-Baptiste. Her two sons, the living and the dead, had taken possession of the little girl.

'What am I, then, to my children?' Pauline suddenly asked herself. She stopped outside the threshold of her room, where Crazy-for-her was expecting her. She felt another pang in her heart.

'And what about him? He's been so long-suffering, yet what is he to me? Baptiste, my poor Prince de Nemours, poor love of my youth, I don't know why, I can't love you as I used to. Love has expired in me, desire has perished. My fond and absurd Prince de Nemours, how long will you keep open the book of our first encounter, the book of our thunderbolt passion for each other? You see, I've lost the page. The book has fallen out of my hands. I've lost all the pages. I probably can't even read any more. I can't spell love, I don't know how to say it, or read it, and neither you, Baptiste, nor Delombre can teach me to read again. Your patience has been wasted. Sacrificed for nothing. Throw your books away, both of you!'

It was then that she heard the wind outside, beating against the walls, gusting over the roof, whistling shrilly. She turned away from the door and crept away from her room. She went downstairs.

The wind was circling round the farm like some mad beggar come not to ask for shelter but on the contrary to coax everyone away with him on his wandering.

'I'm coming, I'm coming . . .' she repeated. When she lifted the latch the wind wrenched the door out of her grasp, slamming it so violently against the wall that it broke in two. It was a bright night outside. Birds, tiles, branches and various other things whirled round in the pinkish sky. Suddenly there were two superimposed images before her eyes: a bicycle wheel spinning round above a ditch under the pouring rain, and a small wooden grille. The wheel spun round and round, and with every rotation a voice frantic with desire cried, 'I love you, I love you!' And she saw the rain glistening on Baptiste's naked shoulders. The wooden grille also spun round, and at every rotation, a voice entreated, 'Do you love me, do you love me?' And she saw Delombre's tear-filled eyes glistening behind the wooden grille. The two voices and the two images alternated in hurried confusion.

Pauline rushed outside. The wind threw her to the ground. She got up and started walking. The wind kept buffeting her, throwing her off the path. Everything was spinning around her. Earth and sky were just a single huge wheel turning at top speed. Every time she fell she hurt herself, on the knees, elbows, and shoulders. She did not feel any of her injuries. She walked on, dishevelled and harassed by the wind, staggering, falling on stones, then picking herself up again. Baptiste's voice, Delombre's voice. She had to walk quickly to escape them, to leave them far behind. She was almost running.The wind was driving her along. She had to hurry.

There was another voice calling her. So much more urgent and haunting. On her way she passed a dog curled up in ball flying a metre above the ground. It eventually came down on the side of the road. In falling, it broke its back. The howl it gave stayed with Pauline for a long time. But not even this howl could detain her, or make her retrace her footsteps. Another voice was calling her, one that was so much more strident. The sky was still light. The night was pink. The sky moved in vast pink swirls.

The wind assailed the yew on all sides. But the tree resisted. It had dug its roots very deep into the earth, right down into the hips and body and mouth of the child lying there. Little-drum was holding the tree in place.

Around the tree the night was red. A cloud of red berries rapidly whirled round the battered branches. Pauline was encircled by this whirl, enchanted by this dance. She joined the dance of picked-off fruits spinning round like hundreds of frenzied bees. She in turn began to spin round with the yew-berries. As she spun round, she began to pluck the little red berries out of the air and pop them into her mouth. They were oddly crunchy between her teeth; the pulp filled her mouth with a bitter taste. This taste elated her. She could not resist it. She kept foraging for more berries among the broken branches as she went spinning round the trunk. The night was so beautiful, red and pink and shifting. The night called and creaked from every side. The night poured into her mouth and filled it. Red and pink, and pulpy. Little-drum gave his mother his new blood, his vegetal blood, to drink. Bright red and bitter. The night was vermilion, wind-blasted. And Pauline laughed, with a pretty childlike laugh, clapping her hands as she danced. The night was light, and her heart, too, grew light, increasingly light. As light as the little arils flitting in the wind. The night coloured her mouth, and heart, with a taste of merry poison. The voices – Baptiste's and Delombre's – had fallen silent at last. Only Little-drum's charming playful laugh rang out. And her gladdened heart was off, getting lost, in the wind. Then it stopped, and fell silent, and so, too, did the wind. One last thin shower of berries fell from the yew-tree in a bright scattering over Pauline, lying on the ground.

They told Night-of-amber, 'Your mother's dead,' but he had nothing to say.

What mother were they talking about? It was years since he had had a mother. She was the mother of the other boy, the blue Skunk, the one who was dead, and in fact it was the Skunk who had killed her. It was his rotten carcass that was responsible for the yew's branches being covered with those poison-filled berries in the heart of a Midsummer's Night.

'Your mother's dead.'

Who were they talking to? And since she was no more Ballerina's mother than his, he told his sister, 'Mother won't be coming back any more. We won't be seeing her again. She's gone to join her only son. The Skunk.' And when Ballerina cried, he flew into a rage.

Meanwhile, Crazy-for-her would not hear of it. He quite simply denied it. He did not see Pauline's dead body, or attend the burial. He shut himself away in his room as she had once done. He did not shut himself away, pretending to wait for her – why should he wait for her, since she was there with him? Not just with him, but inside him. Not even inside him. She was him. He became Pauline.

He began by putting on make-up, painting his face, wearing his wife's clothes. They took away from him the trappings of his disguise. Thadée came to see him every day, and tried to talk to him, but Baptiste turned a deaf ear. Neither Thadée, nor Mathilde, nor Rose-Héloise, nor his daughter Ballerina could get through to him.

'Just leave him to his madness,' said Night-of-amber. 'In any case he's always been crazy. He's never been anything else but a quivering dog lying at his wife's feet. Just leave him in peace to gnaw on the bones of his love, otherwise he'll bite you.'

Father Delombre came as well. He sat in front of Crazy-for-her, searching his lunatic gaze for access to his reason and his heart, but found none.

'What's that black-cassocked crow doing here?' Night-of-amber said of Delombre. 'He can stammer and caw as much he likes, but he's wasting his time; that nincompoop father of mine can't hear anything now. In any event he'd better not try to flap his smelly wings near me or my sister, or I'll burn his plumage and smash his beaky face!'

But Delombre never went near Night-of-amber. He could tell perfectly well that the young boy hated and despised him. After all, had it not been so with nearly all the Peniels? Mathilde, Rose-Héloise and young Heart-breaker, and especially Night-of-gold-Wolf-face? All of them bore in their hearts such anger and violence, such rancour against men and against God; they bore their anger bred of suffering like pus in the furrows of a badly treated wound. And he could only suffer for their wounds.

Delombre had heard speak of Violette-Honorine, of the miracle of roses and blood wrought in her body, of her long agony and very saintly death. So what mystery was it that affected her, from the day she was born, whose whole life had been nothing but obedience to grace? But was not grace such as this a madness, some obscure irretrievable disaster? The thought of Violette-Honorine tormented him, for through the young woman's holiness and martyrdom the question of grace defied him, terrifyingly. Confronted with it, he measured his own weakness, cowardice and impotence, and the contradictions within him. He desired nothing so much as to be filled with this grace, dazzlingly transfigured by it, and feared nothing so much as to be stricken by this same grace, this havoc. His fear increasingly got the better of his desire; a physical, almost animal fear, that kept rearing up inside him and bucked his desire every time he tried to take the leap into the infinite void of faith. And the voice that entreated him, subtly and stubbornly, then became sorrowful. 'Do you love me?' the voice implored. His desire wanted to answer 'yes', but his fear cried 'no'. Pauline's death, Baptiste's madness, and their son's hatred only increased the urgency and pain of this obsessive question.

Crazy-for-her was blind and deaf to everybody. He became Pauline. It did not much matter to him that his wife's belongings and clothes were taken away from him: he did not even need to dress up any more. The transformation took place inside his body. His hair began to grow, his skin became more delicate, and smooth. But his metamorphosis soon developed into a strange disfiguration. Day by day his muscles disappeared, his flesh sagged, his skin softened, like pap in milk.

Everything about him began to sink inwards. His flesh collapsed in on itself – not only his face and torso, but also his genitals. Even his voice ended up sounding hollow. This inversion of his body occurred gradually. Soon he was incapable of getting up, of walking; he was no more than a thin bundle of rags, lacking any muscle. Then his bones, too, softened, turning cartilaginous.

Crazy-for-her lay formless and weightless in the middle of his bed. He kept his eyes wide open all the time, day and night. But his eyes were so sunken in their sockets, it was almost impossible to see them. In any case his gaze, too, had turned inwards. This gaze now followed only the slow progress of his hollowing.

He ceased to speak. His tongue shrivelled up in the back of his throat like a tiny glass leaf. Similarly, his ears, mouth and temples caved in on themselves, becoming deeply indented in him. He seemed to be nothing more than a mould of himself.

His genitals completely retreated, burrowing ever deeper inside him, mining a hole in his body. This inward sinking of his genitals ravaged everything inside him, and as the sinking progressed the emptiness within his flesh mounted.

Pauline penetrated him with her absence: a flurry of wind like a trickle of silence. He felt himself slowly departing, carried off by Pauline, eroded by Pauline's disappearance. He became Pauline's disappearance.

His genitals kept on digging inwards, penetrating his own ruined body, driving the emptiness all the way back to his heart. He entered into Pauline's absence; he slipped towards extinction. The emptiness reached his heart, then this last muscle in his body, a thin membrane grown concave, in turn collapsed and failed without the slightest sound.

'Well,' said Night-of-amber when his father died, 'there's nothing left now of the brother's era. The blue Skunk's had his day. He carried off mother and father in succession. But he won't get us. We're nothing to do with him, and nothing to do with them any more. Let the big yew-tree gobble them up!'

It was above all the days of his childhood that had come to an end; his body was starting to change. He was now erecting, in strength and desire, in the middle of his own reinvented body, his father's lost genitalia.

His body was changing, and the world around him, too, was thereby transformed. His gaze, and all his senses, changed rhythm and dimension; the places that had so enchanted his childhood suddenly seemed constricting and charmless. He felt the want of space, he dreamed of other vastnesses, of broader and farther-reaching roads, of stronger winds. He dreamed of other company than that of these slow-witted and taciturn peasants bred in the soil of Blackland, or the dull provincials that were his schoolmates at the lycée in the small market-town where he was a weekly boarder. He dreamed of more exciting encounters. He dreamed of taking Ballerina with him far away from this austere and boring land. He repudiated his family, his memory, his childhood. He yearned for cities, for the advent of strangers in his life, to surprise and amaze him. He wanted to leave.

And he did leave. In the year following his father's death he left Blackland, the market-town and the provinces. He finished his schooling with such success that he won a grant to go and continue his studies at university. The world was at last going to open up to him; the big city summoned him. Paris, that distant, almost alien place, was going to become his own. Night-of-gold-Wolf-face had met his greatest love there, and there young Benoît-Quentin had encountered the only love of his life. The war had robbed them both of their beloved. But the time of war was over – was he not the postwar child? The child of the post-brother era? In any case he wanted to be a youth without memory, without attachment or nostalgia. He repudiated his land that was too dark, covered by forest and traversed by a river that flowed too slowly, that could carry nothing but the shadow of clouds. His remote borderland. Forgotten by history. He remained true only to Ballerina.

Yet he had to leave her behind. He could not take her with him to Paris, although she, too, had to leave the farm. Thadée and Tsipele gave her a home and brought her up with their daughter Néçah. They became for her what her parents had never managed to be: with them she discovered affection and peace. The love that bound them was a happy love with no ghosts coming to haunt it. Indeed, happiness seemed to have attached itself as firmly to them as unhappiness had to her parents. But above all she experienced something of childhood other than what Night-of-amber in his jealous passion had always imposed on her. Childhood was no longer solely that rebellious, brutal age full of anguish and threats. Childhood became another kind of age that was all sweetness and patience. And this she owed to little Néçah. It was as though fear, doubt, and sadness had no hold on her cousin; she was not even remotely susceptible to them. So in her company Ballerina forgot her own sadness, and lost her doubts and fears.

Ballerina did not deny her memory the way Night-of-amber did. It was simply that her memory – the sick, tormented memory she had been given from birth – was as though cleansed and purified by Néçah's mere presence.

Néçah had a gift of movement. Her every gesture was an accomplishment, seeming to create not so much a pattern in space as a script. A light, fluid script undulating in the transparency of the air, moving round things like those pale-purple, luminous jellyfish floating among algae and corals. A deep-sea script, a script from the depths of time, calmly and precisely displaying its white signs. For it was precision and dexterity, more than gracefulness, that characterized her gestures. Every object she touched became a curio, assumed the infinitely subtle weight of things rich in resonance and reflections. Things pregnant with mystery. Perhaps it was from growing up among the curious bric-à-brac in her father's shop that she acquired this kind of rapport with objects that was full of ease and delicacy. Even though still very small, she did not upset things, she never stumbled, and had never broken anything at all. Her body dwelt in space wonderfully, yet without seeming to occupy it. Ballerina had only to take hold of Néçah's hand and she immediately felt calmness and serenity settle within her and around her.

Néçah was not very talkative, and scarcely ever played outside. She liked to stay indoors, to be among things. She could spend hours contemplating an object, a piece of cloth, or even a few crumbs scattered on the corner of a table. It was with her that Ballerina learned to look at things, to touch them and listen to them. By virtue of her mere presence Néçah rid Ballerina of the abruptness of manner she had contracted from all the time spent playing with her wild brother. And she thereby transformed her fondness for music, which until then had been basically motivated by the need to escape Night-of-amber's influence; it became a genuine passion that she worked at with a great deal of concentration and perseverance. Music acquired a physical shape, that of the cello. And Ballerina applied herself to treating this instrument the way Néçah dealt with objects – with adeptness and seriousness.

Ballerina's first music teacher was thus a three-year-old child who knew nothing about music and was even a stranger to the world of sound. But this child had such an intimate knowledge of the world of things, and dwelt in their mystery with such familiarity, that she caused a kind of breathing to occur in each object, a kind of writing to appear in space. A writing that was patience through and through. It was essentially this that Ballerina learned from her: patience. Patience of movement, and of the ear, patience of the body. Infinite patience of the body that submits to the mystery and demands of the instrument's body.

But before long Thadée and Tsipele, astonished by the remarkable progress Ballerina was making, decided she ought to leave the village of Montleroy to go and study her art in depth with real teachers. So Ballerina, too, was to leave the remote bordercountry of her childhood, high above the Meuse. But the town where she was to go to boarding school was also on a border and there, too, a river flowed, not lying deep at the bottom of fields, but on a level between the streets and houses. A river neither the source nor mouth of which was located in the country's interior. A border river, with vines and forests along its banks, a river of countless fables and poems. A legendary river, mingling in its waters the echo of the languages spoken on the banks either side of it, languages sometimes sung and sometimes yelled.

Night-of-amber and Ballerina: they both left Blackland, their village perched on a height, that seemed to touch a sky so low the clouds wandered in the fields like herds of silent cattle. Their village enveloped in the grey mists that rose from the Meuse at nightfall. The rivers on which they were going to live flowed much more strongly, with waters less grey and sleepy. The Seine and the Rhine. Each of them, leaning over these new waters, was going to discover in themselves a face that was differently lit, a gaze unlike their previous gaze to settle on things and people.

Blackland retreated into its isolation, more than ever a borderland, lost in oblivion and indifference. The time when wars had regularly raised it on to history's prow was over now. Over for good.

But the time of war was not at all over. In fact it had never ceased. In its impatience and intemperance, the time of war had simply changed location. It liked to carry its fury elsewhere, always elsewhere, that is to say, more or less everywhere.

The time of war had abandoned Blackland; it no longer entered across the frontiers. It even played itself out far from any of the country's borders. This time the continental population was going to be able to keep its distance from war and remain safe. At least for the most part, for there were after all conscripts. Conscripted to go and fight. Heart-breaker was one of them.

Heart-breaker, who had taken so long and had such trouble emerging from childhood, was immediately summoned by war as soon as he reached the age of majority. He could not understand why or how he had been found and summoned in this way. He could not understand whose was the anonymous, imperious voice that called him up out of the blue without asking his opinion. He did not understand anything. He left as he had always lived, at least until the last few years, in simple obedience. As soon as he set off, he found himself in the same distress as before. The army, the war. These as yet still abstract words had the bitter redolence of those other words that had for so long held him prisoner: boarding school and orphanage.

He crossed the entire length of the country by train. He had never travelled so far in his life before. But he was still a long way from reaching the end of his journey, even when the rails ceased and land gave way to sea.

The army, the war. When he reached the end of the rails the two words were coupled with two other new names: Marseilles and Algiers.

Marseilles and Algiers: the names of cities. No, for him, from the outset they were names of anguish, of total solitude in the midst of the mob. And it was an enormous mob, of men, only men, gathered on the parade ground of a big assembly camp. Men from every corner of the country, of the same age as he was. Young men, with shaved heads, their eyes still full of spirit, who still laughed like adolescents. Any traces of childhood in these men had been concealed under brand-new fatigues. They were all herded inside that vast enclosure and kept waiting there. The wait was endless, punctuated by cries that came over loudspeakers. These cries were a list of names delivered like axe-blows, that cut into the mob, breaking it up only to reshape it. At each cry a man rose, separated himself momentarily from the mass, then disappeared again into the crowd already formed by the roll-call. Dozens, hundreds of names, yelled out from A to Z. The parade ground was now just a vast alphabetical list. When the alphabetical list was ended, and sorted out, the voice over the loudspeaker began to bellow out orders. The long-awaited order finally came: embark ship! The alphabetical list immediately began to stir, to jostle and low like cattle. It became a bestiary.

Embarkation took place that evening. The wind had risen. A sea wind with a sharp tang. Heart-breaker had never experienced one like it; this wind went to his head like an acidic wine. A huge procession passed along gangways that creaked in the wind. One by one, men loaded with kit-bags and haversacks climbed on to them, calling out their names to a junior officer who caught the name on the wing and checked it off on his list.

Now alphabetical list and bestiary became confused; the men whose names had been called out disappeared into the ship like the pairs of animals that boarded Noah's Ark. But these human beasts were all male; there were no females at all with them. So it was not for the survival of their species that they were packed into the ship's bowels. They were setting sail towards violence.

'And the earth was corrupt before God, and the earth was filled with violence. And God saw the earth, and, behold, it was corrupt; for all flesh led depraved lives. And God said unto Noah, I will put an end to all flesh, for the earth is filled with violence through them; and, behold, I will destroy them with the earth.'*

* Genesis 6: 11–14

It was true that many of the men embarking would disappear for ever from the face of the earth, and among those destined to return a great number were to lose something of their soul on the way.

Darkness descended. It was an intense darkness illuminated with stars. When it was Heart-breaker's turn to climb the gangway and give his official name – Yeuses, Adrien – as though tossing fodder to the junior officer, he suddenly gave a start. For one last time he looked up, into space, at the sky, at the night. It was to the wind that he addressed his name. Was he also registered on that vast black list riddled with twinkling stars? Yeuses, Adrien. But this name was foreign to him; it choked him as painfully as his heavy soldier's boots hurt his toes. Back home on the farm, with those that had become his family, he was never called anything but Heart-breaker. But here a name like that was inadmissible, unpronounceable. The gangway creaked, and black slimy water sloshed against the sides of the ship. This harbour water was nothing but a viscous lymph leaked from the rusted guts of these big ships that already, a few years before, had taken aboard countless other soldiers and transported them to Indochina. These unseeing ships always headed for war.

This greasy lymph was not the sea. It was not the sea he had dreamed of. 'Yeuses, Adrien!' called out Heart-breaker, and a moment later he was engulfed in the hold, still dazed by the wind from the sea and the brilliance of the stars, and by the avowal of his name to the night. Yeuses, Adrien was going to war.

Another darkness reigned in the hold, a thick, noisy, nauseating darkness that gripped him by the throat. The salt tang here was mingled with the reek of rust and fuel oil, and soon the stench of men packed in like animals prevailed. This stench could only worsen during the voyage, with sweat, urine and vomit. The flesh revolted in anticipation. The seasickness that afflicted most of the passengers turned the men even more into beasts. Strange beasts seized with retching and convulsions and acid sweats, as if they were undergoing some kind of ecdysis in order to take on a new skin. Skins that came with bullets and knives. 'There's worse to come, boys!' they were told in loud hearty tones by the regulars, boasting stripes and experience, who were to be responsible for their training and for keeping up their morale.

They arrived in Algiers the next day. But Algiers, like Marseilles, remained just a name. They did not go into it. They glimpsed from afar the walls and roofs of Algiers. White-Algiers stood silent, crushed beneath a low-cast, leaden sky. They disembarked and immediately set off on another journey, this time by train. They travelled away from the sea, and the town. They crossed vast landscapes planted with cork-oaks, pines and fig-trees. The sky remained low-cast, colours were lack-lustre, shapes stricken with immobility. The air was close, the heat sticky. Then they got off the trains and climbed into trucks. They kept going further up country; they were being taken into the North African heartland. The wind made the trucks' tarpaulins flap and the dust in the road swirl. A sense of dryness so far totally unfamiliar to him then overcame Heartbreaker, straining all his senses. He observed with surprise and detachment this strange landscape interminably passing by. This ochre-coloured stony ground endowed with a harsh beauty was implacably alien to him and yet he could not tear his eyes away from it. He looked as perhaps he had never looked before, with extreme concentration, with rigorous attention. Although dead tired, he would have liked to drive on indefinitely like this, at high speed, in a straight line, crossing this austere emptiness for ever. He forgot why he was there; his mind emptied as they sped along the road. He had only a keen impression of rapid flight, of dizzy escape. Towards nothing, towards no one.

Yet it was to a very particular place, where there were other men just like him, that he was taken. Where he was confined, to be subjected to training. The long journey was over and its purpose revealed.

'You'll see, boys! We're going to make men of you!' it was announced to them in proud promissive tones. So that was why they were here: so they could be made into men. But then what were they before they got here? Were they not already men? So what new kind of man were they expected to become?

They had left their homeland and crossed the sea like the animals Noah had embarked. But unlike Noah, who had fled violence, in order that the covenant between God and all flesh on earth be renewed after the flood, they had come along to fight against others. Without even wanting to, without even realizing it, they had come along to suffer the consequences of being oblivious of the covenant and violating the principle of brotherhood.

'And for your own lifeblood, also, I will require an accounting; from every beast will I require it: and from man, even every man's brother, will I require an accounting for the life of man.'*

It was all very well for war to change location, to change form, weapons and soldiers, what was at stake remained eternally the same: every man that shed another man's blood would on every occasion be called to account.

But what Heart-breaker learned in the weeks following his arrival in Algeria was not to account for the life of man, whosoever the man might be, but on the contrary to call others to account, to claim revenge for the life of his comrades.

For when, on that calm and silent night, lit by a very slender crescent moon, he came across the emasculated bodies of eleven of his companions nailed naked, like large flayed birds, to the doors of the houses in a deserted Arab village, it was rage, undiluted rage, that overwhelmed his heart. Overthrew his heart. An icy rage, as pure and sharp-pointed as the crescent moon hanging over the mountain.

* Genesis 9: 5

Grief did not give rise to pity, sorrow, or distress; grief came upon him too suddenly, too utterly. It threw him into outright terror, and immediately turned to hatred. Total hatred of the enemy, and desire for revenge.

Eleven bodies gleaming white beneath the limpid brightness of the moon, splayed in a cross on the doors, their faces and genitals mutilated, their hearts ripped from their breasts. Faces and genitals confounded, hearts plucked out. Black holes, gaping on this side of the night. Black holes in which the wind moaned. The wind that came down from the mountain, rose from the desert, crept out from under every stone, and came rushing simultaneously from every corner of space. The wind blowing in the cavity of bodies pitted in three places.

The wind. The wind of the Flood. The wind of oblivion and denial.The strident wind, drowning out with its cold neutral voice, devoid of modulation and intelligence, the other voice that expressed itself in words: 'I will require an accounting for the life of man.'

The wind, extraneous to words, whistling its cry of rage and hatred. The shrill wind, silencing the voice that eternally calls to account the man who takes another man's life, and inciting only the exactment of revenge for the spilling of a man's blood. The sour, piercing wind, like a soughing of blood.

And that night, too, Heart-breaker's gaze reached to the extreme, travelled outside of his body and riveted itself until blinded in the mutilated flesh of his companions. Eleven young men with gouged-out eyes, plucked-out hearts, chewing grotesquely between their white lips on the shapeless mess of their severed genitals. The world at that moment ceased to exist, the word 'man' lost its resonance and the word 'life' lost all meaning. The world was no more. Soldier Yeuses could not become a child again, and did not want to be a man. He had toppled out of the rhythm of the ages. From now on he was cast out of time. He was reduced to nothing but the madness of his devastated gaze, nailed naked to the doors of the village.

And the moon hung above, so slender and white, like some forgotten comma chalked on the immensity of the sky wiped clean by the wind to give prominence to emptiness, obliviousness and death: the emptiness of the world, obliviousness of the covenant, and the senseless deaths of the men.

The moon, up there, above the earth, an icy comma between the living and the dead. A thorn-like comma between murderers and victims – a very thin, moving comma, slipping from one to the other, able suddenly to turn from one against the other.

3

It had been raining for days. A light, monotonous rain. It was the beginning of autumn. The birds were beginning their great gathering in preparation for migration. On the electric wires that stretched out along the roads, on the wooden gates and fences round the meadows, on the edges of roofs – everywhere, the birds huddled together in their hundreds, conferring about their imminent departure in vast clamorous twitterings. Night-of-amber, too, was getting ready to depart. He was leaving Blackland the next day and taking the train to Paris. His case was packed. It was virtually empty. He had so little to take with him – a few clothes, a little linen. He owned nothing, and did not want to own anything. He was off to the city, to find eloquence and books. He was off to find words. At last he was wresting himself from the heavy silence of the earth.

He sat there on the edge of his bed. He watched evening fall, he listened to the birds about to leave, the quiet continuous drizzle of rain. He did not stir. He was alone in his room, his fists clenched in his lap. The evening twilight was slowly obscuring the space around him, objects dissolving one by one in the increasing darkness.

'Let the shadows devour them all!' he thought. 'Let night swallow up and obliterate all the objects, furniture, even the walls of my room. Will I not be in a new room tomorrow, a strange room that's completely bare?'

The house was steeped in silence. But the farm was so empty now, what noise could there have been? His parents were dead, Ballerina had moved out to live with their Uncle Thadée. Only Mathilde remained, austere Mathilde reigning over the deserted farm, always carrying on her hip the big bunch of keys that opened the doors of the rooms and cupboards. A bunch of keys that opened only on absence and coldness now. There was also Rose-Héloise who had moved next door, in the low-built wing of the farm where Two-brothers and then Thadée and Tsipele had lived.

But Rose-Héloise made no sound. She spent her nights endlessly brushing her hair over and over again. Since Heart-breaker had gone to Algeria, she could not sleep. Yet every evening she would put on her night-clothes, draping herself in a long white nightgown, then sit on a little stool almost at ground level, and tip her head forward, with her forehead on her knees, and stay like that until morning, brushing her hair mechanically, to stave off the boredom of insomnia and chase away her anxiety. Yet her anxiety would not allow itself to be chased away in the least; it got into her hair and tangled it. Heart-breaker had stopped sending news and this silence terrified her. She sensed that the war had wounded him, had mortally wounded him, not in his flesh but his soul. 'What had he seen? What had he done over there?' she kept wondering, as she brushed her hair.

Her hair eventually took on the purple hue of the birthmark on her temple. But the war was nearing an end and Heart-breaker would soon be back. She did not doubt his return. And yet this imminent return did not calm her anxiety.

'Who, but who will come back?' she wondered. 'Will he still be Heart-breaker? What have they done to him? What has become of him?' Was not war a monstrous, obscene and insane mother who only carried men in her deformed womb to deliver them anew with the tranquillity of their memory and of their soul amputated for ever.

That was war; the war was and remained that monstrous mother who unflaggingly swallows men up in her insatiable belly and crushes them body and soul. Heart-breaker, the little orphan rescued from distress and loneliness by Rose-Héloise's love, was gobbled up by this avid mother. Heart-breaker was no more. The mad devouring mother had triumphed over the adoptive mother, had stolen her child. The mother named war had defeated the loving mother, reminding the child that he had never had a real mother, that actually he was nothing, no one's offspring. Heart-breaker was no more. His place was taken by Yeuses, Adrien, a squaddy in already worn and soiled fatigues.

Soiled with blood. The blood of a man, the blood of another. Blood that dried badly, formed crusts, left indelible marks. Blood whose crusts turned into ulcers that penetrated the thick fabric of fatigues and struck deep into the heart, making it gangrenous, its scabs of madness and rage spreading everywhere, into the conscience and soul. And Rose-Héloise sensed all this. She sensed that her adopted son, her chosen child, would not come back to her as he was when he left, but that another man whom she did not know would return in his place; a man she had not seen grow up, a man too quickly and too brutally begotten by this thieving, scurrilous and insane mother, war. Then, not being able to talk to anyone, and unable to shout or cry, Rose-Héloise kept brushing her thick hair that with the passing nights turned purple.

Yeuses, Adrien was making war. He was making it as ordered to, for finding himself back at square one again, forsaken as he was from birth, he regressed to that state of submissiveness and unhealthy obedience in which he had for so long languished during his life as an abandoned child in an orphanage. But the orders here had changed tenor. It was no longer simply a question, as before, of reciting correctly his prayers, lessons and La Fontaine's fables, of keeping quiet in class, in the refectory and the dormitory, of lying asleep all night like a stone figure on a tomb, with his hands laid completely flat on the top of his sheet so as not to succumb to the very wicked temptation of pleasuring himself. That was all rubbish here. The squaddies could yell and curse to their heart's content, they could stuff their faces with the grub served in their mess-tins in the canteen, and wank themselves stupid under the old blankets in the barrack rooms. The orders here, while still ultimately directed at the soul, were intended not to make it dry and starchy, but rather to dislodge and eradicate it.

Yeuses, Adrien had seen his companions nailed and emasculated under the crescent moon. He had seen this and it was a sight of such violence that his gaze had not wavered. He had not turned his eyes away from it; he had stared coldly at the eleven bodies until his gaze was completely fixed, until he could not see. Eleven bodies. His comrades. Still so young and, like him, called up against their will. Young men whose faces still bore the imprint of childhood, with laughter still in their eyes. Their childhood had been plucked from their hearts, their youth from their bodies, and the laughter from their eyes. Their hearts, and genitals, and eyes had been plucked out of them. Yeuses, Adrien remained obsessed by this vision. And he did not much care about calling others to account or being called to account for the life of man; he wanted revenge. The violent taste of blood had taken possession of him.

Blood: ebb and flow. A perpetual tide that comes and goes between victim and assassin, drowning them by turns, as if a very strong wind was always blowing on men's blood, on their spilled, wasted blood, to send it rushing in all directions.

Yeuses, Adrien was making war. The wind blew around him. The wind had blown on the blood of his companions as on a great fire, stoking its redness, its burning. Its bite. The wind had blown across the eleven bodies bled white, that no earth, no dust covered, to raise the cry again and again. This was the way of war.

'For the blood she shed is in her midst; she set it upon the bare rock; she poured it not upon the ground, to cover it with dust; that it might cause fury to come up to take vengeance, she set her blood upon the bare rock, that it should not be covered.'*

Yeuses, Adrien had heard that mounting, howling cry; he had heard it in his rage. The cry of bodies without burial, the cry of blood on bare rock spilled by the fellaghas like a sacred and perfectly barbarous offering to

* Ezekiel 24: 7–8

their land. He had not let that cry rise beyond human measure, and go soaring to the far side of night. He had intercepted that cry, deviated it from its course. Had not let it climb endlessly. He had not let his comrades' blood cry from the ground to God. He had deflected the cry of pain towards the earth, the very same earth on which the enemy had spilled that blood, and had thereby perverted the cry into the ravines of vengeance.

The very silent cry of his flayed companions had entered inside him and imposed itself as the enemy had wanted: as perfectly barbarous. A sacred blood, from which all sanctity was excluded.

Yeuses, Adrien was making war as ordered to. He spent days and nights combing the mountains in search of rebels, shooting at fleeing figures, throwing grenades into caves, setting fire to villages and entire hillsides in order to force out and kill the enemy ambushed in every cranny of this hostile land. Orders were given, he obeyed. He obeyed all the more because the rebels remained invisible; he was only chasing shadows all the time, shadows that constantly rose from some mysterious hell to sow all around them terror of their cruelty. Fire against fire, death for death, hatred against hatred. Blood for blood.

The shadows of this invisible enemy were so big, so dense, that they eventually cast their dimness into Soldier Yeuses's eyes, a dimness in which everything was confounded. All those of the enemy race were swallowed up without distinction in the same loathsome, menacing obscurity. Old people, women, children, all in collusion, all *fells*, all guilty.

Jebel, hell. The war was constantly restricting its vocabulary. Vast tracts of land were thus expelled from physical human geography and shunted into a grotesque catastrophe-stricken geography. 'Liberation!' they cried on the one hand, and to liberate their land and pay tribute to it, they put it to fire and sword. 'Pacification!' they proclaimed on the other, and to pacify the foreigner's land of which they wanted to remain master they allowed themselves to be corrupted by his violence and insanity. Liberation, pacification: the words of deaf people, words that lost their human face, so that in the end there was nothing left but that - jebel-hell – to sum up the immense weight of their inanity, the gravity of their lie.

So, in whose eyes had the earth once again grown depraved and filled with violence, with the result that throughout whole areas men, together with their villages, their families and their livestock, should be wiped off the face of the earth, with no concern for sparing the just and the innocent?

In the eyes of men, solely of men, greedy for land.

Jebel-hell. Landscape of rock, thorns and scrub, and on its mountain-sides trees consumed by flames and blown to shreds by rockets. A landscape that Soldier Yeuses scoured endlessly, armed to the teeth, with his eyes fixed on the ground, trying to detect footprints in the dust.

Soldier Yeuses made war to the point of brutishness, chasing the invisible enemy without respite. For the rebels always seemed to vanish in the daylight, to dissolve into the night. The night was their territory. So far, Soldier Yeuses had killed nothing but shadows.

However, there came a day when someone stepped out from this mass of shadows. Someone of flesh and bones and blood, of skin and nerves. Just the day before, the soldiers on the side of Pacification had lost another three men, killed by those fighting for Liberation. They had been found lying across a path, mutilated in the face and groin. Lying on their backs in the heat of the sun, they smiled a manic smile, with their mouths ripped from ear to ear. Not far from there, on a path descending from an isolated mountain village, a young boy was arrested. He was coming down from his village driving a skinny black goat that trotted along in front of him, and which he was taking to a well. The little goatherd got no further; it was he that was put on the end of a rope and taken to the camp. He could not but be an accomplice of those who had assassinated and mutilated the three soldiers. The victims' comrades were beside themselves with anger and hatred. They wanted the culprits. They needed a culprit. At least one. They began by questioning the boy. What did he know? What had he seen or heard? Where was the rebel hideout? He must know, he had surely seen something. Did he not have brothers and cousins fighting with the rebels? Yes, of course, like everyone here. What did it matter whether the brothers and cousins were fighting voluntarily or had been press-ganged into it. They were with the rebels; that was enough.

It was enough to cast doubt on the boy, to identify him with their clan. They bombarded him with questions, driven home with a lot of slaps and kicks. But the boy, terrorized and stupefied by the repeated slaps, said nothing. The more he remained silent, the more the others lost patience. The slaps gave way to punches. The boy began to bleed from the nose and from his eyebrow.

Was it the sight of blood that suddenly fired the anger of the men leaning over him? The fact is, they redoubled their blows.

'That's enough!' said one of them finally, breathless with exertion. 'We'll never get anywhere like this.' Then addressing the beaten-up boy slumped in his chair, he said, 'Now, let's get serious! You talk, or else it's the electrodes. We've wasted enough time already.'

The boy did not respond. He could not breathe: his mouth was full of blood; they had broken his ribs and dislocated his shoulder. He was trying desperately to recover his breath, but did not even know where to find it, in what recess of his body to retrieve it.

'Come on,' said the man, 'let's take him and put the wires on him.'

They had to drag the boy who was already unable to stand any more. He was as limp as a bundle of rags, and all disjointed.

'Hey,' said the man, 'you're coming apart. But you haven't seen anything yet. Now, you'd better talk, or watch out for your face and ballocks.'

Soldier Yeuses was called to help, to continue the interrogation. He came. He did not shrink before the boy who was thrown to the ground in the middle of the low-ceilinged room where they had dragged him. After all, it was only one of those bastards that had taken a bit of punishment – nothing more than he deserved, and especially after what Soldier Yeuses had seen done to his friends; in fact nothing more than was justified. Yeuses, too, wanted some culprits on whom to take revenge for his comrades at last. So let this one pay for the others. For once he had one of his enemies, for once they had managed to catch one of them alive, to snatch one out of the shadows, there was no way he was going to let him go!

Let him talk, let him confess, let him at last put faces and names to the assassins, so that his need for revenge might come out of the shadows as well. Once more the soldiers bombarded their hostage with questions, abuse and threats. All of them wanted to know, wanted him to talk, to denounce the culprits. Their prisoner could only groan and gurgle, his mouth gummed up with thick saliva and clots of blood.

And the more he remained silent, the more their obsession with finding the culprits closed in around him, focused more intensely on him. On him alone, who was at their mercy. With every passing minute, every passing second, he became the culprit.

He was the culprit. Jebel-hell was him. He, that shapeless heap sprawled on the ground. In that moment he bore responsibility for all the crimes, all the atrocities, mutilations and castrations committed against their comrades.

'So, are you going to spill the beans, *fell*, or do we fry your ballocks?' said the one in charge of the interrogation, wiping the sweat trickling from his brow. They were all hot, as though drunk with the heat. Their faces, necks, hands were lacquered with sweat. Even their eyes seemed to shine with sweat. A sweat that was secreted from much deeper than their skin, that rose from their innermost flesh. A sacred sweat secreted by anger, hatred and passion. For there was passion involved now. There was hunger. There was madness. In the men's bodies, hearts and eyes, there was truly madness. A madness of blood and suffering. They had to reverse the flow of blood, and suffering, and bring it to its extreme limit. Perhaps even already at that moment it was no longer a question of making their hostage confess information that he knew nothing about, but simply, solely, to make him confess the secret of suffering, of man's cry. The secret of war. And this secret was a confusion of fascination and repulsion, pleasure and distress. A very archaic secret that resided in the most obscure recesses of the flesh, the deepest recesses of memory. Of desire and of fear. It was this that the faces of the soldiers crowded round the young goatherd, and Yeuses's face, exuded. All of them were giddy with the desire to penetrate the secret of war, of the reason for war. It was from the depths of their souls that their sweat rose.

Only the boy was not sweating. He was bleeding and he was cold. He was shivering. He was cold enough to weep, to die.

'Right, that's enough! Get your clothes off. We're wiring you up. You've asked for it,' said the one in charge of the proceedings.

The boy did not stir, so the others tore his clothes off, forced him to squat down, then slipped a long metal rod under his folded arms and legs.

'Go on, Yeuses,' ordered the head of the operation, 'turn the juice on!'

Stupefied by the heat, the sweat and smell of blood, Yeuses obeyed as meekly as ever. He turned the handle of the little box that he held firmly between his knees, as though it might have been a coffee-grinder. The current flowed into the metal rod through the wire they had attached to it, while the other soldier applied the end of the second wire running from the box to various places all over the boy's body. The boy screamed.

'There, you see, you haven't lost your tongue,' said the man applying the wire. 'So, are you going to give us those names?'

But the boy persisted in not knowing anything. The wire was applied to his lips, and heart, and anus. His screams grew louder. Yeuses did not hear these cries any more – it was as though he had been anaesthetized by them. He steadily turned the handle up to the levels required of him. He heard only the cries of his comrades, those in the village beneath the moon, and those on the path in the heat of the sun, found dead and mutilated. But this appallingly hunched-up pile of flesh, with a gourd-like head and swollen eyelids that no longer allowed even the semblance of an expression to look out of them, was nothing. Not even a man. He had no face – it was just a puffy mess. He had no expression; he shouted in an incomprehensible lingo; and already he stank of stale blood.

Yeuses turned the handle. Would the enemy never emerge from the shadows, then? For even now the enemy remained a faceless shadow, devoid of humanity and of meaning. Had this hostage had a face, an expression, a voice, perhaps Yeuses would have halted his mechanical gesture, but the hostage was submerged in his suffering as though in mud, becoming a shapeless, ugly, screeching thing that rendered totally banal the torture they were inflicting on him. A nasty, groaning, convulsive, hunk of meat , with no age, history, or identity. So where was the enemy?

The master of ceremonies conducting the interrogation suddenly stuck the wire on the boy's testicles, and gave an order to Yeuses: 'Turn it right up!' The whole point of the proceedings finally became clear: by their redoubled rage they were to avenge all injuries done to their own. They were finally getting down to what war, every war, was all about: ballocks against ballocks. A matter of honour between men, the great, ever-recurring tragedy of male private parts erected in pride, power and dignity. Yeuses meekly turned up the power. The boy collapsed at the end of his cry; he lost consciousness, falling face down on the ground, his limbs twisted round the metal rod. With the wire still in his hands, his interrogator turned him over with a kick in the side. It was then that Yeuses saw the child.

For this chance enemy they had lighted on, for want of a better, was still only a child. A poor kid of scarcely eleven, with a smooth-skinned body, a rounded tummy, and small unformed genitals. War had revealed what it was all about only to return him to the edge of an abyss of absurdity and pain. They were torturing a child. The madness of war carried to its limit had just shattered and collapsed, and the victim's beaten-up face, which had been lost from sight, came back into view in the most unexpected, irrational and overwhelming manner, in that other intimate part of the body. Right in the middle, in the most secret, most vulnerable part of the body. A child's body.

The perspiration that had been sticking on his skin suddenly stopped pouring from him, and turned into a cold sweat. Yeuses stood up, throwing the box to the ground. A tremendous coldness came over him. He felt himself shivering. He was cold with the child's coldness, he shivered with his shivers. He was engulfed in the child's fear.

'Hey, what are you doing?' asked his colleague, who had not let go of the piece of wire. 'We're not finished yet.' And to start the proceedings again, he gave the boy a violent kick in the back to bring him round. At the same time Yeuses grabbed the metal rod with which the victim was trammelled, and with both hands brought down it with all his strength on the skull of the soldier he had so meekly obeyed until then. The man collapsed in a heap, rolling close to the child. The other soldier who had taken part in the interrogation began to back away and instinctively made a furtive move for his gun. But Yeuses had already rounded on him, still holding the metal rod.

'Get out of here,' he said to him, 'get out of here at once.'

'Don't fool about, Adrien,' the other took the risk of mumbling, 'come on, don't fool about . . .'

'I told you to get out of here,' Yeuses repeated in icy tones.

The other backed out, his hand clenched on his weapon.

Yeuses locked the door and returned to the middle of the room, where the two bodies lay. Oddly, the soldier was in the same position as the child, lying on his side, with his limbs folded. He did not move; he was not breathing any more. He was dead, killed instantly. He had not suffered any pain. His face expressed only great astonishment. The little soldier who wanted to play at being the grand inquisitor was astonished that there should have been such a sudden reversal of roles: he had died before the hostage. War, of which he had made his profession and even, with the passage of time, his mistress, would thus never cease to surprise him. It had just revealed itself to be much more unpredictable and treacherous than he had thought. He had not died a hero in the midst of battle, but as a common torturer in the close confines of a low-ceilinged room. And now he lay there, no longer a soldier, certainly no hero, and not even a torturer any more, but simply, perpetually, a victim.

Right next to the dead soldier lay the child. He was shivering. Yeuses saw long shivers run over his skin, in all directions, interminably, as if his every nerve was twitching. Yeuses knelt beside him, tried to lift him as gently as possible. But the final kick he had been given must have broken his spine, and he gave a shrill scream. Yeuses wrapped his arms round the boy and held him close. The child's head fell back on his shoulder. He felt the little boy's shivers running over his own skin, penetrating inside him. He in turn shivered; the child shivered inside him. He stroked the boy's head and face. He wanted to comfort him, to wash him clean of defilement, to relieve him of his pain. He began to rock him almost indiscernibly, to lick the wounds on his face. He licked him the way a beast licks its young to which it has just given birth. He spoke to him, too, in an undertone, with immense tenderness. He spoke to him as a mother speaks to her infant. The child was moaning now; he was not screaming any more. Fear and pain were slowly ebbing out of him. Along with the blood continuously flowing from his mouth.

'Tell me your name, your name, tell me your name!' Yeuses murmured to him tirelessly.

That name, just that name, was all that he wanted to know now. Not the names of his enemies, nor the names of the culprits, the assassins. Enemies have no names, nor do assassins. They lose their names, as if cruelty and crime obscured and destroyed all names. And if ever the assassins had a name, at that moment it could only be his: Yeuses, Adrien.

It was the little boy's name that he wanted to hear. To save it from death, silence, oblivion. To save it from war.

'Tell me your name, your name, tell me your name . . .' he repeated in a manner of entreaty. As if the salvation of the world at that moment lay entirely in that sole name. As if his own salvation, the salvation of Adrien Yeuses, depended on that name. As if the peace of all his companions killed in the mountains, and thrown across the path, was also dependent on it. As if forgiveness for the soldier lying beside them was bound up, too, with that name.

He did not demand to be told that name, he begged. He begged, for himself and for the other fellow, the soldier betrayed by his war-mistress. Peace and forgiveness resided solely in the mystery of that name. Forgiveness.

'Tell me your name, your name . . .' he implored, stroking the little boy.

The child eventually stammered out, 'Be . . . Be . . . Belaid . . .'

Belaid. So the child had heard him, he had responded. In the depths of his agony he had found the trust and the strength to make a gift of his name to Adrien.

'Belaid . . .' Adrien repeated softly.

Belaid. At this name, the war laid down all its weapons. The war that for him had raised its weapons, flags and fury on behalf of every one of his murdered companions, all at once admitted defeat at the mere name of one of his enemies dying in his arms.

Adrien clasped the child to him, rocked him in his lap, supporting his head on his shoulder with immense care. He chanted his name in a murmuring voice, as if by the force of repetition he wanted to rid him of all the injury that had been done to him, to polish him like a stone. Belaid ... This name unfurled inside him its lament, its melancholy and beauty. Bringing tears to his eyes. This name, continuing unceasingly to let its mystery unfold within him, caused Adrien's tears to overflow. He did not even hear the shouts outside the door, the hammerings on the door. He heard only the murmur of this name in his heart, the trickling of this name down the walls ... Belaid, Belaid ...

The door gave way. Five armed men appeared in a shattering glare. A scorching blaze of light entered through the forced door like an avalanche of yellow-saffron waves. The blazing light of the sun beating down on this war-torn earth.

But since the war was over, what was this too harsh and incandescent light, and what were these men doing here, with their hands close to their hips? Did they not know, all of them – the sun, and the soldiers – that the war was over, that it had capitulated before the name of Belaid?

Completely blinded, Adrien had difficulty making out what was happening. He was now so far removed from it all. The gigantic shadow cast by the men pounced on him even before the soldiers reached him. He huddled round the child's body to protect it from this enormous shadow trying to engulf it. Yet the child sank into the arms of this shadow; his head became heavy, incredibly heavy, against Adrien's neck.

They tore the child's body from his lap, twisted his arms behind his back and tied his hands behind him. They forced him to his feet and made him walk. All this happened very quickly. But just as he was leaving the room, and crossing the threshold where the light shimmered, he looked back, casting a final glance at the motionless child who lay completely stiff on the ground. Then a great cry took hold of him. He began a tremendous howling, resembling the way the local women modulated their wails of grief and affliction. The child's body tore itself from Adrien's heart, the name of Belaid rent his belly. He screamed. In order to share this name that he could no longer carry alone, to surrender it to the wind. So that the wind might go sobbing Belaid's name across the whole world, so that everywhere that it went it might bend men's knees, might force all wars at last to lay down their weapons. He screamed. But the wind only carried Adrien's sobs astray across the mountains, scattered the name of Belaid in the desert sands. No one heard this name, no one committed it to memory. History has no use for the names of dead children mourned by failed soldiers. Belaid's name was thrown in prison along with its sole custodian. Belaid's name was put in irons. Belaid's name then became Adrien's torment.

So who was going to come back? Who? Rose-Héloise wondered. Would that person still be Heart-breaker, the son found after so much loneliness, the son given to her as a blessing. What would the war have done to him?

The person who was eventually to return would never be the same again. The war had cast him into perpetual alarm, in the name of a foreign child whose face and eyes he had not even seen. The name of a little peasant-boy from the jebel, dying in his arms, had driven out of him – far, far away – any other name. The little goatherd had robbed him of his name, his soul, and his wits, leading them into the desert, there to lose them, to surrender them to the wind and sand.

Rose-Héloise waited. She did not sleep, she did not dream. She brushed her hair.

Nicaise, who lived in the shed next door, often came to watch her. He felt attracted by this woman with purple hair flowing to the ground like silent tears. When he entered the house, and saw her sitting in her night-dress, with her head bowed forward over her lap, he would crouch down in front of her, gently take the brush from her hands and begin to smooth her hair. He loved this thick, purple hair that smelt of ivy and vines. They did not speak to each other. She let him do as he wanted. Sometimes he would stop brushing, and taking her hair in his hands bury his face in it, thereby rediscovering an obscure mixture of terror and delight, that feeling of loss and forsakenness that he had experienced on the day of his return to the village at the end of the war, when his mother had hugged him in her arms, pressing him to her apron stained with the blood of his father and brother, who had been killed in the wash-house.

They did not speak to each other; they had nothing to say. Like all those wounded by war, grief, sorrow or shame, they had no words equal to their distress and fear. They had only gestures and looks. Gentle, crazed gestures that performed a magic ritual to exorcise the pain of remembrance, anxiety for the days to come, and present loneliness. The gestures of survivors trying to regain their hold on life, their place in time, and to rediscover the inclination towards desire. So they communed in silence amid the hushed, silky whispering of purple hair.

Nicaise loved Rose-Héloise, and his love developed into desire for her. He abandoned the young woman from Montleroy whom he had been walking out with for years. He could no longer go near any other woman's body but that of Rose-Héloise, although he had not yet touched, or even seen hers. It was that body alone that he desired, the body of a woman more than ten years older than him, folded in silence beneath a weeping of purple hair.

And his desire for her was obsessive. Was her skin, under her night-dress, as white as the fabric of her garment, and was the bush covering her pudenda as purple as her hair? It was her, and no other woman, that he desired. But nor could he put his desire into words, so it was also through gesture that he expressed it. He expressed it very slowly, gradually, through incomplete gestures, until she discerned the call of his desire, and responded to it.

And Nicaise finally discovered Rose-Héloise's nakedness. He knew her body – her skin so white, and her purple pudenda. The ritual of their gestures became a body ritual. They made love every night, all night long. They lost themselves in each other like swimmers diving into deep waters. They made love on the ground, in a silence so great, all that was to be heard was the murmur of their blood flowing in their hearts and limbs.

Night-of-amber watched evening fall. His last evening in Blackland, his last night in the bedroom of his childhood and adolescence. The birds finally fell silent, the rain continued its desolate, monotonous drumming. His mind was empty of all thought, but for Ballerina's name, her face and her voice. Ballerina, his sister, his jealous love.

'In your name there's the word "ball",' he had often told her. 'Your name opens like a ball. A magnificent ball at which only the wind whirls round.' The violent wind of his desire, for at this ball he wanted to be the only dancer, the only partner of his little sister, whom he already dreamed of as his lover.

'But am I not going to lose her by leaving?' he wondered, with his fists clenched in his lap.

He finally rose and began to undress in the middle of the room.

It was then that it reappeared. It came and settled on the window ledge. With a sharp tap of its beak it broke a pane of glass and flew into the room. The floor was strewn with broken glass and rain. The bird came straight towards Night-of-amber, who was half-undressed, and perched on his shoulder. Night-of-amber lost his balance and fell to his knees. But he did not cry out; he did not take fright. He could not see the bird. He simply felt the clutch of its claws on his neck. He knew at once that it was back – the bird made of metal and canvas that the wind had snatched from his hands and carried up into the clouds all those years ago. His steel-jackdaw, his silver-swallow was back, his kite that had gone off to puncture the sky, to make an assault on a ne'er-do-well God.

The bird of his anger was back.

The bird began to flap its wings against Night-of-amber's temples, then released its grip and came and stood in front of him, on the ground. At last Night-of-amber saw it. The bird's wings and back were covered with ocellated green and purple feathers whose disks were ringed in blood-red; its head and throat and breast were as though enamelled with fine gold and silver scales. Its tail, which was very broad and long, opened into an ivory-coloured fan.

The bird rose by slowly beating its wings and came and landed its claws on Night-of-amber's eyes. The boy toppled backwards, his head hitting the floor. Coloured circles began to spin round under his eyelids that were locked under the bird's feet. The circles widened in luminous waves, then flowers sprang up, spreading their petals like crystal corollas at the bottom of a kaleidoscope. The flowers wilted and were swallowed up in a vast, greenish, globuliferous darkness, and myriads of little white fish covered with sharp spines came swirling into view. They in turn vanished into the now purple darkness. Then signs that were unfamiliar to him, half figures, half letters, appeared, advancing by fits and starts, like sea horses. These hybrid signs did not allow themselves to be read, they were written in brief flashes, and kept spinning round. And they rustled beneath his eyelids like crumpled paper. In Night-of-amber's squeezed eyes a book was striving to be written, a story was gathering its words in haste and disorder. But the darkness again swept everything away, swallowing up the book, drowning the signs. A white, powdery darkness. Night-of-amber sank into a deep sleep. And he dreamed.

★

Two big horses, one bay, the other white, trot ahead of him, drawing a sledge on which he is semi-reclining under blankets and furs. He can see only the enormous rumps of the horses, with an icy sheen on them, and their gently swaying necks. Their manes are almost motionless, so incrusted with frost are they. The countryside around is extraordinarily flat. A snow-covered plain extending as far as the eye can see. A plain swallowed up in the distance by gloomy forests.

The horses are skirting the forest. The trees are not trees but huge lecterns made of dark wood with a reddish gleam. A forest of lecterns. He notices in passing that all these lecterns are decorated with birds that have large outspread wings to support the book-rests.

He suddenly realizes there are no longer two horses trotting ahead; they are women advancing. They are naked. Their hair is like the horses' manes, rigid with frost. They walk slowly. The reins he is holding pass over their shoulders. Their upper bodies lean slightly forward as they walk, drawing the sledge. They walk in step, and at each step their hips sway in unison. The very gentle roll of their buttocks lulls him, sends him to sleep. He falls asleep and in his dream begins to dream.

He dreams within his dream, lying beside Ballerina under the blankets and furs. He dreams that he is hugging Ballerina, caressing and kissing her. But the little girl's body grows colder and colder in his arms, beneath his lips. So cold that his hands and lips begin to bleed. And this coldness that chaps and hurts him wakens him from his second dream. He wakes up completely bewildered in the first dream.

His sledge-team is still moving through the same landscape, but very fast. He cannot tell any more whether they are horses or women ahead of him. He would like to stop speeding along like this; he pulls on the reins, but the horses, or women, far from slowing their gallop only go faster.

He must have been thrown from his sledge, for now he is all alone, on foot in the snow. His sledge-team has disappeared. Woodcutters enter the forest of lecterns. Each of them carries an axe on his shoulder. And suddenly, all together, they begin to strike at the lecterns. But their blows make no gash in the lecterns, which are no longer made of wood but of iron, and a chorus of shrill, clear sounds rises into the air. To this chorus the woodcutters add their voices, for with every blow struck, keeping rhythm, they give a kind of deeply modulated grunt in a rough voice. Then the birds wrest themselves from under the book-rests and take flight. A slow, ungainly flight.

Armed with a very long-barrelled, shiny, silver-coloured rifle, he shoots at birds hovering in the sky. But the birds do not fall; they continue to fly low around him.

He wanders into the forest that the woodcutters have left now. Rust has already attacked the iron lecterns. Indeed, they are so corroded they are the mingled colour of bronze, blood and gold. Some large books lying open on the book-rests let their pages flutter. The texts are illegible. He goes up to one of these books and tries to decipher the text, but then realizes the pages are not covered with letters, but bird-droppings. Very regular bird-droppings, arranged on finely traced lines, like notes of music on a staff. He can still hear, fading into the distance, the lingering echo of the dual chorus of axe-blows and woodcutters' grunts. And he thinks, 'This is perhaps the score for the noise they are making.' But there is immediate laughter that rises all around. It is the birds that are laughing.

The birds laugh, and their laughter is that of humans, piercing and mocking, and their bodies, too, become human. They are now men flying all around him, laughing heartily, and beating their wings.

He fights with the bird-men. He fights with an axe. One of the bird-men sets foot on the ground and comes to fight hand to hand with him. It is a strange tango that the two of them dance, completely entwined together. They dance among the lecterns, among the books whose pages flap, this way and that, like the bellows of an accordion.

The lecterns turn like windmill vanes, and the wind makes the pages of the books flutter. The pages tear, and go flying in all directions. Pages of antiphonaries.

The bird-man, in his dance, makes him arch backwards, forces him to touch the ground, and throws him violently on his back.

When Night-of-amber woke towards dawn, numb with cold and aching all over, the bird had disappeared. The rain had stopped. A humid wind entered through the broken windowpane. He put his clothes back on and got into bed fully dressed, but continued to feel cold. He fell asleep again, into a deep, finally dreamless slumber. He got up just in time to leave for the station. He then began to doubt the bird's strange visit. The broken windowpane could very well have been caused by the wind. But as he hastily washed, he was surprised by his own face in the mirror: the fleck in his left eye had, as it were, become detached and kept moving across his iris in every direction, like a frenzied and flamboyant wasp. The gold fleck's crazed flight in his eye was never to cease. From then on, everyone would call him Night-of-amber-Wind-of-fire.

At midday he boarded the train to Paris. Rain had started to fall again, but so finely it was no more than a drizzle. Someone on the platform came up to his compartment and tapped on the glass. He could not see who it was, for all the drizzle trickling in blackened streams down the filthy window. He lowered the window and leaned out. His grandfather was standing on the platform, uncovered in the rain. They looked as if they had never seen each other before. They saw each other as never before, from so close. Their faces were almost touching, one upturned towards the other, and the other bowed over it. Their breath clouded each other's face. They stared directly at each other in total silence. Their gazes had such a distance to travel. Each one positioned at an extremity of time.

Night-of-gold-Wolf-face, weighed down with so many

years that he no longer kept count of them, and so much memory confused with forgetting. Night-of-gold-Wolf-face, the very aged son of his mother-sister, the fresh-water exile who had five times taken a wife to establish himself on earth, and who had seventeen times fathered children. Night-of-gold-Wolf-face, the man of every war, who had taken part in none of them but had given as hostage to each of them his beloved wives, and sons and daughters.

Night-of-amber-Wind-of-fire, just turned seventeen, already a rebel against his memory. Night-of-amber-Wind-of-fire, the son betrayed by his mother, the orphan captivated by his sorrow and loneliness, who had known no other love but the love fraught with excess that he bore his sister. Night-of-amber-Wind-of-fire, the child born after all the wars, and who had all by himself invented his own war. The madly vengeful child, the jealous adolescent. The lover of words.

They confronted each other.

'You?' Night-of-amber finally said to the old man whose presence on the platform astounded him. He did not really know his grandfather, who had always kept his distance from everybody and never seemed to have taken any great interest in him. Night-of-amber could not believe that the old man had come for him.

A first whistle announcing the departure of the train shrilled down the platform.

'There,' said the old man, 'there . . . since you're going there . . .' But he could not find the words, and seemed deeply distressed.

Night-of-amber, still bowed over him, waited. A second whistle was blown, doors slammed shut. The old man jumped, a gleam of panic flashed across his eyes.

'There,' he said again, 'in the town where you're going . . . there's a park . . . a park with gravel paths . . . if ever . . .' A final whistle sounded that set all the carriages rattling into motion, so that Night-of-gold-Wolf-face's voice was lost.

Night-of-amber stayed for a moment with his head leaning out of the window watching his grandfather's figure on the platform gradually become smaller. Then everything disappeared: the station, Night-of-gold-Wolf-face, and even the landscape steeped in a greyish mist. Night-of-amber sat down again and closed the window. The appearance of his grandfather just as he was leaving troubled and even annoyed him.

'So what did the old man want?' he wondered. 'What did he want, with all that stammering about "there"? They should all leave me in peace, now that I'm getting away from them at last. Yes, I'm going there, far away from them all, and I don't want to see them ever again!'

He snuggled down in the corner of the seat and went straight to sleep.

Meanwhile, Night-of-gold-Wolf-face was returning to his hamlet. He did not even know himself why he had gone into town like that, at the last minute, to see his grandson on the station platform. What did he want to say to him? He had not been able to find the words – as the words to express what he wanted to say were not to be found. For what he wanted to say lay so far beyond words, so deep in the flesh, within his heart.

There, it was there, in the city, before the Occupation, that he had met the woman who had won his heart, never to let it go again; the woman who, when she disappeared, was to cast his heart into hell for evermore. Perhaps he had wanted to see once again, for the last time, the train leaving for Paris? Perhaps he had wanted to tell his grandson, 'When you're there, go to the Parc de Montsouris, and listen closely to the footsteps of the women walking on the gravel. For I'm sure that you can still hear hers there. I hear them all the time. Her footsteps, so lithe and unhurried, on the avenues in the park, on the streets of the town, in the district of Auteuil, along the riverbanks . . . Your footsteps, Ruth! Your footsteps inside me, at every moment, but your heels rip my heart, hammer at my memory, and pierce it with holes . . . Your footsteps,

Ruth, coming towards me, and I am continually waiting for you, but at the same time your footsteps move away, keep moving away, and I am waiting for you, outside of time . . . Your footsteps, Ruth, that keep leaving trails of ashes all through my body . . . Oh, Ruth! Your footsteps that are constantly moving away from me, your footsteps that leave me lost in hell . . . Ruth! Ruth!'

And old Night-of-gold-Wolf-face wept as he climbed back up to his hamlet. He wept as he had never wept in his life before. He wept in Ruth's lost footsteps. He wept as he walked, and as he walked he stamped the ground with all the strength in his feet, as if he wanted to leave behind traces of his own footsteps, in case Ruth were to come looking for him . . . in case his beloved were to return from the dead and try to find him.

NIGHT OF STONES

1

The train came into the station. Night-of-amber-Wind-of-fire was still asleep, with his heading resting against the window. He woke slowly, sluggishly, as if he had to rise from very deep down through sea-green waters. He was alone in his compartment, although a greasy smell still hanging in the air, of pâté sandwiches, garlic sausage and bananas, mingled with the stale smell of dark tobacco, testified to the recent presence of other travellers. He took his case and went out into the corridor. The carriage was empty. He got off the train. The platform, too, was already deserted. Every platform. It was drizzling, just as it had been in Blackland. Night-of-amber-Wind-of-fire was amazed by all this emptiness.

'Where am I?' he wondered, still not properly awake. He suddenly had the alarming impression that he had got off at the wrong station. In fact he felt he had arrived in the middle of nowhere. Through the mist of drizzle he read, on large signs, written in big white letters on a blue background, the words 'Paris' and 'Gare de l'Est'. This only half reassured him, and the feeling of having ended up nowhere persisted. He walked the whole length of the platform, his carriage being at the end of the train, and through the station. But as he was about to emerge into the street, he stopped, turned round, and made his way to the waiting room. He had so desired and looked forward to this city, and now that he was about to enter it he was suddenly scared. He did not feel wakened enough from the torpid slumber that had rendered him senseless for the entire journey to sally forth straight away. He felt himself to be a stranger. He had a need to go and sit among a crowd of other strangers, people leaving, waiting, in transit. He remained there for a while, watching people sleeping where they sat, following the to-and-fro of the impatient pacing up and down among their luggage, observing the anxious who jumped at every announcement that crackled over the loud-speakers and kept feeling for their wrists under the sleeves of their coats in order to study the hands of their watches, as if the time were a mad and cunning bee ready to fly off at whim.

He finally left the station. He saw nothing of the city because he immediately plunged into a metro entrance to travel directly to the university halls of residence where he was to stay. But his subway journey was never-ending because he made the wrong connection three times. When he finally reached his destination dusk had fallen. A damp grey dusk. His room was cramped, the yellowed paint on the walls was flaking in places. Everything seemed tiny – the space, the bed, the wardrobe, the window, his own life. Tiny and so dismal. He threw his case on the bed and immediately went out again. Already he needed some air, some space. He did not take the metro again: he walked. He wandered aimlessly through the streets until late, only interrupting his stroll to buy waffles or chestnuts from street-sellers, not so much from hunger as from want of something to do, and above all to fill his mouth with a feeling of warmth. He ate as he walked, dropping in his footsteps bits of chestnut that were too burned, like a distracted Tom Thumb, perfectly indifferent to which way he was going. He came to Boulevard St-Michel, and walked down to the fountain. In the greenish rippling light shed by the street lamps the statue of the Archangel dragon-slayer seemed to tremble slightly and cast into doubt his triumph over evil.

He began to walk over Pont St-Michel, and stopped half-way across the bridge. The waters of the Seine steeped in darkness were black, like a flow of lava running between the riverbanks. The rain was incessant, fine, grey and relentless.

The rain dispersed the passers-by. No one loitered, especially not on the bridges where the wind blew even stronger, condensing the cold sting of drizzle. Night-of-amber-Wind-of-fire was the only person to pause a while in the very middle of Pont St-Michel, his face turned to the wind, looking towards the cathedral's pale facade. A man who had just hurried across the bridge suddenly stopped, looked round, and gazed for a moment at this peculiar dawdler, with his elbows on the parapet, looking out over the river, heedless of the bad weather. In the end he came back towards him and leant on the parapet, too. He remained like that for a moment in silence.

'Were you there?' he suddenly decided to ask Night-of-amber-Wind-of-fire.

The latter jumped, and gazed in surprise at this stranger who had accosted him with an absurd question.

'Sorry?' he said.

The other man repeated, 'Were you there?'

'Where? Was I where?' asked Night-of-amber-Wind-of-Fire, completely baffled.

'Here,' said the other. 'Here, this time last year, the night of the great Arab-bashing . . .'

Night-of-amber-Wind-of-fire just could not make sense of the stranger's questions. 'I don't understand you,' he simply confessed.

'Ah!' said the other, looking rather disappointed and embarrassed. 'Seeing you here, in this place, in such bad weather, exactly a year later, I thought that . . . that perhaps you . . . you were remembering . . . well, I don't know . . .'

'But what are you talking about? This is this first time I've ever been in Paris. I arrived this afternoon.'

The other gave the ghost of a smile. 'I'm sorry,' he said, 'forgive my mistake.' Then he added almost as an aside, 'Pity . . .' His smile had already faded.

'What's a pity?'

'Everything,' said the other, shrugging his shoulders.

'That I'm in Paris? That I arrived only this afternoon? That I'm on this bridge for no reason?' It was Night-of-amber-Wind-of-Fire who suddenly felt like talking, detaining the stranger just as he sensed that he was about to walk off.

'Yes,' replied the other, 'perhaps that's it. I'm sorry that you're on this bridge for no reason, with no memory or awareness of what happened here.'

'Well, explain to me what this reason is,' insisted Night-of-amber, adding with a laugh, 'go on, tell me, if I like it, I'll adopt it as mine!'

'I don't think you'll like it. I really don't.'

'Why not?'

'Because there are deaths involved.'

'Deaths? What deaths?'

'Deaths. Tens, hundreds, perhaps more. It isn't known how many, and probably never will be. There were dead everywhere, on the embankments, on the pavements, in the Seine. It was just about a year ago. October 17th, to be exact. It was raining like today. Just like this evening, the same stupid drizzle. Yes, the same weather, the same darkness, the same indifference in the city. There were lots of them. They came in from the suburbs in their thousands. Women, men, old people, even children. They were marching peacefully, without shouting, without waving banners. They were well dressed. They were in their Sunday best, as they say. They came to demonstrate to uphold their dignity. They ended up having their faces smashed with heavy sticks and truncheons. You see. It all happened very quickly. They got themselves bashed over the head, killed, like that, in their Sunday best, without really having time to understand what was happening. Afterwards, there were women's shoes lying all over the pavements, in the street, in the gutters. I remember those shoes, yes, especially those shoes . . . because it was so absurd, so scary, so . . . oh, there isn't a word to describe it . . . it left a sense of terrible anguish, and terrible shame as well. All those shoes lying scattered around, their walk ended. All those shoes put on to go and march in pursuit of dignity, but leading only to ignominy and death. And blood everywhere, in the road, and in the Seine . . . a terrible, lasting anguish. And a terrible shame . . . for us.' He fell silent. Without turning to look at Night-of-amber, who saw him only in profile, with his gaze fixed on the river, he had spoken in a slow, faint voice, like someone remembering, who suddenly, in his surprise, terror and sorrow, cannot but remember, and talk, and let the words flow from him.

'But what do you mean by "they" and "us"?' Night-of-amber-Wind-of-fire asked abruptly, the stranger's words remaining just as obscure to him.

The other gave a start. 'The Algerians, of course!' he exclaimed. 'The Algerians that were killed that night! Have you never heard of the massacre that took place on the night of October 17th, 1961? Never?'

'No.'

'What about Charonne? That at least means something to you, I suppose?'

'Yes, of course I've heard of Charonne!'

'Of course!' echoed the other, but in a bitter, disillusioned tone of voice. 'Of course you must have heard of those killed at the Charonne metro station. Everyone's heard of them. But the great Arab-bashing of October 17th, no, nobody knows anything about that. No one knows, or wants to know. It's been torn from the calender, that date, and that night wiped from the memory of every good Frenchman, consigned to oblivion, obscured in falsehood and denial, like the bodies in the Seine. Yet another lacuna in History's pig-headed memory. What amnesia, what absent-mindedness! Don't you think?'

Night-of-amber, roused in turn by the other man's agitation, felt like retorting sharply, 'I don't care a damn! I don't care a damn about all your dead, about any dead, about any wars. I don't care a damn about my own dead! Besides, I was born after the war, after all the wars! I don't care a damn about History. I couldn't care less about being French! I might easily have been born somewhere else, in Finland, Zaire, Laos, or Panama. What difference would it make? I might even have been born on one of those tiny islands lost in the middle of the ocean, thousands of kilometres from any continent, or deep in the hinterland somewhere. French! So what? An accident of chance, among many others. I might not have been born at all. I'm on my own in this world, like everyone else, except that I fully accept this solitude. I've no past, neither a family past nor a collective past. I've no country to which I owe allegiance. I've no memory, especially! I don't want any. I live only in the very fleeting, present moment. A scintillation of discrete, independent, whirling moments. My only duration, my only love, is my sister. My sister, whose name begins with a ball. I don't care a damn about anything else! If I've left my home and my family, it's precisely in order to have done with any kind of past, or memory, to break free of all recollections and sorrows, with all that cock that only gives rise to pointless regrets, cloying nostalgia, ridiculous and harmful remorse, sneaking, futile sorrows. Here I am on the bridge for no reason, and I don't want to give myself any. None at all! So your stories that not even History wants to know about leave me completely cold! Your stories! What a bore! That's all we ever hear – stories about dead people, about people who have been killed. When the hell is anyone going to talk to me about the living, about strong and happy people, full of desire and pleasure in this world? When? I'm on this bridge now, without the slightest reason, and I'm happy here. I'm here only by a freak of chance. I'm seventeen and I want to live in an uncharted age, full of youth and innocence. So there! Do I have to yell it in your ears to make myself clear?'

'You're quiet,' the other remarked.

'I feel like shouting,' was all Night-of-amber replied.

'Well, go on and shout, then. Our Lady opposite will perhaps answer you. She's heard others before. But she doesn't care either. For, you see, she's asleep. She's sound asleep. She's been asleep for centuries, inside those beautiful white stones, as though in a tomb. She's asleep and can't hear us. And she can't hear us because we don't know how to speak to her. That's the truth of the matter. Because we don't even know how to look at her, to see her, through the thickness of all those stones erected in her name.'

'What are you on about?' Night-of-amber cut in, half baffled and half annoyed. 'You're raving!'

'Perhaps,' said the other. He remained silent for a moment, then continued in a completely different, recitative tone:

'To be sure, if I didn't have a certain faith
That God by his grace has given me,
Seeing Christianity only derided these days,
I would be ashamed of having been baptised,
I would regret being a Christian
And become pagan like our early ancestors.
At night I would adore the rays of the moon,
In the morning those of the sun . . .'

'A sermon followed by a recitation of poetry?' Night-of-amber interrupted him.

The other laughed. 'Don't you like my recitation?'

'No, it's inane.'

'You don't know the first thing about it,' the other replied calmly. 'Have you never even read Ronsard? For me, his "Remonstrance to the People of France" retains its power intact, even if the context is totally different. Anyway, I'm boring you, aren't I?'

'No, it's not that you're boring me.'

'What then?'

'You annoy me. I told you, you make me want to shout.'

'And I feel like a drink,' said the other, seemingly quite unaffected by Night-of-amber's surly and arrogant manner. 'How about going to a café?'

'Why not?' agreed Night-of-amber, who in spite of everything could not bring himself to part from this speechifying and provoking stranger.

'Which way do you want to go? Towards St-Michel or Châtelet?'

'Whichever you like, I don't know my way round here. I've only just arrived.'

The stranger led him off towards Châtelet. As they walked down the Boulevard du Palais, he stopped for a moment and pointing to the massive pile of the police headquarters, he said, 'That's where they wanted to come. It was towards that building they were marching.'

Night-of-amber immediately cut him short. 'Who's "they"? The dead in their Sunday best? The little shoes that fell off the women's feet?'

The other did not reply straight away. It was only when they reached the Pont au Change that he spoke again. 'I was there, too, that night. I was at St-Michel, in a café, when it broke out. I was there and I saw it. I saw that crowd marching quietly and without anger. I saw how the police suddenly charged, encouraging motorists to drive straight into them. I saw how they were cudgelled indiscriminately – women, men, and old folk. Because they were Arabs, and we were at war with their people. I saw ... Sometimes I wonder what I saw, since nobody, or practically nobody, wants to discuss it, to admit to this crime. For that's exactly what it was: a crime. A senseless crime, with no justification, committed without warning against unarmed people in the capital of a country supposed to be that of the "Rights of Man". A crime committed coldly by fellow citizens. Fellow citizens, compatriots! These completely harmless words sometimes take on a curious resonance. A contradictory resonance, depending on the period, and on events. During the Occupation these words must have chimed sadly with unhappiness, fear and anger. But that night these words were consonant only with shame. Shame, revulsion, disgust and pity, too. Hardly a year gone by and already forgotten, or worse, denied. The war's no sooner ended than everyone wants to sluice everything away; the two countries involved are both eager to purge the national conscience, to wipe clean their memories. Nations always have two memories: a very, very long memory – long and hardy – for their own glory and heroism, and even longer for revenge. And then a short memory, very short, for shame and defeat. Beyond this atrophied memory lurks an even more degenerate faculty: the rejection of memory, the denial of any memory associated with a bad conscience and guilt. Now, one evening I saw a few hours of our history in the making, very quickly in the making, very violently improvising as it went along, and being immediately obliterated. And this was just a few yards from Notre-Dame.'

'I don't see the connection,' said Night-of-amber.

'It may not be very obvious, but it isn't completely non-existent either. For that night there was something of a crusade about that horde of cops charging against the followers of Allah. The cross against the crescent, even if in the event the cross was in the form of truncheons. That's what an atrophied memory leads to: constantly rehearsing the same violence, the same witch hunts. After the star, the crescent.'

'I don't think the cops are great devotees of Our Lady,' said Night-of-amber. 'As a matter of fact, nor am I.'

'You don't surprise me.'

'And you? You seem very enamoured of Your Lady, but you speak in the tone of a betrayed and resentful lover.'

'Betrayed, no, but resentful, yes. Only it isn't with her that I'm disillusioned but with the use made of her name. Not even disillusioned, but revolted, disgusted. By the use so often made of the names given to God and his saints, in every religion. There's always a return to venerating idols, fine, conquering, hate-filled idols, all made of gold and armed with weapons, and the icon is forgotten. Again a matter of betrayed memory.'

'Right now, you're simply forgetting your invitation to go and have a drink. You talk too much; you've made me thirsty.'

They finally made their way from the Pont au Change and went and sat in a café in Place du Châtelet. It was still sprinkling with rain, a huge veil of fine drops misting passers-by and buildings.

They were the last to leave the café, when the waiters were already stacking the chairs on the tables and sweeping up. Once they were out in the street, a completely drunk Night-of-amber gave a cry.

'Well, what did you see?' asked the other. 'Nerval's ghost in top hat and tails slipping out of the theatre through the stage door?'

It was only that he had caught sight of the tower of St-Jacques, looking so spectral under the drizzle and terrifyingly like a giant arm raised in the darkness to fell the city. They staggered on for a while. They had given up talking, but the other fellow was whistling the tune of a popular romantic song, 'What's left of our love?' They turned down Rue St-Denis, which was lined with glum-looking prostitutes, their thighs reddened by the cold. On his first night in Paris, Night-of-amber-Wind-of-fire, who rejected all memory and all past, wandered down one of the most ancient streets in the city, one of the most burdened with the past.

Rue St-Denis, the great sacred way, the route by which the kings and queens of France entered the city on their accession to the throne, when they made their way to Notre-Dame for the Te Deum. Rue St-Denis, the great funeral way along which, when their reign was at an end and their life over, sovereigns took leave of their city and their people with great ceremony and returned to the basilica to deposit their remains there, to perpetuate in stone the royal legend.

Rue St-Denis, last stopping-place of those on their way to the gallows at Montfaucon, and who, just before they went to swing for their crimes right above the city, received here three pieces of bread and a cup of wine from the very bare hands of the nuns belonging to the order of the Daughters of God, and singing in their clear voices the psalms of penitence. Rue St-Denis, opening its gates of asylum in the evening to the homeless, who, for want of a bed on which to lay their poor-man's carcasses, for a couple of sous could come and sleep here, at Fradin's flop house, and hang their heads,. ringing with tiredness and hunger, over a rope strung between two walls. Rue St-Denis, a terrible maw sheltering in the depths of its caves of miracles a nation of ragged shadows – swindlers, crooks, all kinds of con men, expert in the art of stage managing their absolute destitution, trading on a fabulous horror show to exploit people's pity and mercy.

Rue St-Denis, that bears the name of one of those fools of God who, after being decapitated, picked up his own head from where it had rolled on the ground and took it to wash in the water of a fountain. Rue St-Denis, a place that long before it acquired this name, long before there was a city here, even long before the advent of men and history, saw the very great and fantastic procession of elephants that passed by, drinking from the waters of the Seine.

Night-of-Amber-Wind-of-fire lurched his way along Rue St-Denis, beneath the shining gaze of the prostitutes. An entire guard of gazes, shining with make-up and neon, fixed on the man passing by. But he only noticed their knees, the roundedness of all those naked knees lacquered with rain, slightly bent beneath the weight of bodies weary of displaying themselves so. Rue St-Denis, a long roadway planted with round and glistening knees, like plane trees along an avenue.

They eventually reached the Gare de l'Est.

'Well, what do you know?' exclaimed Night-of-amber. 'Back to square one!'

'How about taking a train, any train?' his companion suggested.

'Definitely not! I've absolutely no desire to go back to where I came from. A train going south, from the Gare du Sud, or west, from the Gare de l'Ouest, fine. But not east. No way!'

'There is no Gare du Sud or Gare de l'Ouest,' said the other. 'They have other names, but I can't remember them.'

They entered the station, and walked on to a deserted platform. They walked to the very end of the platform and stood there for a moment, facing the rails that disappeared into the night. There was nothing going on. The city seemed to have dissolved in the darkness and the rain. All movement had ceased. They stood at the end of the platform as though on the end of a mole lost in the open sea, forgotten by boats.

'Let's go and sleep,' said Night-of-amber. He could not stay awake any more. He felt that before long he would collapse in a heap. They returned inside the station and went and lay on benches in the waiting room. They fell asleep there, in the dim light accompanied by distant sounds, not waiting for anything.

It was in that light that he woke up. He felt even more disoriented and lost than when he had got off the train the previous day. He had a terrible headache, and his jaw and hair felt stiff. His companion had disappeared. Night-of-amber had difficulty gathering his wits about him and recalling precisely the events of the night before. All that kept running through his mind was the tune of 'What's left of our love?' He got to his feet and walked out of the waiting room. Suddenly he stopped.

'But I don't even know his name!' he said to himself.

He felt a great bitterness at the idea. So he would not see his companion of an evening ever again, that young man with straight fair hair that kept falling in his eyes, who talked non-stop, passionately and volubly. The fellow had talked to him about everything he did not want to hear mentioned – war, memory, faith, political commitment. And yet he had heard him out, only contradicting him to encourage him to go on talking. Actually he had listened to his voice more than what he had to say – the rhythm, tone and expression of his voice. War, history, faith, politics, all these things remained totally alien to him, deprived of meaning or interest. What he had just woken up to for the first time was simply a feeling of friendship. A feeling that was still unrefined, lacking in ease and sophistication, and with which he felt a bit lost and uncomfortable, as though dressed in a brand-new suit that is all crisp and starchy. A feeling of which he was not in fact even aware.

He took the metro again to return to his hall of residence, and arrived back just when everyone else was getting up. Standing outside the door of his room, yawning so hard his eyes filled with tears, he was rummaging through his coat, searching for his keys, when he pulled out of one of his pockets a piece of card torn from a packet of Gitanes. The little black silhouette of the dancer on a blue background appeared distorted before his eyes that were misted with tears and blurred with tiredness. As he played with the piece of card, twisting it in his fingers to make the dancer spin round, the card turned over. On the back were scrawled a name and telephone number: Jasmin Desdouves, OUR 5903. Night-of-amber finally got the door open and threw himself fully dressed onto the bed. Before falling into a deep slumber again, he said to himself, 'I'll call him tomorrow.' And then he was asleep.

During his early days in Paris, Night-of-amber-Wind-of-fire saw Jasmin Desdouves regularly. He put into this new friendship the same passion that he had until then invested solely in his fondness for his sister. They met in cafés, cinemas, parks or libraries. Jasmin Desdouves was a few years older than Night-of-amber, and was at that time preparing a Masters thesis on Victor Segalen, while Night-of-amber was enrolled at the Sorbonne as a first-year student of philosophy. He was still no more interested than before in the disaster of war, in different memories of history, in religious matters or political problems, but he was none the less close to his friend, sharing with him a similar way of thinking, of responding to things, of dealing with reality.

Reality. They treated it as a raw material, as stone to be cut and sculpted, as clay to be worked and shaped, as a body to be set in motion, placed on stage – a combination of drama, dance and song. Reality was to them a perpetual invitation to dream and use their imagination, a constant incitement to adventure, desire, and travel. For the two of them, seated at bistro tables or on benches in parks or by the river, were constantly travelling. They travelled fabulously, in the land of reality, in the provinces of time, each of them following his own route.

But however deeply the route of one plunged into the depths of the imaginary and into the magical power of poetry, it never strayed far from the rest of humankind, or from the present, while the route that the other followed went zigzagging freely through the most fantastic geographies, resolutely removed from men and events of the day. Jasmin pursued the exoticism inscribed within the real, such as Segalen and St-John-Perse responded to with wonder and praise, only for a better appreciation of the presence of man amid the immensity of things and of time, and in order then to confront the present in the full knowledge of the world's most obscure undercurrents and those of history, and in the knowledge especially of the infinite strangeness of the human soul. He listened to the poetic word to detect in it the muffled rhythm of constantly advancing history, underlying the world's song and giving that song a human dimension. Of words, he required gravity, uncompromisingness and appropriateness, in order to be able to discover in the weight of language the very weight of time as it accumulated from age to age, the weight of man and his soul. He had the capacity to be ever mindful of man, of his frailty, folly and dignity combined. Of the work accomplished by poets he expected only what one of them had said of it, that 'it's enough for the poet to be the bad conscience of his time'.

This bad conscience of his time and his people, he bore within him not as a mere reproach or a confused and unhappy sense of guilt, but as a demand for honesty. For him, it was not a matter of wielding words as a sermon, but as a constant appeal to others, a call for attention, lucidity and goodness. The years of his adolescence were accompanied by the distant sound and fury of the war in Algeria. He had grown up with this distant sound, and was grieved by all the violence used on either side, grieved by the blindness and hatred that had fossilized in the hearts of so many of his own people. He knew that he was too deeply involved in the history of his people not to share the sufferings as well as the disgraces of his people, but more importantly, he felt such a strong sense of solidarity with his fellow human beings – all those fellow human beings appointed in equal measure throughout the world to endure the trial and mystery of their presence in the world – not to feel as much anger as sorrow and pity when violence and injustice was done to them. Only through words addressed by man to man was Jasmin Desdouves in full communion with reality, and with its fantastic imaginary reverse side. His relationship with reality was one of friendship, and with man one of fraternity.

Night-of-amber-Wind-of-fire did not so much commune with reality as try to carve through its very density paths of escape by which he could go rushing off towards greater vastnesses. Rushing breathlessly, out of sight, towards greater freedom, to zones exempt from every form of bondage, to greater wildnesses beyond the bounds of humanity. It was himself that he pitted against reality; as a stag frays its antlers on tree trunks, he frayed his heart on every dream and desire, on every excess. His forlorn heart in which his mother's cry was lodged like a dark thorn, tearing his childhood and wounding to the quick his trust in others, alienating him from his own, from history and from God. His pained heart on to which his sister's name was directly grafted.

Night-of-amber-Wind-of-fire very soon abandoned the university's vast amphitheatres and lecture halls. He preferred to go and pass the time in other places. He often went to the big greenhouse in the Jussieu Gardens, where he liked to be confined in the very clammy and seductive humidity of the plants and flowers. He could remain there for hours, getting intoxicated by their scent, colours and shapes. Their often contorted shapes, sometimes inelegant but always beautiful. Garishly beautiful, like those giant orchids with petals more fleshy than a bitch's tongue, of violet, purple or orange. Flowers with lips too heavily rouged, flowers with bright mouths, flowers with whore's tongues, flowers with fabulous pudenda. He immersed himself in the sultry fug of the greenhouse as in the body of some huge, polyanthus woman, her loins damp with sleep and spent with pleasure. When he emerged from that vegetal den into the fresh air outside he felt overcome with dizziness, exhausted and ecstatic with desire. He went to see the animals in the zoo, not to watch them circling round in their miserable enclosures, but to catch in their eyes, narrowed with boredom, the gleam of a deeper and more ancient look, and to draw from their rumps and flanks, grown thin through immobility, the thrill of a prodigious leap about to be made.

Then there were the stations, those vast waiting halls filled with movement, those huge covered bazaars of people pacing up and down. He never tired of haunting them; he liked to identify the rogues among the crowd – the pick-pockets, those seeking to prey on lost-looking country girls, illicit vendors of transport tickets, drug pushers, con men touting for unclassified hotels or clandestine brothels. He observed their sly manoeuvres with the same distant curiosity with which he observed the travellers, or porters on the lookout for tips. In fact they were all on the lookout for something – the right time or the right person. The right moment to board a train, to find the awaited relative or friend, to rob a passer-by or take advantage of the guileless. Looking out for the other person in an animal-like way, looking out for the time with anxiety. Time ticking past second by second on the giant clock faces, as though to stress the ruthless erosion of time.

There were also the race courses, markets, stadiums, airports, department stores, swimming pools. He had to go wherever it was crowded. He had to get lost in every throng, the better to detach himself from it, to rally himself in his proud, fierce solitude. He would spend the whole day wandering in all these congested, busy, anonymous places. Things had to be lively around him; there had to be talking and jostling. He needed constantly to seek out the smell of human beings so as to trace in it the underlying whiff of the animal lurking in every person – whiffs of madness, violence and desire so ill contained by their citizens' attire. Occasionally he had even gone into the big hospitals. St-Louis, Trousseau, Lariboisière, Cochin, Pitié, Salpêtrière, Hôtel-Dieu, Diaconesses, Necker, or Notre-Dame de Bon Secours – he went trailing his boundless hunger for human folly down their corridors, like an alley cat prowling among open dustbins in some backyard. Through open doors he could see patients lying in their beds. He was immune to their suffering, distress, and terror. All he saw were degenerating bodies, defeated bodies still fighting, as best they could, to save themselves from the clutches of death.

And it was precisely this he came to spy on: the magic of the body's dissolution and corrosion, the mystery of extinction already at work in the living flesh. Work of darkness, turning blood into mud, skin and heart into callus, presence into absence. Work of darkness that did not precede any work of light but ravaged human matter, destroying organs and dislocating limbs, devouring faces, gradually reducing them to nothing. But this work of nothingness that he witnessed resulted in a work of ruddiness, for there, too, he rallied not only in his solitude and pride, but in the plenitude of his presence in the world, in the vigour of his youth and all the energy of his desire. When he left these long and labyrinthine hospital corridors whose whiteness was soured with the smell of ether and carbolic, he would walk through the streets inhaling the city air as he might a sea breeze.

That was how Night-of-amber-Wind-of-fire spent most of life during the first year: walking. A continuous stroll through the city, amid crowds, smells and noises. A stroll in the course of which all his senses were multiplied. He had hundreds of eyes, ears, nostrils, fingers, always alert at every moment to catch the flavour of the animate and inanimate. At the end of his walks he would often meet up with Jasmin, the only person in the city, for him, to have detached himself from the crowd, to have acquired a face and a name. His only friend, his double, his opposite. And far away, beyond all these streets, bridges, and buildings, there, in bordercountry, was Ballerina.

There, somewhere that had become nowhere, was his sister. He did not see her any more, and would not see her again for a long time. He had no wish to return to Blackland. He was more determined than ever to have no further dealings with his family. There was only his sister – his dream of her, his desire for her. He wrote to her continually, letters that he never sent. He knew very well she would not have read them. The girl to whom he wrote could have no address; she lived nowhere. She inhabited a dream. He wrote to her to rend the space between them, to trace a path through this desert. He wrote in order to pin down, in black and white, the infinite pain of his impossible desire for her, as well as the magic fulfilment of this desire.

And this was how he experienced the city – as a crazy, manifold letter addressed to nobody, to everybody, to absence. All those giant placards carrying multi-coloured advertisements of the most garish and touting kind, and those newspaper kiosks covered with headlines and pictures that changed every day – who they were addressed to if not to hurried and distracted passers-by? And those who scrawled their thoughts on the walls – slogans, lines of poetry, criticisms or demands – and those who chalked their destitution on the pavements where they squatted to beg at knee-level – who did they all address themselves to if not to stone and asphalt? Tarmac, stone, cement, hard and opaque materials grimy with smoke, eaten away by pigeon shit and dogs' piss, strewn with cigarette-butts, and spattered with spittle and puddles of oil and petrol.

And all those plaques stuck up by the entrances to buildings indicating that such and such a musician, writer or painter, such and such a great man listed in the encyclopedia of proper names, lived, created or died here, at such and such a time – who were they signalling to, what were they signalling? And all those commemorative plaques set in the walls of houses and public buildings all around the city, recalling the name and age of those who had been shot by the occupying forces – who or what were they challenging if not memories in disarray, already averted from the past. For the city was like a cemetery, covered with epitaphs, signs and dates, words written in absence, condemned to oblivion.

Those who had been creative, those who had given their life, here, at this particular place in the city, were not actually here any more, and never would be again. Neither here nor anywhere else. They were dead, no longer of this world. That is what the plaques said: such and such a person, who once lived and loved, no longer lives here, no longer dwells here. Here nothing. All those plaques merely indicated points of contact, already long in the past, between time and space. Those plaques merely marked where the stridence of time ripped through space in order to create sites. Those plaques were merely white scars left on space by time, scars in stone for ever drained and exhausted of the blood of the men named on them. Jasmin always read these plaques whenever he came across them; he read these names out loud. To wrest them from the silence of the walls, from the deafness of stone and marble. From the stone of fossilized history, from the marble of oblivion and silence. Once he stopped in the middle of a street, caught hold of Night-of-amber by the arm, and set him in front of one of these plaques.

'Look,' he said, 'do you see that name? Who cares about it? Little bunches of municipal flowers are left there to wilt from time to time, on every national anniversary. These names chill me. This one was riddled with bullets on a December morning of 1943. He was seventeen. But his youth was of no importance to those who gunned him down.'

'Perhaps it was of no importance to him either,' said Night-of-amber.

'Perhaps, yes, but the two things are completely different. And anyway, perhaps he had been denounced, like so many others. Given away by his neighbours, his concierge, or even someone close to him. What does it matter? All informers are alike. And in those days informers were much more numerous than anyone wants to admit now, but it is so much easier to rat on somebody than to confess. They squealed quietly in the dark, concocting their letters of denunciation on the sly, out of self-interest, jealousy, fear, or vengeance, or even out of sheer pleasure. They wrote to the enemy; they who were under occupation wrote to the occupation forces, participating of their own free will in the work of hatred and destruction going on around them. They wrote to death, so that death should on no account be left unemployed. But they remained in the murky shadows from which they had meticulously corresponded with death. They retained their monstrous anonymity, from beginning to end. Just imagine if the names of all the informers, traitors and assassins were known, and posted on walls instead of the names of those, always belatedly, celebrated for their work or honoured for their courage. Perhaps to cite all of them the city would have to expand? But history does not mention those names. History does not know how they are spelt, or how to pronounce them.'

'Of course not,' Night-of-amber contented himself with replying. 'If plaques had to be put up to record the name of every fool and bastard, the city would be stricken with a terrible, galloping, plaque sclerosis. Not a wall would remain free of it.'

Night-of-amber-Wind-of-fire walked through the city as though it were a black book full of violence and delightful oblivion. He had no memory, did not believe in responsibility, or care a damn about history, and had no fondness for people.

He did not like people, though humankind intrigued him. He saw man as nothing more than a beast half alienated from his original animality, half lost since he had crawled out of the earth and mud. A beast grown monstrous because of its incomplete mutation, with its shark's belly, its magic, totem-like phallus, its unpredictable unicorn's heart, sometimes so tender, sometimes so cruel, and its neck so grotesquely contorted towards the abyss of heaven.

It was this failed mutation that fascinated him. What obscure coupling had produced this strange human offspring? Did it result from fornication between the beasts and the gods, or the elements and the gods? Or perhaps from some mysterious amorous struggle of a very barbaric nature that took place within darkness itself?

Humankind was simply a coagulation formed in the caverns of the night, a malign tumour that had grown in the void and proliferated.

In the beginning were the Shadows and these Shadows concealed in the chaos of their black entrails Night-above and Darkness-below. One tore the other, sowed in it the seeds of its desire, violence, and cry.

In the beginning were the Shadows. And this beginning had never been, and kept beginning over and over again, without end. In the end would be the Shadows. This end was already, for ever and ever, in perpetuity.

At that time Night-of-amber-Wind-of-fire developed a passion for the great legendary cycles that recounted the birth, life and battles of the gods, as well as for the great epic stories relating the adventures of men-heroes. He preferred Hesoid's Theogony to the Bible, and Homer to any history book. He was a great deal more fired by the fierce battles of the Titans, Cyclops, Hecatoncheires, Furies and Giants than by the exodus from Egypt, or the wars fought by nations throughout the ages. His favourite was Cronos, last-born of the Titans, and his interest ran out with the advent of Zeus, who established the rule of the

Olympians, when already a certain principle of order and light that he was averse to began to prevail.

Cronos, though, was rebellious, cunning, and violent. The one who had castrated his too oppressive father with a cut of his flint scythe, and then stuffed his brothers back into his mother's teeming wound. The one who had coupled with his sister Rhea, on whom he fathered six children that he later devoured.

Rhea: this sonorous name enchanted him. On his long walks, he sometimes repeated it to himself, like a spell. The nature of time in history was indeed very mysterious, as Jasmin said. But for Jasmin this meant that everybody's responsibility was boundless. For, he claimed, 'This responsibility is so great that it binds us to each other, not only in the present, but just as much in the past and the future. We are the contemporaries of both our most distant ancestors and descendants.'

Night-of-amber, however, felt himself to be a contemporary only of the Titans.

He hung up on his bedroom wall a reproduction of a painting by Goya, depicting Cronos, huge and distorted in the darkness from which he loomed, in the process of tearing to pieces the body of one of his children. This rigid body in the grip of its carnivorous father fascinated him; its trunk was decapitated, the arms half rent off, but the buttocks, thighs and legs were still intact and looked like those of a live person. The rounded, somewhat heavy buttocks, set in shadow, occupied the centre of the painting. They were a woman's buttocks. Night-of-amber decided that this must be Demeter, mother-to-be of Persephone, Queen of the Underworld and of the Dead.

Rhea, the sister penetrated, impregnated by her brother. Demeter, the daughter devoured by her father. The naked daughter holding up like a torch, to the gaping mouth of her father, with his bulging eyes, his flowing mane of hair like white flames, one of her lovely arms all mangled. In the evenings Night-of-amber would gaze for a long time at this monstrously beautiful image. At night he would dream of this body: the woman with the chewed arm, and rounded buttocks, mounds of soft clay indefinitely moulded by his desire. Rhea, Demeter, Pauline, Ballerina – he confused these names and faces in his dreams. He dreamed that he was Cronos wolfing down his brother, Jean-Baptiste, with the enormous resonant belly, like a purple drum, covered with sores. He dreamed that he was Cronos ripping to pieces with his teeth the body of Pauline, his traitor-mother, tearing off her head, shoulders, and breasts. He dreamed that he was Cronos cutting off his crybaby father Crazy-for-her's genitals. He dreamed that he was Cronos bearing down on Ballerina's frail body, his hands gripping her buttocks, his phallus lodged inside her.

No, it was not about himself he dreamed; it was not even he who was dreaming. It was the flesh dreaming within him, tormented by the most intense desire.

But he very soon deserted his room, and forgot the image. From the day he met Nelly, he had somewhere else to sleep. She was his first lover. She was exactly twenty, with splendidly rounded buttocks. Her face was rather plain; passing her in the street, he would not even have given her a second look. Yet it was in the street that he had encountered her, but from behind. He noticed those buttocks as she walked in front of him. That day she was wearing a tight, satin-like, purple skirt that showed her legs to above the knee. He continued to follow her wherever she went, his eyes riveted on those purple-moulded, purple-lacquered buttocks, intent on their rhythmic swing, and the subtle play of light on the satin-like fabric. He eventually accosted her in the shop she entered, a record shop on Avenue des Ternes. He went up to her and gently removing from her hands the record she had just taken from a rack, he went and paid for it at the desk and came back and gave it to her.

Then he said with a charming smile, 'I'd like to listen to it, but I don't have a record-player.'

He improvised this gambit with equal bluff and candour, and it worked. Seduced, the girl suggested by way of thanks that he should come and listen to the record at her place. Less than an hour later Night-of-amber-Wind-of-fire lost his virginity to the strains of Schumann's Fantasiestücke, which the girl had picked out completely by mistake, having gone into the shop to buy Elvis Presley's latest album.

Their relationship lasted nearly a year. He was never in love with her. During the day, each of them would do their own thing, she going to work and he on his walks. He never asked her any questions about herself, and took no interest in the rest of her life. He lied about his own life, his past and his studies, for fun, out of indifference. He lied about everything except his feelings.

'You know, I don't love you, Nelly, I only love your butt. I find it terribly attractive.'

He said this without cynicism, even rather kindly, and always concluded this declaration of not loving her with an adorable smile. She never responded to these blunt confessions. In fact she made no demands on him, and seemed to expect nothing of him. She simply took what he had to offer her – his smiles radiant with youth and his desire for her. But occasionally a curious look came into her eyes that were suddenly clouded with doubt and distress. He never noticed these looks, having never really paid attention to her eyes. It was enough for him that she should be equipped with the buttocks, thighs, and hips of Demeter, the daughter gobbled up by Cronos, swallowed by that enormous black mouth of madness. He liked to take her from behind, to clutch her by the hips and press his belly against her warm, soft-skinned buttocks, and to come inside her with blind sensual pleasure. Then he would rediscover that obscure joy, momentarily magnified and all-powerful, that he had known as a child in his tenebrous retreats where he reigned as a rebellious and solitary prince.

He left her as soon as she imposed on him her face, her look, her being. It was a summer evening, and it had been raining. One of those tempestuous rains that within a few seconds inundates the sky, the streets, the trees, then retires just as quickly, leaving everywhere a chill, intense light, like the brilliance of grey-blue satin.

When the rain stopped Nelly threw the window wide open and leaned out over the drenched street to breathe in the air that had at last been refreshed. Then she turned to Night-of-amber-Wind-of-fire and, covering her eyes with her hands, in a playful tone of voice she sprang on him the question, 'Do you even know what colour my eyes are? Tell me.'

No, he didn't know. He would not even have been able to say whether they were light or dark. He did not reply. She waited, determined, hidden behind her hands.

He eventually hazarded a guess. 'They're brown.'

She removed her hands, revealing her face. She suddenly had a very hard, almost violent expression. The eyes that she pinned directly on to him were the exactly the colour of the sky after the downpour. Slate-coloured. Anyone would have thought she had torn two little bits of sky from between the roofs to stick them in her eyes. He felt disconcerted and, before long, uneasy. He was seeing her for the first time. Her features looked drawn, with a puffiness about her eyelids and mouth, as though she were on the point of screaming, or weeping. He could think of absolutely nothing to say to break the heavy silence that had fallen between them. The sense of awkwardness that had stolen into him suddenly turned into a wave of anger. Everything happened independently of their reason or will – the direct look that she gave him like a slap in the face, a look so blue, so naked and piercing, levelled at his heart, without warning, like a challenge, and a reproach; and the fury that rose inside him, through his whole body, a hatred of her that suddenly blistered his nerves. What did she want? What did she expect of him? An expression of gratitude, an apology, a declaration of love? Well, she could go to hell. Trying to touch his human feelings in this way, she had homed in only on what was most deeply and obscurely animal in him, and roused a tremendous anger in a heart more untamed than ever. He was seized with a burning desire to slap her, to tear off her face like a strip of wallpaper stuck on a wall, to dissolve the blueness of her eyes in acid. A desire to strangle her, decapitate her. To throw her head out of the window. A desire to bite her, to tear her to pieces – head, shoulders, arms. To keep only her hips, her smooth buttocks, her full thighs, her rounded knees, her hot cunt. To make her once and for all what she had actually always been, a lovely headless body yielded to the frenzy of his desire; Demeter's arse.

It was she who broke the spell by speaking.

'The party's over,' she said simply, in a very calm but expressionless voice. 'Get out of here, this minute. I don't want to see you again. Ever. You're not going to play with me like a doll any more.'

He contented himself with saying, 'Fine. I'll be off then. Actually, it's better this way, because you're beginning to get on my nerves. Your stupid little blue eyes have left me with no desire to screw you!'

He gathered up his belongings and made for the door without paying her any further attention. As he was about to leave, Nelly rushed at him and scratched his face with all the strength in her nails.

'Bastard! Bastard!' She hissed the way that furious cats do. He grabbed her by the hair and, violently pulling her head back, he bit into the hollow at the base of her throat, drawing blood. Her cries were immediately choked, and she raised her hands to her neck. She staggered, her breath taken away.But the rage that had just exploded inside him, that she had just conjured up in his face by raking him with her sharp nails, did not subside. Flattened against the door, the skin on his face scratched raw, he stared at her, motionless. She was holding her throat and rasping, hunched in pain. He felt the blood from her scratches running down his face, reaching his mouth. He licked his lips. He detected a taste of iron, of stone, in his blood. A taste at once very insipid and very powerful. Outside the sky had darkened; evening was closing in. His face was on fire. His mouth kept emptying, and filling with moisture, redness, and hunger. His face was like a burning stone, his tongue was turning into flame. Wild, liquid flame. He walked over to Nelly, slapped her three times in a row, then kneed her hard in the stomach. She collapsed.

Shadows filled the room. The furniture and objects, even the walls, were beginning to dissolve, distorting space. He said nothing, and she was no longer crying. She was dragging herself around on all fours, choking, as if groping about on the ground in search of her lost breath. But her breath, too, had dissolved in the evening's gathering dusk. He came and crouched behind her. He caught hold of her hips, pulled her towards him, threw her dress up over her back, and tore off her knickers. She tried to escape, but he was gripping her too strongly, with one hand. With the other hand he unbuttoned his flies. His movements were precise and swift. And there, kneeling on the floor, riveted to the girl who was no more than a curled-up heap already half obscured by the shadows, he took her by force. Nelly's forehead struck the ground, the cry or sob that assailed her died in a gurgle in her wounded throat. But he heard nothing. He was not himself any more, and she was no longer Nelly. They were nothing, either of them. Nothing at all, nobody. A single misshapen body, consumed with fury and pain. He was no more than a dog mounted on her. A dog of stone and shadows.

He left her like that, curled up on the floor, grotesquely uncovered. Without a backward glance, he left her there, bruised and humiliated. He did not even close the door after him. He just walked out. He walked all night long. The cry she had hurled at him before clawing at him kept ringing inside him, throbbing in his head and heart until it made him feel sick. Bastard! Bastard! It was a cry that clawed at him now, through his whole body, from inside, much more surely than Nelly's nails. And he was aware of the absurdity of this insult, an insult that fell far short of the act he had committed. He had hit her, hurt her, raped and sullied her. He was much worse than a bastard. What he had just done was criminal. But he could not admit to being guilty. Was he not the postwar child, the child that came after death, and therefore absolved of all remorse, all shame and guilt? Was he not the person without memory or past, and therefore free of all obligation? He resisted the insult thrumming at his temples, denouncing him to his own conscience. Bastard! Bastard! He resisted this attack of conscience, a conscience perturbed and involved for the first time ever. He resisted this unfamiliar feeling of culpability, this dizzying and hateful unease of culpability. Bastard! Bastard! The walls of the city crowded in on him; his footsteps echoed weirdly on the pavements. Each of his footsteps seemed to carry the echo of that insult.

He could not admit to it, absolutely not. He would not on any account admit to it. He was indeed the postwar man, coming after all wars, of yesterday, today and even tomorrow. He would never concur with Jasmin's ideas. He felt solidarity with nobody.

He belonged neither to war nor peace. He had never known peace. He belonged out of time, beyond the pale. He belonged only to the moment, the furtive moment that sprang from nowhere, unconnected with the past, unlinked to the future. He would find a way of silencing this cry that Nelly had fired off inside him. He would find a way to stop it reawakening that other cry – his mother's cry, that September cry, that had destroyed everything. Both war and peace. He walked on, between the facades of the buildings, like a sleepwalker. His head was burning and his temples hurt, as though crushed by the stones of the walls.

And suddenly the name came back to him. He had just come into a very long, straight, empty street. The diffused light of the street lamps perforating the darkness cast a metallic sheen on the puddles of water left by the rain. That splendid name with its crude, incantatory sound: Rhea. The name drowned out the insult, and drove away Nelly's cry. And his mother's cry.

★

Rhea! The sister-goddess possessed by her rebel brother. Rhea: it had the ring of a hatchet-blow. The name struck at every step, cleaving the darkness, smashing the stones. The walls moved aside, the street opened up into a gigantic avenue lacquered with dark blue and pools of silver. Rhea, Rhea. The name rent the town like a bronze plough-share. And he walked right down the middle of those stone furrows sown with darkness, his head held high. He was not walking any more, all of a sudden he was stamping. This movement turned into a jitterbug dance.
He made his way through the sleeping city in the manner of a savage sovereign lord. He was not guilty; he was free, and supremely indifferent to others. He who as a child had crowned himself Prince-very-dirty-and-very-naughty, that night declared himself Prince-lover-of-all-violence.

Rhea, Rhea! The name clattered at every footstep. With every click of his heels. It was no longer a name in fact, but a sound. Not even a sound, but a noise. An original noise, endowed with the explosiveness of the greatest burst of laughter, with the force of rhythm, and crackling with darkness.

With every step Night-of-amber-Wind-of-fire moved further away from Nelly – any memory of Nelly. He moved further away from everything and everybody, even Jasmin. He strode resolutely towards solitude, pride and anger.

With every step he moved further away from himself. He advanced like a boat with no crew or captain aboard, left to the mercy of every current, of the most contrary winds, and the treacherous songs of the sirens. He felt strong, magnificently strong, and absolutely free.

Rhea! A cry of pleasure and defiance.

2

Rue de Turbigo. It was there that Night-of-amber-Wind-of-Fire moved to when he left the university hall of residence. He had always hated that big dormitory partitioned with concrete walls, where even the beds were like desks. He found a job as a night porter in a little hotel near the Bourse, so that he could pay for a private room in town.

Five evenings a week he went to the hotel ceremoniously called At the Sixteen Golden Steps, in honour of the great classical-style temple that stood near by. Five evenings a week he, who was so hard up the whole time, came and spent the night under the hotel key-board, in the shadow of the god of Finance's holy of holies. This was where he studied, amid the ringing of the telephone and the clinking of keys swinging on their hooks. He would slip behind the long reception desk covered with tourist brochures, sit in the yellow-coloured vinyl-leather chair, and there, in between dealing with clients who came up to find out what time breakfast was served or some good place to go in the capital, by the acid glare of the ceiling light, he read the works of authors on his degree syllabus. He opened his books right under the neon tube that cast a chilly and greenish halo round the whiteness of the pages and the skin of his hands. After several hours' reading, his fingers often looked to him like those of a drowned man, with olive-coloured nails, and the print on the page ceased to be letters of text that made sense and turned into impressions of rusty nails scattered over pages made of plaster.

These little nails then began to dance in his eyes. They clung to his eyelids like crinkled eyelashes, and composed themselves into strange alphabets. Indecipherable alphabets. The entire world, of things and individuals, gently drifted into a blur, became indefinite, and unreadable. This always happened towards dawn, the time when tiredness sends shivers of silence, coldness and absence of mind running through a person's whole body.

Letters, keys, and nails were really all one and the same, fluttering and clinking beneath his eyelids. He would get up, cross the deserted hall, and step outside for a breath of fresh air to perk himself up. The street was almost always empty at that time, as was the Place de la Bourse, just at the end of the street. He gazed at the fake temple squatting on its pillars, like the legs of some giant beetle, inside its rusted railings. A giant, massive scarab. A sacred scarab, like that of Ancient Egypt, preserving under its folded wings of stone the echo of the fabulous clamour that daily exploded within its belly. Quotation of stocks, invitations to tender, share trading . . . With piercing cries, shouting, bellowing, and hooting, an entire race of numbers-men came and celebrated here, with fantastic hysteria, at once unbridled and formalized, the great financial ritual. A race of devotees in impeccable suits, their shoes polished to perfection, their ties neatly knotted round their puffy throats, their freshly-shaven faces gleaming with lavender-scented sweat, their rigid bodies in the grip of an almost undetectable trance, of monetary delight. The Bourse, enormous and silent in the night, a dung beetle rolling in a closed circuit the murky sun of the great barbarian bourgeoisie's wealth. The Bourse, a mock temple glorifying the most profane values, honouring the most insolent of gods.

Alphabet, keys, and nails. All these formed a strange whirl in Night-of-amber-Wind-of-fire's eyes whose gaze on the street and square was that of a diver rising suddenly from the deep. But he liked this mysterious hour at dawn when the cycle of time began to enter the process of switching from night to day, when the city that still lay fast asleep prepared to waken, when his own tiredness was about to return. For it was the time when, after that brief pause at the hotel entrance, he went back into the hall, emptied the thermos flask of coffee he had made for himself, and finally plunged into the texts on the sole syllabus of his desire. That year his favourites, in no particular order, were Heraclitus, Empedocles, Aeschylus, Sophocles, Plotinus and Schelling.

He did not go back and sit on his chair, but began to pace about, reading in an undertone the book he held in his hand before his face. He needed to move, to zigzag to and fro, to articulate the words, to roll them in his mouth. He needed to read with his whole body – muscles, nerves, mouth and feet – and not just with his eyes following the lines and his fingers turning the pages. He endeavoured to read these authors in their own language and this exposure to languages still not very familiar to him demanded of him an attentiveness that was all tension and alertness. The letters then turned themselves more than ever before into keys and nails that he had to learn to twist and turn, extract and fix. For these books were like the sacred Scarab that constantly begets itself: they could discharge within them the black sun of strife, and the fall, of the great divine drama, the world's genesis, and man's folly. This Scarab would never cease to roll in all directions the black sun of the Book – books by the thousand, endlessly recommencing. Because for Night-of-amber-Wind-of-fire the question posed by Schelling – What keeps back the imminent golden age when truth becomes fable again and fable truth? – remained for ever open. Anyway, perhaps it was not a golden age, but rather an age of onyx or obsidian, an age of lava and wonderful mud? Yes, the question remained open, open like a wound, and that is why books never came to the end of it, all taking up the question and re-examining it again and again. The question of origin, of meaning, around which the pages of books perpetually flapped, wings and membranes of the magic Scarab.

At eight o'clock in the morning Night-of-amber-Wind-of-fire finished his shift. He left the hall, turned white with daylight again, and walked back to his lodgings along Rue Réaumur. On the way, he stopped off at a café on Boulevard de Sebastopol, where he bought himself a glass of rum at the counter in preparation for his daytime sleep.

★

Rue de Turbigo. It was there that he shut himself away every day to sleep in the room that he rented. Three metres by four. He had solved the problem of being cramped by opting decisively in favour of emptiness. There was not even a bed. He slept on a mat, wrapped in a blanket that he folded up as soon as he got up. In one corner was a trunk, in which he stuffed all his personal belongings – his clothes and things. There were a few shelves for his dictionaries and the few books he owned. He was enrolled at several libraries. In all things, even reading, he lived by borrowing, never possession. By the window was a folding table. The chair, too, was a folding one. There was also a little gas heater standing on his case in a corner of the room. In his case were piles of letters. He never opened it; he only half-opened it every time he wrote to Ballerina, in order to toss in the sealed and stamped letter.

He continued to write to her, and not to send his letters. Letters that were sometimes very brief, sometimes very long. Insane letters, in halting words made more so by the muteness to which they were destined. Love letters as mad as they were arid. For his love was arid. He spoke to himself, in a void, in her absence. He did not even know now what face the object of his desire had. It was more than two years since Night-of-amber-Wind-of-fire had left Blackland and he had not been back to see his sister again. In any case Ballerina was not living there any longer; she had already gone to Strasbourg.

The letters piled up inside the case – a poste restante for lost words. He always took great care to seal the envelope, stamp it, and address it legibly to the person to whom it was written: Ballerina Peniel. Only the address was not always the same and often between the first name and the second he would stick in another word. Ballerina Crypt Peniel. Ballerina Arrogance Peniel. Ballerina Orient Peniel. Ballerina War Peniel. Ballerina Archipelago Peniel. Ballerina Rail-car Peniel. Ballerina Body Peniel . . . As for the places it was addressed to, these were always verbs and

adverbs, words of geography in action, in motion and tension. He wrote to her at: Eternally Running, Admirably Wanting, Shouting Immensely, Nonchalantly Suffering, Swimming Crookedly, Fabulously Digging, Bitterly Set To A Rhythm . . .
All the letters went into the case. Ballerina's name was shut in darkness; silence surveyed the place-names composed of verbs and adverbs. He had written to her, and that was enough. And it was enough, because nothing ever could have been, anyway. His love for her was too vast, too demanding. He had written to her to no purpose, quite absurdly. He had written to her in words torn from his body, the body of an intemperate brother, an imaginary lover. In words removed from his body like bits of skin, concretions of flesh, precipitates of saliva and blood.

He spent little time in his lodgings. He slept there, and wrote there. His life took place outside, always divided equally between solitary study and wandering through the city. He did not see any more of Jasmin. Since that evening when he had so brutally raped and violently attacked Nelly, the city had become for Night-of-amber-Wind-of-fire a free zone where everything was possible, where everything was allowed. And where the things that Jasmin said could therefore be nothing but ridiculous verbiage.

He wandered through the streets, sometimes amusing himself by following passers-by – not those that were going to work or returning home, for he could not attach himself for long to their footsteps. The footsteps of domestic animals, plodding and without surprise. It was those that passed by chance, walking aimlessly, and only able to arrive nowhere that he liked to follow.

So it was that he met the two strange characters that became his companions for a while. The two Vowels, as he called them. There was O, and there was U. The closed vowel and the open vowel. O was Ornicar. Everything about him was indeterminate, indeed ambiguous – his age, where he came from, what he thought, even his race.

Night-of-amber encountered him in the street, behind an oyster-seller's stall. Not that he was an oyster-seller. Night-of-amber-Wind-of-fire never actually knew quite what Ornicar was, what his origins were, or how he spent his life.

It was a summer evening. He was walking down a street that was oppressed by the heat and emptiness, one of those streets deserted every August by its inhabitants who migrate to the sea or the mountains. Passing in front of an oyster-stall attached to a large brasserie that was closed for the holidays, he heard a sound completely out of the ordinary. A kind of long echoing vibration, pitched from deep to shrill. He stopped, but could not see anything. He looked at the sign above the stall: 'Oysters. Seafood. Crustaceans. Shellfish.' A fishing net, spangled with dried starfish, covered the wall inside the stall. A few empty crates were piled up in a corner. The peculiar note rose to total shrillness, turned into little squeaks, then descended again, plunging deep as though to the bottom of murky waters, to lurk there. Then the note became syncopated, fragmented into an echo. In the end Night-of-amber-Wind-of-fire wondered, 'What sings like that?' He asked himself the question out loud, so intrigued was he, and not expecting any answer. And yet an answer came.

'A rorqual!' shouted a gleeful voice. A curious little fellow then emerged from the stall's shadows. He was unkempt, and looked like a jack-in-a-box. His colouring was indefinable: something between swarthy brown, olive and orange-tinted ochre. He had a long, wasted face, a very thin mouth, slightly almond-shaped, narrow eyes of bluish black and astonishingly shiny. In fact, on closer inspection, his skin appeared to have been stretched and sewn up again, as if he had been seriously burned, and he looked more as though he were wearing an already shabby and badly fitting mask than as if it were his real face. There was indeed something second-hand about that too tightly drawn countenance; it might have been taken apart and put together again a very long time ago, in early childhood, and when he grew up the seams had cracked and the mends had swollen.

'A rorqual!' he repeated, dusting himself down. Then he jumped up on to the front of the stall and sat there cross-legged.

'Ah, yes, a rorqual!' he declared for the third time with an air of triumph.

'I heard,' Night-of-amber-Wind-of-fire said eventually. 'Is that some kind of parrot, or what?'

'Oh,' exclaimed the other, looking shocked, 'you don't know about the happy humpback whale, the enormous baleen whale with black mottled skin that leaps and sings among the waves?'

'No, but you don't look anything like that. You look much more like an eel.'

'You didn't see me properly,' said the other. 'Look!' And with that, he lay flat on his stomach on the wooden display-counter, lifted his feet like a flipper and began to swell. For he did really manage to swell, and his skin turned black, and he resumed his long, underwater ululations. Then he flopped over on to his back.

'Well?' he asked, completely out of breath.

'Not bad,' Night-of-amber conceded, 'but more like a sea lion than a whale.'

The other looked vexed, and sat up again. 'What about you?' he eventually asked, stretching himself. 'What animal are you?'

'It depends on the day,' replied Night-of-amber. 'Humans are like Noah's Ark: they all have a representative of each animal species inside them. But generally they let the poor wild creature expire of boredom and oppression, deep in their constipated guts, out of fear, stupidity, shame, or even tactfulness. Let's say that I'm a walking zoo, but of carnivores mostly – canids, to be more precise.'

'But you know,' said the other, having cadged a cigarette from him, 'I don't restrict myself to whales. I'm an animal that metamorphoses. I'm nothing absolute, nothing definite. To tell the truth, I actually think that I'm an animal that doesn't exist: something between a griffin, a salamander and a dahu.* A dahu especially. My own mother could never find me. I was no sooner born than I vanished. To be absolutely honest with you, even I never managed to catch up with myself. It's a long time now that I've been pursuing the chase, but there's nothing to be done about it, I'm elusive.'

'In short,' said Night-of-amber, 'from what I can see, you're god.'

'Damn it all!' cried the other. 'How did you recognize me?'

'Easy. God or the dahu, what's the difference? Neither of them exists, but people spend their time running around after them.'

That was how Night-of-amber-Wind-of-fire met Ornicar, the dahu-god. The person who had no memory, who rejected history and saw himself as the contemporary of the Titans became friends with the person who did not exist. Their relationship was founded on nothing but the most preposterous derisiveness and ludic behaviour. At the age of twenty, Night-of-amber-Wind-of-fire suddenly began to regress to a constant state of unrestrained childishness. They went about everywhere arm in arm, through the streets and the bars of the city, always on the lookout for some trick to play, for some dramatic stunt to pull off. The one who did not exist was above all a person who did not work.

'How do you expect me to work?' he said. 'I've no identity to declare. I've no papers, nothing, no identity card, no residence permit, or passport. It's only natural, since walls can't keep me out. Who would want to employ someone who doesn't exist, who doesn't know where he comes from, or even his own name?'

For in spite of searching his memory, he was unable to identify any trail, any dates, places, or individual that

* A mythical French Alpine goat

might help to define the event of his birth, or the story of his youth and childhood. He did not even know what he was doing here, in this country, in this town, or how he came to be here.

'Basically,' he would sometimes say, 'I'm probably a kind of mandrake. I must have been born of some hanged man's sperm that fell on the ground of some foreign land. But where? And when?'

The only genealogical tree he was ever capable of establishing was that hypothetical gallows, the devil of a way from anywhere. But he was remarkably good at catering for his inability to work, thanks to his inexhaustible faculty of imagination and metamorphosis.

'Since I'm only a mirage, a subterfuge,' he said, 'I may as well take the art of illusion to the extreme.'

And he cashed in on his very elastic appearance, by offering to the crowd his talents for metamorphosis.

His talents in this area were boundless; he could transform himself in any kind of animal whatsoever, from a little mouse to an elephant, rhinoceros or hippopotamus, including insects, fish, and birds, and he was wonderfully successful in imitating the calls and songs of each one. He could contort himself incredibly, and take on any colour of the solar spectrum, he could puff himself up or contract at will, to the greatest amazement of the onlookers who never failed to stop and gather at the sight of such an unusual spectacle. In short, he lived very well on the art of being a non-existent person.

But was that really living? The fault in him kept worsening, the sense of being abstracted from himself and from the world only increased, and became a chasm. A chasm of distress and total solitude that he eventually fell into.

Night-of-amber-Wind-of-fire, who had never seen Ornicar as anything other than an exceedingly cheerful fellow, and had made friends with him on that basis, had no inkling of the obscure distress eating away inside him, no presentiment of his collapse. It was enough that Ornicar should amuse and amaze him. He had never questioned him on the causes of the frightful botchery to which his face and even his whole body seemed to have been subjected, as though after some awful disfiguration. Just as he had never tried to penetrate the obscure reasons why his companion always refused to let him visit the place where he lived in the suburbs, or why he systematically collected every glass jar and bottle he could find, or why, again, he always took extreme care to avoid walking or resting on people's shadows cast on the pavements or against a wall, as if they were sacred and terrifying markings. Fads among others of this demented dahu-god.

The fall of the dahu-god was sudden and drastic. It happened one mild and sunny April afternoon. Ornicar had taken by storm the statue of Balzac standing proudly, with his dishevelled hair and considerable paunch, at the crossroads at the end of Boulevard Raspail, in the shade of the trees that were just regaining their foliage. That afternoon Ornicar was playing at imitating the snowy owl. He was perched on the statue's shoulders, uttering a series of raucous cries that had put to flight all the sparrows around and attracted curious passers-by. Soon a crowd of intrigued onlookers had gathered at the foot of the Balzac monument. A very small boy detached himself from this group and came forward a little, pointing with his finger at the freak gesticulating up there and laughing. But his mother had immediately caught him by the arm and drawn him back towards her, standing him against her white dress and holding him by the shoulders so that he did not wander off again. Standing very straight, and not moving, the little boy remained obediently with his mother, but with his finger still pointed at Ornicar. A tiny child's finger.

'Craowoo, aowoo, aowoo!' cried the owl Ornicar, who from one second to the next seemed to be covered with white feathers, and whose eyes dilated, taking on the hue of molten gold. The crowd watched open-mouthed this extraordinary metamorphosis. And he, from the top of his perch, stared bizarrely at the finger of the little boy he had just noticed in the crowd. That tiny finger that all at once denounced him to his own memory, to the impossibility of his memory.

'I'm a snowy owl!' he suddenly began to announce between two cries, his voice altered. 'A bird of the attic nights. I nest in stone and coldness, I feed on stars and lemmings, and on nights when the moon is full I tear up the shadows of the great white birches, quivering on the snow, to feed them to my little ones. Craowoo . . . My hunting area is vast, illuminated by snow and silence, I carry the shadow of my wings to the seashore and over the frozen waters of the lakes. I sometimes fight with seagulls, grouse, and wild geese. I even attack penguins, seals, and the occasional bear. As for men, if I happen to come across one, I swoop down on him, I peck at his neck, then I pierce his eyes and go and feed his saliva-soaked gaze into the squawking beaks of my dear little ever-ravenous young. Craowoo, craowoo . . .'

What he said was so incoherent and bawled in a voice so grating that the people assembled round the statue could understand almost nothing. But people never listen to the speeches of lunatics, they watch them gesticulating and shouting from a safe distance. They let them expurgate in their stead the monsters and terrors teeming inside their own hearts, and which they keep securely fettered. They watch them daring to perform this task of extreme audacity and grotesque pain with an avidness matched by repugnance.

For the crowd that day quickly realized that the cheerful eccentric perched on Balzac's neck had just exceeded the limits of role-playing, had stopped performing, and was toppling into the night of insanity. Those that were laughing at the start of the spectacle rapidly stopped laughing. All faces froze, all mouths fell silent, all eyes opened wide. A man was in the process of losing his sanity, right there in front of them. A man was in the process of ceasing to exist to himself, right there, just above their heads.

'Craowoo oo aowoo ooh!' Ornicar compulsively beat

his wings in empty space. He was a dull chalky white, and his voice kept rising and rising, becoming inaudible.

'I nest in the void. I nest in hunger and cold. I've flown the world over, with my wings spread wide, but I've never managed to find myself. I've never found myself because I've never existed. Never, never, never, nn . . . ever . . . but where? Ah, but where is . . . ?' His voice suddenly cracked, and at that point his question and his sanity were gone for good, as though caught unawares and overcome with dizziness by the answer that was not to be found. And he fell astride the statue, with his knees squeezed against Balzac's ears, his fingers clutching the hollow eyes, and his head thrown back. He would have remained there indefinitely if they had not come to move him. The fire brigade had to be summoned to fetch him down. They arrived with a great furore, and raised a ladder against the statue. They had to twist his fingers one by one to loosen his grip. Then they brought him down like a stiff and dislocated puppet, bundled him into their van and drove off with him at top speed through the warm streets of the city. And so the chase for the dahu-god came to an end. He was then confined in an asylum. And he who did not exist let strange hands lay him in a white bed, like a stone figure lying on a tomb. He was never to regain his reason, nor the power of speech or movement. Everything in him was petrified. Of all the animals in his magic bestiary only one remained faithfully attached to him to the end: the dahu. The dahu had lain across his heart and was keeping watch over him.

As for the bailiffs, when they entered his apartment after his internment to draw up a list of his assets, they discovered one of the most bewildering collections that might ever be found: the whole place was chock-a-block with thousands of glass jars stacked from floor to ceiling, all filled with excrement. No furniture, no other belongings, nothing. Just a string hammock, hanging in a corner among the piles of jars. No bailiff in living memory had ever seen a horde like it: so much human shit so reverently preserved for years and years. But all this fossilized crap had none the less failed to fill the breach that opened in the soul of one who never managed to exist, of one whose body and memory had been consumed by history.

So it was that Ornicar disappeared from Night-of-amber-Wind-of-fire's horizon. But his horizon was shifting and forgetful. As was that of the other person with whom he struck up a friendship at about the same period – the open vowel U: Ulyssea.

He also met her in the street, one night when he was on duty at the Sixteen Golden Steps Hotel, and went to stand at the door for a few minutes to get a breath of air before immersing himself in his favourite reading. An immensely long, gangling shadow suddenly came round the corner of the street that was usually so deserted at that hour. For the shadow had preceded the body that cast it, and it was flanked by a second shadow of a very bizarre shape. The bodies finally appeared, making their double shadow sway gently in the light of the street lamps. The person approaching was walking on stilts. She was dressed in a full, loose dress of silky grey, and wore over the upper part of her face a bright-red mask with a long thin beak. On the end of a long green-satin leash held in her hand was a miniature llama.

She advanced on her thin legs with ease, bobbing her curious, wader-bird head at the second-floor level of buildings, whistling the tune of 'The Sad Waltz'. Just a few notes, always the same, sung quietly. In a little girl's voice. The llama trotted along beside her, holding its head high. It kept its eyes almost completely shut; they had an albino creature's pinkness. Night-of-amber-Wind-of-fire left the doorway and came towards them. As soon as he found himself standing in front of the girl, who towered over him, he in turn began to whistle, with lively insistence, choosing a different tune, that of 'Invitation to the Waltz'. The girl began to laugh. She laughed the way little children do, in light melodious bursts. She climbed down from her stilts, taking the hand offered to her by her chanced-upon chivalrous knight.

They spun round together for a while in the middle of the street, singing together. When they finally came to a halt, slightly breathless from their improvised waltz, Night-of-amber-Wind-of-fire retreated a few steps and introduced himself with a bow.

'Charles-Victor Peniel, night porter.'

'Well,' said the girl, 'my name's Ulyssea and I'm a bird.'

'Really? What do you mean by that?' he asked.

'I'm mean a migratory wader-bird.'

'Pity, I'd rather you meant a street-walking bird.'

The girl was not at all offended by this remark and even agreed to follow the night porter to the hotel reception area and share his flask of coffee with him.

She tied up the llama at the hotel entrance, leaving it to look after her stilts, which she propped up against the wall. She sat cross-legged on the counter, and lifted the mask from her face, so that the beak was like a curved horn over her forehead. Night-of-amber-Wind-of-fire noticed that she had a very decided squint in her right eye, and he thought that with this louche look she could not dare plague her lovers by training her eyes on them directly, to get them to say exactly what colour her eyes were.

But most of all he thought this little squint-eyed bird was extremely disturbing and desirable. And he did not deprive himself of thinking this out loud. The girl took this second remark just as easily as the first. She unfolded her legs and slid down on to Night-of-amber-Wind-of-fire's lap – he sat facing her in his chair – and let him remove her clothes. He took her like that, straddled across his thighs, like an amiable and flighty doll. Outside, the miniature llama's pink idle gaze filtered over the deserted street.

Ulyssea was one of those travelling people who go from town to town, with their vans full of costumes and props, putting on shows all over the country and even across the border. She belonged to a troupe of actors, jugglers and acrobats, who were stopping over in Paris. But what she liked more than anything else was to wander about, perched on her stilts, all on her own with her llama, through the streets of sleeping towns; to go gliding through the darkness between the facades of the houses with their shutters closed on the dreams of those asleep inside; to cast her long thin shadow on the pavements, very quietly tapping out her mounted footsteps.

In fact it was always during the night that she came to visit Night-of-amber-Wind-of-fire. He would hear the approach of a peculiar sound, like the quiet tapping-out of a tune in the silence of the deserted street. He would see the shadow of her figure and that of the llama creep up to the doorway of his hotel and dissolve in the pool of bluish neon light, from the hotel sign, splashed on the pavement in front of the entrance. Then she would jump to the ground, leave the animal tied up outside, slip into the hotel reception area and join Night-of-amber behind the counter. It was right there on the floor, under the key board, on eggshell-coloured limestone tiles, that they made love.

Ulyssea was a wonderful storyteller. There seemed no end to the number of stories she knew, gathered from here and there in the course of her travels or perhaps stolen from sleepers dreaming aloud in their bedrooms. But it was mostly her way of telling them that created their charm. She had the voice and laughter of a child, and there was immense grace in the way she bowed her head while speaking, and waved her hands about. Hands so tiny that Night-of-amber-Wind-of-fire could contain both of them in just one of his.

There was a greyness about all her stories, a silky grey that was very gentle and rather sad. Sometimes it was the story of a shadow that had lost its man one day on the banks of a river whose name it could not remember, and ever since then it had been going down all the rivers in the world, on a raft of woven reeds and rushes, in search of the body so unexpectedly taken from it; sometimes it was the story of a little girl fed since birth on nothing but pancakes of dust, who had become like a little mouse; or else the story of a miraculous tree of ashes covered with silver fruit at every new moon; or the story of a king whose kingdom gradually turned to smoke, and his castle into mist, which were eventually blown away by a gust of wind, and the dispossessed king went wandering about his non-existent kingdom, begging, carrying his wife the queen, who had gone mad, on his shoulders; or the story of an old woman whose hair suddenly began to grow in the form of raindrops, and who went and plunged her head in the sea so as not to feel the trickling coldness of her hair constantly running down her back; or the story of all the statues in a town that one day decided to wrest themselves from their plinths, niches or fountain basins to go and establish themselves as a free people outside the town which belonged to men; or else it was the story of the fisherman who one day drew up in his nets the body of a drowned young girl incrusted with thousands of silver seashells . . .

There was always a greyness about her stories, and a little coldness in her heart. That is why she could never keep still, and had to keep moving from town to town. Always moving on, and on, never taking root, never getting tied down in a place. Always moving on, and on, rediscovering the supple rhythm of walking, striding freely, recapturing the light-footedness of wandering. Always moving on, and on, walking through life like the common crane, with that detached and graceful air, drifting with the wind. Ever a fugitive, with passing time.

She moved on. She took to the road again, with her llama and her companions. She did not warn Night-of-amber of her departure. She simply stopped coming to visit him one night. For several nights he waited for her, behind the reception desk, for the time noticing its ugliness, vulgarity and coldness. He could not concentrate on his reading; against his will, something inside him kept listening for the least sound from outside, distracting him from his work. The quiet tapping of her stilts on the street, the soft rustle of grey fabric floating round her body, the dissolution of that double shadow falling into the bluish pool of neon light at the hotel entrance, the silent figure of the pink-eyed llama – it was all this that he waited for. Hoped for. And that very high-pitched voice of hers, prattling on, telling her stories, a melancholy child's stories, and her tiny hands, her stifled laughter, and the freshness and taste of her skin, her breasts, her mouth, and the weight of her body, so light on his own, and . . . and . . . and . . . It was a long of list of indefinable things that made him wait so expectantly, in a state of amorous alertness. Ulyssea. He heard her name murmured quietly in the silence – a show-girl's name, the name of a wanderer and a sleepwalker. Ulyssea. Her name seemed to clink on the key board behind him. Ulyssea. He heard the whisper of her name with the turning of every page of the book he was absentmindedly leafing through.

Ulyssea. He heard the singing of her name to the distant tune of 'The Sad Waltz', as it whirled round, in a transparency of emptiness, with a barely audible rustling of grey satin. The name was running away from a ball, a night-time ball . . . and this name became confused with that other name that opened with a ball. Ballerina. Ulyssea had run away only to let little Ballerina more easily find her way back into Night-of-amber-Wind-of-fire's watchful heart.

This went on for several weeks. Several weeks during which Ulyssea's name swept over his skin like a shudder, knotting his throat and his stomach, hammering at his temples. Try as he might to deny or escape the discomfort of unassuaged desire, the sadness of waiting in vain, his malaise persisted. Then he lost patience with himself. He rebelled against the cunning and hurtful power the girl's name had over him. Damn it all, he, Night-of-amber-Wind-of-Fire, was not going to let himself be caught, at only twenty years of age, in the sticky spider's web of amorous feeling! He was angry at having allowed himself to be touched by that disgusting languor, and he was even angrier with the girl who was gone.

'Ulyssea,' he cried out at last, 'I'm quite capable of doing to death your wheedling name! I'll reduce your memory to dust. So, take yourself off on those wretched stilts of yours and don't ever come back! Let your wings fly you to hell, you short-sighted little tramp, with your ghastly midget llama!'

And he did to death Ulyssea's name, just as he had unfrocked Nelly's name, put Jasmin's away in a cupboard, and forgotten Ornicar's. All that remained was his aching nostalgia for Ballerina.

Rue de Turbigo. He lived there under an angel's wing. A sculpted angel, on the facade of his building, by his window. A lanky angel, excessively long in the leg, whose body was draped in the folds of a narrow robe that covered its feet. It looked rather like the body of an eel-like fish. It was three-stories high, gazing down on the street with utter indifference, with a ghost of a little smile, as vague as it was foolish. The outspread wings behind its shoulders and framing its head were ridiculously out of proportion with the length of its body. If ever this stone angel had been seized with a whim to detach itself from the facade and go flying off around the neighbourhood, it would have fallen straight on the road, betrayed by those absurd, graceful little appendages. The face of this angel was fairly inane; the face of a well-fed adolescent, with a flat nose and forehead, rounded cheeks and with a funny, rather doltish, little smile playing on its lips. An expressionless gaze. There was really nothing sublime about this fish-like angel, but it nevertheless had a bland innocence, a pleasant unconcern, a curious indefinable something that Night-of-amber-Wind-of-fire liked.

'My neighbour is a stone angel begrimed with the sweat and smut of the city,' he used to say. 'It doesn't chat, and it doesn't move. It stays there, pinned to the facade, with its idiot smile and vain grace. It's not a guardian angel, more of a cretinous angel. The citizens' angel, if you like! The real face of God, in fact – the mug of a poor mindless creature that doesn't give a damn about what goes on below.'

And strong in this scornful assurance, he rewarded the Turbigo angel every day by opening his shutters beneath its wing with a look full of condescension.

In fact he eventually brought this look to bear not only on his stone neighbour but on all the people he passed in the street. By dint of immuring himself in his haughty solitude, and rebelling against all form of attachment, he lost the thread that leads to others. And if ever this thread happened to be lying in his path and he mistakenly picked it up, he would immediately break it in a rage.

But this thread was a strange thing that kept turning up unexpectedly, in the most unlikely guises, and every time he had to cut it again, his anger increased.

So it was that he met the old woman one day, coming upon her in the labyrinth of the city. An old woman selling lemons. A woman so old, so ugly and crooked, that she looked as if her age could not be measured in years, and there seemed nothing human about her. She stood all shrivelled in the middle of the pavement with an old basket set between her very red, almost purple, bare legs, one hand stuffed in the pocket of a short ragged overcoat too big for her, and the other hand held out in front of her, displaying a lemon on her palm.

A lemon of such a bright, luminous yellow it looked like a burst of sunshine. At the mere sight of it, the mouths of passers-by filled with all the tang and savour of the day. And the old woman presented it to the world like a strangely insolent challenge.

'Look!' she seemed to say. 'This ugly old woman has in her possession one of the secrets of the world. Here, in my hand, I hold your thirst. I also hold your tears, lymph, humours, saliva, sweat, urine, all your acid and translucid fluids. I have total power over your bodies. And I will do violence to you, if I so please. I will poison your fluids, I will taint them all!'

Her eyes were no bigger and with no more colour in them than lemon pips, her skin was yellower than the rind, but of a murky, brownish, very lack-lustre yellow. She stood absolutely still, all bowed over the gleaming lemon on her beggar's hand, like a statue of a grotesque and wrinkled angel offering to the world the sacred heart of some young solar god that had only that moment been sacrificed. An immemorial moment.

'One franc a lemon, one franc!' she murmured in a toneless, very thin voice. She kept repeating her little phrase for a few minutes, like a litany, then fell silent again, with no change of expression or pose, without even bothering to look if anyone who might hear her was passing in the street. Maybe she was blind, wondered Night-of-amber-Wind-of-fire, who watched her for some time at a distance, from the pavement opposite.

'One franc a lemon, one franc, one franc a lemon, one franc, one franc a lemon, one franc . . .'

Occasionally a passer-by would notice the old woman, and go and buy her fruit. But it was never the one displayed in her palm that she sold. As soon as a client came up to her she would bend down over her basket to take out another. An old, misshapen lemon with a rind that had turned soft with spots of blue. Unsold lemons from Les Halles, spoiled fruit picked from the crates thrown out when the market closed. That was what the old woman was selling; that was her pitiful pauper's ruse. She dumped the rotten fruit in the cheated buyer's hand and quickly pocketed the coin without saying a word, as if her entire vocabulary was limited to those few words: 'one franc a lemon, one franc'. Although unpleasantly surprised, the buyer never dared complain, let the matter drop out of pity, and walked off with distaste, holding at arm's length the mouldy fruit, and wasting no time in chucking it in the gutter once around the corner. Perhaps these clients had a confused feeling that basically this swindle was quite fair, that the poverty-stricken old woman had only given them a just return for their scant pity. A mouldy lemon in exchange for their undistinguished charity.

'One franc for pity, one franc!'

★

Night-of-amber-Wind-of-fire eventually went up to the old woman to buy a lemon. He just wanted to get a closer look at her, to let his curious gaze dwell on the wizened face of this ridiculous and squalid trickster.

'How much?' he asked and immediately the mechanism went into action.

'One franc a lemon, one franc . . .'

Her eyes were whitish, almost entirely covered by the soft, rheumy skin of her eyelids. Her mouth was toothless and her lips flabby, which weirdly distorted the curve of her nose and the prominence of a chin that bristled with long tendril-like hairs. He took a coin out of his pocket and held it out to her. She then bent towards her basket, but he stopped her, saying, 'No, you old witch, I want that one, the good lemon, not a rotten one from your miserable rubbish-bag!' And he made as if to seize it.

But the old woman's hand immediately closed round the fruit with a dry crack of her knuckles, and she gave a peculiar high-pitched cry, like the squeal of a saw. And the look she fixed on him was truly that of a little girl seized with terror, and madness. Her penetrating cry actually sounded like a baby's cry.

He then turned away without challenging her any further. The old woman was too weak to be trifled with. And then that scared expression, that appallingly wild look, that horrid whinging unnerved him. He did not like being caught unawares like that. He only wanted to call her bluff, rile her, have a little fun at her expense. But the old woman was absolutely off limits, already far too sunk in her distress and destitution. And he felt in some confused way that something like pity had found its way inside him, had touched him. Now, he hated that insidious feeling above all others. He had long ago determined once and for all that pity smelt bad, that it stank like the feet of a fat wheezing trouper. He could not bear that this fetid smell should treacherously infiltrate him and turn his stomach. So he walked off. But he had no sooner reached the end of the street than he turned round. The old woman was trotting along, still clutching her fruit in one hand, tucked under her throat, and holding her battered basket in the other hand. She was going. His curiosity returned, and he decided to follow her.

He followed her for a long time, but she took such small unsteady steps that he felt he was getting nowhere. Time spent in her wake was time slowed, inspissated, weighed down. He eventually had the alarming feeling that his body was slowly turning to stone, that his feet were melting into the asphalt. He wanted to stop shadowing her, but he could not. Something in the old woman acted on him like a magnet. Something more and more stubborn in him persisted in following her. The air was very mild, and yet he had to battle his way forward as though there were an extremely strong wind blowing against him. The old woman, however, moved on unperturbed, tacking between the walls, the passers-by and the cars, like a boat sailing against the wind. Like Charon's bark.

It was a very narrow, steep street. He was panting, but she was not. At last, half-way up the street, she came to a halt in front of a big carriage entrance. She set down her basket, gathering all her strength to push open the heavy door. In fact, she only had to open a crack, and she slipped into the building. Night-of-amber-Wind-of-fire rushed after her, and opened the door in his turn.

But there was nothing behind the door; there was no building behind the façade. A vast building site gaped there, a wasteland of deep holes, turned-over ground with weeds and nettles growing here and there; heaps of debris were piled almost everywhere, machines and tools were stowed in a sheet-metal enclosure. A whole row of old houses had recently been demolished. All that was left standing were some of the outside walls, perhaps to be included in new constructions. Nothing of this was visible from the street. The façades on the outside were perfect *trompe-l'œil.* But there was nothing *trompe-l'œil* about the other side of them; rather, they were eyesores. The remains of old apartments, and traces of the floors and rooms where generations of tenants had lived, were still discernible. Strips of wall-paper, rusted and twisted piping. In some places there were even bits of staircases, and Night-of-amber noticed a derelict lavatory. The white enamel throne, polished by the evening light, sat there in splendour, suspended over empty space. A few pigeons were perched on the edge of the bowl, dozing, with their heads between their wings, sunk into their necks.

So was it here, on this building site where work seemed to have halted, that the old woman had made her lair? But in which corner, under what roof? There was everything here but roofs. There were only walls, bits of things, fragments of staircases. Night-of-amber-Wind-of-fire ventured further into the building site, searching every corner, trying to run the old woman to earth. After all, she could not have just disappeared. Yet he could not see her anywhere, and he could hear no sound. Some cats wandered among the rubble in silence.

The light was slowly fading. Banks of vaguely orange-tinted clouds drifted immensely slowly above the city, noise of which, heard in this enclosure, was subdued. So had the old woman stricken everything with slowness, muffledness, disappearance?

All of a sudden he felt caught in a trap, a prisoner of the now invisible old woman. She had made him follow her into this gutted and baleful place. She had drawn him from the city, from sound, movement and the crowd. He thought he was the hunter and he turned out to be the hunted. The old woman had cast a spell over him to make him pursue her, to take her revenge for being affronted by him. Then he was suddenly seized again by that insane fury that had already exploded inside him once before, the evening when he had raped Nelly. He felt overtaken, body and soul, by a tremendous anger, a wild hatred towards the old woman.

'If I find her, I'll kill her!' he said to himself, without even thinking about the meaning of these words.

A sound finally caught his attention, the sound of someone climbing steps. He was startled; it was such an unexpected sound in this devastated place.

It was her. The old woman, over there, climbing up the wall. She was toddling up the wooden steps of the remains of a half-collapsed staircase on the wall with the overhanging white enamel seat attached to it. Could it really be that she was ascending towards the can? What was she going to do up there, what was she going to say?

'One franc a lemon, one franc . . . One franc the city, one franc . . .'

With her short, man's overcoat covered with stains and full of tears flapping round her, with her bare legs covered with purplish-red scabs, her completely wrinkled and livid face, her eyes the colour of plaster, her toothless mouth, and her shapeless basket full of rotten lemons, she had the grotesque and terrifying appearance of a witch going to cast a spell. A spell against the city.

'One franc the city, one franc . . .'

She was ascending the pulpit to curse the city, to hawk it to Death. She was going up to the can to sow and spread a plague over the city.

Night-of-amber-Wind-of-fire went over to the staircase. It was so broken-down, the wood so rotted by the rain, that it looked truly impossible to set foot on it without the whole thing collapsing. Furthermore, there were many steps missing, sometimes five or six together. And yet the old woman doggedly continued her climb, her head bobbing furiously, regardless of the danger. Night-of-amber-Wind-of-fire stood right next to the staircase and called out to the old woman.

'Hey! Where are you going? You're mad! This staircase is going to collapse. Come back down!'

He did not even know what he wanted with her any more; she kept surprising him, provoking in him sometimes amazement, sometimes anger. She kept eluding him. She did not so much as cast a glance at him.

'I'm talking to you!' he shouted at her again. 'Who are you? Answer me!'

She continued, unperturbed, now climbing steps that did not even exist. She was climbing up the side of the wall, scaling empty space.

'I know who you are,' Night-of-amber then began to yell, 'I know who you are! A human spectre, one that met with a bad end, a sneak, a gorgon of the Apocalypse! But I shan't let you bring your curse against the city and the living!' He did not even know whether he was joking, or dreaming, or whether he was genuinely afraid. One thing was certain: the old woman was a provocation to crime, whether the crime was conducted by her or against her.

'One franc for death, one franc, one franc for death, one franc . . .'

Darkness slowly filled the building site, dusk dispelled the clouds. Just a few trails of orange-pink still frayed out here and there, above the rooftops, over to the west. The air was cooling, the walls were getting damp. Night-of-amber-Wind-of-fire picked up stones and bits of iron. He exerted himself throwing them at the old woman, but he missed every time. His stones smashed against the wall, merely wakening the pigeons asleep among the struts supporting the wall, and also wakening his memory.

Time flipped over. All of a sudden Night-of-amber saw himself back in the lower depths of his untamed childhood; the abandoned factory warehouses, the old bunker deep in the forest, the latrines with the rickety door with its heart-shaped light. The shrines of his anger as a rebel child. Little Prince-very-dirty-and-very-naughty was rising like a phoenix, resuming his strength and his battle, merging into Prince-lover-of-all-violence.

Time flipped over, went into a spin. The present was no more than a point where past and future were scrambled together. Night-of-amber recovered all his madness, all his fury as a child.

That old woman, up there, scaling the darkness flanked by empty space, was Lulla, of course! Lulla-my-brawl, his first playmate, his first love. Lulla-my-brawl grown infinitely old. Lulla-the-tramp, the Black Sheep. He began to laugh, to cavort around the wall with great cries, as in his playgrounds of yesteryear.

'Hey, Lulla-my-crone, Lulla-my-ugly, come down, come here so that we can fight! Come on down here, my darling-loathsome, I'll bite your buttocks as I used to – your witch's buttocks, right to the bone! Come down, I tell you, come at once, I'm ordering you, I'll mount you as a wolf mounts his female, and I'll scratch your back and sink my teeth into your neck, your loins, I'll break your jaws and limbs. I'll make fertile again your ancient womb, and father on you young with jackdaw heads and toad's legs that will peck open your belly with their beaks. I'll fuck you to death!'

When he looked up at her he saw that she was sitting on top of the wall, on the toilet, whose white enamel bowl gleamed in the twilight. Her basket was laid on her lap and she was rummaging inside it very intently. Then she straightened up a bit on her seat and began to chant her litany in her expressionless voice.

'One franc a lemon, one franc . . .'

And every time she uttered her little phrase she extracted a fruit from the bottom of her basket and threw it at Night-of-amber-Wind-of-fire.

'One franc a lemon, one franc . . .'

But just as the stones he had thrown did not reach her, so the fruit she was now bombarding him with all missed their target. They did not even reach the ground. Every lemon, in mid fall, in the very momentum of its fall, was transformed, and turned into a little humming bird of a very bright yellow that suddenly reversed its flight and soared straight up into the sky on a shrill note.

He did not know any more what was really happening. He had followed the old woman into the backyard of his own past, into the debris of his repudiated memory. It was his 'third eye' that had seen all this, the oneiric and furious eye that sometimes blurred his vision in order to pierce the density of the visible, to breach time. The old woman, through his own folly, had wakened in him this third eye with its hallucinated gaze that could suddenly start dreaming while he was wide awake. The old woman, with her smell of musty flesh and rotten fruit, already turned blue with decay like his brother's skin, had opened up again that round cyclopean eye like the hole left by a bullet shot into the middle of his forehead. Straight into his heart.

. . . Like the skin of his brother with the swollen belly . . . his dead brother held for three days in his mother's arms . . . his drum-brother rolling on his purple paunch his mother's piercing cry . . . the brother who from deep in his grave brought forth in the branches of the yew-tree a lovely spread of red poison to make his mother lie down with him again, for ever . . . and his father turning himself inside out like an old glove with a hole in it . . . His brother, mother and father, how he hated them all! Even now they were coming for him again, to hurt and torment him, to make him suffer. But for how long? Ah, if he had only had the old woman in his clutches at that moment, how he would have beaten her! He would have slaughtered her.

Night-of-amber-Wind-of-fire fell ill after that encounter with the old woman with the lemons. That very night he had been taken with a fever and had to go home to bed. He rolled himself up in his blanket, and spent three days, curled up on his mat, shivering and sweating. And the whole time he had the fever, he had to endure the stridence in his ears of the note sung by the lemon-humming birds. In his delirium the old woman took on the face of his mother, she inverted like his father on the point of death, and the lemons swelled up like his brother's belly.

One night he even saw the neighbouring stone angel break away from the wall and come and rest its head against his shutters, slyly watching him through the slats, trembling and suffering. It too resembled the old woman, sniggered quietly, convulsively beating its truncated wings.

He had to battle to the point of exhaustion against this monstrous resurgence of memory, to return them all to oblivion – his brother, mother and father. He had emerged from this illness thinner and weakened. He had recovered from it feeling more alone and more at a loss than ever. He tried to cope with this old distress and terror by writing. He warded off the note – the old woman's cry, the humming birds' cry, his mother's cry – with outpourings of words, written down, as they came to him, on bits of paper. They were short pieces, hastily scribbled down.

Not even a cloud to look at
Mother has eaten them all
The sky has the wishy-washiness of cloudy dishwater
The wind is lying low like a big ailing dog
The light is rusted and trembles between its paws

Someone turns over in his sleep
his temples blue with sweat
in his paper sheets with a blood border
He has been robbed of his dreams, everything stolen from him
His mother's the thief, she took his heart
to colour her excessively pale cheeks
to redden her madwoman's cry

Words have been lost
all words, all names
far from pages and mouths
they roll with the marbles of clumsy children
down the avenues and out of town
along with chipped marbles and plane leaves
they go and get lost far away, beyond the suburbs
Out of town

His mother often came and spied on him
from behind his bedroom door

she halted
in his sleep he could detect her
his brother's death stank so
in the folds of her dress and the furrows of her wrinkles

Bronze flies with gold reflections
devoured his eyelids
like dung beetles
and a haggard angel waded
in his liquefied dreams

His brother pissed from the bottom of his grave
and his urine splattered the wind
with bright-red poisonous berries
and his mother who liked to make jam
pulped the pretty urinous fruit
in her mouth
with the reddened sugar of her cries

For days he spilled out words like this by the yard, then he threw the whole lot into his suitcase, along with the letters to Ballerina. And then he stopped. All of a sudden he said to himself, 'That's enough time wasted, no more fooling around. It's not a matter of self-defence any more, but attack.' And he came to a decision: 'I'm going to kill the next person who reopens this wound of memory in me. Whoever it is, I'll kill them.' This idea strengthened in him, and he finally convinced himself that only a crime could free him from this long-standing pain, this betrayal.

One day as he opened his shutters he greeted the Turbigo angel with this announcement: 'Hello, stupid! I'm a murderer. My victim's out there somewhere in this city. I'm going to find and execute that person.'

The angel's foolish smile remained unfailing.

3

He did not go looking for his victim. It was not up to him to go looking. Let his victim come to him voluntarily. Let the victim identify himself to his anger, offer himself to his violence. He would certainly know how to recognize his victim when that person appeared. Then he would accomplish his task of murder, his task of liberation. And by the same deed he would finally sever the obscure ties that still fettered him to his old wound, thereby severing all those ties still binding him to other people.

'If necessary,' he said to himself, 'I shall tear the person's heart out, in order to banish my own heart into exile for ever, outlawing it. Yes, I shall tear his heart out to make an irredeemable savage of myself and become an absolute barbarian. Then I shall set up my life in total rupture with men and with God. That's what I have to do, consummate that rupture.'

This idea had sway over him, not as a confused thought or hazy delirium, but quite the contrary, as a very precise axiom on which he wanted to rebuild his life. An axiom as clear and distinct as the one thanks to which Descartes had regained a firm footing and confidence at the height of his doubt, and on which he had then been able to build his phenomenal philosophical monument. An axiom to equal 'I think, therefore I am.'

During the course of his studies Night-of-amber-Wind-of-fire had turned this infinitely incisive little phrase this way and that in every direction, without ever managing to get properly to grips with it. He had put as much absurd effort into toying with Descartes' reflection as Monsieur Jordain had put into fussing over his compliment to the Marquise. But all that was irrelevant now, the terms of his axiom derived from a completely different vocabulary – that of crime. All that remained was the shattering force of a self-evident truth snatched from the most profound doubt; of the pain of a much misguided thought all of a sudden being established as a sovereign principle. The absolute necessity to commit a murder so as to be done with his past, his memory, and his torments, and put an end once and for all to any form of pity, and even feeling in general: that was his self-evident truth. His beautiful, dazzling axiom. To kill, in order to liberate himself of everybody and everything, including himself. To kill in order to live at last in total freedom, beyond the law.

He did not go looking for his victim; he let the victim come to him. This took time, but the victim came.

It all began with a song, as in a musical comedy. But the song weighed sixteen tons and the musical dealt with mortgaged souls.

> Some people say a man is made out of mud
> A poor man is made of muscle and blood
> Muscle and blood, skin and bone
> A mind that's weak and a back that's strong . . .

It was a remarkable voice, so solemn and deep it seemed to well up from the entrails of a man crouched underground. The voice of a black man. Night-of-amber-Wind-of-fire could not understand any of the words, so much did they rumble deep down in the singer's body, but it was not a matter of understanding. He heard. The voice came surging out of an open window, like an enormous roller, immediately flooding the street along which he was passing. He stopped, enveloped by that wave of terrible mellowness.

> Sixteen tons and what do you get?
> Another day older and deeper in debt.
> St Peter, don't you call me
> 'cause I can't go
> I owe my soul to the Company Store . . .

The voice swelled, in a spate of distress and beauty. It

took over the listener's entire body, flowed between his flesh and skin like a sweat of mingled blood and tears and darkness. Darkness of flesh doomed to tribulation and shame. Blood of flesh the colour of darkness, sweat of a heart the colour of tears.

I was born one mornin'
when the sun didn't shine
I picked up a shovel and walked to the mine . . .

The voice was so dense, so ample and majestic in its lament that the whole city seemed upset by it. Night-of-amber had the feeling that the ground was beginning to move, as if a dizzying landslide was being set in motion by a surge of mud rising from the bowels of the earth. Before very long the walls were going to break loose and go lumbering off through the shattered streets like a herd of despondent men walking to the mine.

Sixteen tons and what do you get?
Another day older and deeper in debt . . .

Third floor. Night-of-amber-Wind-of-fire identified the window from which the voice was coming and plunged into the building, taking the stairs four at a time. The door of the apartment from which the song emanated was not closed. He pushed open the door that stood ajar without even thinking of knocking. He came into a dark corridor, steeped in a smell he did not recognize. A smell at once sweet and bitter.

St Peter, don't you call me
'cause I can't go

Sounds came from a room off the corridor, accompanied by a girl's smothered laughter. He walked down the corridor and came to the doorway of a room with the shutters half-closed. It was more cluttered than the storeroom of a natural history museum. A great muddle of motionless creatures were packed together in the semi-darkness, on the walls, tables and shelves . . .

I owe my soul to the Company Store . . .

Night-of-amber noticed they were almost exclusively reptiles: lizards, vipers, slow-worms, and grass snakes preserved in liquid, the skulls and skeletons of various serpents displayed under glass, and a whole group of animals stuffed and mounted, uncoiling their long, shiny and supple bodies like algae. Rattlesnakes, najas, cobras, varans, and pythons, poised with their mouths open, their little glass eyes staring blinding at one another.

The eyes of the person who came into the room also had a curious glassy, or rather metal-like, gleam. He was barefoot and completely unbuttoned. He did not seem at all surprised by the presence of a stranger in his house. It was he who spoke first.

'Do I know you?' he asked simply.

'No.'

'So what are you here for? Who sent you?'

'No one.'

'You want to buy?'

Night-of-amber thought he was selling his stuffed animals and replied, 'No, certainly not.'

The girl he had heard laughing appeared.

She was also barefoot and wearing nothing but a man's shirt that came to half-way down her thighs. Night-of-amber noticed the curve of her breasts under the shirt, and noticed too that she had adorable, little, round feet. She examined the intruder from head to foot and seemed to find him to her liking.

'Who ith it?' she asked her companion.

'A guy who just says no. Don't know him,' the other replied laconically.

'Ith that true?' she said to Night-of-amber. 'Do you always thay no?'

'No, of course not,' he exclaimed, unnerved by the girl's seductive glance and her slight lisp.

'You see,' the other fellow remarked, shrugging his shoulders.

'Yeth I do,' she laughing, 'but what I thee ith charming.'

Night-of-amber finally explained himself: the magnificent voice heard from the street, the door left ajar.

The voice repeated its lament for the last time.

St Peter, don't you call me
'cause I can't go
I owe my soul to the Company Store.

To modulate those final words the voice seemed to have completely liquefied into a flux of mud.

I owe my soul . . .

Like a very flowing tide of molten lava. Throat transformed into geographical fault, belly into resonance, reverberating and amplifying the deep vibration of the moaned murmur of a gashed heart. Then the song went silent and the voice subsided. Different music had immediately followed, introduced by the braying voice of the radio presenter. A twist tune that had the girl bopping. She moved her body delightfully. She was quite small, nicely rounded, with very short curly hair of a striking reddish-brown and an apricot complexion. Everything about her was similarly rounded and lively and bright.

Night-of-amber quickly forgot about the song. It was the girl now that interested him. He stopped answering no to the other fellow's questions. Inconsequential questions, constantly skipping from one subject to another, and interspersed with fits of hysterical laughter as irrelevant as bursting into sobs would have been.

'Don't pay any attention,' the girl said finally, 'he's just smoked a joint.'

He must have had a good deal more than one.

But Urbain Malabrune was prudent; he only took soft drugs, whereas he dealt in hard drugs. He had developed his business partly thanks to the snakes that were a real fetish with him. In fact, according to the Chinese horoscope, his sign was the snake.

'The snake is supposed to be the complete opposite of man,' he used to say, 'and therefore man's worst enemy, his rival, his evil double. But a rival is always an excellent friend, at least it's a genuine equal. I train snakes. They are my vertebral column.'

He had trained them above all to be his go-betweens.

'They're perfect allies,' he explained to Night-of-amber one day. 'They have a slow, steady digestion, so the capsules stuffed with heroin or coke that I make them swallow are unlikely to get thrown up inopportunely into the hands of inquisitive customs officials, who anyway, like all laymen, are much too averse to the sight of snakes to amuse themselves by going and examining their stomachs and feeling their bellies.'

Night-of-amber-Wind-of-fire never became one Urbain's clients, but he did make friends with him, in so far as such a term had any meaning between two people of their kind. As for the girl, he made her his mistress. Her nickname was Infante, but all the people that hovered in Urbain's obscure wake were called by nicknames. Night-of-amber met a few of them at parties arranged by Urbain who liked to surround himself with courtiers – his acid-head nobles, as he described them with a mixture of scorn and admiration. Among his most remarkable peers were the Scribe, the Lunatic and Pallas.

The Scribe belonged to that category of people that time never seems to affect, and who retain for decades the physique of an eternally young man. He was an outstanding calligrapher and lived by his art. But his profession was twofold: on the one hand, he designed announcements of every kind for clients as precious as they were moneyed, on the other he counterfeited documents and signatures for clients who were even more moneyed, and above all much more perfidious. In fact he showed a reverence towards writing equal to that of Urbain towards reptiles, because, he would say, 'when you succeed in copying perfectly other people's handwriting you acquire a magic power over them; it's like stealing their soul. You invest yourself more or less with the power of life and death over them, so compromising, and indeed fatal, can certain written words become.'

Moreover, his great regret was to be living in a country whose days of war were over, a time of proven advantage to the secret side of his art. He retained a certain nostalgia for the recent period of war in Algeria that had afforded him some splendid opportunities to produce some extremely costly counterfeits.

The Lunatic was a cyclical hermaphrodite, belonging to one sex or the other according to the lunar calendar. The only constant was his homosexuality, because when he was a man he took a lover, and when she was a woman she took a mistress. When the male triumphed in him then he was seized with an intense exuberance that often verged on aggression, and when the female predominated in her she fell prey to a deep melancholy.

As for Pallas, a tall, dark woman with an angular face of austere beauty, she was named after the Queen of Spades, an unlucky card to have in your hand, for like her, she had the art of sowing discord and confusion and of steeling words like blades.

Among all these characters of greater or lesser wickedness, either by nature or for fun, and some of them even by vocation, only Infante seemed devoid of any ill-will. She rubbed shoulders with them all, not paying any attention to their malice, never minding about their rivalries and jealousies. She went about lisping gaily like a child, heedless of everything and everybody, always in pursuit of her sole pleasure. While the others assiduously cultivated a militant immorality, she contented herself with being in the simplest possible way what she was innately: a cheerfully amoral creature. So she was actually the sanest and least tormented of this group.

For Night-of-amber-Wind-of-fire the days of his friendship with Jasmin were completely over, as were the days of his camaraderie with Ornicar. It was no longer a question of friendship or camaraderie but of a community of interests, a conspiracy for ludic evil. The same was true of his relationship with women. All loving feeling was banished; it was just a conspiracy for sensual pleasure.

But someone else turned up, from outside this group, who upset all the rules of the game. Where spades were trumps, he cut a heart. In fact he was not even of any suit – he entered the game unexpectedly, in the manner of a joker. Everyone attributed to him whatever value they wanted to.

It was the middle of winter. The wind whistled along the walls. The pavements crackled with frost. Pigeons that had died of cold were occasionally to be found in the gutters. Urbain and Night-of-amber-Wind-of-fire were returning home one evening, slightly drunk. It was still far from being morning. Night-of-amber lived more than ever at night, although he had already long given up his hotel porter's job. He had joined forces with Urbain, for whom he worked as a kind of secretary. He was in his final year of study and would be submitting his thesis in the spring: a study devoted to the concept of betrayal, for he had chosen not an author but a theme. The theme on which he had built his life, like a cacophony around a cry.

As they were about to part at the corner of the street, a smell came upon them. A smell of hot bread that was utterly delicious in the biting cold of dawn.

'I'm hungry!' Urbain immediately exclaimed.

The smell came from a small open window in the basement beneath a baker's shop. They saw a light cloud of steam floating just above the pavement, unfurling in the chilly air. They went closer. A light was shining in the basement. Urbain crouched down to the window and looked into the bakery.

'I can see the baker's boy,' he said, 'he's putting some enormous loaves into the oven . . . Hey! Just look at those croissants on the table over there!'

Night-of-amber also bent down. He saw the white figure of the baker's boy busy at the ovens, and the huge tray covered with croissants and brioches.

There they both were, crouched in that soft cloud of warm steam, smelling the bread that was baking and the melted butter in the pastry of the croissants and brioches that had just come out of the oven, and it was not pangs of hunger they felt but a terrible, enormous greediness. A greediness such as they had not experienced since childhood. And it was that, an overwhelming childhood taste, that suddenly wakened inside them, catching them in the stomach and in their mouths, in that chilly hour of dawn. They stared agape into the bakery, their eyes wide open, enraptured, their figures clutched to the grill over the window. Urbain whistled, the way little boys on the way to school do to hail a friend, and he called out to the young baker: 'Hey, baker, we're cold and hungry, give us a bit of bread or one of those golden croissant!'

The boy looked round and came and stood in the middle of the room. He peered up at them, his face, streaming with sweat. The thick glasses he wore were all steamed up, and he took them off to wipe them with his handkerchief. He was bare-chested, his chest that of a skinny adolescent, all hollow. He put his glasses back on and smiled at the two men who had just called to him and continued to beg for bread and croissants.

'I'm coming!' he said. He had a falsetto voice.

He came out and joined them in the street. He had put on a thick woollen jacket and carried in the crook of his arm a big paper bag stuffed full of croissants, chocolate-filled pastries, and brioches. His hair was white with flour.

'Here,' he said, holding out the bag to them with a shy

and gentle smile. He watched, motionless, as they emptied the bag, and he kept the same smile the whole time they were eating.

'Baker,' cried Urbain at last, his mouth still half full, 'that was fabulous!'

'Oh,' said the boy, blushing, 'I'm not yet a baker, I'm just an apprentice.'

'Well,' said Urbain, licking his fingers, 'as far as I'm concerned, you're the baker king!'

Night-of amber was inspired by the absurdly grandiloquent story-teller's tone that his companion had adopted to go further: 'To show our gratitude, you can make a wish and we'll grant it immediately. For, you see, right now, we have all the power in the world!'

'But I don't want anything,' said the boy in his little falsetto voice. 'If you enjoyed eating them, so much the better. It's given me pleasure, and that's enough. Well, I must be getting back now.'

But Night-of-amber insisted. 'Is there really nothing you'd like? You must have a wish, now! Go on, tell us what it is, and no sooner said than done! But be quick, for our power is erratic.'

The boy's smile became even fainter and his voice even shriller. Lowering his head slightly, he murmured, 'I'd very much like to find a friend . . .'

'Is that all?' exclaimed Night-of-amber. 'Then your wish is granted. You've found one – me.'

And to prove to the baker-boy the truth of his words, he scribbled down his name and address on the paper in which the croissants had been wrapped, which was all spotted with grease and sticky with sugar. Stammering, the boy took the paper and hastily returned to the bakery. The other two went on their way. Their mouths were already losing the taste of the warm croissants and soft brioches, as that of the alcohol and tobacco they had indulged in too freely during the evening returned to them. And similarly they were losing that brief flash of childhood that had seized them.

Just as they were about to separate, Urbain asked Night-of-amber, 'By the way, did you really give your address to that sucker?'

'Why, of course!' he replied. 'I wrote "Night-of-amber-Wind-of-fire, at his place under the wing of the huge angel that looks as ridiculous as birds with very large spans". With that, the nincompoop's welcome to search for me.'

And that is exactly what the young baker's boy did: he searched. For he took absolutely seriously what Night-of-amber-Wind-of-fire had said. His innocence was so great, so pure, that it bordered on simple-mindedness. He was so devoid of any wickedness, it was impossible for him to suspect the least falseness or irony in others. So, when he got back to the bakery that morning, and uncrumpled the piece of greasy paper that Night-of-amber had scribbled on, and read that address, which was more incomprehensible than a Chinese puzzle, not for one second did he doubt the seriousness and sincerity of the man who had declared himself to be his friend. Of course he understood nothing of that absurd charade, but he was not at all alarmed by it. It did not even surprise him. Like those youthful princes in fairy stories who, in order to conquer their realm or meet their beloved, have to undergo trial by ordeal and contest, and survive a thousand mysterious detours, so he reacted in the face of the enigma: he accepted with calmness and confidence the difficult task imposed on him. And so, day after day, he conscientiously paced the city, street by street, tracking down every statute of an angel to be found, on the trail of the promised friend who had immediately disappeared.

For he felt so alone in this city where everything and everybody were unfamiliar to him. He had arrived only a few months before, and the vast urban space crammed with buildings, monuments, cars, and beset by a brutish, hurrying throng, by noises and shouts, completely bewildered and even distressed him. It was the first time he had left his home, his village. His island.

A tiny place, detached from the mainland, a bar of sand and rock dropped into the ocean, set amid wind and brightness. His village. A few very white houses with rounded tiles, huddled among the vines fringed with poppies, tamarisks, pines and salt marshes. It was there by the salt marshes that he was born and had always lived: in the middle of the sea, in front of salt gardens that dazzled with a very soft, bright light, amid total transparency. A transparency that still sparkled and tingled in his heart, making him feel more than ever an islander, in the middle of this enormous and opaque city. He had not made friends with anybody since his arrival in Paris. He spent his life, between his two basements, that of the bakery and that of his lodgings, confined in solitude, a solitude that day by day weighed more heavily on him. So, when the two strangers called out to him from the street that December morning, and one of them offered his friendship with such assurance, he felt suddenly relieved of the oppressive burden of the total solitude in which he had been isolated by his exile in the city. Someone was going to get him out of his den. So he had spent a long time searching.

And he had found what he was searching for. One day, there he was, gaping up from the pavement in Rue de Turbigo, beneath the plinth on which the invisible feet of the angel rested. As soon as he saw it he knew that was the one – the angel under whose wing his long-sought friend had his place. For it was truly immense, its thin figure extending three stories high, looking quite extraordinary stuck to the facade of such a building. He gazed at it so long his vision began to blur and he had a stiff neck from looking up at the windows sheltered under the wings. Then, forgetting his shyness, he plunged into the entrance hall and rang the bell on the concierge's door. She did not know anyone by the name of Night-of-amber-Wind-of-fire, but he recalled so precisely the stranger's face and appearance and so accurately described him to the concierge that she eventually recognized the tenant he was talking about, and told him on what floor and at which door to find him.

He went straight up the stairs without stopping, and arrived at Night-of-amber's door quite breathless. Without further reflection, he knocked. Several very resonant knocks. An even more resonant silence then descended, filling the landing, weirdly accentuating the shadows, the angles of the walls, and the shape of his hand left resting on the wooden door, fingers tucked in. And he felt his heart pounding very fast, and the blood rushing to his temples, and his eyes misting. The sound of footsteps came in answer to his knocks. Footsteps that sounded as sharp and resonant as his knocks – there, behind the door, approaching. And the door was suddenly thrown wide open. They stood there, face to face, in the doorway, planted on either side of the doormat.

Night-of-amber opened his door so suddenly in fact that the visitor's hand that had been resting on it then dropped into empty space, and in falling landed on Night-of-amber's chest. He did not step back, but simply gazed in surprise at this stranger who seemed to be seeking support against him. But the visitor recovered himself, withdrew his hand, and eventually said in an uncertain voice, with his head bowed, 'You don't recognize me?'

'I simply don't know you,' Night-of-amber replied rather coldly.

Then the other began to speak very fast, stammering breathlessly. 'Yes, yes, you do . . . that is, yes and no . . . don't you remember? The croissants, the brioches . . . Although it's true, it was a long time ago now . . . it was very cold . . . at the beginning of winter . . . Do you remember? There were two of you, in the street, it was still dark, you . . . I'm the baker, well, the apprentice . . . You called out to me, you were hungry and . . . oh, I don't know what more to say . . . You told me to make a wish, and that . . . well, that . . . it's a difficult thing to . . . My friend, that's what you said. That you'd be my friend . . .'

'Ah!' said Night-of-amber, in such a detached manner that he seemed to imply that even if he did have any recollection of the scene, it was of no interest whatsoever to him.

'You know,' said the other, 'I've been looking for you for a long time . . . well, you see, there are so many angels in this city . . . statues, I mean . . .'

'Loads of angels in Paris?' exclaimed Night-of-amber, amused. 'Well, what do you know! Surely there are more bloody nuisances than angels, unless the angels are pests as well?'

'Am I disturbing you?' asked the young baker, immediately anxious.

'Well, after all, we disturbed you at work one day, didn't we? So perhaps that does give you the right to turn up out of the blue and disturb me in my idleness. And besides, I'm surprised, you have the perseverance of an obtuse angel . . . Since you're here now, you'd better come in!'

He went in, and stayed with Night-of-amber-Wind-of-fire until evening. For despite his manner of an awkward and stubborn angel, his thin falsetto voice full of hesitation, and his myopic eyes hidden behind thick glasses, he kept on surprising his host. They sat cross-legged on the floor, like two tailors, face to face. One talked, for hours, and the other listened.

One talked as he had never before dared, or even known how to. He talked about his island, lost out there off the coast of Charentes, about those salt gardens with their dazzling white pyramids, and about his father the salt-worker, silently raking that nacreous powder deposited by the sea. His father, the sun and the wind, all three united in a magic task to deliver fire from water, to cristallize the foam. And he, the only son, the puny child, made ill by the wind.

For the wind made him ill, just as it had eventually driven his mother mad. The wind, the ocean, his mother, all three disunited, in violent discord. His mother would scream when the wind blew too strongly, she would break everything in the house. She was scared to death of it. She died of that fear. For it was by screaming against the wind, stronger than the wind, to silence it, so as not to hear it any more, to drive it far from her island back to the mainland, that she burst the veins in her throat. One day her mad-woman's cry put an end to her life, and choked her in a bleeding sob.

Then his father suddenly became old, very old, long before his time. He had to stop work, he had to abandon his big salt gardens, his beautiful castles of foam, taking to his bed in a so-called rest home. And he, the only son, left his island, and travelled far from home, from the sea and the wind; far from old age and death, far from madness. He came to be swallowed up by the city.

But the gaze he cast on the city was the opposite of Night-of-amber's gaze. He had the gaze of a poor devil, of a man-child suffering from being so alone among the crowd and quietly, passionately begging for other people's recognition and affection. Above all, his gaze was of infinite tenderness, so unlike, so radically unlike that of Night-of-amber that the latter could not understand him, but nevertheless felt curiously arrested by him, like a hunting dog surprised by a totally unfamiliar smell it cannot identify, so it does not know what animal's traces it has come upon. Those of some small prey, or on the contrary of some large predator? And it was this ambiguity, this doubt, that kept him with his visitor, listening with unaccustomed attentiveness.

The baker's boy had a rather absurd name, his mother having given him her own, a woman's name, simply shorn of its final vowel. He was called Roselyn Petiot. It was only owing to the loss of a final mute e that he did not have exactly the same name as his mother. But owing to the loss of what other mysterious letter was he not a complete man, that his body was still not fully formed? For at over seventeen years of age his body still remained that of a pre-pubescent boy.

And this late-developing, immature body he now, for

the first time, entrusted verbally to someone else. A stranger, in whom from the very outset he placed his entire trust; through whom, perhaps, he was attempting to relieve his shame and suffering. And all the time this confession lasted, Night-of-amber-Wind-of-fire, squatting on the floor, felt a strange and violent pain come into his groin, tense between his hips, and shoot up his back, like women's menstrual pain. As if Roselyn's words were gnawing at him from within, in the most intimate parts of his body; as if Roselyn's confession suddenly threw his own virility into alarm and panic. The virility he had erected for himself on the very ruins of his father's, and had forged in the image of Cronos. And that evening, when his visitor finally left, he went to see Infante and remained closeted with her for several days of constant lovemaking. To get rid of that obscure pain in his back and stomach.

Infante's desire was insatiable. Her body was ever a gateway to an infinite labyrinth of pleasure, and Night-of-amber never tired of caressing it in all its roundedness. Even when asleep, his hands continued to explore her body, and to embrace it. His relationship with her was like the relationship that a spoiled and greedy child has with pastries, sweets and ice cream . . . food that is not at all necessary but pure indulgence, if not caprice. Luxury food that has nothing to do with hunger, but simply desire, in which the smack of genuine hunger is even destroyed and lost. He gorged himself on her pretty body, in the grip of an attack of bulimic gluttonizing. To the point of nausea.

On the evening of the fifth day of being closeted with Infante, when he suddenly woke with a start on the carpet where they had rolled together in a heap of crumpled sheets and blankets after their afternoon frolics, and he saw the nakedness of their bodies illuminated by the red glow of the setting sun, it appeared to him as if they were two flayed bodies with bleeding limbs, their faces and hands consumed by flames. He even thought he could detect the stale smell of blood. The smell of blood spilled to no purpose, and already fetid. The suddenly nauseous smell of their bodies exhausted by incessantly rubbing against other. The smell of lovemaking reduced to capricious fornication soured by the ebbing of assuaged desire unrelieved by any real tenderness. The smell of fucking and sweat turned cold. Then all at once Infante's body, that lovely intemperate body that had always given him pleasure, separated itself from him, from his flesh, from his manhood, and rolled far away from him. He got up and dressed in a great hurry, and left without waking her. Ran away, with a strange taste of foul blood all over his body.

Roselyn Petiot returned several times to visit Night-of-amber-Wind-of-fire, who was as much irritated as intrigued by the runtish baker's boy and the great woes of a young, lovesick country bumpkin that he hopelessly trailed round. Night-of-amber still could not form a definite opinion about the boy. The vague disquiet that Roselyn awakened in him was much stronger than the scorn he inspired at the same time. This congenital fool, this nothing little squirt, as Night-of-amber inwardly designated him with disdain and ill-humour, nevertheless kept obtruding on his thoughts, unsettling something elusive within him.

It was quite simply that Roselyn niggled at his memory, threatening all the defences he had been erecting for years in his heart and his conscience, as if, in the naive and very sincere way that he spoke, the other was in the end only confessing to him his very own anguish – his old, disavowed anguish relegated to oblivion.

For a whole month Roselyn's visits continued, becoming ever more frequent and ever longer. And Night-of-amber could not help looking forward to them, while at the same time dreading them. He let him talk, talk endlessly, about his island, about that maddening wind, about his father with a gaze devastated by the sea, the light, the salt and in the end by grief; and about his mother who had been robbed by the wind of her reason and her life. A mother as mad as his own mother, uttering the same cries, like thorns in her son's heart, and a father as weak as his, suddenly shrinking into his body under the shock of widowhood. Roselyn often spoke, too, of a young woman called Thérèse; he had known her since childhood, from the time when she used to come to his island regularly on holiday. He spoke of her as if she might have been his sister, an older sister, loved without jealousy. And this also reminded Night-of-amber of his own history, of Ballerina. Thérèse did not live in Paris, but she was going to come soon. She would be coming to see him, Roselyn, and this promise filled him with infinite joy. He wrote to Thérèse every week, and he did not throw his letters into the bottom of a suitcase. He sent them to her, every one. And she answered them.

It was in all these things that Roselyn disconcerted Night-of-amber; he presented him with a reverse image of himself, a curious negative. The similar hurt that had marked them both from the outset had become submissiveness, tenderness and humility in the one, rebellion, anger and pride in the other.

But the day came when this difference that drew them together as much as it set them apart turned to discord. For by talking so freely, with his confessions and remembrances, Roselyn's quiet voice had eventually opened up countless breaches in Night-of-amber-Wind-of-fire's memory, and so destroyed his defences that it had wrested from silence his entire past. His painful, hated past.

Once again his enemy-past was making its return, doing violence to him again. Not through the ugliness and madness of a woman, but the simplicity of speech and purity of heart of an overgrown child lost in the city.

The city, always the city, with its encounters, fortuities and snares. He thought to find oblivion here. He had carefully laid plans to be in constant flight. He had wanted to silence for ever this deadly refrain of betrayal, to smother it among the stones and asphalt, but the city kept turning against him and betraying him in its turn. Once again his entire past was being thrown back at his heart like a dirty old rag. His mother, father, brother – a vile, three-headed beast that was definitely never going to let itself be decapitated, that kept returning to grimace in his dreams.

Then Night-of-amber flew into a rage against both the city and Roselyn.

But the city itself flew into a rage, against everything. It, too, turned violently against its past, its history. It became angry and called for rioting. For spring that year not only brought the trees in the parks back into blossom and made verdant again the chestnut and plane trees along the avenues, it also, very oddly, brought the streets themselves into blossom. Extravagant graffiti festooned all the facades with their slogans and sketches, like webs of red ivy. Posters splattered the walls with their paper brightness that strove to be more brilliant than daylight. One of these posters announced, 'Beauty is in the street.' It showed a young girl running forward, her arm raised to throw a stone. A stone against everything, against everybody.

Such was beauty during that peculiar month of May that did not herald the cherry season but the season of paving-stones – a shattering of stones. The paving-stones actually took on the colour and flavour of cherries, at least for those who proclaimed, 'I delight in paving-stones!'

The paving-stones were loosened, and began to roll down the pavements like pebbles.

'Underlying the paving-stones is the beach!'

But the paving-stones were even more than that; they turned into words, a great alphabet of stone.

'I love you! Oh, say it with paving-stones!'

Even love was declared with paving-stones, like beauty, like the happiness that some had decreed a 'permanent state', while others loftily declared, 'Bugger happiness!'

The transmutations of the paving-stones were infinite; they took the place of gesture and word, of speech and action. Of power. For all these paving-stone enthusiasts wanted to establish a new power – a power that was all pleasure and imagination. And they wanted it immediately.

'Pleasure here and now!'

Then, equating elections with fraud, they traded their ballot papers for paving-stones, which seemed a lot quicker and more effective.

Cars exploded, lighting up the sides of the roads where they were parked, enormous balls of flame that crackled like fireworks. For even in its anger the city retained a festive air. Suddenly people did not cross their city any more as if it were a boring maze of streets marked out by daily life, but went running in every direction, shouting at the tops of their voices, storming buses, factories, public buildings, schools, and universities, constantly taking each other to task in astounding exchanges. For words came out from under the stones, sprang up everywhere, as cry, song, chant, provocation. Space and time in the city were no longer ruled by order, work, and habit, but had pitched over and become the space and time of a gigantic fair-ground where everything was chaos, enthusiasm, surprise.

'We must systematically explore chance!'

The city was playing at revolution, and some people believed in it, but it was only a flash in the pan, and among those in the front line on the barricades, who thought themselves real little soldiers fighting valiantly for joyfully singing tomorrows, more than one was rapidly disillusioned. The tomorrows soon grew hoarse and very out of tune, and became incoherent again. In fact some of the rioters themselves, more astute than their comrade paving-stone enthusiasts who thought themselves to be inspired realists by 'demanding the impossible', were wary early on and warned unambiguously, 'Comrades, you're straining at gnats and swallowing camels.'

The city flew into a rage and improvised a lightning war, a little springtime guerrilla conflict. But from this, too, Night-of-amber-Wind-of-fire found himself excluded. He passed it by as he had always passed history by, whether it was shod with boots stinking of death and clicking with madness, or thin-soled tennis shoes with badly-tied laces.

He confused everything – the city, Roselyn Petiot, and

the nauseous awakening of the family hydra. He and the city's anger became confused. There were the same cries, the same clashes, the same fires and explosions in the streets and in himself. Stones and bodies, everything was being torn up and overturned. Underlying the paving-stones was the beach. Underlying oblivion and denial was memory.

The city flew into a rage, and the rioting intensified day by day. Those who wore their youth like a buttonhole red carnation dug up the paving-stones in the streets, removing from beneath their feet the heavy rocks of the past begrimed with boredom, slimed with antiquatedness, in order to decorticate their society and open it up to a more rhythmic movement of history. They wanted to live, and not simply remain alive. They wanted to live their youth.

Day by day anguish embedded itself in Night-of-amber-Wind-of-fire, and his rage increased. It was his memory consumed with grief and madness, haunted with the cries of traitors, that he wanted to dig up, to turn completely upside down. To decorticate his heart at last, for ever. He wanted to live without memories, without suffering. To rediscover oblivion, lying beneath his memory laid bare once more, once too often. A second oblivion of infinite profoundness. A wonderfully enduring, narcotic oblivion, replete with innocence.

Then one day, when he had been tried to breaking-point by this maddening memory, and his nerves could not take any more, he remembered the promise he had made to himself more than a year earlier: that he would kill the next person who dared to reopen the wound of his memory. Whoever it might be. And just as the city was having fun playing at war, he decided to play the murderer.

A murderer. For this time he was ready to kill. Deliverance through crime, he said to himself. Beyond crime, liberty. Beneath crime, real life.

A murderer.

Had he not finally found his victim? Had the victim not

come to him of his own accord, in all heedlessness and stupidity? Yet it was not that Night-of-amber had not done everything to deflect him, but the other had persisted in tracking him down, and finding him. Then, as if he were up to nothing at all, provoking him with countless roundabout words that had opened up as many wounds in his memory. And as many cries.

This fool with a ludicrous name. An aborted female name! With an even more absurd family name to follow it. And who dragged around, along with all that, an overgrown child's body destined to total impotence, and wittered on for hours in a falsetto voice, staring at you with a cretinous expression in those little red-herring eyes hidden behind his big bottle-glass lenses that were always misted with tears – well, when all was said and done, the stupid sucker had certainly gone out of his way to become a victim! He bloody well deserved to get himself bumped off.

To get himself slaughtered.

A slaughter. That was indeed what took place.

For Night-of-amber-Wind-of-fire acted on his promise. But as soon as he did so, he was overtaken by his action. Everything happened very quickly, as if without his knowledge, almost. His role in this killing of which he was the instigator was not even that of the murderer; worse, perhaps, he had the role of the person who delivered the victim to his murderers. The informer, the black muse. The most vile, most abject role. That of the traitor.

It was into the hands of his partners in ludic evil that Night-of-amber-Wind-of-fire delivered Roselyn. All the time he had been receiving the baker's boy's visits, he had said nothing about him to Urbain, for he would have been ashamed to admit to his association with such a person, an association that, on close consideration, was beginning to take on the obscene appearance of friendship. But when he found himself cornered, with his memory laid bare, he rebelled and, turning against the one who had backed him into this corner, he conceived the idea of taking revenge on his persecutor by handing him over to Urbain and his accomplices. With their out and out cynicism, they would surely manage to inflict on Roselyn Petiot a punishment equal to his offensive foolishness.

They did indeed. They managed to find a humiliation equal to Roselyn's total humility, to subject him to an agony equal to his very great gentleness. Not equal but, by reversal, out of all proportion to them. For everything was reversed; the victim's extreme goodness and simplicity inspired his torturers to a cruelty and sophistication just as extreme.

And Night-of-amber-Wind-of-fire served as an intermediary between them all. He was the traitor, who brought the victim – his friend – into the hands of his executioners.

The traitor, who topples, with his hands and soul bound, into the darkest night.

Into absolute night.

NIGHT OF MOUTHS

1

The train sped on. Night-of-amber was not asleep. There was no place inside him for rest any more. Oblivion was for ever denied to him. Through the sun-drenched window he saw a countryside in blossom passing by, and a smooth, blue sky. But these images did not impinge on him, they merely skimmed over his absent gaze, drifting past at a distance. His eyes remained obstinately fixed on another image: Roselyn's face.

Roselyn's huge grey eyes, filled with tears and terror.

Roselyn's mummified body.

On his mouth, all brown with caramel, all stuffed with colours.

And on Thérèse, too. On Thérèse's body.

Her hands. Her hair and breasts. And her half-open lips, so solemn and lovely.

He could not see anything else now. And this taste of salt in his mouth. An infernal thirst raged in his mouth. A thirst that came to him when he saw Roselyn on the brink of death, and had not left him since. He was insanely thirsty. Was it from having licked the tears of his victim, as if those tears contained all the water from the salt pans on his island? He felt as if he were dying of thirst. But he knew he would not die. And anyway, if even he did, this thirst would torture him in death. He felt that, too.

He left Paris at first light. That was the end of Rue de Turbigo. The stone angel had dislodged him from there with a bat of its wing. How that angel's foolish smile sent a pang through his heart now! He went by himself, he fled like a thief. A thief that had lost everything, a thief that had robbed himself. He left his few belongings behind – his trunk, his books, and his clothes. He left everything under the angel's empty wing. All he took with him was his old suitcase. His case that contained nothing at all

– nothing but sheets of paper all marked with burns and full of holes. When he opened the case where he had for years been stuffing his letters to Ballerina, his writings, his notebooks, all the words escaped.

All the words, letter by letter, in their thousands, suddenly flew off in a tremendous vortex of signs like tiny insects of ink. A black, jingling myriad of key letters. And all these detached letters that had gone mad scattered through the room, smashing into the walls and windows. Not a single word remained written; every sheet of paper and envelope lost its writing and bore only the reddish traces of burns. Paper made lacy with holes, fluttering in the bottom of his suitcase. Not a single word had survived. He immediately shut his case and without waiting any longer, without worrying about anything else, he fled. He left on foot, walked for the last time up Rue Réaumur to Boulevard de Sebastopol, then down Boulevard de Strasbourg. He walked fast. His case was light. He did not stop on the way or look back.

Yet the city was still in a ferment, with disorder on the streets – corridors on which no one passed by without calling out loudly to each other. People ran about, some singing, others shouting, everyone in a state of excitement, and arguing. The city had opened up without limit to verbal self-expression. A manifold, lively, shifting self-expression that at every moment improvised speeches, songs, slogans, abuse or striking aphorisms, and above all exchanges between strangers. A self-expression so intoxicated with itself, so bemused by total freedom, that it was occurring everywhere at the same time, even without always knowing what to say, as one of the most pertinent graffiti of the day admitted: 'I've something to say, but I don't know what.' What counted above all was the act of speaking, the impetus given to verbal expression. Some people openly made love in the streets, thereby putting into practice one of the slogans in vogue that spring: 'Unbutton your brain as often as your flies.' Just another way of playing at Revolutionaries with no risk but that of casual sex.

But he saw nothing, and had nothing to say. Roselyn's grey gaze blinded his eyes, the taste of salt dried his mouth. To what man or woman in that crowd, heady with its own rebellion, could he have spoken of what so violently gripped his heart? He was out of play. Where heaven on earth reigned for everybody else, and freedom of speech triumphed, for him everything had turned into hell on earth and silence. Even writing had abandoned and disowned him. He who had thought of himself since childhood as the accomplice of words found himself suddenly deprived of all verbal expression.

Nor would he ever submit the thesis he had just completed after six years of study. He had left it behind along with all the rest, amid the disorder of his abandoned room. What he had worked on so hard, with such passion and dedication, did not interest him any more. A jumble of words that had lost all meaning. In any case, all those words that he had so long deliberated, so meticulously weighed, had perhaps also melted like wax ink, burning the pages, just like the words of letters and notebooks. What did his arguments and research into the concept of betrayal matter, now that he himself had become a torturing incarnation of the traitor?

The train sped on. The whole countryside was a face. Roselyn's face.

He let him come back to visit him, and won his complete trust in order to overcome his chronic shyness.

'Roselyn,' he said smoothly, 'I'd like to introduce you to some other friends of mine. They would be so happy to meet you. One of them has invited us to a party. It'll be very informal, I assure you, and there won't be very many of us. Anyway, I'll be with you, I won't leave you alone. Truly, it would give me so much pleasure if you came.'

Roselyn was reluctant. He was afraid of people, just as a child is scared to be among adults it does not know, but his friend insisted so much that he eventually agreed. 'Well, I'll come if you want me to . . . but, you know, I'm shy . . . I'm not used to going out, and being with other people . . . We won't stay long, will we? And you won't leave me all alone them, will you?'

Night-of-amber promised.

And he strictly kept his promise, in reverse.

The party was held at Pallas's place; she had a huge apartment on Rue de la Butte-aux-cailles. This party was prepared with skill and most of all excitement. Its organizers were Urbain, Pallas, the Scribe, the Lunatic and a few others besides. Infante did not come; in her search for purely personal pleasure she was otherwise committed that evening. Night-of-amber was the instigator of the party.

It was he who had proposed the idea and presented it in such a way as to appeal to his accomplices: to trap the baker's boy, that puny idiot, that tearful little runt, to keep him in their sophisticated clutches, and play with him, like cats with a mouse, until he was dead.

Night-of-amber-Wind-of-fire and Roselyn arrived together. As soon as they entered the apartment the door was carefully closed behind them. All the others were already there, waiting. They were all most elegantly dressed. Night-of-amber led his friend into the big reception room where the party was to take place. He held him by the shoulder. Trembling all over with shyness, Roselyn only remained upright thanks to that familiar hand laid on him in a comforting and affectionate gesture. He had brought a box of sweets – boiled sweets – and he held his little package awkwardly clasped in his hands. As soon as they came into the room they were struck by the intensity of the lighting. All the lamps were lit. The hostess and her other guests were seated side by side at the long dining table covered with a magnificent linen tablecloth of dazzling white, with their legs crossed dangling in space. The table was not laid; there was no crockery on it. Pallas and her companions seemed to want to substitute themselves for the place settings.

None of these smart seated figures said a single word at

the entrance of the newcomers; they contented themselves with a perfectly chilly stare directed at the baker-boy in his Sunday best.

'Here he is,' announced Night-of-amber-Wind-of-fire. 'Allow me to introduce my very dear friend Roselyn Petiot. I bring him to you as a present. I hope you find him to your liking.'

Roselyn was already completed baffled. All of a sudden he could not even recognize his friend's voice. Never before had he heard Night-of-amber speak in this cutting, cynical tone of voice. And the hand laid on his shoulder suddenly felt terribly heavily, like a concrete paw fastened on to him. That roughly pushed him into the middle of the room. Under that bright light and those lofty gazes. For as soon as his introduction was made, Night-of-amber-Wind-of-fire had actually given the boy a hard shove and turned away from him. And Roselyn found himself all alone, seized with dizziness, nervously fiddling with the string on his package of confectionery. He was no longer capable of moving, or speaking, or especially of looking at anyone.

'Well, Monsieur Petiot, step closer, come over here!' Urbain finally addressed him. 'This party is in your honour, I hope you'll prove worthy of your reception. Come on, come closer!'

But it was only by making a gigantic effort that Roselyn still managed to keep himself standing; if he took the least step, he would fall. He stared in desperation at the toes of his shoes.

'Really, Monsieur Petiot, don't just stand there, like a picket for tethering goats to, right in the middle of the room,' said Pallas. 'At least come and bring us that ridiculous little package you're clutching convulsively to your stomach! Tell us, what's inside it?'

Then, still with his head lowered, Roselyn held his arm out straight, into empty space, and stammered, 'Sweets . . .'

An enormous burst of laughter exploded at the table. Roselyn's hand was trembling so much that his package ended up by coming undone; all the sweets rolled on to the ground. The laughter redoubled.

'Monsieur Petiot is actually a goat,' quipped Pallas. 'Look, he's just deposited his constipated little sugar droppings right in the middle of my room!'

'Your behaviour is indecent!' continued the Scribe. 'That's nothing short of incontinence!'

'You know,' added the Lunatic, 'the wolf had much less reason than that for gobbling up Monsieur Seguin's goat, so we beg you to learn to control yourself, for if you act the goat too much, we'll have to play the part of wolves!'

Then they all began to jeer at him, delighting in repeating his name as if it were a completely grotesque word. Only Night-of-amber-Wind-of-fire said nothing. He stood apart, leaning against a wall, and watched Roselyn, while smoking a cigarette. Roselyn finally looked round at him and gave him an imploring look, but he was met with only an infinitely distant and scornful gaze. Then his last strength deserted him, his legs could not support him any longer. His knees gave way, and he collapsed on to the floor, among his sweets, and began to cry.

'Monsieur Petiot's incontinence truly knows no bounds,' observed Pallas. 'Now he's crying!'

And the sweets moistened by his tears stuck to the floor.

Night-of-amber was not even listening any more to the sarcastic remarks of ever increasing virulence made by his accomplices. He heard only the whimpering of Roselyn who lay crumpled up on the ground. And he felt a rising disgust, as well as anger. He eventually tore himself away from the wall, crossed the room and came and grabbed Roselyn by the hair.

'Now that's enough,' he shouted. 'Get up, you wimp! Stand up, you spineless creature! And stop snivelling. These floods of tearful piss are disgusting! Be warned that we hate wimps, and pity revolts us. If you carry on blubbering like that, I'll crush you like a cockroach. Now, get up!' And forcing him to his feet, he dragged him by the hair over to the table to the shouts and applause of his accomplices. Then he threw the boy at their feet.

From that moment everything moved very quickly. They all began to drink, getting inebriated on a very special cocktail prepared by Urbain, and on the words, insults and teasing that they heaped on the baker's apprentice. They made him take his clothes off, and having blindfolded him they amused themselves by pushing him round in every direction, sneering mercilessly at his nakedness – his larval nakedness, of a man not fully formed, with a hollow chest, skinny limbs and a little boy's genitals. They broke his glasses, whose big lenses diminished his myopic eyes to moth holes. Night-of-amber did not touch him again; he contented himself with watching the others do their worst to him. Having handed over his victim as fodder, he returned to lean against a wall. He laughed, and it was a continuous laughter that was more and more piercing. A laughter he could no longer even control, as if it were the drink concocted by Urbain that had instilled the laughter into him. A crazed laughter that made him grind his teeth and seemed to whet the fury of the others to ever greater violence. He felt his nerves being bared one by one, stretching to breaking-point in his flesh. He felt his sanity waver, teetering in a harsh, acid light, where everything stood out with terrifying precision. He felt his vertebral column running through his back like a steel stake, and his heart spinning rapidly like a ball of flame. He felt his penis grow painfully erect, acquiring the hardness and roughness of a stone. Erect without desire – a muscle tensed by anxiety, stiffened with cold.

And he heard it again – his mother's cry rising from deep in his entrails, tearing through his stomach. The cry of both their mothers, his and Roselyn's. Everything began to get confused. The farm at Blackland encircled by forest and Roselyn's island encircled by the sea. Isolated bits of land and rock. Death prowling in the forest, among the age-old trees, and the wind blowing in from the sea, whipping up the waves like an armed rising against the land. And the tears of their fathers, the same soppy fathers, the same widowed husbands. Tears that had flowed from their grief-stricken bodies, like a loss of semen exhausting their virility. And his sister and Thérèse, the younger and elder sister, both in a remote, distant place, on the far side of dream and desire.

Into his eyes, dilated by the fiery drink, came dancing the reeling figure of Roselyn, spinning round in its pitiful nakedness. That pale skinny body, that pre-pubescent carcass, writhed like a white flame before his eyes. A salt flame. He laughed.

'More! More!' he shouted between two great bursts of laughter. 'Spin the top again!'

Roselyn said nothing; he was not even whining any more. He let himself be tossed about like a scarecrow. He seemed to have taken leave of his body. The blindfold over his eyes was soaked with sweat and tears; his mouth grimaced in a kind of rictus that resembled a trembling smile.

'Round and round, little baker's boy!' cried Night-of-amber-Wind-of-fire, flattened against the wall. 'The corn needs grinding. Hotter, hotter, the bread needs more cooking! Go on! Spin round, get hot, burn, whirl, little baker's boy, if you want to become king of bread-making! You wanted a friend? Haven't you found one? A nice multiple friend. Don't you wonder at the reception we, your friend, are giving you?'

But actually what Night-of-amber-Wind-of-fire was hearing as he shouted his derision, was this, nothing but this: 'Round and round, dear twin of my neglected and betrayed childhood, dear twin of my distress and loneliness! Keep spinning till everything's exhausted . . . until my unhappiness of old is consumed, until my old hurt is cleansed and purged. Spin round, I command and beg you! Free me of my memory, free me of my past! Spin round and round and trample under your thin, bare feet all those cries of our mothers, those sobs of our fathers – reduce them to dust! I beg and command you! And then drop dead afterwards, to put an end for ever to all remembrance, all pity, all weakness! Spin round and die, little baker's boy, to free me for ever from myself!'

★

Which of them all had the idea for the final scenario, he could not remember. It was the 'multiple friend' they had all become who must have suddenly had the inspiration. The beautiful white tablecloth was cut up into strips and they laid Roselyn on the bare table. And there, while some of them kept him down and prevented him from thrashing about, other applied themselves to wrapping him up in these strips. From head to foot. They wound him in these wrappings like a mummy, with slow and very meticulous movements, without talking or shouting any more. The game was turning serious now. The wretched baker's boy did not make them laugh any more, for his swathings gradually rendered him more and more magnificent. It was no longer a matter of derisively swaddling him, but of preparing him for sacrifice. And their silence intensified Roselyn's terror. Only Night-of-amber-Wind-of-fire continued to let out his piercing laughs.

When the bandages reached his chin, Roselyn tried to lift his head and cried out, 'Night-of-amber! Don't let them kill me . . . they're going to suffocate me . . . save me, I beg you . . . I'm scared! Don't let them kill me . . .'

Hearing himself appealed to by that beseeching voice, Night-of-amber-Wind-of-fire's laughter stopped dead. Who was calling him? What for? Was it that mummy lying there, that cloth figure on the dining table? That bundle of rags? Which dared to beg for pity?

'Who do you take the two of us for?' he then shouted in anger. 'Lazarus and Jesus, perhaps? I'll have you know that I do everything in reverse. Not resurrection, but the celebration of destruction! Not salvation, but total damnation! No pity, only wrath and fury! You wanted my friendship? I gave you much more than that. I made you a present of my hatred. Stay in your bandages! Be shrouded in the whiteness of death! And give up the ghost! Really, what impertinence, what insolence! He's offered a lovely death in white linen embroidered with exquisite little flowers in white thread, and, what's more, made to measure, and he, the baker's boy, dares to complain? I'll ram your reedy-voiced pity down your eunuchoid throat!'

The others resumed their task of binding him up, but still leaving his mouth free. They also made a slit at eye-level. Then they paused, to observe him at leisure fighting against suffocation and to feast on his frightened animal gaze. He could only breathe through his mouth. The air whistled between his dry lips. And suddenly Pallas suggested, 'How about letting our guest sample the sweets he so kindly brought us? After all, what proof have we that he did not poison them?'

Delighted with this idea, they hurried to pick up the boiled sweets that had fallen on the floor and stuffed them into his mouth. Soon the sugar began to melt in his saliva, clogging the sweets together into an incrustation that stuck to his teeth and slowly blocked his mouth.

They watched the thin, white mummy struggle desperately to wrest himself from the restraint of the bandages and the occlusion of the sugar. They listened, fascinated, to the very hollow and increasingly rapid beats of his frantic heart pounding under the cloth. They admired the way that mouth changed with sugar of every colour – red, green, orange, pink, violet and yellow blending together, and trickling in long threads of thick saliva like a seeping of resin. Shiny globules, in which the light played, bubbled between his lips then burst with a little dry sound.

'Bravo!' cried Urbain. 'Didn't I say you were the king of bread-making? You're much better than that, dear baker's boy, you're the emperor of confectionery!'

It was then that Night-of-amber approached the table. He moved the others aside and, bending over Roselyn's mummy, tore from his eyes the blindfold the embalmers had put on again while stuffing him with sweets, so as to concentrate their attention solely on that sugared mouth. But he wanted to see. He wanted to see Roselyn's eyes to catch the brief glimpse of death in them.

But he caught nothing at all. Quite the opposite, it was he who was caught. Beyond all measure.

It was the first time he had ever seen Roselyn's eyes.

Eyes no longer masked by spectacles, no longer deformed by thick myopic lenses. Eyes dilated with anguish and suffocation. Huge eyes, of ash grey, very pale and luminous. Eyes filled with tears made iridescent by the light.

Roselyn gazed at him. But did he recognize him in the state of total terror in which he was foundering? In any event there was no trace of hatred or resentment in his gaze, nothing but an abyss of amazement and sorrow. It was the gaze of an eternal child whose innocence and goodness were not even affected by the betrayal that the person he had chosen as his friend had just committed against him.

Night-of-amber-Wind-of-Fire grabbed the head of the mummy with its mouth filled with red and orange-coloured sugar, and with big eyes the colour of ashes; he lifted it in his hands and bowed over it. In those eyes that were mirrors he saw the reflection of his own face. His miniature portrait quivered in the silvered moistness of Roselyn's eyes.

How deep was his image going to go? To Roselyn's heart? To his soul? And suddenly that word, which never had any meaning for Night-of-amber-Wind-of-fire, sprang up inside him with a vengeance and began to acquire a life of its own. To take on a terrible power. He felt his face completely toppling in Roselyn, and plummeting down to his soul, the soul of a dying man.

For Roselyn was dying, there, in Night-of-amber-Wind-of-fire's hands. He was going to penetrate the mystery of death, taking with him the image of his friend, his treacherous and murderous friend.

Night-of-amber felt hopelessly lost.

'Roselyn, Roselyn,' he called in a murmur, 'don't die . . . I beg you, don't die!'

But already the ash-brightness in Roselyn's eyes was beginning to dull, and Night-of-amber saw his reflection grow slowly muddied, and slip towards the pupil's gaping hole. He clutched the dying boy's head in his hands, he clung to it.

'Roselyn, Roselyn, I beg you . . . don't leave me on my own . . . don't go away like that . . . don't go with that reflection in your eyes . . . Roselyn, save me . . .'

And he wanted to say, 'Don't take my soul and die, save both of us! Come back to life! Give back my soul that you're stealing from me . . .' He wanted to say absurd things whose meaning still completely eluded him but whose power tore at him like claws. And he wiped the boy's sweat-covered brow and wet eyelids. And suddenly he began to lick him.

He licked his face, his eyes swollen with tears and terror, his lips glued with sugar. He tried to bite into the enormous incrustation formed by the melted sweets in order to break it, to free the boy's mouth, to let him breath and speak again. He wanted to hear him; to hear him say, 'I forgive you.'

He managed to crack the sugar shell, but just as he succeeded in doing so, he felt a very faint breath on Roselyn's lips that hesitated at the brink of this narrow vent and lightly touched his own lips. But this extremely tenuous breath immediately failed. It failed at the very contact of their two mouths pressed against each other. And this breath began to ebb away, then very slowly died. And at the same time Night-of-amber-Wind-of-fire's reflection died in the leaden grey of Roselyn's eyes. Night-of-amber saw the tiny portrait of himself slide into the pupil and go spinning down as though falling to the bottom of a well.

He felt the weight of the head he was holding in his hands become at once limper and heavier and the sweat on it turn chill. Then he began to rub his face against Roselyn's half-bandaged face, to lick his eyelids and lips, mixing the sticky taste of the sugar with the salty taste of tears and sweat. And he bit into the ribbons of linen the boy was wrapped in, tearing them to shreds, and moaning. For he could only moan, as if everything in his mouth had also begun to melt – words, cries, questions, appeals, like a thick, scalding syrup, mingled with salt. And that was the taste of his soul that he had lost as soon as he found it, that cloying, enervating, immensely thirst-making taste. Sugar and salt.

The train sped on. Through the half-open window the smells of spring entered the compartment and seemed to brighten the mood of the travellers who were unwrapping some food. Some rubbed apples on their sleeves to make them shine before biting into their juicy flesh. Night-of-amber-Wind-of-fire felt nothing, neither hunger nor desire. His mouth remained parched by the sharp taste of salt and the caustic taste of sugar. A taste that was all violence. His mouth, even more than his eyes, remembered.

There was no other memory but body memory. An animal memory, entirely of the senses and passions. And inside his body with its bared senses, inside that flesh of a wary beast, the unexpected had settled, something his reason still could not conceive of, something totally out of place – the weight of a soul.

But all weights, and memories, and tastes became muddled inside him. Weights of bodies and souls confused, memories of eyes and mouth and skin. Salt and sugar blended in the extreme, to the point of unassuageable thirst. To the point of torture. Weights of that other combined in a single block, and in counterbalance to this hidden and terrible heavy weight was the totally gentleness of the weight of Thérèse's body.

Thérèse. He had spent only one night with her, but that night was enough to have overturned everything inside him, for ever. He knew that not for a long time, a very long time, would he be able to approach other women's bodies, even as he knew just as well that he would certainly never see her again. She had turned his body inside out like a big glove made of flesh, she had torn him away from himself as no woman before her had ever done. She had introduced him to another kind of pleasure. Through her, he had plunged into the deepest night of the flesh. Into the body's primordial darkness.

★

He rubbed his face against Roselyn's so hard, and so frantically licked that sweat- and tear- and melted-sugar-stained face that he ended up giving it the polish of a stone. Then he turned from the table on which the mummy with the washed face and cleansed lips lay, and fled from that place where neither space nor time existed any more. And as he fled, he picked up Roselyn's jacket that was thrown on the floor with his other clothes. When the door slammed behind Night-of-amber-Wind-of-fire the others who had been standing there, watching, pulled themselves together, and Urbain declared in a bitter tone of voice, 'I'm disappointed in Peniel! Basically, he and this sucker were two of a kind. But now, let's call it day. We've got to get rid of this body as quickly as possible.'

'You're right,' said Pallas, 'the evening's over. The table needs clearing. We've finished with dessert, so remove the leftovers for me.'

Urbain and two other guests were detailed to remove the leftovers in question and make sure they disappeared. They went during the night to throw the baker's boy's body into the waters of the Seine, quite far outside Paris, over towards Nogent, taking care to weight it with some heavy stones so that it remained very unobtrusively at the bottom of the river for as long as possible. But to be even safer, they smashed the jaw bones and all teeth beforehand, so that the body could not be identified in the event of being discovered, even in several years' time.

Night-of-amber-Wind-of-fire did not go home. He went to Roselyn's place, having found the keys in the boy's jacket. It was the first time he had ever been there, their meetings always having taken place at Rue de Turbigo. A basement flat with barred windows that looked out on to the street at ground level. Seeing these windows up near the ceiling, Night-of-amber remembered what Roselyn had said to him on the subject of the feet of passers-by, about women's shoes in particular, and women's ankles.

'People always think it must be very unpleasant living in

the basement,' Roselyn said to him one day, 'well, I like it, because I see hundreds of women's feet and legs. And then I like to listen to the sound of their high heels on the pavement. The sound of footsteps approaching, passing and moving away, if you listen to it carefully, can be as unsettling as a voice. From seeing all these feet, and listening to all these footsteps, I've ended up being always able to tell what kind of body is passing above, what kind of woman, and even sometimes to imagine their face and their eyes. Have you noticed how a person's way of walking and the echo of their footsteps matches their expression? I've several times fallen in love with women when all I've seen of them are their feet and ankles. They walked briskly . . . stepping along so briskly, so prettily . . . I would have blushed to see their eyes!

But that night no woman came along, making the unsettling sound of her heels echo outside the small basement window. Total silence reigned in the bedroom and in the street. A silence so pure it seemed to deny the existence of the city all around, and to spring from elsewhere. From Roselyn's dead body, perhaps. From his mouth lacquered with sugar. From his smashed jaw.

This silence intrigued Night-of-amber. Such a silence in the heart of the city, and a city still disturbed by rioting, was incomprehensible. Standing in the centre of the room, he listened to this extraordinary silence. And that was how he fell asleep, standing, looking up towards the ceiling, his eyes lost in the silence.

The silence was broken around dawn, with the first glimmerings of light. It was dispelled, swept away with a broom by the caretaker of the building zealously cleaning her little patch of pavement. And the sound of the broom sweeping the ground invaded Night-of-amber, entering his head, his eyes and his mouth. Then the enormous pulse of the city had begun to beat again on all sides, and its noise to rush back like the blood of a wound, eventually reaching Night-of-amber-Wind-of-fire.

He shook himself out of his strange torpor. He had slept the way horses do, and his knees hurt. So he began to pace the room into which daylight was slowly descending. And this infiltration of daylight within these walls covered with posters, pictures and photographs terrified him. For with it, his conscience returned. All his memories of the day before slipped in with the rose-tinted brightness of the morning and came and settled around him, one by one.

Faces emerged from the walls: huge posters of singers and actresses; and humbler portraits of strangers – Roselyn's relatives, no doubt, people from his village. And among this crowd of faces, some enormous, some miniature, everywhere were photos of gulls, sea gulls, all taken in full flight.

Faces and sea birds gobbled up the whiteness of the walls, pitted the room like a sand-castle attacked by the wind. And the birds wheeled round these faces that might have been overturned boats, or wheelbarrows filled with salt.

Wheelbarrows filled with salt – that was how the portraits suddenly appeared to Night-of-amber-Wind-of-fire. And not only the portraits of the stars and those of the Petiot family, but every face whatsoever was equally that, and only that: a wheelbarrow of salt. And this image terrified him.

So he averted his gaze from the walls to escape this convoy of salt faces, and looked at the furniture and things in the room, inanimate things. All was in perfect order in the little baker-boy's room, an impeccable tidiness prevailed among his belongings. On a shelf above the bed he noticed a few books and a shoe box. He looked through Roselyn's suspended library; it was as limited as it was eclectic. There was a dictionary, a collection of songs, two books about cakes and pastry-making, a large illustrated book of fairy-tales, an anthology of French poetry, an old missal, and a dozen novels. Night-of-amber-Wind-of-Fire took the books down one by one and leafed through them.

As soon as he opened the dictionary a shower of petals

and dried leaves fell out. Roselyn used his dictionary as an herbal. Traces of pollen and colours of flowers stained some pages, encircling columns of words with halos of blue, pink, ochre or purple-violet, crimson or mimosa. His eyes scanned a list of words encompassed within a purplish oval: nativity, natrium, natrolite, natron, natter, natural, naturalize, nature, naught, naughty, naumachy, nauplius, nausea, nautch, nautic . . . A sweetish smell in which were mingled the slightly dusty smell of the paper and the scent of the faded flowers emanated from this herbal of words. Words lost for ever, words that Roselyn would never visit again. Night-of-amber-Wind-of-Fire snapped the dictionary shut.

He picked out the collections of songs. Old love songs all repetition and sweet refrains. Did Roselyn sing at home in the evenings? Maybe his falsetto voice could pitch itself correctly in music and at last feel comfortable, and forget the awkwardness connected with the shrillness of speaking.

The books about cakes and pastries contained mouth-watering pictures to look at, masterpieces of sugar, cream, nougatine, crystallized fruits, almonds, honey and chocolate. Was this what the little baker's boy dreamed of – managing to fashion with his own fingers such wonderful desserts created out of desire and conceived solely to satisfy desire – a crazy, childish desire, a purely oral desire.

The end paper of the book of fairy-tales bore a dedication written carefully, with slightly trembling zeal, in already fading purple ink: 'For our darling Roselyn who so likes to dream, on his seventh birthday. With all our love.' And below were the date and two signatures: 21st September 1958. Mama and Papa.' Roselyn would have been eighteen that autumn. Would he finally have become an adult? Would he finally have stopped dreaming like a naive little boy, and trembling in front of others, mistaking fire and flames for phantoms of friendships?

With each book Night-of-amber was caught in the toils of further questions that kept bringing the same torment. He tossed them one by one on to the foot of the bed. He also threw down the missal without even bothering to open it. 'It's bound to be his First Communion missal,' thought Night-of-amber. 'It must be stuffed with ridiculous pious images.'

He then took down the anthology of poetry and began to skim through it distractedly. One poem caught his attention, halting the rustling of rapidly turned pages. A poem by Verlaine, from the collection 'Wisdom'. The song of Gaspard Hauser.

> A quiet foundling,
> Rich only in my steady gaze,
> I approached men of the cities:
> They did not find me shrewd . . .

Once again, Night-of-amber-Wind-of-fire slammed the book shut. Was there not one word, then, that did not force him back to Roselyn? Gaspard Hauser, Roselyn Petiot – men with such a steady gaze, with a peace and gentleness in them that do violence to men of the cities. Men-children who have no place among men of the cities, whose place lies in the depths of the forest, in the midst of rocks and salt marshes, among woodland- or sea-birds. Whose place is elsewhere, wherever . . . but not here, not here! Night-of-amber-Wind-of-fire abruptly stood up and began to pace the room again. He stamped about angrily in his distress, and again flew into a rage against his victim.

'But, tell me, why, why did you not defend yourself? Why did you come and surrender to me so easily, arouse my fury, and drive me to crime, eh? Why did you turn me into a murderer?'

Gaspard Hauser, Roselyn Petiot. He had totally confused them now. And then other verses came to mind, Georg Trakl's 'Song for Kaspar Hauser', which was even more painful, more oppressive than Verlaine's. And these shadow-laden verses rose to his mouth like a flow of burning saliva.

Austere was his dwelling-place in the shade of the tree
And pure his countenance.
God spoke to his heart in a gentle glow:
O Man!

His footsteps found the town at evening silent;
The gloomy lament from his lips:
I want to be a knight.
But forest and beast followed him,
House and dusky garden of white men
And his killer sought him.

Spring, and summer, and glorious autumn
Of the just, his light footstep
up to the dreamers' dark rooms.
At night he remained alone with his star;
Saw snow falling on the bare branches
And the murderer's shadow in the dusky hallway.

The silver head of the unborn dropped.

Every word took on extraordinary weight. Every word pronounced itself inside with distinctness. Indeed, the weight of these words was so heavy that he had the impression his jaws were going to crack. He wished he could bite the earth. 'The gloomy lament from his lips' . . .

Night-of-amber-Wind-of-Fire tried again to take his mind off his distress. He turned back to the bed. 'That shoe box must surely contain bags of marbles or old miniature cars,' he said to himself. 'It would be typical of Roselyn to have religiously kept his kiddy's toys.'

He needed something to fiddle with, he, too, to forget himself in a moment of childhood. The box was light. A cardboard box that had contained a pair of pumps the design of which was drawn on a label beneath which was written Vitello Verde. He opened it. It was three-quarters full of letters. Letters neatly sorted into bundles with elastic bands round them. He picked out the biggest bundle; they were letters from that young woman Roselyn had so often spoken of. He read the name and address on the back of the envelopes: Thérèse Macé, 3 Rue des Alouettes, Nevers, Nièvre. And he read the letters, the whole bundle, at one go. This correspondence extended over a period of more than ten years. The first letters were those of a little girl to a little boy, then of an adolescent, and finally of a woman, but still written to a child. An eternal child whose pureness of heart, goodness and simplicity seemed continually to enchant Thérèse. To worry her sometimes, too. Roselyn must have written a great deal about Night-of-amber, for in her most recent letters Thérèse often returned to this subject, asking questions about the man she referred to as 'your mysterious friend whom I find as odd, indeed suspect, as the wildly fantastic address he gave you when you first met.'

When all was said and done, what did this Thérèse know about him? And what did he know about her? Only this: that she had known Roselyn since childhood, that she was unfailingly fond of him, that after much moving around the country, she had finally settled in Never, where she now worked as a bookseller, and that the tone of her letters was remarkable for its clarity, delicacy and thoughtfulness for her correspondent. Nevers? Why Nevers? And where exactly was Nièvre? Night-of-amber-Wind-of-fire wondered as much at the name of the town as at the position of the region. Why on earth had this woman, who seemed to have travelled so widely, to have for so long remained undecided between different places, ended up in this little market town planted in the middle of the country? Nevers. He repeated to himself the name of the town as though trying to fathom the reasons why Thérèse had settled there, but in fact it was the English word 'never' that kept coming to mind. He meant to say Nevers, but he invariably heard 'never'. Never again, never more.

This Thérèse intrigued him. He had a vague sense that the way out of the terrible labyrinth in which Roselyn's death had confined him must reside with her. Never-ending, never, never. He felt a growing need to meet her. A need that soon became imperative.

He went rushing out, and ran to a post office. The facades of the buildings were rosy in the morning light, and the water running in the gutters looked fresh and very spring-like. But he saw nothing, felt nothing.

'Come urgently. Stop. Awaiting you at Roselyn's. Stop. Night-of-amber-Wind-of-Fire.' Then before handing over his telegram to the clerk, he added to it, 'Awaiting you. Urgent. Come.'

He felt such a need to see her that he invoked her arrival by constant repetition of this incantation, unreasoning reiteration of these words. He immediately went back to Roselyn's place, as if Thérèse might arrive there from one second to the next, simply because he had just now asked her to come, and shut himself up in the bedroom once more. He remained confined within those four walls the whole day, rummaging among all those now useless things: objects, books, clothes. He read the letters, looked through the books again, turned the clothes over this way and that, fiddled with bits and pieces, as if trying to track down in everything some secret about Roselyn. But there was nothing out of the ordinary to find, no mystery to uncover or penetrate. Roselyn had always been a creature of such transparency that no shadow could linger after him. And Night-of-amber only kept coming across the very thing he most feared: Roselyn's extreme simplicity, his child-like levity. His innocence and fragility.

Night-of-amber-Wind-of-fire dozed off during the afternoon. He had not eaten anything since the day before, and his head was spinning. Everything was spinning round, even the dream that he had.

He is walking straight towards the sea, but the sea retreats as he approaches it. He makes arduous progress, for he is pulling a heavy wheelbarrow; his wrists are tied with string to the handles of the wheelbarrow. It is full of large crystals of salt. Their brilliance blinds the sea gulls gathered all around, beating their wings and crying.

The sea keeps retreating. But he is not moving any more. He is now freed of his wheelbarrow. The birds have disappeared; just a few carcasses and a few feathers lie scattered here and there on the ground. The ground is neither earth nor sand nor pebbles, but salt that violently reflects the light.

The light is a very white, vibrant light. The sky slowly revolves. Seated on a swing, with his back to the sea that has turned dark green, he is holding a shoe box on his lap. When he opens it, a fantastic cry emerges, escaping from it like a lark that flies straight towards the sun, rising sharply. Shatters, and starts again. The cry of woman who has gone mad.

A man tries to write in the salt, but the wind keeps obliterating his words. Yet he does not grow tired of trying, and keeps retracing the same signs with equal diligence, and constant patience.

The wind chases the words away like clouds, like frightened birds. Never, never. The man writing with his fingers in the salt is blown away with the words; he goes tumbling along with them in the wind.

Above the sea, drawn like a broad stroke of green across the horizon, a low window lights up. A hand has just pulled back the curtains. Thick curtains of bronze velvet. A woman's hand – her other hand rests on a man's shoulder. Both of them are young, their faces full of seriousness and hardness. They resemble each other – brother and sister. Indeed, they are so alike they look like the masculine version and the feminine version of one and the same figure. But they stand next to each other like two lovers. Their eyes are smarting with tiredness, insane desire, blighted love. So filled with passion and sorrow are their eyes, it seems that if they suddenly turned to look at each other, their faces would explode and shatter like plaster. Their mouths are dark red, almost brick-coloured. They move their lips almost imperceptibly. Rain starts to fall, soon veiling the windowpanes. Their faces tremble a while longer behind the streaming window.

A girl, sitting cross-legged, right on the sea shore, is sewing. She holds in her fingertips, with their chewed fingernails, a very fine, silver needle that chirrs like a cricket.

'The sea is torn,' says the girl without looking up from her task, 'it needs mending.'

The sea is an enormous tarpaulin of oily green, with a big knife-slash at the hem. Night-of-amber-Wind-of-fire recognizes the girl: it is the sister who was standing at the window. She is dressed in the same material as the sea. Her cheeks are hollow, her mouth huge, magnificent. Her lips the colour of brick.

The girl is down on her knees, searching with her hands for something. She seems nervous. Her hair is all dishevelled. Night-of-amber-Wind-of-fire watches her, but does not see himself, all the time keeping out of his own range of vision. Likewise, he does not hear his own voice; yet he must have questioned the girl, for she replies, in a strained, muted voice: 'You can see very well what I'm doing! I looking for his kisses. His kisses in my hair. The wind blew in my hair and robbed me of all the kisses my brother buried in it. They fell on the ground. Please help me find them!'

She looks up at him for a moment: her eyes are dark purple, her lips cracked by the cold, salty wind blowing strongly over the beach.

'Help me, I beg you!' she says again.

The brother and sister are lying side by side on the beach. Their heads, arms and sides are touching. They are naked, wrapped from their ankles to their shoulders in a piece of the green tarpaulin. A shred of the sea. Going up to them, Night-of-amber-Wind-of-fire sees the fine silver needle briskly flitting round them, whistling – it is sewing them together, skin to skin. They have the same eyes, gleaming like pebbles thrown to the bottom of a well and circled with shadow; their mouths, too, are similar: wide, with beautiful, firm lips, slightly revealing their teeth.

The needle sews and whistles. It is sewing their lips together now. But from beneath their lips reddened with blood wells a moan. Their mouths' muted moan.

'Never, never. I want to be a knight. I want to be your lover, I want to be your mistress. Never-ceasing. Never-failing.'

The needle pricks their kisses, ripping them. A little blood pearls on their lips and salt crystals spangle their eyelids.

The wind has blown away the big green tarpaulin. The sea is gone; it flaps in the sky with a sound of heavy wet fabric. Dogs with the heads of fish – wonderful heads covered with silvery scales iridescent with countless reflections – are walking about on two legs, standing upright like human beings, and pushing wheelbarrows. There are hundreds, perhaps thousands of them, in procession across the deserted beach. A crazy beach that has lost the sea. Their wheelbarrows are full of sweets. Green and purple boiled sweets.

The sand, which is actually salt, slowly covers the bodies of the sibling lovers, building a mausoleum over them. The salt-sand turns the colour of ash and glistens.

The dogs with fishes' heads have disappeared. Only a single, huge one remains. Its body is that of a big greyhound, with a gleaming, light-grey coat. It is standing on its rear legs very upright. It half-performs a few dance steps, leaping higher and higher. Its suppleness is remarkable. The rhythm of its movements increases.

The greyhound with the fish's head is stretched out at the foot of the mausoleum built of sand the colour of ash and salt. It very softly modulates a long, extremely melodious, gentle moan. The sand crumbles and disperses. The dual body of the lovers – the brother and sister sewn skin to skin – reappears. The girl's dishevelled hair is full of sticky green and purple boiled sweets. Her brother's kisses. The sibling lovers sleep, temple to temple, with the same slightly tense smile on their chapped lips. A weary smile.

The greyhound has rolled over on to its side. It now has Roselyn's face.

'I want to be your friend,' he says in a murmur. He is trembling, and trembling . . .

He woke with a start. Someone had just knocked on his forehead, right in the middle of his dream. Knocked on his temple. He got up with his heart pounding, completely bewildered, not knowing exactly where he was any more. The knocks continued on the door, and there was something very patient and stubborn in the way they were repeated. Outside the light was just beginning to fade.

Thérèse was standing on the threshold. She had no luggage. As soon as he opened the door, she rested on him a piercing gaze that was very green and dark beneath the blonde fringe covering her brow. She did not offer him her hand or even say hello.

'Where's Roselyn?' was all she asked, in a slightly hollow voice that seemed to echo in the silence a long time after she stopped speaking.

And still totally wrapped up in his dream, he replied with a vague gesture at his face, 'He's there . . . he's trembling, and trembling . . .'

'But you're the one that's trembling!' she then remarked.

And he slowly backed into the room, with his arms folded over his chest, his eyes wide open and imbued with sleep, staring wildly at the young fair-haired woman standing in the doorway.

She came in, closed the door, and walked towards Night-of-amber-Wind-of-fire. The girl's footsteps on the floor resounded in his head, and in his heart. She walked inside his body.

'Ah!' he exclaimed softly. 'Your shoes . . . your shoes are green, with high heels!'

Thérèse came to a halt in the middle of the room and looked at her feet in slight surprise. 'Well, yes. Why the amazement? Have you never seen a pair of green court shoes? They were a present from Roselyn. He sent them to me this winter. I like them very much. I wear them all the time.'

She was dressed in a pleated skirt of a light, grey, silky fabric, a pale-green cotton jacket, and a scarf with grey and pink flowers that she wore over her shoulders. Her hair was pinned up in a bun, and two thin silver pendants danced from her ears. Even more remarkable than her dark, green eyes was her mouth, which was wide, like a wound, and solemn.

She talked a great deal. About Roselyn, about the island where she had known him as a child, about the friendship between them that they had never lost despite leading such different lives and living so far apart. She talked about herself as well, but not much. About her life, for a long time nomadic and irresolute, and recently settled at last. In Nevers.

Not once did she ask that question again: 'Where's Roselyn?' As if she had understood from the very beginning. Understood that Roselyn was nowhere, nowhere in this world. That from now on he dwelt only in them: in her, the friend who had always loved him like an older sister, and in this man with gold-flecked eyes the colour of amber, who had loved him like a crazy assassin. For this, too, she sensed: that Night-of-amber-Wind-of-fire had driven Roselyn out of this world, and that driving him out had been his own ruin. And that he had called her to his rescue, to the rescue of a murderer overwhelmed by the horror of his deed. She did not revolt at this, she did not even try to find out what had happened, or how, or why. It was too late for that. The only thing that mattered now was to save Roselyn's memory; not just a purely formal memory without content, but a true remembrance replete with the presence of he who was now gone. All this she sensed in a very confused way, but with tremendous power.

Darkness fell, and the two of them were still there in the

room, sometimes seated, sometimes pacing around, talking. Then the talking stopped, as if all the words had been used up, or had suddenly broken, or dissolved in the shadows slowly filling the room. The sound of the city reached them. They could hear cries in the distance, crowds marching and rioting, police sirens, the shatter of breaking glass as stones were hurled at windows. All around them, in the streets, everywhere, young people were claiming their rights. Their right to speak, their right to desire, happiness, and pleasure. And the two of them, there, deep in their burrow, below the level of the street, listened to that great clamour of celebration and revolt with a curious mixture of astonishment and indifference. They were the same age as the demonstrators running about above their heads; they might have joined them; they might have been among their own with them. But at that moment their youth was being played out elsewhere.

Far from the city, far from any crowd, far from history. Even outside of time, perhaps. Somewhere in the margins of time, on the outermost fringes of eternity. Their youth was as though suspended, in exile, even – their youth was at that moment hostage to an absent person.

They fell silent. She took off her jacket. She was wearing a plain black top with the scooped neckline of a leotard or swimsuit. She sat completely still, on a chair in a corner of the room. He remained standing by the bed, with his back against the wall, his hands crossed behind him. He was looking at her. And suddenly she made that wonderful, overwhelmingly beautiful gesture: she leaned her body slightly forward, stretching out her neck and raising her head sharply towards Night-of-amber-Wind-of-fire, and she placed her hands on her breasts, with her fingers fanned open as if she had just felt a pang of sorrow or surprise in her heart. And slowly she rose from her chair and came towards him, her breasts still contained in her palms, her outspread fingers pointing to her throat. Her eyes were open wide, almost staring, and their expression was completely wild. Her lips were parted, and trembling slightly. He, with the wall, as it were, part of his body, felt himself topple backwards into the thickness of the wall.

Thérèse walked straight towards him, and the sound of her heels reverberated in the wall, and carried through every basement in the city. Was this, then, what the demonstrators had exhumed by taking up the paving stones in the streets – this crazy sound of footsteps, the footsteps of a woman in green shoes, a woman struck with amazement and tenderness, an insanely beautiful woman? Was this, then, the prize of this entire battle launched by young people armed with shouts, and stones, and songs – these simple footsteps of a woman in high-heeled shoes, hammering the city's underground silence in order to send them travelling all across the world, through earth and body, among the living and the dead? These footsteps of a woman trampling on the hearts and blood of men, bruising their muscles and nerves, leaving them ravaged with desire. These footsteps of a woman resonating even inside his mouth, destroying all speech, creating a hunger, a thirst, that would remain for ever unassuageable. These footsteps of a woman inside a mouth that was falling victim to insane love, that was becoming an abyss haunted with cries and kisses.

She walked straight towards him, came right up against him. Their hips were touching, their breaths mingled. Then they roughly laid hands on each other. They grabbed each other by the shoulders, by the neck, by the hair, no sooner having taken hold of each other than pushing each other away, only to be able to seize each other again.

Her unfastened grey skirt slipped down her thighs with a very quiet rustle, falling to the ground and fanning out in a huge corolla. Her pleated, circular, ash-grey skirt lay on the floor at the bottom of the bed like a nimbus of the moon.

Thérèse's skin in the darkness also had that pallor and whiteness. Her very slight body hardly weighed at all on

Night-of-amber's body. Only her loosened hair had any weight, being so long and thick.

The train was getting close to his home now. And it was that weight, the weight of her blonde hair, slipping from one shoulder to the other, falling back, mingling with shadow and smells, allowing itself to be imbued with caresses, laden with kisses, that he still felt in the hollow of his hands, on his neck, his chest and his belly.

He felt for ever bound to that body, that hair. What Thérèse had revealed to him of the body, of fulfilment and desire, no other woman had ever led him to suspect, whatever the pleasure they might have given him. She took him into those sea-bed geographies extending to infinity below the skin – a dual geography, in herself and in him; alien geographies that yet coincided through an obscure and very powerful network of fault-lines. She brought him to the peak of tenderness, she taught him total self-abandonment and self-oblivion in the other, to the point of perdition. Of wonderment and terror. For this joy attained in the flesh's far side of the night, in the exhaustion of caresses and kisses, in the blinding of gazes, was also a terror of the senses and of the heart.

And in the body's far side of the night to which she thus led him, he found Roselyn again.

Roselyn drifting on the surface of the water, who had to be towed from the river down to the sea, who had to be helped to drift without bumping into anything, without fear. Roselyn floating like a light raft covered with salt, his cargo of tears and human sweat returning to God. Would he find comfort there?

And in Night-of-amber-Wind-of-fire's eyes the images suddenly blended. He saw those long barges laden with sand that he had so often followed on the embankments alongside the Seine, walking towards the Ile des Cygnes, down to the Pont de Javel, out towards Issy-les-Moulineaux, and a name came back to him: Morillon-Corvol.

The name of sand-pit company began to resonate inside

him, with a strange rhythm, until it became a light and gloomy melody. Morillon-Corvol – it was a beautiful name. A name that went with the current, a name linked with the sand, a name that daily traversed the city in silence, without the citizens lending much importance to it. Yet at that moment it seemed to Night-of-amber-Wind-of-fire that this name, which suddenly came back into his mind, was one of the city's magic names. And this name turned over in his mouth with infinite sweetness.

This name only served to mask another, unutterable name: Roselyn Petiot, a name it masked, but above all transported, passed on.

Morillon-Corvol, Roselyn Petiot – drifting sand, drifting salt, flowing down stream, through the middle of the city, unnoticed by the men living there.

Everything became increasing muddled inside him. Images, faces, and names. Roselyn Petiot, Morillon-Corvol, Gaspard Hauser . . . and then those of Ballerina, Thérèse, and even of Georg Trakl and his sister Gretl . . .

Gaspard Hauser, Morillon Corvol, Roselyn Petiot . . . And just as sea gulls always fly in the wake of barges, other names came echoing back to him, wheeling in the wake of these original names; the names of all the men and women he had met during his six years in Paris: Jasmin Desdouves, Nelly, Ornicar, Ulyssea, Urbain Malabrune, Infante. And Thérèse. Always Thérèse.

Thérèse who broke away from him in the morning, and got up. And he, left lying in the sheets like a ship-wrecked man, without moving, without saying a word, watched her dress. He was so full of her, so drained and turned inside out, he was so crazy for her, that he was incapable of making even a half-gesture to detain her. He remained curled up on the bed, watching her, with eyes only for her. For he sensed that she was going to take away with her the secret of the crime she had detected in him from the outset, that she was going to take away with her the most obscure part of himself, and also carry off the most vivid memory of Roselyn. That she was going away so burdened, with such imponderables, such mystery, that already she could not look back any more, or linger. That she must not on any account look back; that he could not in any case detain her. That she was going away, and they would probably never see each other again.

She put on her grey skirt again, her black top, jacket and flowery scarf. She stepped back into her forest-green shoes, picked up her bag and disappeared. She did not touch anything in Roselyn's room, and took nothing away as a souvenir. She had come only to save Roselyn's memory from falling into oblivion; that was all she had come for. She had come to save him from death, despite the crime committed against him.

Night-of-amber-Wind-of-fire spent the rest of the day in the same position, curled up in the warmth of the sheets that retained Thérèse's fragrance. He did not go out until after dark. He wandered aimlessly about town, then drawn to the river, he headed down to the embankment. And an absurd idea suddenly possessed him: he boarded a river launch, sat down at the largest table in the restaurant and ordered a meal. The waiters in white jackets regarded this client with surprise, almost as an intruder, for the restaurant was empty, the evenings that spring not being good for tourism and local citizens much more seriously occupied elsewhere. They observed him, too, with distrust: being so untidy, with that strange half haggard, half hunted look that he had, would he be able to pay the bill? When he gave his order, the waiters stared at him astounded, if not in panic, for he ordered no less than every dish on the menu: some fifteen starters, as many meat and fish dishes, all the vegetables, salads and cheeses, and finally a dozen desserts. Likewise with the wine. Then he asked for the table to be laid for three people. And, there, all alone in the middle of the restaurant, presiding at his big round table crowded with bottles and dishes, he poured drinks for Roselyn and Thérèse.

He ate and drank in a completely chaotic way, picking

at each dish, sampling every wine. The launch crew gathered round to watch, dumbfounded, while this crazy client guzzled in silence. But he paid no attention to them; he observed the embankments slowly slipping past, while nearby a harpist in attendance picked out the notes of a tune of dubious charm that he did not even hear. He kept his eyes fixed on the embankments, listening only to the lapping of the water outside the illuminated room's picture windows. And he wept. Every dish had a taste of salt, all the wines were sticky and sweet. But he ate, nevertheless, forcing himself to swallow everything. For he was not eating for his own pleasure. He was eating like this for the others, in order to nourish them – Roselyn, Thérèse, and Gaspard Hauser, too. Towards the end of the meal, by which time he was completely drunk, he pushed aside all the plates cluttering the table and grabbed the centrepiece bunch of lilacs. And he ate the flowers as well. In order to deck with flowers Roselyn, Thérèse, and Gaspard Hauser, too.

He got home feeling sick and drunk, and spent the night vomiting and crying. It was not until morning that he felt more or less recovered. Round about dawn, in the coolness of daybreak. And he decided to leave without waiting any longer. He fled his room and the city, a total outsider to the joyful anger being celebrated there by young people from whom he had set himself apart. He had spent the night vomiting up his youth. He was now ageless. But in any case assassins are always ageless; as soon as they accomplish their crimes, their age teeters, shatters, is lost – it divorces itself from them, and the age of their victim is added to it.

Day and night. From these, too, he found himself excluded. He fled the city before the fullness of day. He fled the day.

The day. He went through it without seeing it; he broke it like a pane of glass. The day, which bore the initials of his lost friends. All his betrayed friends: Jasmin, Ornicar, Urbain, Roselyn. He had never been able to take anything from them, or to give them anything. He had understood nothing about them: Jasmin's rigour and excitement, Ornicar's distress and madness, the wickedness rooted in Urbain like a challenge, Roselyn's immense goodness . . . Of all these things he had been capable of choosing only the worst. He had allowed himself to be seduced by the most facile, blackest, most cowardly charm, that of evil. Instead of trying to cure Urbain, he had hopelessly aggravated his condition.

The night, too, he went through, breaking himself. For the night was stronger than he was, and it was the night that won. The night written by those women who had been his lovers: Nelly, Ulyssea, Infante, Thérèse. He had done violence to the first and humiliated her, repudiated and cursed the second, played with the third until these games cloyed, but the last had left him destitute of himself. She had reduced to nothing his violence, his arrogance and his ludic behaviour of equal intemperance and irresponsibility. The last had closed the night behind her, had slammed the night on him like some huge iron door.

The train entered the station. No one was waiting for him. No one in his family knew that he was coming home. Would they even remember him at Blackland, after so many years' absence, during which he sent no news, and had no news from them? He did not even know where he was going home to, nor whom he would find there. He stepped down on to the deserted platform. It was a brilliant day. He was so thirsty, it made him weep.

2

But people of the land have a deep memory, much deeper than that of city people. It is rooted in their bodies like the roots of their trees in the soil.

He returned to his childhood home. It was Mathilde who greeted him. An unchanged Mathilde, her large, hate-filled virgin's body, still sombrely dressed, the heavy bunch of keys to her domain clinking on her hip. She greeted him as if he had left the day before and had just returned from a trip into town.

'So, you're back, are you? Will you be staying long?'

He found his room empty, full of damp, dust and darkness.

'No one's been in here since you left,' said Mathilde, opening the door into it. 'I always keep the rooms of those who have gone closed. Here's your key.'

Rose-Héloise still lived in the low-built wing of the farm, and Nicaise was living with her; since those nights that she spent waiting up for Heart-breaker's return, when Nicaise came to visit her, he had never left her again. It was they who now did the heaviest work on the farm.

And Heart-breaker, the adoptive son Rose-Héloise had so keenly awaited, her elected child she thought to have saved from loneliness and misery, was there, too. He was next door, in the shed, where he lived like a savage.

For he finally came back from the war; deemed to be insane, he had not been executed for the crime he had committed on his fellow soldier during the interrogation of the child.

But in fact, no, he had not really come back from the war. He had left his reason there. His reason was still rusting in irons in the depths of the cell where they imprisoned him after the crime. He had actually lost everything there – his youth, his joy, his heart. His sleep and his breath. He was no longer capable of loving since then, anything or anybody. He no longer knew how. On his return he had barely recognized Rose-Héloise. His memory of the child that had died in his lap never left him, driving everything else from his mind. The weight of that child's body, and with it the weight of all the others who died in the war, that of the soldier whose skull he had shattered no less than that of his mutilated companions, and even that of all the enemy fighters killed in the mountains, bore down on him terribly. He was buried under the weight of all those human beings killed in the war. He had difficulty breathing, so heavy was all this in his arms, on his shoulders, in his lap, and he dragged himself about, rather than walked, always panting when he spoke. At night no sooner had he fallen asleep than he would wake up again. He woke with a start, short of breath. Sometimes, when the pain became too acute, crushing his chest and lying too heavily on his lungs, he would throw himself on the ground, and there, beating his chest with his fists, begin to wail like a woman in mourning. It was a very long wail that he would then modulate, an ululation at once strident and syncopated, after the manner of the women of those parts. And if Rose-Héloise, alerted by that cry of distress, came running to comfort and console him, he would roughly push her away, chasing her out of his den. No one could console him. Only Belaid might have done so. But Belaid had gone off into the heart of the desert and could not hear him. He was leading his goat from well to well through the vastness of the sands. His black goat with beautiful brown eyes with glints of bronze in them, and its very thin flanks. But all the wells were dry and Belaid kept moving on; he did not have time to turn round, to listen to Heart-breaker's cry, to come back to him. Belaid had to go on and on, he had to hurry off, in search of water for his goat, whose big eyes were burning with thirst. And Heart-breaker kept being left on his own, all alone on his little patch of land in bordercountry, far away from the sea, perpetually far from Belaid's country. He remained alone, breathless and sleepless.

Once Night-of-amber-Wind-of-fire learned of what had happened to Heart-breaker – that he had come back from Algeria out of his mind, after blindly taking revenge, for the crimes committed against his comrades, on a child, whose only fault was to belong to the enemy race of the moment – he kept hovering around him. But he never dared to accost him or even to try to speak to him. Actually he feared him as much as he sought him out. The other reflected his own crime like a distorting mirror, a magnifying mirror that terrified him. Heart-breaker was expiating his crime in the manner in which he had committed it – beyond reason. The gleam of intelligence that flashed through him when the child died in his arms almost in the same instant destroyed him, so overwhelming was the self-evident truth that then revealed itself to him: that man is so absolutely forbidden to kill a fellow human being that whoever flouts this prohibition kills himself in killing his victim. And it was this, the violence of this incontrovertible, self-evident truth, that Night-of-amber-Wind-of-fire had some inkling of, while at the same time rejecting it with all his strength. He, too, had killed, but totally gratuitously, in time of peace. Cold-bloodedly. He, too, had been caught unprepared, overwhelmed by his crime. But he was nevertheless still holding out. He was holding out against the dizzying insanity that had overcome Heart-breaker, and even more against that other torment: the torment of admitting his crime, not simply to others but also to himself. He refused to make a true reckoning of the full extent of his deed, for such a deed was out of all human proportion, and so could only really be measured by God. Now, he could not submit to the idea that God existed, and he desperately strove to stifle the pangs of doubt that anyhow continuously gnawed away at him. He refused to have to endure, like Heart-breaker in his madness, Cain's indefinite exile in the far corners of a land for ever hostile and silent. So he admitted his crime to no one: not to any other human being – for he despised all judgements deriving from human morality, which he considered obtuse and cunningly self-interested, just as much as he despised all those enshrined in the law, which he compared to a crafty and ruthless horse trader – and certainly not to himself, so as not to give his conscience the chance to speak, for in the state of distress to which he had reduced it, it would only have been able to speak in terms that he most abhorred: terms of guilt, remorse and repentance. And eventually in even worse terms. Of God. So, he sheathed himself in silence. But his refusal only made his exile worse.

When he first came back to Blackland, Night-of-amber-Wind-of-fire kept away from the others as much as possible, contenting himself with just prowling now and then round Heart-breaker, his obscure and wretched double. He set himself to work, and learned to tend the land and livestock. This work exhausted him and brought him no pleasure, for he was still unskilled and inexperienced, but it was precisely this weariness that he sought, this stupor that overcame him at the end of the day, and drained him of all thought. He did not read or write any more. Words, all words, terrified him. He did not even try to obtain news of Ballerina.

The others expressed no surprise at his return after so many years, nor at the fact that he should set about working the land so zealously. The reasons for this behaviour did not concern them. Night-of-amber was one of their own, and that was enough: he was entitled to his place on the farm. In any case, who would have been capable of showing concern? Mathilde only had time for her land; Rose-Héloise only minded about Heart-breaker, and Nicaise only about those two; as for the other Peniels, they all lived away from the farm: Thadée and his family at Montleroy, and Night-of-gold-Wolf-face at Mahaut's place with his two last-born sons, while Ballerina had long been a stranger to Blackland. And then Night-of-amber-Wind-of-fire's arrival was a relief to Mathilde, Rose-Héloise and Nicaise, for they could no longer cope with all the work by themselves. Heart-breaker was now no use at all; he could only wander around his shed, looking haggard, and stopping every three steps to catch his breath.

Yet Night-of-amber's presence soon ceased to be a support, for despite all the care and effort he put into his work, the results proved disastrous. Every piece of ground he ploughed became arid and stony, and not a single seed he sowed germinated. Nettles and brambles rose in his wake. And the same was true of the animals – all those he took care of fell ill and even died. The curse on Cain that he had tried to escape had also fallen on him. The fields refused the labour of his hands, the paths rejected the traces of his footsteps, the animals wasted away. Everything that came into contact with him, soil and livestock, grew sterile.

Mathilde came to him and accused him angrily: 'What have you done! Look at what's happened to our farm since you've been here! I don't know what contamination you've brought back from the city, but you can't go on destroying our land like this for much longer. My land! For I've been battling with it, day in and day out, for more than sixty years now, to make it strong and fertile, and now you come and bring death here, just like in the days of war! Where the hell did you get your Jerry hands? Because, word of honour, if we let you carry on, you'll soon have laid as much to waste as those soldiers from out of hell. Bah! You're just like all the men in the family: you can't stay put. You have to go looking elsewhere, traipsing around all over the place, and when you come back with your hang-dog expressions, you've lost your wits or your soul on the way! My brothers went off, all of them, in turn, and the ones that came back were only shadows of themselves; the others died, the devil only knows where! As for my father, the one time he took it into his head to leave his land and waste time in the city, he knew no better than to bring back a disastrous woman. A foreigner, together with her bastard daughter, and both of them with death at their heels! So my father . . . But don't let's talk about that any more . . . We're talking about you, who are so like my father! For you take after him more than any of his sons ever did. It's as though the same demon is in possession of your hearts. But I'm staying the course, I'm holding out, I'm safeguarding this land where I was born, and this farm I inherited from my mother. I'll save them, yes, I will. Come what may, I'll save them from every scourge, and if necessary I'll drive you off them!'

Night-of-amber-Wind-of-fire stopped working in the fields, in the meadows and in the cow sheds, but he did not leave the farm. He had nowhere else to go. The land where he had come to find refuge rejected him. But, he knew, wherever he might go, it would spurn him. The land is the same everywhere. And he did not want to go back to cities any more. He could not live among men of the big cities again; he was now afraid of city-folk. When he fled like a thief from Paris, it was all the cities in the world that he was fleeing simultaneously, for his laughter, his own laughter, the nasty, crazy laughter that had seized him that May evening when Roselyn had been put to death, still made the walls, streets, and windows shake, everywhere. Whatever town he went to, that laughter would have followed him like a dog ready to bite, and would have driven him away. His laughter haunted the town, every town, making millions of windowpanes rattle. He heard this laughter at night; it went through his dreams, and ran through his sleep. And that is why he truly had nowhere to go. Not even away from the earth, not even on the moon where men had just landed for the first time. There, too, the nasty laughter would still follow him, always. He did not care that it was now possible to go walking about on the moon, since he, and so many other men like him, could not even go about freely on the earth.

So, not knowing where to go, he decided to stay. Every place was the same to him, equally hostile and arid. The curse on Cain had been thoroughly visited on him, so he might as well suffer the loneliness and bitterness of exile where he was. He would remain as a stranger on his native land. But he would remain there for ever. Still and always, he persisted in being self-willed, his back turned resolutely on God. No, he would not admit his crime, he would not ask forgiveness, neither of men nor of God, even if Roselyn's failing gaze continued to carry away his image and steal his soul. There was still too much pride in him. Pride and rebellion. At least, there was in him a lasting memory of pride and rebellion, now grown hollow.

Since he could not, after all, remain on the farm without working, he decided to learn how to fashion wood. He would become a carpenter. And he who had so detested trees in his childhood went back to them. To their broken bodies, torn from the earth, cut off from their roots. Like him.

Night-of-amber-Wind-of-fire was suddenly stricken with sterility. Rose-Héloise was similarly stricken with fertility. She had long since passed the age when blood marks the mysterious rhythm of the body. But the mystery of the body is infinite, as long as the cries or murmurs of the heart mount freely through the obscure closeness of the flesh. The purple birthmark on her temple that had bled its colour into her hair all the time that Heart-breaker was away at war, now all of a sudden changed the direction of its flow once more. Blood rushed to her womb again. Blood began circulating inside her like fertile spring-water. And she conceived a child by Nicaise. But she knew at once that this child would not really be her own. This child was so late, so marvellously late, in coming to her, after her time. It had only been granted to her to give birth in order to answer Heart-breaker's beseeching appeal, to bring back to him and reconcile him with the child of his anguish, grief and madness. And this child that was at last going to save her chosen son from the clutches of that mother-ogress, war, she welcomed as an unhoped-for guest is welcomed. Through this late motherhood, it was a little as though it were Heart-breaker she was giving birth to, restoring him to the world and to life. She invested all her hope in the child growing inside her body, and in her heart, too, for she sensed that by its mere arrival it would be able to create a rift in time and blaze a trail for all of them through the density of their unhappiness and free them from it and bring them all together again.

The child stirred oddly inside her; it seemed to be swimming in the waters of her womb. Sometimes she had the impression that it was touching her heart.

'It's the child's foot,' she said, 'its tiny, light foot, like a little bird's, I can feel it against my heart, as though it were trying to find support.' And she drummed on her belly with her fingertips, conducting an obscure dialogue with the child. During the last month of her pregnancy, a kind of murmur rose within her – a few notes sung very quietly, like the chirping of a little sparrow hidden in a thicket.

As her confinement approached, this murmur grew louder, and acquired resonance within Rose-Héloise's body. It rose to a high pitch in a tuneful whistle and Rose-Héloise's skin gradually lightened, as though she were illuminated from within. She had the pinkness tinged with straw-yellow of a glass with a candle burning in it.

She gave birth in her bed; no woman came to help her. Only Nicaise was there. It happened one June evening, towards the end of the hay harvest. The smell of freshly cut hay filled the air, pervading the land and the houses. Even pervading their bodies, a sweetish, heady smell, combining pepperiness and sugariness.

The smell of hay came through the open window, carried by the warm wind. It circled round the room, stole into the curtains, rested on the sheets; it scented the napes of necks and quivered on hands. The child was born into this smell of hay, and it was amid this smell that it gave its first cry. A clear, fluty cry. Nicaise took the child and wrapped it in a cloth.

'It's a son,' he said, bringing it to Rose-Héloise.

'It's my son,' said Heart-breaker. There he was, standing in a corner of the room. They had not seen him enter. He was standing by the wall, with a far-away expression. He seemed to emerge from the wall as if he had walked through it. He stepped forward after a few moments and went up to Nicaise, moving rather like a sleepwalker, slowly reaching out towards the child. He appeared not to see anything else in the room but the infant. He gently took it from Nicaise's arms and, clutching it to his shoulder, went out into the yard with it. Nicaise made as if to follow him, but Rose-Héloise held him back by the hand.

'Leave him,' she said simply, 'let Heart-breaker take the child. Leave them both.'

He stood in the middle of the yard. The child cried again: an extremely high-pitched, sharp, piercing cry. Then what happened was this: the forests all around shook themselves, the trees swayed as women's hips do, sending a great clamour rolling through their branches. And suddenly thousands of birds rose into the air: bullfinches, orioles, thrushes, and buntings. The smell of hay burned in the air as strongly as incense. It was into this smell that the birds flew. The sky was no more than a smell. An aroma of freshness and dryness, sugar and salt, pecked at by the sparrows in their exhilarated flight. Heart-breaker felt as if the ground had been cut out from under him, and his legs gave way, as though he were bowing under the weight of this fantastic smell of hay. All of a sudden a terrible pain rent his stomach. He collapsed in the middle of the yard, still holding the child to his body. Evening was falling very gently, swelling the June sun to an almost purple red, the colour of the child's hair. A fieriness also swelled in Heart-breaker's entrails, licking at his back. He rocked his shoulders violently, crouched on the ground, with the child cradled in his lap. His face and body were streaming with sweat. He huddled over the child, shivering and moaning. The child did not stir. He had gone to sleep in Heart-breaker's lap. The birds flew off in every direction, covering the earth with their song.

The evening warmth intensified the smell of the hay. The sky was an orange red, with long banks of frilly, apricot clouds. The sun slowly darkened behind the trees –

purple torches undulating in the wind. Heart-breaker gave a final, strident and syncopated moan that scattered the birds. Then there was silence. A tremendous silence, all over the land. The wind fell. Only the smell of hay persisted. Heart-breaker slowly fell over on his side, with the child curled up in his arms. The sparrows swooped down into thickets and gardens, and immediately soared out of them again, carrying in their beaks clusters of red currants or black currants, whose berries they crushed in flight. A fine, sour rain sprinkled the air. For the third time the child gave its new-born baby's cry. A playful cry, like a burst of laughter. And this cry was at once taken up by the birds returning to the forest, a long undulating echo in the purple-coloured darkness. Heart-breaker stood up, reeling, and began to breathe deeply of the evening air. He breathed it until he was giddy. The child waved its arms about cutely in his arms. Its skin and hair had that smell of hay.

Heart-breaker gazed around in astonishment, as though he were rediscovering the land, the woods, the farm, after a very long absence. He gazed in wonderment. He breathed, and his breathing was full and calm. And that was how the world appeared to him in that moment, full and calm. He breathed the world. He breathed the world in the child's hair. And suddenly the smells of over there came back to him. All the smells. Over there, far from his land, on the other side of the sea, where his mind was shattered. His memory came surging back to him. But he was not afraid any more, and no longer fought against it. He let it submerge him. He wept in silence, his teeth clenched, his eyes wide open, and he gently stroked the child asleep in the crook of his neck.

'Belaid,' he murmured, 'Belaid . . .' But that was all. The days of letting the dead child's name be stifled in a welter of tears and vain words were over. This name had finally wrested itself from the madness of a frozen memory and bounded into the rediscovered space of love.

He returned to Rose-Héloise and Nicaise, holding the child out to Rose-Héloise.

'He's hungry,' he said, handing back the child that was waking up. Then he walked away. He walked for a long time through the meadows. His head was spinning. He lay down at the foot of a haystack, with his face turned into the stubble. And there he fell asleep. Now he was able to sleep. His wandering was over. His wandering and his torment. Belaid had at last found the well in the desert where he could water his goat.

A well in the desert. On the very far side of night, where day dawns again and memory returns. The colour purple – night, day and memory. The colour purple, forgiveness and hope.

The child was named Felix. But he was so playful, so affable, that everyone just called him Fé, as if a single syllable with a slight whistle to it more suited his impishness. The fleck in his left eye was not golden but purple, like his hair. Like the world according to Heart-breaker.

And just as little Fé had caused the sparrows of the woods and fields that had gathered in the sky to fly off when he was born, so he seemed to attract people; he was the Peniels' lure. With his arrival, life resumed at Blackland and thereabouts; life emerged from its reserve and loneliness.

It was about that time that Ballerina reappeared. Like her brother Night-of-amber-Wind-of-fire, she had been away from Blackland and her family for a long time; she had spent her life elsewhere. First of all, in Strasbourg, where for years she had been at boarding school, studying music, and now in Grenoble, having moved there recently. She taught music there, in a lycée. She could have continued her studies, gone off to other countries to further develop her art and perfect her playing with new teachers, but the unexpected suddenly turned up in her life and deviated her from her course, and from her destiny.

The unexpected was called Jason; he was around thirty years old, with periwinkle-blue eyes; he was American, and his talent in life was for living. He had been away from his country for some ten years, and in that time he had travelled all over Europe. He liked cities, old cities with narrow streets; churches peopled with marble saints and gilded angels made of wood; and big tea-rooms decorated with mirrors and velvet hangings, where he liked to spend hours reading and watching people. He was always reading, and his memory was vast; he remembered all these books. But he remembered them in such a way that his memory was not so much like a library as a vast aviary or a big greenhouse, because he had no sooner read the texts than the words began to proliferate in him, transforming into images, sounds and movements. The texts came to life inside him – a strange, entirely cerebral life, but intense and somewhat eccentric, too. He looked at people with the same bright, piercing eyes with a slightly crazed expression that he brought to bear on books.

And, as it happened, it was in a café that Ballerina met him, when he was passing through Strasbourg. But he was just passing through everywhere, even his own body from which he often seemed surprisingly absent. What Ballerina first noticed about him were his hands, which were very light-skinned, with long, thin, slightly nervous fingers. Extraordinarily supple, beautiful hands. His least gesture was marked with a disturbing gracefulness, or rather delicacy, for there was something fragile about those perpetually moving hands, a barely detectable tremble in them. He did not so much touch things as skim their surfaces, caressing rather than taking hold of them. And Ballerina was at once reminded of Nęah, the only person she had met until then with a similar gift of movement.

She raised her eyes from the man's hands to his face, and studied him closely without reserve, for she was observing him in reflection in the big mirror opposite, without his noticing. He was reading. Ballerina had fun deciphering the title of the book he was holding, from the words reversed in the mirror:

ЯƎTИUH Y⅃ƎИO⅃ A ƧI TЯAƎH ƎHT

But her gaze was so insistent that she finally alerted the man whose image she was examining. He looked up from his book and gazed back at Ballerina. Their eyes met in the mirror. She blushed at being caught out in her curiosity like this, and immediately switched her gaze to another corner of the café. But in an amused voice, with an accent that gave it a slight lilt, he said, 'Here I am!'

And she, without thinking, said, 'Where?' In the mirror or in the room, or even in the book? At that moment she would not have been able to say, so much did the stranger with the delicate hands seem to her like a dream. A beautiful, calm dream appearing on the surface of a mirror, and slow to decipher.

She made that dream her beloved. And her beloved she made her life. At first sight. It was a Monday. The following Sunday she left Strasbourg and went to join Jason in Grenoble, where he had decided to stay for an indefinite period, for he never measured time. His peregrinations from town to town were over; he had been through them all, from Dublin to Leningrad, from Stockholm to Syracuse, from Lisbon to Istanbul. Now he was turning towards the mountains. Actually, it was towards the mountains that he had always been travelling. He had taken all those detours to the four corners of Europe only the better to circle round them, imagine them, desire them, for he was one of those people who find only by dreaming, who arrive only by running away, and who love only in anticipation. Strasbourg was his last stop. A three-day stopover; his meeting with Ballerina took place on the morning of the first day. She acted as his guide to the town.

When they left the café she led him through the old lanes to the cathedral. It stood at the end of a little street, a proud, unusual building, its pink stone softly lit up by the rather cold morning light. They walked slowly round it, examining the doors, and stopped in front of the south entrance to look at the two spandrels depicting the Virgin: on the right, the coronation, and on the left, the dormition.

'Dormition?' repeated Jason intrigued, not knowing the meaning of the word Ballerina had just mentioned.

But when she explained what it meant, he found it so bizarre he began to laugh.

'That's wacky,' he said, 'but also very lovely. You Catholics are rather cracked! Dormition . . . a pretty crazy word, really . . .' Then he examined the sculpture again with great attention, studying the extraordinary circle of saints' faces bowed over the Virgin's body, faces strangely alike in their grief, their gazes lost in the distance – the distance of an unphraseable question. And standing among them, in the centre of the arch was Christ, he, too, with his sweet, sad face bowed towards the dead Virgin. Yet she was not lying there in death at all; her body seemed still so full of life beneath the wonderful folds of her gown, as though about to rise again, to start dancing, and there was an expression of sovereign calm on her face. A sleeping body with the vibrancy of a dream. No, the bed on which she lay was not a death bed, on the contrary it was more like the bed of a newly delivered young mother. And indeed the child was there, standing on Christ's left arm. For the Christ figure was holding against his heart his own childhood, at once immortal and infinitely vulnerable. And only the child's face returned the Virgin's expression of great calm.

'A pretty crazy word . . .' Jason repeated, as though in a dream. Then turning to Ballerina, he added, 'But beauty is always a little crazy, isn't it?'

'Sure,' she agreed, 'beauty is just as crazy as a flash of lightning.'

Then she suddenly drew him into the cathedral, exclaiming, 'Quick, quick, let's hurry, the big clock is going to strike twelve!'

Midday did indeed throw the astronomical clock into a state of hyperactivity, setting in motion all its fabulous temporal bestiary: the angel with the hammer and the angel with the sand glass, death striking its bell with a bone, and the big cockerel flapping its wings and giving piercing cries – these together orchestrated the procession of Apostles in front of Christ with his hand raised in blessing. But this was only the dramatic staging of human time, all comings and goings, clamour, changes and transformations as evidenced by the four ages of life trotting along in front of death. On other tiers of the clock, astral time, the time of eclipses, lunar and solar cycles, continued its impassive and complex progress in perfect indifference to that of mankind, which was too hectic and always in a state of alarm. For men, there was noise, hurry and turbulence, for the rest a simple quiet play of pointers imperturbably describing the abstract march of pure time. Jason musingly wondered according to which of all these calendars the strange time of the Virgin's dormition might be measured. But Ballerina tore him away from his dreamy question by brightly pointing out to him the alcove at the base of the clock where the chariot of the planetary divinity that ruled each day passed.

'Today is Monday, Diane's day, the moon.' She had eyes only for human time, and no thought for anything else, that wonderful time of meetings and desire, of surprises and of love. Monday, the first day of the week, the first day of Jason. Jason, who had at once become for her, for evermore, the first day of her youth. Her real youth, discovered at last. Jason, Monday, day of her joy.

Monday, the first day of Jason, the first night of bodies offered to each other. It rained during the night. A slow rain that streamed constantly down the walls and shutters, like a very soft whispering of young women between themselves. The very gentle sound of running water, the very quiet, light sound of crumpled sheets in which the bodies of the two lovers kept slipping towards each other, into each other. Skin on skin. Hands and mouth on skin. Tireless the rain, insatiable their skin. Ever more enraptured with touching, exploring, feeling. They wrapped themselves up in each other, steeping themselves in each other, in the half-light of the sheets, amid the murmur of rain and the smell on their skin. They became so tightly bound together they could no longer tell their bodies apart, and their kisses had the rain's softness. Their mouths acquired the deepness of night.

In the morning Ballerina went out on to the balcony. The floor of the balcony was covered with very clear water that gleamed in the light of dawn. Gleamed like metal, like her own face reflected in that pool of rainwater. She leaned over her reflection in the water, over what was such a new image of herself; her eyes shone like pebbles in a mountain stream, and her mouth flashed like glass. And suddenly she exclaimed to herself, 'Beauty is upon the earth!' She exclaimed this in a rush of insane happiness, standing there, completely naked, on the edge of a hotel-bedroom balcony, above the rooftops of a town where people were still sleeping. It was not a reference to her own beauty, but another kind of beauty that had descended on her, dazzling her. The beauty of being totally wrested from oneself, ravished by the other, turned back on the other. And those eyes glistening there in the water were not just her eyes – they were her eyes looking at him. Eyes completely besotted with the other. Eyes that had become mouths whose gaze was all desire and pleasure; eyes that had become mouths in which gaze and kiss were one. A mouth as deep as night, vaster than day.

Mountains. Mountains carry the echo of voices much further, very much further, than the rooftops of a town. They carry the echo so far in fact they sometimes seem to be denouncing the voices to death. Ballerina did not care for mountains. They inspired her with vague anxiety, a curious unease. She could not see in their enormous mass spiked with peaks and glaciers, fraught with abysses and ravines, anything but a monstrous outcrop of land, the angry ground puffing up its matter with violence. When she picked up her cello, she never sat facing the view; she always played with her back to the window. She could not have played looking at the mountains; that formidable pile of rocks, snow and ice seemed so opaque to her that her whole body felt weighed down and crushed at the mere sight of it. Her hands would then tense on the bow, and the instrument itself seemed to turn into a dead weight, too, and lose all resonance. But she was so happy living with Jason that as soon as she saw him again in the evening she forgot the oppressiveness of the mountains, albeit so great.

She loved the nights, because darkness swallowed the mountains and brought Jason back to her. And she dreamed of those huge lakes he often told her about – the big lakes back home, in the far north of his country, near which he was born and had grown up. In summer he swam in them, in winter he skated on them. Lakes whose waters were sometimes turquoise, sometimes periwinkle or forget-me-not blue. Waters so deep that he had never seen the bottom. Waters deep and vast as childhood, like his childhood, the childhood of a dreamy and solitary little boy from North Michigan. He would say to Ballerina, 'You'll see, I'll take you there, and you'll be amazed by my lakes.'

But it was that turquoise-coloured, translucid, lakeside childhood he kept talking about that amazed her, because from her own childhood she retained only a sense of fear and distress, a terrible feeling of darkness. Her childhood was spent in the depths of gloomy forests, full of dampness, purplish shadows and murmurings. Forests haunted by a dual violence – that of her dead brother, the big purple Skunk, and that of her living brother, the jealous rebel.

So it was that Jason's childhood became a legend to them both; a fairy tale round which they constantly wove stories, even projecting it into their future life with talk of the child they would have. They always imagined this future child with the face of a little girl that each of them modelled on the other's features, and they gave her a silly and charming nickname: Lilly-love-lake.

For her, it was just a dream, a lovely dream that was all desire. For him, the dream was all nostalgia, a slow and perpetual drift against desire. Childhood lingered in his heart, magnificent and enduring, an invisible, gracile little figure that continued to skate and swim inside him. Lake of his memory, periwinkle blue, reflected even in his eyes. As soon as he was old enough, he left his country to go in search of another past, one more ancient, more turbulent, more diverse than the too sweet and timeless memory of just his own childhood. He left to try and become truly adult. And that was what he had come looking for in all these town of old Europe – a past moulded by history. But his stowaway childhood came with him, in his eyes and hands; it continued to gleam in his gaze, to dance in his movements. His childhood did not give up; it travelled through all the towns without ever abandoning its grace and unselfconsciousness. And it was his childhood, buried deep in his heart, that had spurred him on until he left the towns and turned to the mountains. Despite all his efforts to become adult, something inside him resisted it; he could not make his mind once and for all to enter that adult world ruled by work, efficiency, duty and responsibility. So he slipped away quietly, irresolutely taking refuge in unspecified time. He kept saying, 'Soon, soon, I'm going to end my great holiday and go back to my country and start work.' And he accompanied these imprecise words with an even vaguer gesture.

The mountains for him were the last stage before the end of his everlasting holiday. And that is why he gave himself up to them body and soul, with stubborn passion, as though he had to drag to the top of its highest peaks that ineradicable childhood that was preventing him from becoming fully adult. Up there, in the perpetual snows, he would lay down his own childhood, and surrender it to infinity, to eternity. Dormition. Up there, between ice and sky, where the ice never melts, where the sky remains always an intense, pure blue. Up there, amid perfection, in the silence and stillness, he would lay down his childhood and commit it to the mountains. He wanted to conquer the dormition of his childhood. Afterwards he would come back down among men, and mingle in the crowd; he would go back home and start work.

Ballerina did not like the mountains. Deep down, she was jealous of them. What was it about these rocks and ice, this witch with sharp shoulders and flat sides, that so enchanted Jason? He seemed to become day by day ever more spellbound by them. Ballerina could not understand that when Jason got kitted up to go climbing, it was his own childhood he was girding himself with. All that she could see was that he was going away from her. Then she directed into her music the obscure and terrible jealousy eating away at her heart. She put into her playing all the violence of her offended love, as if trying to find through the fantastic sonority of her instrument the true expression of her disturbed passion, and to relieve it.

3

But the summer that she came to Blackland to see her family again, and introduce Jason to them, she felt happy and unburdened of her jealousy. She did not want to stay at Upper Farm. She remained in the village with her Uncle Thadée, and found young Nęah there, in her unchanging gracefulness. Nęah's smile was so luminous, it not only lit up her own face but also the faces of all those around her. She was imbued with the beauty of the stars and the radiance of the moon, as if her father had engendered her from his seed mingled with star dust. With her, and with Thadée and Tsipele, Ballerina rediscovered that same peace the three of them had already given her in the past. Their presence, their true and strong sense of happiness comforted her, who was incapable of experiencing anything without doubts and anxieties. But it was not with star dust that her father's seed had been mingled to beget her, but with tears. And those tears still flowed in her blood, upsetting her too fretful and fearful heart at the merest trifle.

During that summer she also saw a lot of Chlomo who had recently turned to the village and opened a shop, too. He had become a clock-maker, but while his job consisted mostly of repairing watches and clocks, his passion was to invent new machines for measuring time. Among his numerous creations he had created a clock that was particularly beautiful in its austerity: it was black, grey and ivory in colour, and there was something terribly inflexible about the advance of its slightly stumpy-shaped hands that stubbornly kept pointing back to an earlier time, like fish swimming against the current to reach the waters upstream where they were spawned, in order to reproduce there and perpetuate their species. This clock measured what had been Chlomo's parents' time, their time that was broken off in mid course. Seeing it, Ballerina was reminded of the remarkable female figure standing in the background of the spandrels dedicated to the Virgin on Strasbourg's cathedral – the figure representing the Synagogue, paired with another symbolizing the Church. One stood with an ineffable mixture of pride and anger in her whole body, the other in an attitude of glory. A blindfold covered the eyes of one, while the other's brow was graced with a crown. The blindfolded figure held in one hand a broken stave that pointed up the intricate lines of her lovely arched body, and a parchment in the other hand; the crowned figure held the sceptre of power. But the blindfolded figure with the anguished body expressed such power, will and distress that Ballerina's attention was always drawn to her rather than to the other. And the blindfold seemed not so much to signify blindness as to suggest alternative sight; in fact there was a kind transparency about the blindfold, and detectable beneath it were eyes that remained wide open, regarding the world with an indomitable gaze that was both gentle and untamed in its sadness. This statue's hips were caught in the same movement as those of a fisher woman drawing in her nets, pulling them out of the eddying current. It was her crumpled parchment that she was thus rescuing from oblivion, for there remained things to read, to read and understand, in this text discarded by the other woman crowned in glory who seemed to triumph at her side.

Chlomo loved Ballerina. He felt more closely bound to her than to any other person, even his sister Tsipele. He could not have explained the origins of this attachment that had come into being at Ballerina's birth, and even before her birth. In all these years when they lost sight of each other, he had never stopped thinking of her. And now he was seeing her again. She was eighteen, in the first full bloom of her beauty, and she was madly in love with another man. She was even more beautiful for being in love. Her dark purple eyes took on mauve reflections when she laughed while talking to Jason; her step became more supple, her body more graceful when she walked at his side.

But the way that all the Peniels had of throwing themselves with reckless abandon into love, as though into an abyss or a burning fire, was completely alien to Chlomo, and the terror of loss and pangs of jealousy were equally unknown to him. He loved Ballerina even in her passion for another, and he felt no jealousy towards Jason. Actually, the three of them got on so well, they liked to spend their evenings together. They would meet in Chlomo's shop when he finished work, and stay there talking, and sometimes remaining silent, too, musing amid the sound of the countless clocks that hung around them. They ate supper together, then drank wine, beer or rum. Jason preferred bourbon and always brought a bottle of Four Roses to put a bloom in the glasses at the end of every evening.

Jason talked a great deal then, in his fluid, lilting voice. He talked about all the books he had read, all the towns where he had lived, all the people he had met, and those lakes that had charmed his childhood. And about the mountains, too. About the mountains especially, he had a great deal to say. Then he would wave his hands about, sketching vertiginous summits in the air, peaks glinting with ice, vast, smooth expanses that were all the more alluring for offering less grip. He evoked the silence that reigned at high altitude, even more radiant than the ice-encrusted rocks. Silence, brightness and solitude. And the blue, that icy blue of absolute pureness, of the sky stretched out between the ragged mountain-crests like a sheet flapping in your face, depriving you of sight. For there was a constant duel between the body and what the eyes could see, the body always wanting to climb higher than the eyes could see, to exceed the limits of vision.

Ballerina talked about her music. Sometimes she brought her cello and played for Jason and Chlomo.

As for Chlomo, he never spoke about himself, or the childhood from which he had been so violently wrested, or his recent past, when he had travelled. He preferred to tell stories.

Yet Chlomo once happened to betray his feelings, but only Jason noticed. One evening, made drowsy by the confused murmur of the clocks and by the alcohol she had drunk, Ballerina dozed off, with her head resting on Jason's lap. Chlomo watched her sleep; he gazed at her hair tumbling down Jason's legs. And desire had suddenly seized him by the throat like a sob. To escape this moment of panic, he drained his glass of bourbon in one, and launched into an absurd story that he made up as he went along. A story without an ending.

One fine day a woman broke an hour-glass – out of clumsiness, or anger, or even perhaps impatience at the slowness of time, he could not really say. And there was no end to the amount of sand that was spilled. Night and day, week after week, the sand poured out like blood from a wound that nothing could close or heal, and it covered everything. The sand buried the town, then the countryside and all the villages around, and the rivers and ponds, and the hills and forests. The whole country was transformed into desert. An infinite desert of white, ivory-coloured sand of very fine and smooth grains. And the woman walked barefoot through the desert, on and on, without end, sowing in her wake the traces of her footsteps. As there was no wind the footsteps remained there. And one day these countless footprints set off walking on their own. They wandered all over the place, roaming the whole desert, until they completely covered the entire expanse. Then the woman stopped, not daring to trample on them.

And there Chlomo stopped. His story did not lead anywhere. He did not even know what he was talking about. His ridiculous story had not even taken his mind off Ballerina. His eyes remained riveted on her, on her tumbling hair, on her lips. He poured himself another drink. Jason did likewise and, emptying his glass, tried to keep the story going. He suggested that woman began to blow, to blow very hard, without pause, then the footprints blew away like clouds of may-flies, and soon disappeared, after which the woman set off again. But towards what, he did not know.

Ballerina, opening her eyes, but with her head still resting on Jason's lap, took over. Her idea was that the woman started crying. And these tears flowed just as the sand had flowed, endlessly, thereby washing away all the footprints, then the woman was able to continue on her way again.

Chlomo, half-drunk by now, grew irritable and declared that the woman had neither blown nor wept, but bled, and that each drop of blood as it hit the ground had turned the footprints into desert roses. Roses so red, red with the woman's blood, that the sand had caught fire and the whole desert had gone up in flames. And the woman, too.

Jason intervened and said that the desert roses did not burn at all, but began to proliferate and build up into a crystal mountain that the woman climbed with her bare hands and feet.

'But in that case,' said Ballerina, 'the woman will cut herself and bleed again, and the desert will catch fire, and the story will never end.'

'Of course it will,' shouted Chlomo, his eyes now fixed on the label of the empty bottle, whose four little roses danced in his eyes like fireflies. 'I'll make the woman start walking again, and come out of the desert, and in order to achieve that I'll hurt her more than the flames if necessary . . .'

'But you don't enter into it,' Ballerina told him, 'it's a story and you've no business being in it.'

'No, he's right,' said Jason, 'since we're inventing the story, we can do what we like.'

'Anyway, it's a stupid story,' said Ballerina, already dozing off again, with Jason's hands resting on her hair. She smiled faintly in her sleep.

Chlomo began to smoke. His features were drawn; his eyes could not settle. Jason very quietly withdrew his hands and stuffed them in his pockets: he had understood. Chlomo's heart suddenly became transparent to him. A heart assailed by a love that was no more going to lead anywhere than the absurd story he had started making up a moment ago. But was there any way out for himself either, he wondered. Had he not always been looking for one in order to free himself of his childhood? And then love, too, was just a story, so often crazy, and sometimes very painful. But while Jason had claimed that you could intervene in the stories that you invented, he was much less sure that you could intervene in love. The heart, to be sure, was a lonely hunter. A blind and stubborn hunter, sometimes to the point where it went mad. A ridiculous hunter that sometimes went so far as to kill itself.

They stopped talking, and remained there in silence until dawn. All three of them: three hunters devoured by their own quarry.

Ballerina spent as much time with Chlomo as she spent avoiding her own brother. When they saw each other again after so many years they found almost nothing to say to each other. They stood there face to face, in oppressive silence, with a terrible bitter taste in their mouths. What could Night-of-amber-Wind-of-fire have told her? The six years he had spent in Paris were reduced to just a few days. Those few glaring days centring round Roselyn, the friend he had betrayed and sent to his death, and this crime put everything else into the shade. Roselyn's mouth crammed with the sickening sugariness of sweets made wet with tears, sweat and saliva dried Night-of-amber-Wind-of-fire's lips into silence. That mouth sealed with the sugar of death compelled secrecy. Words had got limed in the stickiness of boiled sweets, all speech had sclerosed and could not be articulated. And he dared not look his sister in the face for fear that she might see in his eyes the reflection of Roselyn's terror as he died.

But Ballerina had no more to say than he did. Her brother had no understanding of music, and as for Jason, she stubbornly refused to talk about him. She was too well acquainted with her brother's jealousy, from having suffered it all through her childhood, and from her own experience of this same sickness she was now suffering. In this they were too alike: both were only capable of loving to an extreme, in fear and jealousy. So they remained close-lipped about their experiences, tensed in silence, one suppressing his shame, the other her love. Night-of-amber-Wind-of-fire did not even tell his sister about all the letters he had written to her, all those words he had dedicated to her like so many calls for help and songs of love. Like so many frantic kisses. Nothing of them remained. The letters had burned, the words disappeared, the calls were lost and the songs had fallen silent, choked in a cry. And the kisses had fallen into the void. The void of a love that had never truly existed. So now there was a great unease between them.

Ballerina went once to visit old Night-of-gold-Wolf-face, over at the Three Spell-bound Dogs. But this man who was her grandfather inspired her with an even more powerful sense of unease than her brother. Basically, she knew nothing about him but the local legends that had grown up around him. When anyone came to see him, he would sit very upright facing his visitors, but hardly spoke at all. His mouth remained stitched up by the word that had pierced his heart more than quarter of a century ago already: Sachsenhausen. His ripped and stitched-up mouth.

Indeed, to which world did this man, soon to be one hundred, belong? It was not very clear whether it was that of the living or the dead. Time acted on him in a strange manner. It took its toil on his heart and memory, but seemed to spare his body. He still stood his ground as firmly as ever, and not a single white hair had sprouted in his brown mop. He spent the whole day walking in the woods – what he did there, no one knew. And his shadow went with him everywhere, unfailingly light and dancing. It was said locally that he spoke to his shadow and that his shadow answered him. Some even described having heard moans from his father's seven tears that he wore round his neck as white droplets on a string. Or perhaps it was the soul of the wolf whose utterly shabby pelt he always wore on his shoulders that would start whining like that on certain nights?

Mahaut and he lived together like two strangers. But they had thrown in their lot together and remained under the same roof like two pillars supporting a common loneliness. If one were to go off, this loneliness would have collapsed, unbearably exposing their absence from the world. With them lived their two sons, September and October. These two sons, old Peniel's last-born children, had to raise themselves, in the shadow of the great beeches. In the shadow, above all, of their mother's madness. But one found his way to brightness, while the other buried himself in the deepest area of gloom.

September and October built a greenhouse near the house. At first it had only been for fun, then their fun had grown into a job for them. The greenhouse expanded; they cultivated flowers, fruit and vegetables, which they went and sold in the village. But only September went to the village. October could not bear the presence of anybody, and the sight of strangers terrified him.

When Night-of-gold-Wolf-face came home from the woods in the evening and saw the figures of his sons against the light in the greenhouse, he thought he could feel the shadow walking in his footsteps begin to tremble almost imperceptibly, as if something very ancient, buried very deep beneath the ruins of his memory, had suddenly surfaced in his heart again. Something from the time when he was not yet entirely a land-dweller, when he was a fresh-water traveller. Something from the time when he was a child, gliding slowly on the Escaut, between the total distress of his father and the extreme goodness of his grandmother, Vitalie. The greenhouse erected by his sons, this long and fragile glass structure standing so lightly on the ground, reminded him of his ancestors' barge. The same drifting in stillness, the same dreaminess, flush with the sky, the same complicity with solitude and silence. A like sweetness, too. But he would immediately turn away and trudge off, removing his shadow and mind far away from all nostalgia, for any remembrance of sweetness caused untold pain to his heart buried under stones of grief. And it was at those times, perhaps, that the strange moans began to emanate from his father's tears hung round his neck.

And it was true that sweetness hovered round that house of glass inhabited by a solely vegetal world. No noise, no agitation. A haven of calm and light for the two brothers, where they could forget the terrible shadow of their mother locked up in her past. There, among the plants, a damp and gentle, almost silky, silence reigned. A palpable silence, laden with innumerable fragrances. There, the two brothers spoke to each other in an undertone, as if afraid to disturb the sweetness of the place, and the slowness of time.

Then the sweetness of this place began to glow in the evening, lending a lunar brightness to the light in the greenhouse. And it was not just Night-of-gold-Wolf-face who felt a mysterious lump in his throat, like a sob of tenderness, at the sight of this glow; all those who saw it felt a curious pang in their heart as well. For Chlomo, this glow was like a pause in time, a comma, slowing the too rapid passage of time. A milky-coloured comma made of glass, suspended in the evening's opacity. And Heart-breaker saw it in the same way, now that he had learned to see the world, and men, and things, afresh, with new eyes, for he now saw the world reflected in little Fé's eyes. This brightness shone for him, too, like a comma marking a pause in time's frenzy, moderating its violence – and not like that chill, sharp-pointed crescent moon that he had seen one night during the war, in an Arab village, shining down from above on the pale and mutilated bodies of his eleven companions. That husk of moon petrified in the dark night of war had blinded him at the time, and armed his heart and hands with hatred and revenge. But the brightness of this glass, showing through the evening, now gave him a deep sense of peace.

But everyone took pleasure in beholding this glow from a distance, in vaguely dreaming as they passed by, without daring to climb up to the greenhouse and go and talk to the brothers working there. Besides none of the other Peniels really knew the two youngest sons of Night-of-gold-Wolf-face. From the time they were born, their mother had so resolutely kept everyone away from her house and her offspring that no one had since been minded to try to bridge that distance.

Yet there was one woman that came. One evening she saw the light through the trees and walked straight towards it. Without fear or hesitation. She was barefoot and wore a simple dress made of coarse cloth, like a hospital gown. Her skin was brown, the colour of earth in the bed of furrows. Her thick curly hair fell untidily on her shoulders and over her brow. She was constantly chewing the ends of strands that she twisted round her fingers. That was how she came into the greenhouse. She entered so quietly that September and October did not hear her. It was only when they were about to leave that they noticed her. She was standing in a corner of the greenhouse, with her head slightly tilted over one shoulder, her eyes lost in space. As soon as they moved towards her, she took fright and huddled among the pots of plants surrounding her, tucking her head between her shoulders and throwing her hair over her face to hide it. September leaned over her and tried to talk to her. But she did not respond to any of his questions. She just whimpered quietly, desperately chewing her hair and her fingernails. She whimpered exactly like a little puppy. Then September crouched down next to her and began to imitate the sounds she made, but in a calmer tone. After a while she fearfully raised her head a fraction and darted a furtive glance at September through her shaggy hair.

He smiled at her. She gazed at September's smile for a long time, first with mistrust, then with surprise, and finally with curiosity. Two steps away from them, October did not move and did not say anything. He watched the woman with bated breath. She finally looked up, and modulating her strange whimpering in a questioning way, she began to play with her lips, then gradually removed her fingers from her face and timidly reached out her hands towards September's mouth until she brushed his lips. He surrendered his lips and then his face to the woman's groping fingers to be explored, she mumbling all the while. When he thought she had grown sufficiently trustful, he in turn moved his hands towards her face and very slowly uncovered it, lifting aside her hair, then touched her lips. And she smiled against his fingers. Then she grabbed September's two hands and closing them round her face, she fell asleep.

She fell asleep with her face locked in September's palms, and he dared not move. Neither did October, who stared at the woman, with his heart pounding. And they remained there till morning, watching over her slumber. But it was in both their hearts that she slept.

The woman stayed. The two brothers arranged a place for her at the back of the greenhouse. Since she could not speak and they did not know her name, September named her Gentle, with such incredible gentleness had her brown hands with their pink nails and palms rested on his lips and body. But everything about her was gentle: her skin, the looks she gave and her childlike smiles, her soft mumblings, her gestures and her walk, her breathing and her sleep. They hid her among the plants and told nobody of her strange arrival in their midst. It did not much matter to them to know exactly who she was, or where she came from. Where she had run away from, dressed in a simple hospital gown. What did matter to them now was that she should stay with them, among the fruits and flowers and shrubs, and blend her silence with that of the greenhouse, and the spicy smell of her skin and her hair with that of the damp warm earth and the scent of the plants and their sap.

Neither of the two brothers managed to teach her to speak. They would no sooner begin to formulate a phrase than she laid her fingers on their mouths as though to follow the sole movements of their lips and not the meaning of their words. So it was she who taught them her language, the language of her fingertips, all touching and caressing. The language of a very small child, constantly feeling the faces and bodies of others. Her language was gentle, dizzyingly so. And their language became that of desire. A vertiginous desire.

And they were overwhelmed by this desire. One evening September stayed behind with Gentle. And he made the discovery of an even greater gentleness than that of her skin so soft and brown. He discovered the gentleness of her flesh, a deep gentleness, like a burst of night mingled with day that opened up to the greatest pleasuring, inside the body. He discovered the moist rosiness that quietly sings beneath the flesh. That sings so quietly, no one hears it without momentarily losing their mind. He discovered the pitching of gentleness into throes of tenderness, and the very suppressed murmur of the blood, with its flow of glistening liquid fires, like a torrent of lava.

October also loved Gentle, and he, too, made the discovery of her body, the hollowness of her mouth-body. He plunged into her as one might sink into the deepest oblivion, as if trying to bury himself inside her, and lose there for ever, the alien voice that came to haunt him every autumn on his birthday. That terrifying voice cast upon him like a spell, like a curse, by his crazy mother. His mother, whom he hated. If ever she had dared to venture into the greenhouse, he would have driven her out under a hail of stones, or dragged her out by the hair. He would have killed her. For she would have been quite capable of bewitching Gentle as she had bewitched him, and destroying the fabulous silence that prevailed in her in order to introduce the terror of that blasted voice. But Mahaut never made so bold as to visit her sons' greenhouse. What they might both be doing there was of absolutely no interest to her. She might never even have noticed the greenhouse.

★

Inside the greenhouse there was an efflorescence of plants and flowers, and an inward blossoming of Gentle's body. She was amazed to see her belly ripen like the fruits; she was panic-stricken when something began to move inside her, kicking out in fits and starts. She gazed anxiously with her childlike eyes at September and October, reaching her hands towards their faces as though seeking from the touch of their lips a response to her disquiet. She did not understand. Only September was capable of reassuring her; October only aggravated her distress, so disturbed was he himself by this pregnancy, as though it was not a child that was going to be born but a monstrous voice that was building up a deadly cry in Gentle's entrails. He did not go near her any more; he was even more scared than she was. September stayed with her and calmed her fears, but he failed to calm those of his brother.

'It's me,' he said, 'I'm the one who brought this blight on her – the blight my mother inflicted on me. That's what's growing inside her: the voice; it's the flood-voice ... the same voice is swelling and mounting inside her, and it's going to tear her apart, and destroy her ...'

Nothing could make October see reason, so much did the voice that took possession of him once a year terrify him. He dreaded its climax months before it came, and then remained ill and exhausted for weeks on end afterwards. And with every passing year the return of the alien voice left him more and more devastated. He could not bear the idea that Gentle should have to suffer this, too, because of him.

Gentle gave birth in the autumn, to a little girl. The mulatto child with her honey-coloured complexion was so beautiful that September named her Wonder. But from the day she gave birth, Gentle was never the same again. She kept to a corner of the greenhouse all the time, and rejected the child. She even rejected September. And at night she dug the earth. She dug without respite, with her hands, like an animal burrowing into the soil to hide itself underground. The child's least prattling alarmed her, as if it might put her own life in danger. The quietness and brightness of the greenhouse that had attracted her when she was on the run were no longer adequate. The birth of this little girl, like a miniature, lighter-shaded double of herself, that was always making a noise, sometimes gurgling, sometimes crying or yelling, had thrown her into total panic. It was as if her own voice that she had for years condemned to silence had wrested itself from her womb, and this banished voice that day by day gained in strength was going to turn against her and take revenge on her. So she had to find some other place to stay, not further away but deeper. For that reason she had to dig. And she dug, and dug interminably, with her bare hands.

She was seeking peace, peace and silence, underground, in darkness. In burial. She wanted to attain total silence. She had to escape any noise, quickly, quickly. And she did. She dug so deep into the earth that she crept down there like an animal into the bottom of its burrow, and disappeared. No matter how deep they dug after her, they never found her. She had plunged into the darkest recess of the earth, and filled her mouth with dirt and silence.

She disappeared the day when the voice that visited October was making its return, as inexorably as the rising waters of the Tonlé Sap reverse their flow. But the onsurge of this voice promised to be so violent this time that October could not bear to have to endure its fury again. When he saw his mother draped in the tattered silk finery and adorned with the extravagant jewellery she invariably wore on this magic date to watch the transformation of her son when the Mekong bestowed its gift on him, and heard her calling him in her strident voice to come and closet himself with her in the sacred room where this ritual always took place, he was seized with such terror, and even more with such anger, that grabbing a pair of secateurs he cut off his tongue and threw it at his mother, like a slap in the face. A bloody slap. Then, with his bleeding mouth distorted in pain, he collapsed in a heap on the ground, banging his forehead on his mother's little feet in their embroidered, black-silk slippers.

NIGHT OF THE ANGEL

1

Night-of-gold-Wolf-face had never celebrated his birthday. In fact he did not know the precise date of his birth. It was some time after the war in which an uhlan had struck his father's forehead with a sabre. He was born of a wound. A war wound. That was a long time ago. But war wounds, like the wounds of love, never completely heal. And perhaps Night-of-gold-Wolf-face was actually born of that double wound. Of war and love.

However, one day he knew that he had lived for a century. He felt it in his body. He was suddenly aware in his flesh of the tremendous burden of one hundred years. Darkness was about to fall on the earth, although it was still early. It was the middle of winter and freezing cold, so cold that night that the sky was turned to stone. It loomed overhead like a gigantic sheet of gleaming black slate, dotted with thousands of tiny stars like little golden tacks. Night-of-gold-Wolf-face sat in a high-backed armchair covered in slightly faded clay-coloured fabric, watching the twinkling stars through the window. They were innumerable, and striving not to let his attention become totally dispersed, he fixed his gaze on one of the countless stars, thereby to keep in check the dizzying sense of emptiness that haunted his heart and soul. But all of a sudden he saw the star he had picked out come shooting towards him and move even more swiftly the other way, receding into the night, both in one and the same motion.

He stood up with a hollow cry, a hoarse and abrupt exclamation of amazement. Detached from its vault, piercing the darkness and ripping through space in two opposite directions, the star had just struck him right in the heart. It had struck him like a short sharp click of the heels; the heels of a young girl stamping the ground to give dash and rhythm to her dancing. But then who was it, in his heart, that was getting to her energetic little feet and beginning to dance?

'And now I'm going to dance barefoot . . .' His heart pounding, Night-of-gold-Wolf-face thought he heard a voice murmuring these words, the voice of a very young and breathless girl. At death's door.

The girl who said this had been dancing barefoot with death for a century. His sister-mother, who died giving birth to him.

Night-of-gold-Wolf-face had just felt this sharp blow strike his heart and indistinctly heard this murmuring when he was seized by the shoulders. Gently, firmly. It was his shadow, his faithful light shadow that had just wrested itself from the ground and risen to stand very upright behind him; its hands were laid forcefully on his shoulders. He heard the shadow say to him, 'Off you go! Go out now. Go and meet them; they're waiting for you.'

This shadow wrested from his body and standing behind him had Vitalie's voice. The tender, urgent voice of his grandmother Vitalie.

'Go, go!' said Vitalie's voice, setting the rhythm to which Night-of-gold-Wolf-face walked. He walked on, with the shadow, lighter than ever, following, pushing his shoulders from behind, sending him along the road leading to Dead-echoes Wood. Before starting out, he girded himself with a broad leather belt with a bronze buckle, as one might saddle a dray horse, so steep and difficult was this walk in the frosty night. So hard-going was it to haul the weight of his years.

He walked towards his past. He climbed towards his memory. Step by step backwards through his life. The life of a hundred-year-old man. And his footsteps were so heavy on the frozen ground, in the silence of the night, they cracked like whips. The night carried the echo of those cracks a long way; the cold intensified the echo. The sky quivered like a glass pane at his passing. The night, in its totality, resonated and cracked. And he climbed the hillside, panting, his brow straining forward. His breath blossomed in the frozen air into clusters of white mist, leaving what looked like a long hedge of light, transparent lilacs bordering his path all the way behind him.

Yes, he advanced with his neck straining, breathing hard, like the thick-set tow-horses of his youth, on the Escaut's banks bordered with birches, willows, elms and white poplars, drawing the dark family barge from lock to lock. From town to town. The barge which his father had named 'Wrath of God'. But that night it was not God's wrath that burdened Night-of-gold-Wolf-face's body as he walked; it was God's distress. No, not God's, man's distress. Just man's distress.

He entered the wood, plunging into it without slowing his pace. The snow was thick and frozen. His shadow was hurrying him along. He did not feel the cold. The cold ran in his blood, in his bones. It was pitch black but he could see every detail of the ground – fallen branches, protuberances of knotty roots, stones, and animal tracks. The night was in his eyes; it was his eyes. He continued until he came to the clearing. To the place where a spring welled up at the foot of a rock. But the spring was frozen and the rock spiked with translucid ice-crystals.

This was the spring that had bubbled up under his neck almost thirty years ago, when he was a man overwhelmed by the revelation of an essentially unpronounceable name, at the end of a war that proved to be the end of a world. Overwhelmed by the revelation of one of God's many names: Sachsenhausen.

A spring of tears shed by the earth over-traumatized by man's violence and cruelty; in fact no beast in this wood ever came to drink from it, as if by instinct the animals sensed the near-lethal bitterness of the spring.

This was the spring that had opened up, like a lock's heavy gates of oblivion, on the expanse of a world turned to desert, on that long-ago night when not even death would have him.

⋆

He was alone in the heart of the wood all muffled with snow, beneath a dizzyingly high and dark sky. A purple blackness, speckled with gold, that cast vague mauve reflections on the snow. The air was so pure, the least twig breaking beneath its crust of ice like a glass fibre could be heard perfectly for miles around. There was no other sound. Just the crash and splintering of dead wood. The whole forest seemed made of glass. He was alone in the silence of the crystallized forest. Excessively alone.

And yet he knew in a flash they were there. All of them.

All waiting for him.

His family. All his family he had so dearly loved. Who were no more. They came towards him, invisible and silent. They came in a circle, all around the perimeter of the clearing. Moving stealthily. Very indistinct against the snow, slender white shadows slipping among the trees.

'You see! You see!' Vitalie's voice kept saying again and again. A voice of mourning very softly lamenting the absent.

But there was nothing to see but a few mauve-tinted white shadows in the starry night, cast on snow harder than polished metal. There was nothing to hear, not even the slightest rustle. Nothing but those splinterings of dead wood, those creakings of bark, on the bodies of trees perished with cold. More and more distant.

'You see!' Vitalie's reedy voice repeated once more. 'You see, I kept my promise, my shadow never left you. Do you remember what I told you the evening when we parted, though our hands remained joined among the potato peelings? Tell me, do you remember?'

'I remember that in morning you had gone,' replied Night-of-gold-Wolf-face.

'I hadn't gone. My love followed you beyond death, I smiled in your footsteps without ever tiring, even when you were lost in the most extreme darkness of this world. What else did I have to give you but my love, a poor woman's love? But what else could my love have done but attach itself to your footsteps? For my love for you was so great, so vast, that even death is too constricting, and could not contain it. But for the truly poor, everything becomes immense, beyond measure: hunger, shame, sorrow and love, too. The poor are dwarfed by everything; their pockets are empty and their hearts crave as their stomachs do. Do you remember? I told you then: my love embraces the sea, rivers and canal, and countless people, men, women and children. I also said to you: you know, they are all here this evening. I feel them around me. I was talking of our family then, at that time. But tonight it is not just the sea, rivers and canals that carry my love for you, but also the land, forests, wind, animals, roses, paths, streams, wherever you have built your life. Ah, tonight, how many are they, the men, women and children, how many are they beside whom, with whom you have built your life?'

'I can't keep count of them any more, I don't know, I don't want to,' replied Night-of-gold-Wolf-face. 'They have built my life only to destroy it.'

But the shadow grabbed him by the hair, almost with violence, and forced him to raise his head in the frost-vibrant wind. And Vitalie's voice said to him, 'Now open up your memory like a free town, lay your heart wide open like a disarmed town. For you see, they're all here. Coming closer.'

There was still nothing to be seen or heard. Even Vitalie's voice fell silent. Had she even spoken?

There was just a feeling. A feeling on the surface of his skin. A light touch on his veins, tendons and nerves. There was just a feeling, in the total frenzy of his senses. Like a gigantic shiver running through his whole body. In a terrible way.

A pelt.

A man's worn pelt, like a beggar's old overcoat.

Night-of-gold-Wolf-face suddenly realized he was nothing more than a pelt. The large pelt of a man, tanned by many thousand suns, weathered by the cold of hundreds of winters, all incrusted with the earth of four seasons, and lashed by the winds from every horizon. The huge pelt of a man, for ever marked by the kisses and caresses of the five women who had been his wives. A hard pelt toughened in the fires of grief for ever smouldering in the ruins of his heart.

A pelt.

The pelt of a man that still bore the smell of wolf, of earth, wind and water. That still retained the scent of a woman in the crook of his neck, in his palms and armpits, and the flavour of their lips deep inside his mouth. The pelt of a man inscribed by time, engraved by history and wars, illuminated by his love affairs, cut to the quick by his griefs. The pelt of his childhood and games, of work, hunger, thirst and weariness. A pelt with sweat and blood on it, a wrinkled pelt. A man's pelt, unique unto itself, worn to a thread, to raggedness.

A pelt.

A gigantic pelt spread over that body's face and every bone, on that night of frost. Frost and remembrance. A drum skin stretched over the heart's resonance. Of enormous size.

A drum skin on which Night-of-gold-Wolf-face began suddenly to hammer. He threw off his jacket, tore off his shirt, and then, bare-chested, began to beat away.

A pelt.

Of grief and imploration. A wondrous pelt, too, that made the dual poundings of his fists and his heart echo in the night, a night giddy and strident with cold.

But who was beating on his skin like that? Was it his fists, his heart, or else the name of every one of those he had called his own, and that had ceased to be? Who was beating away like that, again and again, on his naked chest, on his heart that rang out like a fantastic gong of bronze?

A pelt.

A pelt of cries.

Vitalie. That was the first name. But it was so tender, so intimate, that it flowed like clear water. Vitalie! And he saw the fabulous smile of the woman who had watched over his sleep in childhood, who had comforted him in his childish sorrows and fears. Vitalie, who had never forsaken him, accompanying him everywhere, at every moment, even after her death. Who had attached her light shadow to his footsteps. Vitalie! This name illuminated his heart.

Then came the light and airy name of she who had given birth to him. Herminie-Victoire. His mother, still so young, his sister-mother. His sister who too soon became his mother, and died in childbirth. Herminie-Victoire. The sister-mother, the child-woman who went dancing off, barefoot, with death, because of her fear of life. Herminie-Victoire. Her name passed over his skin like a breath, making his heart tremble infinitesimally.

Then the name that could not be articulated presented itself. The long-hated name. Hated with such violence. The name of terror and pain. The name he had cried 'no' to. His father's name. No. His father's name a thousand times denied. Many thousands of times cursed. His father's name that had been sliced in two. By the cut of a sabre.

Theodore Faustin.

How that name pummelled and scratched against his heart. How heavy this name was, the name of his father who had drowned in the dark waters of the canal, between the lock-gates.

Night-of-gold-Wolf-face felt a rending of his skin, of his heart. He undid his leather belt and whipped his torso to silence his father's name. But the name kept bellowing inside him.

Like a very round, red ball the name of Melanie bounced against his heart. And it was warm, a name still full of life. It was warm like spilt blood. Melanie's name exploded under a horse's hoofs. But the names of their sons immediately came forth: Augustin and Mathurin. His first-born sons. They traversed his heart together. He saw their faces.

They were young, and smiling. But these faces intertwined, intersected each other. Disfigured each other. And the name of Two-brothers clanged in his heart.

The names of Hortense and Juliette resounded in echo to this clanging, filling his heart with bitter tenderness.

Blanche. The name stole into him, so light, and affecting. But he could not keep a fast hold on it. Blanche's name was as fragile as glass, and only allowed itself to be murmured. Her name slowly dissipated in his heart, covering it with a fine and glittery dusting of frost.

The name of his daughter Margot rang like a bell. Sweet, love-lorn Margot. So beautiful on the morning of her wedding. Margot all adaze in the January sun. Margot so light and lovely on his arm.

Broken Margot. Demented Margot. The Jilted-bride. At this name Night-of-gold-Wolf-face felt a pang in heart, rending it like the lace on the old faded petticoats of his wronged daughter.

His heart winced at the name of Elminthe-Presentation-of-the-Lord-Marie. The one he called Blue-blood. The one whose body resonated in love-making with songs and rhythms, with brassy clashes and stridencies. Blue-blood. This name undulated through his heart like a long ivory fish. And chilled it. Blue-blood! The name shattered in a great cracking of bones.

Night-of-gold-Wolf-face wrapped the belt around his torso. As every name struck at his pelt, he had to tighten the girdle to contain his heart-beats that raced ever faster.

Then came the lightest name of all. Violette-Honorine, his daughter, made radiant by the most obscure grace. This name ran through his heart like a child with no time to lose, leaving in her trail an overwhelming fragrance of roses, unless it was blood.

'I am the Child, I am the Child . . .' she murmured as she ran. But she moved so fast that her name was carried away by that other name she had taken during her lifetime: Violette-of-the-Holy-Shroud.

In the wake of this name followed that of her old companion, Jean-François-Iron-rod. His name went by in a fluttering of bird's wings, a vague echo of dove-song. Jean-François . . . his name was consumed in a blaze of fire, unless it was roses. This name left Night-of-gold-Wolf-face with an immense feeling of emptiness and desolation.

Then, unexpectedly, amid a great dissonance of sound, emerged the names of his three most disaffected sons. His sons with the names of archangels, two of them, who knew no better than to sieze the angels' swords and put them to misuse, destined to be assassins, and the third ending up as a gentle beggar. Michael and Gabriel, soldiers of the devil and mercenaries of the Apocalypse, and Raphael, one of the most beautiful singing voices of the century. But their three names entwined in death bizarrely mingled their songs in a doleful cacophony in Night-of-gold-Wolf-face's heart.

'*Und singt ein Teufelslied . . . Nella città dolente . . . Und der Teufel der lacht noch dazu . . . Lasciate ogni speranza, voi ch'entrate . . . Singt ein Teufelslied . . . hahahahahaha! Dove, ah dove, te'n vai . . . Wir kämpfen . . . wir kämpfen . . . wir kämpfen . . . nella città dolente . . .*'

The name of Baptiste seemed to grope its way forward. His son Baptiste, Crazy-for-her, enamoured, to the point of tears and death, of his fair-haired Pauline with eyes the colour of dead leaves. Their names were bound together in Night-of-gold-Wolf-face's heart. Bound like creepers, brambles, thistles. Bound together, they rolled in the trenches of his heart, where the name of Jean-Baptiste, Little-drum, still resounded; Little-drum, who in his day had announced not so much the return of peace as the sudden revelation of an irremediable disaster. These three names were as sharp as thorns in his heart.

*

There was a silence. A great silence in his heart. And a deeply buried weeping at once began to murmur. The name rose within him like a sob. Benoît-Quentin.

Benoît-Quentin! His grandson with all the tenderness of the world loaded on his back. Benoît-Quentin, the child he had loved most dearly. The most child-like of all the children. Benoît-Quentin, his little prince child.

And another name doubled the sweetness and pain of that name. Alma. A double sob choked in his heart.

Benoît-Quentin and Alma. Their names pealed inside him, in his heart, at his temples. He took his head in his hands. He thought he could see the reddish glow of tall flames dancing on the snow. How the flames danced and danced around Alma's little-girl voice as she sang . . .

'*Sheyn, bin ich sheyn, Sheyn iz mayn Nomen . . . A sheyn Meydele bin ich . . .*'

But the flames devoured the song. Thousands of flames, each crackling with the names of Benoît-Quentin and Alma, lighting up their lovely faces and their eyes huge with love and terror.

There was a cry in his heart. A cry that burst from the utmost tips of these flame-arrows. A cry that the bronze-buckled leather belt could not contain.

For then came the name.

The most beloved name. The name that was beauty, all desire and love mingled together. A name of eternal youthfulness, of eternal passion. The name of his greatest love. The name of eternal distress.

The name of Ruth.

And the sky suddenly turned green, forest green, like the dress she was wearing the day they met in the Parc de Montsouris, the day of their separation in the farmyard.

'*Bin ich bay mayn Mamen, a lichtige Royz . . .*' Alma sang. But everything had been destroyed, burned, and all light repudiated. Mother and children, all of them, had been taken away.

Ruth. The name plunged into his heart with a wonderous taste of woman's flesh, horribly tainted with an acrid taste of ashes. Ruth, Ruth, Ruth! The name screamed in his heart, bled in his loins, lacerated his neck and shoulders. Ruth, Ruth, Ruth! The name fought against the flames, the dogs, the armed men, fought against death. The name did not want to die.

Ruth! The leather belt snapped. Nothing could contain the power of that name. The rent beauty of that name. Night-of-gold-Wolf-face fell to his knees. He began to beat the ground with his forehead. He beat the frozen spring as if he wanted to break the ice, restore the water's thrust and flow, restore Ruth's warmth and life, and restore to their four children their stolen childhood. Sylvestre, Samuel, Yvonne and Suzanne. These four names burned in Ruth's name, as fiery brambles. And shed their petals, as flowers of ash. The four names of his murdered children writhed in the flames, disappeared in smoke. The four cardinal points of the entire human race reduced to ashes. To nothing. How was he to find his way in this world after this?

And he chewed on the ice and scratched at the snow until his mouth and nails were bleeding. The frenzied beating of his heart no longer contained by his belt pounded in the silence of the night. Fit to burst everything. Not only inside him, but outside of him, too. Ruth, Ruth, Ruth! His heart battered the earth with such violence that all of a sudden the branches of every tree in Dead-echoes Wood broke. There was a tremendous cracking throughout the forest.

Night-of-gold-Wolf-face turned on his back, with his shoulders and the back of his neck on the frozen spring, his eyes fixed on the frozen sky. The vertiginously high, dark-green sky bearing over him. Like a windowpane.

A windowpane right above the earth. Who was standing behind that windowpane? Night-of-gold-Wolf-face thought he discerned what seemed like a gaze looking through the sky. An impossible gaze, and yet there it was. Like a blind man's gaze, or the gaze of a lunatic.

Night-of-gold-Wolf-face's heart battered against both earth and sky. He had called up his dead, all of his dead. Had named every one. But there was no end to the roll-call. Seemingly, it could never finish. Yet another name sought to be called up. Another name coursed in his blood, rose to hammer against his heart and brow. But he refused to utter this name, refused even to hear it. This name did not belong to any of his family. This name did not even exist. And yet it caused a tightening of his throat, thoroughly oppressing him in his flesh more violently than any other name. No, he could not, would not grant this name any space, voice, or recognition. For if ever this name existed, it did not belong to any dead person. It was the name of death itself. And Night-of-gold-Wolf-face began to hate this name as never before, even in those times of anguish when he had cursed it. It was no longer a question of cursing, or even denying, but of hating. Hating this name to extinction.

The name of God.

Night-of-gold-Wolf-face could no longer contain his refusal and hatred of this name. A cry pierced his heart.

His cry struck the sky like a stone against a window. The sky came down like a shattered pane of glass, at once inundating the earth with torrential rain. A warm, salty rain, like a man's tears. Even more sorrowful than a man's tears. The tears of a God hated by men.

It went on raining all night. The rain streamed down Night-of-gold-Wolf-face's face, in his eyes and mouth, and all down his half-naked body. It melted the snow, dispelling winter. But this was not weather of any seasonal kind, neither of summer, spring or autumn. This rain was out of season. It was raining tears.

And there was no end to the downpour. Night-of-gold-Wolf-face eventually fell asleep under the silently streaming rain that bathed his face and his entire body.

'I'm going to die,' he said to himself, sinking into sleep. 'I'm in the process of dying. I'm already dead and being washed. It's the great ablution of the dead that I'm receiving, the laying-out of the body. But who then is performing this funeral rite? Which of my children? Which of my wives? Perhaps my own dead are the ones who are washing me like this, before taking me to them?

But he was not dying. He was only falling asleep. A long sleep, silky with rain. His heart at last was calm. His heart was cleansed. The rain soaked his face like mud, slowly transforming it into a mask of clay. Obliterating features and traces.

When he got to his feet again among the dismembered trees, in the water-logged clearing, day was already breaking. The sky was as smooth and pale as the face of someone who has been crying for a long time, for too long. The rain had finally stopped. Night-of-gold-Wolf-face felt amazingly light, as if the rain had purged him of his old age, melted away his hundred years. His very shadow had disappeared. He had even lost his lost shadow. And his father's seven tears no longer hung round his neck. They had dissolved, mingling with the streaming rain.

He went back through the forest, now strewn with branches and split bark, and came out into a vast expanse of fields that extended from the edge of the woods. The fields he had made his own. But it was as if he were seeing for the first time this landscape and the terraced village of Blackland that after so many years had grown as familiar to him as his own body.

Nothing was familiar to him any more, not even his own body. At that moment he felt more unconnected with that place than when he first arrived. Yet the cold, rising, winter sun cast the same metallic gleam on the marshes and frozen ponds as on that long-ago day of his arrival. Right at the bottom of the valley the river imperturbably traces its broad, ash-grey, winding course. The wars had destroyed many of the houses in the villages hereabouts, and even reduced to nothing entire hamlets, roads and fields, but they had not affected the river.

The slow, misty waters of the Meuse flowed on in total indifference to history, to time as measured by men. Once again, for the last time, he recalled what Vitalie had said to him in his youth when she urged him to leave: 'The land is vast and surely somewhere there's a place where you can build your life and your happiness. Maybe it's very close by, maybe it's far away.'

It was here that he had built his life. In this place that was neither close by nor far away. Anyway, close by or far away from what? What or whom was it supposed to be close by or far away from? He gazed at the countryside, the fields, farms and river, without the surprise he had felt on the first day, without the attachment or desire of his days of happiness, without the rancour or nostalgia of his days of woe. He no longer felt anything at all.

This place, like every place in the world, was nowhere. Like every place where the time has come for a man to take leave of himself, of his life and body. Night-of-gold-Wolf-face had reached his term. His life had been as long as his lands were vast, but now it was time to construct his demise. His heart was calm, as impassive as the river flowing down to the sea, where it would lose its course, its own waters and its force. His heart was transparent, washed by that night's long-lasting rain. A silent, long-lasting rain, warm and salty like a man's tears. The tears of a man touched with grace at the extremity of his grief. The tears of a man that perhaps had fallen from the face of God. His heart was so calm, already it seemed not to belong to him any more.

Night-of-gold-Wolf-face began to descend the path he had so slowly climbed the previous day. He walked in a robot-like manner through the landscape that had grown so familiar during the life he had lived as a man, and in that moment had also become just as much a fundamentally unknown landscape, in which he was to meet his death as a man. At some point he stopped. He left the path, went a few steps towards the embankment alongside it, and sat down on the slope. For a few moments more he gazed at the sky where dawn was beginning to turn rosy and birds were beginning to revel, then he lay down across the embankment with his face turned to the ground.

There, in the silence and rosiness of dawn, in the short grass crackling with frost, without a word or gesture, he shed the hundred years he had carried from beginning to end as a beast of burden carries its load. He had carried it with occasional joy and pleasure, often with toil and revolt, always to an extreme degree. He very simply shed it. He lay down, with his forehead and palms resting on the ground, and quietly let his heart stop beating.

That morning, when Mathilde rose and opened the shutters of her room at Upper Farm, she thought the air had a peculiar taste, a salty taste as if the wind was blowing in from the sea. And she found a chilly brightness to the sky, an unusal aspect to the landscape. She remained for a long time at the window, studying the sky and surrounding area, but although nothing had changed in appearance, everything continued to seem strange to her.

'It must be because the snow has disappeared,' she thought, 'after the rain that fell all night.'

But an uncertainty became engrained inside her. She felt troubled and nervous, without knowing why. When she dressed and picked up the heavy bunch of farm keys to hang on her belt, as she did every morning, she noticed that all the keys had rusted, and were now reduced to an orange-coloured cluster of warped and corroded metal. As though stained with old dried blood.

The menstrual blood that she had forced back from her womb and banned from her body since the age of twenty. She hurled the bunch of keys to the ground, away from her, with terrible disgust. For it suddenly seemed to her that these rusty keys she had for so long worn on her hip, in the curve of her groin, were in reality a piece of her own entrails. Her female entrails that she had mutilated out of rage and revenge. A cluster of dessicated ovaries contaminated by anger, a coagulation of bad blood oxydized by hatred. The keys she had kept since her father left the farm, like a sacred symbol of her power in the family home, were suddenly no more than offal. The keys to the rooms, cupboards, chests, barns would not open any lock ever again. She felt immured in her room, her farm, suffocatingly cooped up. Insanely immured inside her body, an old woman's sterile, frigid, mutilated body. Immured inside a heart turned to stone because capable only of an extreme, bitter and jealous love.

She paced round the room with her head clasped in her hands. She paced round like a caged animal. She experienced again the great pain that had seized her in the farmyard the day the soldiers came and put her family to fire and sword, the day when the earth was so hard she could not dig it to bury the bodies of those who had been killed. The day when, at the limit of her ressources, she had lain down on the still-smoking pile of ashes where the calcinated bodies were heaped. But she had pulled herself together, and thrust aside the temptation of despair. That day.

That day, when she had called her father, implored him to notice her, to show some feeling for her. That day, when she had wept in her father's arms.

Her father . . . But where on earth was he? She felt cold, and scared, and much more suffocated than on that day, and her father was not with her. And old Mathilde pressed her hands against her temples, and chewed her lips so as not to burst out crying and sobbing. So as not to call out, 'Father! Father!'

She was just a very old little girl, seized with irrational terror, and a completely frantic need to be comforted in her father's arms.

'Father, father, father . . .' she moaned. But he was not there. He did not hear her. He had never heard her. And here was this bedroom door she could not open! She could not even escape, and go running in search of her father. She was imprisoned in her room. A room of such emptiness, reverberant more than ever before with the absence of her father. An intolerable, unbreathable absence. She was suffocating. Then the sense of suffocation grew so strong in her that she seized a paperknife lying on the dresser and simply cut her throat with it.

Mathilde was buried the same day as her father, old Night-of-gold-Wolf-face, thereby keeping her childhood promise never to leave him, right to the very end. Keeping faith, even to extremity, with the insane love of a stubborn and possessive child for a father with whom she had identified her fate.

2

Every place is a nowhere place, as Night-of-gold-Wolf-face had sensed in the moment of dying. Every place, be it empire or hamlet, is but a place of passage. But people passing through places are engaged in a constant relay, taking over and handing on.

At Beauteous-shade, where, after Night-of-gold-Wolf-face's death, Mahaut lived in even greater isolation than ever before, totally rejected by her son October, himself immured, by a barbarous deed, in self-inflicted mutism, life nonetheless went on. The little girl Gentle had given birth to, before disappearing, grew up. She grew up with the name September had given her: Wonder. And this name grew with her. The world was new to her, and by that very fact renewed itself around her. Her childhood brought back to that place a fresh brightness, a previously unknown joy. September guarded this childhood. He drew from it the strength and patience to guard over his mother and brother as well. Fé similarly dispelled the shadows from Upper Farm. With him, Rose-Héloise, Nicaise and Heart-breaker rediscovered the days' zest and beauty, beyond their trials and tribulations.

Yet another child came to Blackland, arriving one autumn afternoon. It was raining. The metallic-grey car coming up the road that led to Upper Farm was hardly visible in the heavily falling rain.

The car entered the yard. A woman got out, wrapped in a white raincoat and sheltering under a big black umbrella. The countryside all around was so grey, it was as though all colour had disappeared from the earth, washed out by the rain. The world that afternoon was reduced to three cold tones: white, black and grey. The woman walked round the car, took a big suitcase out of the boot, then came and opened the passenger door. A little boy climbed out. His hair was a very pale flaxen blond. He stood with his head lowered, looking sullen, clutching a small canvas bag in his hand. The women bent down and spoke to him, but the child remained with his head obstinately bowed. He finally made up his mind to make a move but refused to shelter under the woman's umbrella. He deliberately walked very stiffly right out in the rain, as if he wanted to show his displeasure, to prove how hopelessly alone he was. The woman climbed the flight of steps, set the heavy suitcase down at the door and knocked. She knocked for a long time, louder and louder, before hearing the echo of a footstep in reply. It was Night-of-amber-Wind-of-fire who opened the door to her. After Mathilde's death he had moved back on to the farm, where he had set up his carpentry workshop. He now occupied the large bedroom, the one that had been Night-of-gold-Wolf-face's and then Mathilde's.

'I'm sorry,' he said as he opened the door, 'I didn't hear you.'

He was all covered with fine sawdust that glistened in his hair. He thought the woman was perhaps a potential client, or simply a traveller who had lost her way in the rain and had come to ask for directions.

'Monsieur Peniel?' said the woman in a hesitant voice.

'Yes, but there are several Peniels in this area,' replied Night-of-amber-Wind-of-fire. 'Which one were you looking for?'

'Charles-Victor Peniel.'

'That's me.'

The little boy, who was still standing in the rain, sulking, started slightly at these words and immediately buried his head even further between his shoulders.

'Well, come in,' suggested Night-of-amber-Wind-of-fire. He had not even noticed the child's presence.

The woman turned to the little boy. 'Ashes!' she called out to him. 'Come here!'

But the child remained where he was, wading in a muddy puddle, getting his shoes and legs even dirtier. The woman had to go back down the steps to fetch him and drag him by the hand to the door.

'Let's go in now,' she said. 'I need to talk to you, Monsieur Peniel. It concerns . . . it's about the little boy, who . . .'

But already she was at a loss for words, unsure of how to explain the purpose of her visit, what to say or where to start.

The child cut short all hesitation, all explanations. He had only to lift his head suddenly and raise his eyes towards the man who had answered to the name of Charles-Victor, 'That's me,' and all explanation was unnecessary. For as soon as Night-of-amber-Wind-of-fire saw the boy's eyes, he understood. What he understood was nothing precise or rational; it was in the nature of a brute, self-evident truth that defied logic. He understood as one struck violently.

The child's eyes were familiar to him. Agonizingly, shamefully familiar. Familiar to the point of insanity. They were large, ash-grey, very pale and luminous. Eyes all wet with rain, as though they had been crying.

Roselyn's eyes.

But in his left eye the child bore the Peniel fleck of gold.

The woman did not need to waste much time in explanation and persuasion. She was a friend of Thérèse Macé. She told Night-of-amber-Wind-of-fire that Thérèse had died barely a month ago. But the illness that eventually killed her lasted more than three years. Three years in which Thérèse had fought back. But when she realized she could not hold out any longer, that the end was near, she asked her friend to take her son, after she died, to the man who was his father. She did not doubt for a moment that Charles-Victor could be found, that he would recognize his own son in this child. That he would understand the boy was even more than his son. And that he would take care of him. She did not doubt it, repeated the friend, who for her part seemed to doubt entirely what she was about and the fulfilment of her mission. But Night-of-amber-Wind-of-fire scarcely listened to her. He gazed at the child, with his evasive eyes, his blond hair dripping with rain, and his hands reddened with cold gripping his canvas bag. He gazed at the boy, feeling prey to a very shadowy emotion that was a mixture of consternation, terror and joy.

The woman went off alone. The child stayed behind. He was named after the day on which he was born: Ash Wednesday. In his name was also contained the colour of his eyes. He kept refusing to meet the gaze of this strange man who was supposed to be his father, and remained with his head farouchely bowed, his fingers tightly clenching his little bag. What use to him was a father, a complete stranger that had been sprung on him, all of a sudden, like a jack-in-the-box? None at all ! There was only one thing he wanted and that was to go home, to Rue des Alouettes, in Nevers, with his mother.

Night-of-amber-Wind-of-fire put the boy in the room next to his. He opened the big suitcase and tidied away the child's clothes and belongings. The boy took no part in this activity, as if none of this had anything to do with him. This was not his home; this was not his bedroom. But he did not let go of his little bag; even at the cost of a beating he would not have let go of it. He answered none of Night-of-amber's questions, and would not even let this man come near him, let alone touch him.

Ashes remained closed in on himself with almost malevolent stubbornness, repelling any attempt to approach him, any mark of affection that the others around him tried to express. He refused to let himself be seduced, into being loved or loving anyone else. Day by day his eyes became less a silvery ash colour and more the colour of lead. He remained huddled like a wounded dog in that incommensurable, unconscionable solitude where his mother's death had cast him. He even refused the friendship of Fé, who also lived on the farm and was a little more than two years younger than him. He would not play with any child; he did not want to open his heart to anybody, or to be comforted. He never cried, as if even to cry might be a betrayal of his mother. He kept his tears inside him, deep at the bottom of his heart, like a secret shared with his mother.

Night-of-amber-Wind-of-fire understood this child he knew nothing about. Between the two of them, there was Thérèse. Thérèse who was now dead. Thérèse whom he had only known for the space of one evening and one night; whom he had loved for the immensity of one night. It was already seven years since then. Thérèse, of whom he had forgotten nothing: her body, so tender; her white skin and heavy blonde hair; her grave voice, dark, green eyes, and mouth. Her mouth, wide and lovely as a wound.

Thérèse in her green shoes walking towards him across the rioting city, walking towards him across the room filled with sea gulls, their cries frozen in sugar and salt . . . walking towards him through Roselyn's absent body. Thérèse in her green shoes who came rushing to find Roselyn. Roselyn who was gone. And in his place his murderer was waiting . . .

Night-of-amber-Wind-of-fire understood this evasive, silent and hostile child as he had never understood anyone else before. He instinctively knew everything about him, his thoughts, grief and rebellion. He rediscovered in him the disaffected child he himself had been; the hurt, forsaken, rebellious child. But Ashes rebelled in silence, he suffered in gentleness. As Roselyn, too, must have done when, as a child, he had endured his mother's piercing cries at the rising of the wind from the ocean.

In everything, both physically and in terms of character, Ashes was like a cross between two opposites, as if he were the result of some obscure combination of two irreconcilable beings. There was in him as much of Roselyn as of Night-of-amber-Wind-of-fire, as much gentleness as violence, as much of the victim as the assassin. But his mouth and the inflections of his voice were those of Thérèse.

Night-of-amber-Wind-of-fire understood this child, blindingly so. To the point where sometimes he could not understand anything at all any more. And this child tormented him day and night. He dared not intrude on the forbidding solitude with which Ashes protected himself, because he could not find the hidden path, the breach that would have led him peacefully to his heart. He failed to win his trust. In fact, Ashes showed greater mistrust and coldness towards Night-of-amber-Wind-of-fire than towards anyone else. For the child hated him for being his father, a father unconnected with his departed mother.

Ashes wilfully treated everyone with formal politeness, even little Fé. He was always very formal with his father. Sometimes he even addressed him in the third person, as if he were not there. And he refused to call him 'papa'. He called him 'monsieur'. This determination of the child to impose unbridgeable distances between himself and other people was so unrelenting that Night-of-amber was increasingly overwhelmed by his impotence to conquer his hostility and rage. And the love he felt for his son was so unhappy, so disquieting, that it sometimes came to resemble hatred.

Night-of-amber-Wind-of-fire's turmoil on account of this grey-eyed child whose gaze kept Roselyn's memory alive like a wound, and whose mouth was a constant reminder of his impossible desire for Thérèse, grew to such pitch that it set him even further apart from the others. He was incapable of asking for help or advice from any of his family, being haunted more than ever before by the thought of his crime. He sometimes thought the child with the grey eyes had only come to persecute him, day after day, with the burden of his crime. And he could not admit any of this to the others. So he remained silent, yoked to this orphaned son by a bond as suppressed as it was untouchable.

But this turmoil meant that the day when Ballerina came back to Blackland he could find neither the words or gestures to greet her.

She returned more than a year after her previous visit, but this time alone. She came without Jason, and without the child they had both so much talked about. She came back, carrying little Lilly-love-lake neither in her arms nor her womb.

Lilly-love-lake, the imagined child who would never come into being. Jason-lack, the excessively vulnerable child who would never be an adult.

Ballerina returned with her arms filled with this dual absence, her body consumed with a dual emptiness.

The seasons had passed, and Jason had not noticed years were going by. 'Soon,' he kept saying, 'soon we'll leave Grenoble, we'll leave France, and we'll go over there, we . . .'

But at the end of every autumn, when he saw nature's dazzling flamboyance slowly fading and winter approaching, he would decide to stay another season. He was like the arctic hares and ptarmigans that change their fur and plumage every winter to match the whiteness of the snow; as soon as the first snows fell, his heart turned white and dazzling, crazed with the new climbs it was going to make.

So, at the very beginning of the previous winter, he headed back up to the high pinnacles. Once again he climbed towards the most pure blue of the sky, towards that supreme clarity and absolute silence of the peaks. Once again he set off to conquer the heights to leave his childhood there. But it was himself he left behind there, not even among the peaks, only half-way up. It was himself that he lost entirely. His companions could never understand by what false move or false step he had lost his grip and slipped. They had suddenly seen him break away from the mountain-side and go plummeting into the void. Reduced to tininess, in the void. Perhaps the false move had not come from him, but from that excessively dreamy childhood that still lingered in his heart, hands and eyes. Perhaps the false move had been caused by the mountain, which for no reason had brutally repelled him from its long ice-face. Or perhaps the mountain had repelled him from its side only the better to gather him up again, to keep him all to itself, and hide him. To bury him in itself for ever, deep in a crevasse.

The mountain kept Jason for months. And all that time Ballerina waited. She waited not for them to find Jason's body, but for Jason to come home alive. For she denied the obvious with all the strength of her passion.

'He'll come back one Monday,' she said to herself in the madness of her wait. 'Monday, the day of Diane, the moon. He'll come back one Monday. Monday once again will be the first day of Jason. Monday, Jason . . . Monday, Jason . . .'

But Diane's chariot passed dozens of times without ever announcing Jason's return. For Jason no longer had anything to do with the passage of the planetary gods that ruled the days of men, but belonged to a completely different category of time.

It was spring when they found Jason's body. It was found intact because it was still trapped in the ice. He was lying on his back beneath a sheet of ice, his face turned up to the sky, his eyes still half-open. But one of his hands was slightly mutilated because the ice did not entirely cover the fingers of his left hand, and his index finger, pointing in the air trying to indicate some invisible point in the sky, must have been eaten by some animal, or had simply rotted. It was missing the last phalange. Only that little stump of blackened finger, emerging from the ice, marked him for dead.

And Ballerina saw Jason. As soon as she heard Jason's body had been found, she set off with the men detailed to recover it. She still refused, more than ever before, to believe that Jason was dead. She went up to brave the mountains for the first time. She was in such a hurry to see Jason again, she was the most agile and swiftest of all. She was unmindful of effort, fear or danger.

She reached the place where he fell. She saw Jason lying beneath the ice, with his half-open eyes that expressed nothing but profound surprise, his beautiful hands with their long slender fingers frozen in one of their graceful gestures. How could she have believed in Jason's death? Why should she have believed in it, when he looked almost as he did on the first day they met, on the other side of a mirror. But he was not holding any book this time, his hands were empty. He was the book. The illegible book.

THE HEART IS A LONELY HUNTER

Totally indecipherable.

And yet, at that moment, everyone's heart was more lonely than ever. But what then was Jason's heart hunting? Where was it hunting? And this time it was she who said, 'Here I am!' She did not say it, she screamed it. Lying on the ice above Jason, covering him with her whole body, her eyes riveted to Jason's vacant gaze, her mouth pressed to the ice that made her lips bleed, and beating the ground with all the strength in her fists, she screamed, 'Here I am!'

But Jason did not reply. Only the mountain returned the echo of this cry, amplifying it out of all proportion, from abyss to abyss.

'Here I am! Here I am! Here I am!'

Her cry broke on Jason's mutilated finger. She did not so much see as hear, in the gesture drawn by that truncated digit, the questioning response she herself had made on the day they met: 'Where?'

'Where?' Jason seemed to ask, the blackened stump of his index finger pointing, in total emptiness, up at the immensity of the sky.

Where? This question was always with Ballerina. Where? Where was Jason? And where her joy and love? Where was her youth? Where was Lilly-love-lake? Where her life and what went by the name of death? What was where? Where was God? Where peace and mercy?

There was nothing there. Ballerina found nothing. She could not understand anything any more. She became imbecilic, completely lacking in intelligence. For her, the blackened stump of Jason's finger pointing up into nothingness had replaced thought. Then she began to wander the streets of the city, looking like a tramp, with the eyes of a whore. She walked barefoot, since she could not bear to wear shoes any more. She needed to feel the ground in direct contact with her skin, otherwise the ground slipped away from beneath her. She looked at men with the totally staring eyes of a madwoman, as if to assure herself that Jason was not hiding beneath their exterior. She hated all men for not being Jason. She allowed herself to be taken by any man who wanted her; she did not care, for now her body was just an object, beneath all feeling, emotion and thought. A discarded object that she wanted to mortify even more.

Then she came back to Blackland. She had nowhere else to go. Blackland was the nowhere she knew best. Jason was no longer there to take her to the shores of the great lakes. Jason was no longer where?

Where? Night-of-amber-Wind-of-fire was the last person capable of providing an answer to such an absurd and overwhelming question. He himself was struggling like a snared animal, caught in the toils of guilt that was all the more destructive for his refusal to acknowledge it. It was with Thadée and Tsipele that Ballerina found refuge, as once before. But the refuge she came to find there was more like the den of a bear going into hibernation than anything else. For she was just a sleepwalker when she returned. She could not hear anyone; she could not even see them, Nęah and Chlomo included. All her attention was distracted, dominated by her obsessive question. Where was Jason, and where was he not? And she herself confused her own presence with Jason's absence. She eventually retired to bed. The question dominated her, body and soul. She then sank into a slumber, to pursue her question through an endless dream. She shut her eyes very tightly, the way she used to as a child, when Night-of-amber-Wind-of-fire led her through the forest undergrowth that was haunted by their dead brother, and she was so scared she did not want to see anything of the terrifying world outside. She screwed her fists against her eyes, as in the past, to fill them with darkness and bursts of colour. And she dreamed.

She needed to sleep. To sleep so as not to lose her wits. To dream so as not to lose Jason completely. She needed to dream so as not to die of Jason's death. Not to die of cold. She needed to dream to save them both from the clutches of the ice, to free them from the mountain.

She began to dream the slow descent of Jason's body from the mountain down to the sea. Streams, lakes, brooks, rivers: this was a tortuous descent, through all the waters between. She brought Jason out of frozen waters into deeper and more colourful, running waters. She brought him into the depths of the most fantastic of seas, into green and blue chasms where shoals of luminous fishes dart, and sea horses dance, arching their slender, pinked tails, and jelly fish float by, with their bodies like bell-jars decorated with long translucid filaments. Into chasms spangled with starfish the colour of sand and sun, among bushes of red and yellow algae, spiral-shaped shells, and mosaics of coral. Into purple-hued chasms planted with vast forests of rock, their boughs bristling with golden nodules and blossoming with wine-dark, pink and orange-coloured anemones.

Actually it was her own body she was gradually wresting from death in this way. It was into the unfathomed depths of the flesh that she plunged, into those zones where the blood was thickest, to find the strength and desire to live. For one last time she took Jason into the closeness and redness of the flesh, into the entrails of the world. She wrested him from the mountain, from the ice. She ruptured the stiffness of death to restore to him amplitude, movement and vibrancy. Since death there was, let this death be anything but immobility. Let it become dancing, floating, swimming, music, verve, walking. Anything but immobility.

She dreamed, so that the question of knowing where

men go after death could steal through all the folds of the earth, even throughout the whole universe. So as to imbue her own flesh and her own blood with the memory of Jason. It was not up to the mountain to keep Jason's body, to mineralize his memory. It was up to her, and none else but her, to transfigure Jason's dead body, to restore to him a sequestered and secret life. She fed Jason on her dream; she fed him on the fabulous intimacy of her flesh. That is why she slept so soundly. It was her lover's dormition. A last sleep shared with Jason.

One evening the conflict that kept worsening between Ashes and Night-of-amber-Wind-of-fire finally exploded. The child once again rejected his attempted approaches by retreating stiffly into a silence made proud through grief. Night-of-amber had stretched out his hand in a gesture of affection, to take the boy up to his room, but the child had turned away with an air of indifference and crossed his hands behind his back. Exasperated, Night-of-amber-Wind-of-fire then violently raised his hand against the child's face in a now threatening manner and shouted at him: 'So you didn't see my hand, eh? But now perhaps you'll see it! Tell me, do I have to hit you before you condescend to see my hand?'

Then Ashes, looking him right in the eye, replied curtly, 'I can see it perfectly well. Can you? It's an ugly hand. It looks like a paddle.'

Night-of-amber-Wind-of-fire was appalled by this response. It was true; he had not seen his own hand, had not noticed how clumsy and grotesque it looked, raised against a child, ready to strike him. Then all of a sudden, the whole evening in which he had delivered Roselyn to his death came back to him in a flash. A flash of searing brightness and clarity. A flash of searing sharpness. He saw his hand at the moment in which it had given Roselyn a push on the shoulder, to shove him all alone into the middle of the whitely lit room, all alone amid the laughter and scorn of the others. He saw his hand, and it put him in mind of a face seen under a harsh light. A face congested with anger, its features drawn into a rictus by its disdain for the other in his pitifulness; its eyes blinded by the need to hurt, humiliate and kill the other, the victim.

He saw the hand the child had just denounced, and in it he saw himself as he was on the evening of his crime against Roselyn.

He let his hand slowly drop in empty space. A chilling sweat clung to his temples. In a hollow voice he asked the child, still rigidly holding the same pose in front of him: 'How much more will you make me suffer?'

And with terrifying calmness, Ashes simply replied, 'Until I stop suffering.'

'Get out of here! Get out of my sight immediately!' shouted Night-of-amber-Wind-of-fire, only just holding back the words, 'Or I'll kill you.' For Ashes had just reignited in him the same fury, the same explosion of black despair as Roselyn had, years before.

The child went up to his room, without paying any further attention to him. And he remained at the foot of the stairs, with his arms dangling against his body and his fists clenched. He was trembling with rage, a rage all the more frenzied for feeling ridiculous and impotent. A hollow rage, whistling with emptiness, and with anger, as stabbing as a stake through his spine.

'How much more are you going to make me suffer?'

The question put to the child came back to him, but expressed in an increasingly shrill voice and directed not just at Ashes but also Roselyn.

'How much more are you going to make me suffer?' The question expanded, extending to everybody: Ashes, Thérèse, Roselyn, as well as his parents, his brother Jean-Baptiste, and Ballerina; and finally himself. Everybody, every single person. And God, too.

He left the house, passed through his workshop, where he picked up a coil of rope that he threw over his shoulder, and went out. Outside the wind was blowing furiously.

★

Darkness was falling. The wind was swiftly chasing cohorts of reddish clouds on the horizon. Night-of-amber-Wind-of-fire headed up towards the forest. He made his way towards the wood known as Early-morning Wood, one of three woods in the area.

'How much more are you going to make me suffer?'

The child replied, 'Until I stop suffering.'

All the others to whom this question was addressed surely had this same sole response to offer. But how could you tell when the dead stopped suffering? How could you tell when the dead stopped suffering from all the harm you had done to them, all the hatred you had heaped upon them? And similarly with the living: how could you free them of their anguish and sorrows? Night-of-amber-Wind-of-fire felt as helpless in the face of Ballerina as in the face of Ashes, and Roselyn, and Thérèse. He had loved his little sister so dearly, too dearly, with a sick and jealous love. And now, confronted with her pain and madness, he was without resource. And he was no more capable of helping this unexpected, unhoped-for son whom he loved with a love consumed with guilt. Basically he had never been capable of loving anyone, least of all himself. Since that mad cry his mother had uttered one evening, destroying his childhood at the age of five, love had sickened inside him. Sickened with fear, anger and jealousy. So sick had love grown inside him, it eventually died. It became warped into hatred. He had never been capable of loving. He had done nothing but destroy. He had rejoiced to see death carry away his parents and, no more capable of understanding friendship than love, he had criminally betrayed a friend. A child had come to him, but not even this had succeeded in saving him, as Fé had saved Heart-breaker.

His heart was lost. His mother's cry had irremediably rent it. He was now over thirty, and his heart was black. Black as the night descending on the earth, stony as the path he was climbing. His heart was arid. Not even filled with fire and brimstone, as in the past. Simply arid. Desiccated with misery. He would never be capable of loving.

He plunged into the wood. The night was cold and damp, with a whistling wind. But this was of little importance to a man who had come to hang himself. He took the rope from his shoulder and set about tying a knot. It was at that moment that the other man appeared. A stranger of the same age as him in appearance, and despite the cold dressed like him in just a shirt. A shirt of thick, shiny, blue cloth, like coarse canvas. A loose shirt that flapped in the wind. He was standing a few steps away, with his back resting lightly against a tree, watching him. When Night-of-amber-Wind-of-fire became aware of his presence, he started in fright, then recovering himself he lashed out angrily, 'Who are you, and why are you standing there, staring at me?'

'It's not for you to ask questions any more,' the stranger calmly replied, 'but for me to do so.' What exactly are you doing?'

'Go away! I demand that you leave me alone,' Night-of-amber-Wind-of-fire said curtly.

But the man replied, 'Do you remember the day when you let fly at God your reed-and-canvas bird, sending it up to pick at his eyes and eardrums? Do you remember that very windy day? It's the same wind blowing tonight. Listen!'

And then the man came slowly towards him.

His face was strange, at once impassive and tense. He came up to Night-of-amber close enough to touch him, and the gaze he kept levelled on him was unbearably strong and direct. Night-of-amber-Wind-of-fire seized the rope like a whip, and lashed the man right across the face. He wanted to split the eyes beneath those eyelids, and destroy that gaze. But the man avoided his attack, and managed to grab the rope, which he threw on the ground. Then he pounced on Night-of-amber-Wind-of-fire like an animal of prey, and wrestled with him.

The wrestling went on all night. They fought without uttering a word, their jaws firmly shut, and their eyes fastened on each other, and this silence made their fray even more violent. They fell and rolled on the ground, locked together, and got to their feet again, still locked together. Panting for breath, with their hearts pounding, they kept on fighting indefatigably. The stranger's strength seemed inexhaustible. The first glimmerings of dawn were beginning to break and they were still fighting. Night-of-amber-Wind-of-fire felt so jaded he had the impression of fighting in a dream. He could not tell where his own body ended and the other's began. The blows he landed on the other's body carried as much through his own flesh. But he kept on fighting.

'It's about to get light,' said the other. 'We must finish now.' And as he said this, he caught hold with one hand of both of Night-of-amber-Wind-of-fire's arms and twisted them behind his back, and with the other hand he seized his head by the hair. Then he kissed him on the eyes. Night-of-amber staggered, suddenly overwhelmed by a mighty sleep, and dropped gently to the ground.

When he woke, it was broad daylight. He was alone. The other had disappeared. Close by, where the other had thrown down the rope before starting to wrestle with him, he found the cast-off skin of an adder, which was long, thin and amber-coloured. Around it buzzed a cloud of large flies of glistening green and blue. But Night-of-amber-Wind-of-fire could not distinguish colours any more. He saw everything – the sky and the surrounding countryside – without colour. The world and its inhabitants were to appear to him from now on only in black, grey and white. The fleck in his eye was no longer a bright flame kindling his gaze and reddening his perception of the world. It was an inverted fire consuming his gaze from within.

3

Every place is a nowhere place, but wherever man settles acquires enormous power.

Three times in the past wars had swept across the area of Blackland. Each time the enemy had changed its uniform, its mount and its weapons, but it was the same disaster. Then, after having so often been declared a sacred casus belli, and as such suffered the fate of a piece of meat torn to bits by famished dogs, this poor stretch of land, lost on the far edge of the country, slowly fell back into oblivion. Into indifference and oblivion. And settled there. History went off to carry its battles elsewhere.

And Night-of-amber-Wind-of-fire, who was born after all these wars, and yet kept fighting against everybody and everything, against his own family and his memory, against the living and the dead, first out of anger and scorn, and then for fun, out of cynicism, and finally out of habit, and also distress – perhaps always out of distress - had ended up waging war as well. The one he spent a whole night wrestling with had defeated him, had quelled all rage and hatred in him. The one he spent his whole life fighting against had subdued him. But this subjugation was not inertia, indifference and passivity, it was still tension, expectation and amazement.

He was amazed by everything, so much did his new vision, deprived of any sense of colour, make everything infinitely strange. This colour-blindness transformed the world and the people around him; it was as though he were discovering them for the first time. Discovering in them, to be precise, the area of emptiness, the density of shadowy zones he had not been able to see before. All matter, whether inanimate or of flesh, appeared to him to have a new texture. He detected by sight the porousness of all matter, as if his vision, deprived of the sense of colour, had, by that very deficiency, become confused with another sense: that of touch.

It was that: for him, the visible became tactile. Whether he was confronted with a landscape, the sky, or other people's faces, he always felt the grain of silence in them, the way you feel the grain of paper. The way you stroke someone's skin. And he felt this so acutely, he was overwhelmed by it. At the same time everything looked incomplete to him. Landscapes and faces seemed washy and sketchy. They revealed themselves to him in a state of incompletion that made them both more fragile and infinitely more amazing, for the lines that defined their shape, the features that structured their faces, showed up as fugitive lines endlessly running away, elastic features, in perpetual movement and metamorphosis. And it was this constant amazement that he experienced in the face of everything and everybody since the transformation of his gaze that opened up in him so much tension and power of expectancy. He could not have said what he was expecting, but he would have been even more incapable of reducing the overkeyed expectancy inside him.

After the evening of their clash, Ashes continued to keep Night-of-amber-Wind-of-fire at a distance, but nevertheless his attitude of defiance slightly relaxed. For the child noticed that something had changed in this father he had found only at the cost of his mother's death, and whom he hated for this reason. Something indefinable had changed in this strange father's gaze, and that carried even into his gestures, his voice and his gait. Something indefinable but radical. The child could see this, and although he did not understand what was really happening, he felt profoundly unsettled by it. For it seemed to him that this enemy-father had thereby suddenly ceased to be an opponent, a rival, that anger had no further hold on him, that no provocation could affect him now. It was as if he sensed, in a very confused way but with all his childish wisdom, that Night-of-amber-Wind-of-fire had suddenly unbent and opened up, and that an unsuspected reserve of tenderness was slowly rising to the surface, into his eyes, hands and lips.

All over his body. And this discreet rise of tenderness that he sensed in his father, day by day disarmed Ashes of his defiance and hatred. But thus robbed of his defences, Ashes could no longer protect himself against the grief he felt for his mother, which he would never express. A frantic grief, far too great for a child's spirit, far too violent for a child's heart. And all the tears he had so long suppressed, so as not to admit the reality of his unacceptable bereavement, welled up inside him, invading his whole being. Then the tears seized him by the throat like two unlockable hands.

One night Night-of-amber-Wind-of-fire was woken by a noise coming from Ashes's room. The noise of stifled sobbing. The child was moaning like a little animal. Night-of-amber rose and without hesitating went into Ashes's room. It was the first time he had entered his son's room since the day of the boy's arrival. He approached the bed where the child lay curled up with his face buried in his hands. The little canvas bag was lying at the foot of the bed, wide open and empty. But there was hair strewn all over the bed, all over Ashes's curled-up body. A woman's hair, rolled up in half-unplaited braids, and all of a slightly different shade of blonde. The boy was crying as he lay there, in the middle of his sheets strewn with long hair, like an injured swimmer cast up by the sea, amid fine, pale seaweed, on the white sand of a beach. Like a drowning child rejected by death.

Thérèse's hair. The hair in which Night-of-amber-Wind-of-fire had buried his face and hands for one whole night. And he remembered how the heaviness and fragrance and softness of that hair had ravished his senses and enraptured his heart. It was his skin that remembered, and his entire flesh became memory.

Thérèse's hair now lying scattered around the child, like dead weeds. And the child remembered that first morning when, entering his mother's room as he did every morning on awakening, he had seen her hair shed on the pillow. It was at the very beginning of her illness. All her hair had fallen out, had regrown and then fallen out again. This shedding of her hair punctuated the onslaughts of her illness, after intervals of treatment. Over a period of three years. When she died she had her lovely hair again, for in the end the extent of her illness was such that the treatment that provoked the hair loss was no longer even prescribed. She died with her flesh consumed by her illness and her emaciated face like a wax mask grown transparent. The child remembered that thin face looking so fragile and naked and lost, cradled in hair that seemed to be smothering it. But that night he went to his mother's body that was laid out in her bedroom, and cut her hair. All of his mother's hair was not to belong to anyone but him, and him alone; he refused to share it with death. He stole his mother's hair from death, and every night he went to sleep in the midst of that maternal hair, which he kept braiding, unbraiding, brushing and kissing.

The child remembered. And this was why he was crying – at having to remember. For children's memories are not meant to recollect, to look back on the past and become fixed in that attitude. Their past is far too meagre, too brief and searing, and their memory is a forward-moving force, wide open to the future. Children's memories are meant to skip through the days' unexpectedness as though playing a game of hopscotch. So time was twisted out of joint in Ashes when his memory was suddenly and so prematurely arrested.

He cried, curled up with the hair, the many fair traces his mother had left behind. He sobbed all alone, in the middle of a circle drawn by the hair that death had rendered scentless and silent. He moaned in the core of his fractured and exploded memory.

Ashes, Roselyn, Thérèse: these three became confusing, calling on each other. At that moment Night-of-amber-Wind-of-fire felt he was no more than a conduit, a sound board. He sat on the edge of his son's bed and bent over him. For a long time his hand hovered over the child's head, then slowly came to rest on it. Ashes gave a start, but did not push away the hand that gently stroked his hair. This hand stroked him as gently as his mother's, when she used to come and kiss him in bed at night, before turning out the light, to send him off to sleep more easily. This hand was like his mother's. And his sobbing gradually ceased, and at last murmured in a voice choked with grief, and equally with a sudden burst of insane hope: 'Mama?'

And poised where the voices of the living and the dead converged, Night-of-amber-Wind-of-fire replied, 'I'm here.'

He was there, totally present for his son, and totally loving. He was there, father and mother in one. And Ashes was there – Ashes and Roselyn in one. Then Night-of-amber lay down beside the child, and hugging him in his arms he repeated, 'I'm here. Go to sleep now, go to sleep, my little one.' And he slept, too, with the child held close to him. In the morning when he woke, he saw Ashes sitting cross-legged beside him on the bed, with all the hair gathered in his lap like a bundle of hay. The child looked at him. And his gaze was calm and direct. For the first time his eyes did not evade him any more, were not defiant. Night-of-amber-Wind-of-fire smiled, and the child smiled back, for the first time. A rather timid smile, like Roselyn's, but one that lit up his eyes with such a radiance that their greyness took on a silver hue.

And Ashes was never to lose that silver radiance, so much so that it was soon his turn to be nicknamed, like the other Peniels. They called him Night-of-silver. So night crept into the lives of the Peniels, and so it became part of their names. It crept in like a flow of wax, in which everybody, one after the other, left the imprint of their footsteps and their heart, and inscribed their name both in relief and intaglio. A name read simultaneously by God and mankind, and a name called out simultaneously by life and death. A heart always to be deciphered, footsteps always to be enumerated.

Night crept in, flowing like dark water, like black ink,

into Ballerina's heart. An ink in which a dream was written, in which Jason's long journey, after he was saved from the clutches of the ice, was inscribed, in which his drifting progress was noted. His deliverance. Ballerina was never to bear a child by the man she had so passionately loved, and still loved as much as ever. It was Jason himself who became her child, in the course of this fluid dream the colour of ink. Jason-love-lake. The dream blended everything together: past and present, past and future, river and sea, the sea and the great lakes, the real and the imaginary, expectation and memory, child and lover, joy and sorrow. The dream blended everything into each other: desire and love, love and memory, absence and presence, the dead body and the surviving body. The dream soothed everything. A lake opened up at the bottom of the sea.

One day Ballerina came to the end of her dream. Jason no longer weighed on her, no longer burdened her heart. He had grown light, soft and light inside her, and turned into transparency and brightness in her heart. Jason's whereabouts no longer presented themself as an obsessive and painful question. Jason resided entirely in Ballerina's love: a love turned into memory, her living memory. And Jason moved, breathed, and took his place in the world and in life again, in the space created by that boundless, radiant memory. For love had proved more enduring within her than absence and loss, more persistent than grief. Love had drawn memory away from mournfulness, rescued it from sorrow and regret, and directed it towards joy. A joy that retained in its depths the taste and scalding of tears, but that refused to bow; the joy of having loved with such desire, freedom from care and unrestraint. And this could not be destroyed or lost. This is what the dream had written inside her. The dream had sounded and probed the verb to love like a riverbed, abyss or cavern, an illness or wound, to measure its depth, extent and quality; to measure its gravity. The dream explored the verb 'to love' this way and that, in every tense, to try its resistance, compass and strength. And the dream revealed that to have loved did not apply only to the past but was for all time, present as well as future.

Ballerina woke from her sleep, but the dream was to continue inside her for ever, and keep vigil in the depths of her transfigured memory. A memory always going towards Jason who was at every instant both lost and found. Time could begin again and the years resume their inexorable progress, and one day she might even encounter another love, and later on old age could approach, and overtake her to the point of decrepitude, her love for Jason was immutable. Nothing could consign it to oblivion or perdition, or bury it in a distant past. Jason was an invisible, eternal and wonderful child that was for ever hers, delivered both from age and death.

Night crept in, incessantly stealing into Thadée's eyes, flourishing for him like a book in motion, written in an alphabet of stars. A book about a great deal more than just the history of men. A book about the world's memory. A book perpetually in the writing, in which new worlds were dreamed up at every moment. A book in constant conflagration, where worlds were disappearing at every moment.

In this infinite book in motion Néçah wrote a line. A brief line, of several words. Several names. Several stars. For her seventeenth birthday Thadée and Tsipele organized a special celebration. It was one evening in spring. Tsipele laid the table in the yard, by the flowering lilacs. At the end of the meal she brought out the birthday cake with seventeen candles stuck in it, which Thadée lighted. Seventeen slender, ivory-coloured candles. Néçah opened her hands in front of the flames, as though to protect them from the wind, and her fingers became translucent, like small pink flames. Then she bent her face towards the cake studded with slightly sputtering candles. The scent of the lilacs mingled with the smell of the cake covered with honey and almonds, with the smell of the sugar and wax. And Néçah's face lit up by the glow of the candles was radiantly rosy and transparent. Then, parting her hands, she blew on the seventeen candles to extinguish them all at once. Her breath caught the seventeen flames, but did not blow them out. Her breath took the flames off the candles and sent them shooting into the darkness. The flames went flying off like a swarm of yellow and orange-red insects with slightly bluish wings, and they headed straight up into the sky chirring like cicadas frenzied by smells and heat. Cicadas more frenzied by the darkness and the brilliance of stars than by daylight and sunshine. Streaking through the silence of the night, from one extremity to the other, with a long-drawn-out screeching, as though it were a sheet of glass, they traversed the sky's immensity, then flung themselves into a corner of the sky, forming a new constellation. Seventeen flame-stars that diffused a slightly dim and trembling light up above.

They ate the honey-and-almond cake. And the taste lingered for a long time in their mouths, mingled with that of the night pierced with flames and heavy with lilacs. Nḉah retained in her palms, fingernails and eyes, and on her lips, too, the dazzling transparency cast on them by the candles; she retained it for ever. And her gaze, her gestures and her smile were made even more gentle by it, and even more grave, blessed with such wonderful grace that she amazed all who saw her, even her close relations, and made them lower their eyes with surprise and disconcertedness. And also brought to their hearts, unfailingly, a moment of pure joy.

But this grace that inhabited Néçah was so great, so mysterious, that some days it almost did violence to her. The grace in her was not at all that infinite lightness that in the past had visited Violette-Honorine, the rose-child, the child so consumed with love that mercy had bled from her temple like a wound, for the entire duration of the war; the rose-child that died of loving unreservedly, without a care for herself. The grace in Néçah was so intense it sometimes became a blaze and a burden in her heart and flesh. The blaze of extraordinary hunger, and the burden of fantastic desire. Then she would sit on the steps to the house, or on the edge of a path, and with her hands to her chest, spread open over her breasts, she would start to sing, swaying her body and dipping her head from one shoulder to the other. She sang in a deep, almost hoarse, very warm voice that seemed to rise from the depths of her entrails, chanting a rhythm that rose from the darkness of the ages. And all who heard these deep-toned songs, a woman's songs of explosive beauty that turned into violence and glowing flesh, felt seized with desire. Seized with desire, as though by a driving force, an impulse. It was as if Néçah, since the night of her seventeenth birthday, had been blowing on the world's burning embers, fanning the fires of the sky and the night as well as those that smoulder in the earth and in the flesh of human beings.

Night crept in, constantly passing through the days, lining them as though with a layer of foil, silvering them to make them reflect more brightly, more ardently the light from the sky. It trickled into the blood of men, it swirled in their hearts, coating them with its foil to make them reflect every image, every sensation and emotion, with greater acuteness, sharpness and strength. Night inked the hearts and flesh of the living, the better to inscribe them with the traces of desire, to pen the names and cries of love on them. Night was endlessly opening and deepening and widening like an inkwell. An inkwell of stone, bark, salt, glass. An inkwell of memory.

Night kept spilling its inkwell into the memory of men and their memory was constantly rustling with the very indistinct murmur created by the writing of time, by the past intertwining with the present and reaching towards the future. Night doggedly dictated to men the sayings of memory, of their own memory that they were nevertheless always trying to flee, to silence, to deny. Night stubbornly forced men to commemorate. To commemorate even in the deserts of oblivion. For this ink of night was as much oblivion as memory.

And remembrance flowed in everybody, ever faster, ever further, with advancing age. So it was with Ballerina, released from her grief for Jason by living through loss and recovery, by reversing death's hold on the living through an unexpected gesture matured deep in a dream. So it was with Heart-breaker, released from his madness by wresting the memory of a child from history's amnesia and investing it in another child. In them, memory had regained all its rights, pushed back its boundaries beyond the confines of pain, sorrow and shame. In them, memory had regained scope and movement, and become gravid with much more than mere recollections of others, carrying traces of them, living traces of greater dynamism than formalism. Traces in motion.

And so it was with Night-of-amber-Wind-of-fire. Night had crept into him like heavy and turbulent water, struggled inside him like a dark whirlpool beating against a barrage. Night had let roll within him the deep roar of memory's black swell. Black translucent ink, like obsidian stone. For thirty years. But Night-of-amber-Wind-of-fire had never ceased to put up resistance, to shout no, to raise the breakwater of his cries against these surges of memory. He had cried louder than the clamouring of memory, run faster than the onslaught of those incoming waves from the past. He had destroyed all the echoes in his name, extirpated every root. He wanted to be without any ties or history, without any yesterdays. He had resolutely turned his back on night and invented for himself a day purged of all shadow. He had tried to paint onto night itself a splendid artificial daylight with a big immutable sun of acid brilliance, to dissolve the night with its shadows and echoes. Its embracing shadows, its beseeching echoes. For thirty years. He had painted daylight onto night as though repainting old lining paper to mask the stains and cracks of the wall. He ended up painting with the blood and tears stolen from a young man who was still a child, the better to cover up all the holes and flaws, to brighten the incandescent light of his sun of oblivion, to sharpen its bite. But night was not flat and smooth like a wall, and the victim's blood and tears were not at all acid. Night was hollow, night was a chasm. Night-of-amber-Wind-of-fire had only painted a veil over it. Not even that: he had created the illusion of a veil. The blood was of sugar, the tears were of salt. He had not painted an acid light. Nor even a light: he had daubed a sickly glimmer, much more steeped in shadow than night itself. A cracking, corroded glimmer – crusts of sugar and salt, crusts of blood. A glimmer of nauseating, stifling, dizzing sweetness, and biting, throbbing pungency. He had only painted a cankerous sun with a boring glimmer over underlying night. Over the unfathomable depths of night.

And this cankerous, artificial sun had never stopped opening, bleeding, cracking, and sweating. A metamorphic wound that remained fevered. A wound that for a long time was swollen and ugly. A wound that was struck again by the hand of a stranger who came to wrestle with him. Since that day the wound had changed again; it was transfigured. It still kept opening and bleeding and stinging, but differently. It did not so much bleed as weep tears of blood, and its sweat, too, was of tears. In the place of the artificial sun, a face sweated. The wound became a shroud.

Night transformed itself into a shroud. A great shroud of skin rent all over by memory. Immense was that memory, immense and terrifying, immense and magnificent. It gathered from so far back, from such a depth that it was no longer a swell but came rushing in like a gigantic tidal wave that no reef could hold back any more.

Night transformed itself into a shroud on which, slowly and inexorably, a face appeared. But this face was still silent and expressionless. It remained remote, vague and ambiguous.

And the same was true of Night-of-amber. He felt as if banished far away from himself. Exiled from his own person, deprived of his former vision. Destitute of his anger, hatred and jealousy. He felt as if he were floating inside himself, in the incredible emptiness that had opened up in his heart and mind, and he kept getting lost in this new inner wilderness. He felt even worse than an exile: he was like an extradited person brutally expelled from the place where he had found refuge, and handed over to an external power. But he did not know anything about this external power that had seized him. It lacked any landmark, any shape or boundary; it did not even have a name. It seemed to him that it was even more deprived than he was, even more vulnerable. He felt as if he had been extradited to an unknown country, a country that did not even exist. Extradited to the most absolute nowhere. Extradited to the heart of an alien night; a night turned into shroud, a night that bore a face. The face of a stranger with his eyes and mouth closed.

Then where, from what mouth, did the voice that broke the silence of that alien night come? For there was a voice. A chanting fainter than a sleeping child's breath. But the person chanting was not at all asleep. He was watchful and expectant, seeking and listening. In a state of perpetual entreaty and self-forgetfulness. The person chanting was a man tormented all his life by one single question. A question that was always the same, so plain and simple, had eaten away at him, like rust, day after day, night after night. But for a long time fear had choked his reply.

One question that was always the same had consumed his life, worn his heart to a thread, eroded his body like a tool with its blade worn down. It had even used up his voice. His inarticulate voice that could only stutter, as if fear of replying to the obsessing question that so plagued his heart had interrupted his breathing and speech with doubt and hesitation. A question that was yet so simple, almost absurd even. Absurd and terrible.

'Do you love me?' was the question. Four simple little words in a language everybody could understand, no matter who they were; a language as familiar to a small child as it was to lovers and old folk.

★

'Do you love me?' Four words to take your breath away, and leave you speechless. Four words three times repeated to Peter the disciple – the one who three times replied, 'I am not,' to those who asked him on the night his master was betrayed, 'Are you not also one of this man's followers?' The man he had denied, out of fear, had to die in agony, be buried, disappear, and finally return from the dead in order for Peter to be relieved of the burden of his triple denial. That man had to ask his question three times, thereby saddening Peter whose reply he seemed not to hear, or not to believe, before Peter completely wrested himself from his own being by saying in the end, 'Lord, you know everything; you know well that I love you.' As if at that moment, everything of Peter, including the admission of his love, had shifted from himself to the other, until he was totally subsumed by that other, in whom even the mystery of his own love resided. Then the other said to him, measuring in advance the extraordinary extent of this love grown prodigious through self-renouncement, 'You will stretch forth your hand and another shall gird you and take you where you do not want to go.'*

'Do you love me?' This question had consumed the life of Father Delombre, the stuttering priest who could not but irritate his parishioners and dishearten his superiors. It had worn him out until he in turn stretched forth his hands into the void and awaited the certainty of his own reply from he who never ceased to beg it of him.

He stretched forth his hands into the void, girded his loins with emptiness, and allowed himself to be led like a blind man, a prisoner, out of himself. He had left his parish, which had been taken over by someone else. He had no responsibility, no duties any more. He had no other responsibility but his love, no other duty but to love. He had given up everything and retired into solitude, like the desert fathers of old. But the desert to which he retired was

* John 21: 18

one of trees and brambles, not sand. He now lived as a recluse in Love-in-the-open Wood, in an old hunters' hut made of branches, earth and brushwood. The very same one where thirty years before some hunters and their dogs had sought refuge from the rain before setting off once more in pursuit of game. They ventured out when rain let up, but the light was not good and with the wetness of the leaves they could see nothing but deceptive shapes. There were three of them, and one thought he glimpsed the figure of a young roe-deer. And they fired. There was a cry, a brief cry, as though of surprise, which was immediately choked. A cry that was not the kind that animals utter. Then a sound, that of body softly falling to the ground. The sound of a body that was not that of an animal. The dogs went chasing after it, barking, but the hunters remained there for a moment in silence, not moving. They continued to listen to this double echo that answered their shots; they continued to listen even when everything had fallen silent again, except the dogs. They listened, their hands frozen on the butt of their rifles, their hearts stopped. They listened to a silence that was not that of a shot animal.

It was a child, a little boy of eight. A child that had always loved to run about in the woods, and had been caught in the rain. He had taken shelter under the branches of a hornbeam. The rain started falling again. The hunters picked up the child's body and took it to its parents' house. Over at Upper Farm. Since that day no hunter had ever returned to that place. Joseph Delombre lived there alone now, and no one ever ventured to visit him. In fact no one knew where he had gone; no one cared.

'Do you love me?' He did not even need to answer this question any more, his whole body had become a reply. His already aged body, emaciated by fasting and bearing marks of poverty, nights of vigil and the cold. His human body finally released from his doubts, anguish and shame. A body totally surrendered to the madness of his love; a body turned into transparency. A body that had become pure impulse in its very stillness. And old Delombre understood this: that the one who had for so long asked him whether he loved him had only done so because he could not do otherwise, for he was himself nothing but a beggar, a supplicant. He understood that not only was man crying to God, interminably, without restraint, as much out of anger as wild hope, but also God was crying to man. He sensed that God comes begging to man, and that the greatest humility on the part of men was perhaps to bow down to this God squatting in the depths of their hearts, this God soiled with the blood, sweat, filth and tears of men.

So old Delombre sang, he sang in his wattle-and-daub hut secluded in a thicket in Love-in-the-open Wood. He sang in his faint, very quietly wavering voice that was muffled by the undergrowth.

A voice that no one roundabout could hear or even detect, so tenuous was it, and so close to the ground did it lurk, hidden behind the weeds and brambles and barks of trees.

And yet that voice travelled, carried by the wind. It had grown so light, like drizzle or pollen. It escaped from the undergrowth, stole between the weeds, descended the hill, mingling with the countless infinitesimal noises – rustlings and whisperings – of the earth slowly imbued with evening. It floated down to the river flowing below. And it was there, on the riverbank, that someone happened to hear it.

Night-of-amber-Wind-of-fire was walking by the river, on his way back from Montleroy. The path he took, running alongside the river, was the longest, most indirect way home, but Night-of-amber liked to follow the river's quiet banks, the impassive course of its grey waters. The wind, when it blew across the river's surface, seemed swifter and keener, and the earth nearby had stronger smells. The light especially was different here, as if the water enhanced its brightness, reflecting the countless nuances of its gleams through the grasses and leaves on the banks. And when evening fell the grey darkness, too, was tinged with the water's mauve and green and blue reflections. Night-of-amber-Wind-of-fire could no longer distinguish colours, but he perceived with extraordinary acuity the infinite play of shadows and shadings.

And sounds themselves were changed by the water; they took on a strange, slightly muted resonance, as if the dampness, cold and greyness of the water dulled them, and gave them a matt gold and silver lining. Sounds became almost tangible here.

And so it was that evening. Night-of-amber-Wind-of-fire did not so much hear as suddenly felt the light touch of a sound. Like a breath on the back of his neck. A very light breath that round itself round his neck, then crept down his arms and came to rest in the hollow of his wrists, where the blueness of the veins shows through the more delicate and vulnerable skin. A sound that was a voice, and the voice was singing. And the words of the song began to throb very softly in his pulse, to roll under his skin, to travel up to his heart. Very simple, plain words, the words of a brief prayer sung during the liturgy. The words of the *Agnus Dei*.

But the voice that sang modulated each word with such attention, such passion mingled with joy and supplication, sorrow and hope, that the meaning of each of these words took on infinite fullness, unsuspected gravity. Each word revealed both its meaning and tone, like those flowering waves that appear on the surface of still water when a stone is sent scudding across it, simultaneously funnelling, bursting open, beginning to whirl, and shooting off in a straight line. A line of contact along which the light of grace travelled.

The voice stole inside Night-of-amber-Wind-of-fire, flowing into his blood, penetrating his flesh, overwhelming his heart, sending its words skimming like pebbles. Pebbles of fire and ice, of glass and bronze, both light and dark. *Agnus Dei, qui tollis peccata mundi, miserere nobis.* The voice lingered amazingly on the vowels, opening up to take on an imploring intonation. But there was also a kind of blossoming smile in the sound of this voice.

The voice kept repeating its phrase. Its slow, ever vaster phrase. And the words rippled between shadow and brightness, carrying shadow and light; and floated between distress and hope, tears and smiles, bearing grace. Because borne by grace. And once again the voice took up its phrase. *Agnus Dei, qui tollis peccata mundi, miserere nobis.* The vowels were now gaping, opening up a boundless expanse, like a plain stretching out of sight. Night-of-amber-Wind-of-fire was almost at a standstill, his pace slowed, his hands dangling in space. He examined his hands, as though trying to read in their palms the secret of that voice radiating its song through his entire body. But there was no secret to decipher. Nothing but a moment of mystery to be imparted.

It was completely dark, and the horizon, now lost in shadow, no longer divided sky from earth. The riverbanks, too, were disappearing, and water was becoming indistinguishable from land. But there was still the same continuous, muted sound; the same pregnant, vital smell. The voice intoned its song for the third time. *Agnus Dei, qui tollis peccata mundi, dona nobis pacem.* For the third time the voice swelled on the word *peccata,* modulating the final vowel to a pitch of sorrow, gentleness, and madness. To a pitch where sorrow and gentleness foundered. But the words clung to each other, entwined like convolvulus. Coiling, bindweed words, morning-glories with white flowers. *Dona nobis pacem.*

Morning-glories whose beauty was forged in the darkest night, whose convolutions were at first contortions and their roots brambles.

Peccata. Pacem. Bindweed words that blossomed slowly, unpredicatably. And very surprisingly.

Peccata/Pacem. Two totally irreconcilable words. Two words incredible to find in the same phrase. Two words of radical separateness that only grace could establish any link between. And it was that slender link that old Delombre's voice, in all its tenderness and patience, established.

Peccata-Pacem. Two flowers in one, contorting its body

to raise itself with same energy on the side of both day and night. The voice established the link with the half-day half-night word.

Peccata-Pacem. With mercy destroying the void of sin, wresting itself from the bog of evil. With mercy rending the deepness of night.

Peccata-Miserere-Pacem. The voice imparted the three words of the greatest lament that could ever be sung, the longest entreaty that could ever be suffered – even to a state of wonderment.

THE OTHER NIGHT

Night-of-amber-Wind-of-fire left the riverbank and continued on his way to the farm, where his son was waiting for him. Evening was already giving way to night. The voice heard at the riverside slowly returned to silence. The voice receded, seeming to die. But it did not, could not die. It only returned to silence the better to secure the infinite space opened up by its song, the better to release the power of its words. The moment of pure grace had passed, as moments of insane love do. Then night closes in again. But it is not the same any more. And will never be the same again. Night now bears a hole in its gigantic side. A breach through which daylight might appear at any moment; might burst through and start to shine. Grace is just a brief fissure of lightning. But nothing can close it up again. A tiny fissure, and all around is transformed by it. Not magnified, but transfigured. For everything acquires a face. Not the face of power or glory, but profiles of the poor. And these innumerable profiles, with features running counter to the night, have then to be counted; we have to learn to name them. And every one, unique. Grace is just a pause in which time turns back on itself, brushing against eternity. And afterwards we have to begin again, to get back to work, to start enduring again. Grace is a scythe that sweeps across the world, baring it, exposing it. Then it is impossible to walk, to see, to touch anything without noticing the infinite vulnerability of this flayed world. Grace cuts the five senses to the quick, drawing blood, and from this blood flows a sixth sense. That of mercy. Peccata-Miserere-Pacem. Grace is nothing but that: the imparting of a word. The most boundless of words – mercy.

Night-of-amber-Wind-of-fire climbed up to the farm. He was no longer someone who had been extradited, or even exiled. He was simply a wanderer. A wanderer on his own land. A vagabond who bore God on his shoulders. For there is in God something of the eternal child asking to be taken care of.

He walked on. Night had now completely closed in. It was no longer of water, or earth, or roses, or blood, or ashes; nor was it was of trees, or wind, or stones. It was all these together, all melted into one, like the taste of a strange fruit in the mouth. A mouth blistered with so many cries; cries turned into a simple, quietly murmured song. The night was no longer of the elements, nor of the flesh. It was something other. It was a moving-on.

Night was something other. It was a mover, an imparter, a bearer. God-bearing night.

Night-of-amber-Wind-of-fire was on his way home; it was already late into the night.

Never was the book less about to close. But nor was it going to turn back and start all over again. It had just been interrupted, with such gentleness, such violence, that it could never resume. All words were now put to flight. Words had been caught by surprise, and overtaken by another kind of verbal expression that was neither noise nor complete silence, but something like a very low murmur.

The book was tearing up, breaking apart. It had for so long run counter to the night that it had reached the far end of the night, had toppled beyond night. And the words escaped, racing off at top speed, charging forward, regardless of getting lost, regardless of arriving. The book flicked through its pages, with complete idleness. It had nothing more to relate. It drew aside, giving way to night. Night located in the fissure of words, names, cries, songs, voices.

The book was destroyed, thoroughly destroyed; at a total loss for words. Only the night remained. A night without words.

‘And now this page on which nothing more is to be inscribed.’

Saint-John-Perse
Snows, IV